CASH MONEY CON

D1274212

K'WAN

CASH MONEY CONTENT

ANIMAL

First Trade Paperback Edition: October 2012

Cover Design: Baja Ukweli

For further information log onto www.CashMoneyContent.com

Library of Congress Control Number: 2011943461

ISBN 978-1-9363-9925-3 pbk
ISBN 978-1-9363-9926-0 ebook

10   9

"*The Dream is birthed by a thought and is given heart, soul, and character by the road traveled in pursuit of that dream.*"
K'wan

PROLOGUE

THE RAIN HAD STARTED EARLY. FROM THE dark clouds that had been brewing all morning it looked like it was going to be a full-blown storm, but so far, it had been limited to a constant drizzle. They say that when it rained it meant that God was weeping and if that was the case, then he wasn't the only one because there were at least two dozen tear-streaked faces gathered around a hollowed plot at Rose Hill Cemetery. They had come to say farewell to a soul who was loved by almost everyone she encountered.

Ashanti stood off toward the back of the crowd trying his best to look comfortable. He was dressed in black jeans, a black t-shirt, and had two black bandanas tied around his wrists. Printed on the t-shirt was the phrase "gone but not forgotten" and a picture of the deceased. King James had been pressing him to wear a suit, explaining that it was a sign of respect to the deceased, but Ashanti wasn't trying to hear that. A lot of the people at the funeral knew him and therefore knew how he gave it up, so wearing a suit would've been out of character for

1

him. Respect or not, he would say good-bye to his friend the same way he had said hello: G'd up.

On the other side of the plot someone had broken down into tears which made Ashanti uncomfortable. He had been around death most of his young life, but this was only his second time attending a funeral. The first time had been when his mother passed, and that was only because Social Services made his current foster family take him. She had given birth to him so they would always share the bond between mother and child, but other than that Ashanti felt nothing for her. How could he bring himself to love someone who had sold his sister off into prostitution to pay her own debts and released her baby boy to the streets to feed her demons? He felt no sorrow when his mother passed, only closure, because the one person who had been able to hurt them would never be able to again.

A cold chill ran through Ashanti's body bringing him back from the place his mind was trying to take him. Standing to his left, hands folded over each other and head bowed, was Alonzo. He had passed on the suit also and opted for a button-up and some black-on-black Prada shoes. Alonzo, known as Zo-Pound to those who knew that part of him, was the younger brother of a dude who ran with King James named Lakim. Though Lakim was notorious on the streets, Alonzo wasn't without his fair share of horror stories. He and Ashanti had gotten tight since both of them were reluctantly recruited into King James's crew. Like Ashanti, funerals made him uncomfortable too, but he volunteered to roll with Ashanti when no one else did. Partially because he knew how important the deceased had been to Ashanti, and partially because he knew the parts they had all played in her death.

Ashanti's eyes drifted to two women sitting near the head of the casket. One was older wearing a large colorful hat that he had seen around the neighborhood when he and Brasco were hustling in the projects, but her name escaped him at the moment. Sadness was etched across her face, but she held back the tears that danced in the corners of her eyes behind her bifocal glasses. The younger woman was far less composed. It seemed like every time the pastor opened his mouth the younger one would break out into a wave of sobs and the older one would reach out to console her. Ashanti wanted to go over and offer his condolences but couldn't find the words. What does one say to a woman who has just lost a child? Watching them grieve crushed him, so he turned away for fear that he may not be able to hold in the sadness that filled his own chest. Wanting to focus on something else, he scanned the sea of faces sitting, standing, and some even being held up. Many of them he knew, but there were a few he didn't. At the end of the day it didn't matter who knew who because at that moment the pain they all shared was what bound them. Though he was standing merely a few feet away from her casket, his mind still couldn't process the fact that Gucci was dead.

"You look like you just lost your best friend," someone said from behind Ashanti.

"Something like that," Ashanti said without bothering to turn around. His eyes were misty, and he didn't want anyone to see him on the verge of crying.

"You know, eventually death comes to us all. Some sooner than others."

"You ain't never lied about that," Ashanti said, looking at

3

the casket. "Seems like the good die young and the wicked live forever."

"Indeed, which is why it's up to men like us to keep the scales balanced. Killing is a dirty business, but somebody has got to do it. Ain't that right, Ashanti?"

"Homie, you know me from somewhere?" Ashanti looked up at the man who was addressing him for the first time and was shocked to see who it was.

Animal stood there in all his glory, dressed in a long black trench coat and dark glasses. His long hair blew freely in the breeze.

"Holy shit!" Ashanti staggered backward, tripping over a hill of dirt and landing on his butt a few feet away from the casket. "Animal? No, no, no . . . you can't be here. You're dead, ain't you?" Ashanti got to his feet.

"Dead as a doornail." Animal opened the trench coat and exposed his bare chest for Ashanti to see. There were several bullet holes in his chest, some of which were still bleeding. He walked closer to Ashanti causing him to back up further until he was at the edge of the plot the casket would be lowered in. "They killed me, then they killed my lady, and none of my so-called homies did shit about it."

"I been trying—"

"You ain't been trying hard enough!" Animal cut him off. "Don't worry yourself too much about it though. Hell is pretty nice this time of year, and I've come to give you the full tour." Animal pushed Ashanti into the hole.

Ashanti awoke screaming at the top of his lungs. His head whipped back and forth, expecting to see the dirt walls of the hole he had been pushed in, but found only the pale cream paint of his apartment walls. There was no ghost, and no cemetery. It had all been a bad dream.

He sat on the edge of his bed and let out a sigh of relief. Then he grabbed the half-empty bottle of tequila on his nightstand and tossed it into the waste basket. "No more Cuervo before bed. I'm switching back to dark liquor."

PART I

MO MONEY . . . MO MURDER . . . MO HOMICIDE

ONE

"My baby, please tell me that ain't my baby." The woman burst through the throng of onlookers, dressed in only a bathrobe and house shoes as they were all she had time to grab when the frantic knocks landed on her door. The crowd parted like the Red Sea so that she could get a bird's-eye view of what everyone else had been staring at for the last ten minutes, a corpse under a bloody white sheet.

Alvarez was the first to notice her. The tall Hispanic detective had been standing over the body, picking his teeth with a toothpick and analyzing the crime scene in his mind. Dressed in dark jeans, a T-shirt, and white Nikes, he looked more like a spectator than a detective. "Damn," was all he could say when he saw the distraught look on the robed woman's face.

The robed woman burst through the police tape to where the corpse was laid out, followed by two young ladies and a young man. They all looked distressed. The robed woman went to pull off the sheet, but was cut off by two uniformed police officers. They were a bit overzealous in their handling of the woman, which caused a shoving match between them and the family of the victim.

"They said that's my baby laying there! Get off me." The woman struggled against the cops, which only agitated the already tense crowd.

"If you don't calm down we're gonna haul all your asses in," one of the uniformed officers threatened. He was a beefy white cop with a salt-and-pepper mustache and a thick nose. In his hand he held a nightstick and looked eager to use it.

"Take off that badge and that gun and I'll show you what to do with that nightstick," one of the boys in the crowd threatened, which only stirred up the crowd more. Things were getting ugly.

From his position, kneeling beside the corpse, Detective Brown watched the officers roughly handle the grieving woman and a frown creased his dark face. Unlike his partner Alvarez, Brown was the straitlaced, no-nonsense cop who had a low tolerance for bullshit, especially from other cops. Brushing off the knees of his black slacks he approached the brewing mêlée. "Why doesn't everybody just cool out."

"Why don't you tell these Nazis to cool out?" another boy shouted, getting in the mustached officer's face. In his excitement spittle flew from his mouth and splattered on the officer's face.

"Did this muthafucka just spit on me?" the mustached officer wiped his face with the back of his uniform sleeve. From the shock on the boy's face it was clear that it wasn't intentional, but it was all the officer needed to employ *excessive* force. When he reached for his pepper spray Detective Brown grabbed him by the arm.

"At ease," Detective Brown whispered to the officer. "We're

in foreign territory, and the natives are restless, so we don't need you doing something stupid to put us all in an awkward predicament. These people just lost a family member, so if you can't show respect, at least show a little compassion."

The officer's eyes said that he wanted to try Detective Brown, but he wisely fell back. Detective Brown approached the grieving woman and her family. They cast intimidating glares at him, but he was unmoved. "So this is how you wanna go about it, huh?"

"Fuck that. That's my li'l brother lying out, and these assholes are treating us like criminals," a girl who looked like a younger version of the woman in the robe barked.

"And they're gonna keep treating you like criminals the way you're carrying on," Detective Brown shot back. "C'mon, people. We all know how this is gonna play out if this gets crazy. Them bluecoats are gonna come through kicking ass and taking names, and that ain't gonna bring your family back or get us any closer to finding out who did this. Now, we can do this the easy way and have this woman step over and identify the body or the hard way." He looked over his shoulders at the cops gathering behind him. "Your call."

The woman motioned for her family to be calm and stepped forward. "Please, just let me see my boy."

Detective Brown took the woman by the hand and walked her over to the corpse, where one of the medical examiners was scraping under his fingernails. As they neared the body he could feel her begin to tremble so he squeezed her hand to try to comfort her. "Ma'am, I gotta warn you that this isn't the prettiest scene in the world."

The woman composed herself enough to speak. "I don't care. Please just let me see if that's my baby under that sheet."

Detective Brown leaned in and whispered something to the medical examiner that made her face sadden. With a reluctant nod, she pulled the sheet from the corpse's face. As soon as she laid eyes on her baby boy she broke down. Her eyes were telling her one thing, and her heart was telling her another. Before anyone realized what she was doing the woman snatched the sheet off the body completely and beheld what was left of her son, Slick. His eyelids had been melted shut, and the corners of his mouth were cut back to make it look like he had a permanent smile on his face. Slick's body was covered in cuts and bruises, and his throat had been slit clean to the bone. The only thing keeping it attached to his body were shredded pieces of skin. The most disturbing thing was the word *war* carved into his forehead. She had seen enough.

Detective Brown barely had time to catch the woman when she collapsed into him. She buried her face in his chest, soaking his silk shirt with her tears. Her sobs were so intense that Detective Brown could feel them vibrating in his chest as they came. "I'm sorry for your loss," was all that he could think of to say, rubbing her back to offer some sort of comfort. Being a father himself, Detective Brown could only imagine what she was going through, and the thought of losing one of his own kids scared him to death.

The woman peeled her face from his shirt and looked up at Detective Brown. Her eyes were swollen and red and would no doubt get worse before the night was over. "Who would do this to my boy?" Her voice quivered. "What kind of animal would do this to a child?"

"Don't worry, ma'am; catching *animals* is our specialty. We're gonna get the son-of-a-bitch who did this to your boy,"

Detective Brown assured her. After a few more minutes of consoling and kind words the detective passed the distraught mother off to her family and walked over to join his partner Alvarez, who was scowling over the scene.

"This is fucked up," Alvarez said in disgust.

"Tell me about it." Brown loosened his tie. "How many does that make for us this month?"

Alvarez thought about it for a minute. "Five or six. I lost count."

"And those are just the ones we've been working. Think about how many other poor bastards have been splattered around the city in the last few weeks. Nah, this whole situation smells funny. These people haven't been random shootings or arguments gone wrong. They've been murdered . . . brutally."

Alvarez finally caught on. "Like someone is trying to send a message?"

"Bingo," Detective Brown nodded, "and from the looks of things it isn't a friendly message. Something is afoot in the jungle, and I'd be willing to bet my pension that if we dig deep enough, you and I both know who we'll find tied up somewhere in this."

Alvarez didn't understand what he meant at first but when he really thought about it his eyes widened. "You don't mean . . ."

"Indeed I do," Brown said. "I thought maybe I was bugging when I first started putting it together, but once I really began to roll it around in my mind," Brown shook his head, "this has that little punk written all over it."

Alvarez shook his head in protest. "Brown, I know you'd like nothing more than to slap a life sentence on that whole clan, but I think you're reaching. Besides, the last time I checked, the deceased was an affiliate, so why would he whack one of his own?"

Detective Brown gave Alvarez a comical look. "J, I swear if the brass ever decided to give you a random drug test they'd kick your ass off the force. He's not the deliverer of the message, but the *recipient*. Three of those messes we were called in on were current or past employees. Looks like somebody finally got up the balls to try to put Prince Charming back in his place." Brown's lips parted into a wide smile.

"Damn," was all Alvarez could say once the pieces started falling into place. "If that's the case, then it's gonna get way worse before it gets better." Alvarez shook his head.

"Yup, and once again, we gotta step in to clean up his shit," Brown said, disgustedly.

"The first thing we gotta do is try to get a line on who the new player in the game is. There aren't too many powerful or stupid enough to go at him in the streets like this, so the list of names should be a short one. Where do you suggest we start our search?"

"At the source," Brown said before heading to their car.

Animal stood just beyond the police tape, watching the crime scene among the rest of the spectators. His mane of wild black curls was tucked deeply into a Rasta-style wool cap, and black glasses covered his eyes to protect his identity while he moved within mere yards of the men looking to bury him under a prison for the rest of his days. It was dangerous playing the crime scene so close, but Animal wanted to feel the public's reaction to his handiwork.

When he noticed the black and brown detectives in the sea of blue uniforms, a smile parted his lips. He was both surprised and impressed that they had survived his prison escape a few years back when K-Dawg's men came for him. Los Negro Muertes had been ruthless in Animal's abduction, and to his knowledge, there had been no survivors. The fact that the detectives had not only survived, but had returned to active duty, told Animal that the two men were more resilient than he had given them credit for. As preoccupied as everyone was with the body and controlling the mob, it would've been fairly easy for Animal to kill one, if not both, of the detectives and have a good chance at escaping, but he would let them keep their lives. They'd earned them and were safe . . . unless they came between him and what he had to do.

He watched the detectives hurriedly leave the crime scene and jump in their unmarked car. He had a good idea where they were off to. The Buick zipped up the street and passed Animal, catching him in its headlights. As they passed, Animal made fleeting eye contact with the Puerto Rican detective. There was a brief moment of recognition, then the detective turned away as if he had never seen him. Animal smiled and kept walking toward where he had the rental car stashed.

He felt better after finally being able to spill the blood of his enemies, but Slick had only been an appetizer to the main course. His wrath would be the stuff of legends, and his enemies would feel what he felt—*pain*. He knew before fleeing to New York that the situation was bad, but he had no idea how bad. Though Tionna had tried to assure him that what had happened wasn't his fault, he couldn't help but to feel like it was. Had he been by her side instead of caught up in the madness of K-Dawg and Los Negro Muertes, he could've been there for Gucci. His only solace was that he had gotten to see her for a little while when he returned home, but the homecoming was a bittersweet one.

TWO

ONE MONTH EARLIER

As promised, Red Sonja's plan was to get Animal safely out of Puerto Rico and on his way to New York. It was no easy task, and he had to go the long way, via ship, because the airports were too risky. When the ship he was hiding on reached Miami, Animal was to meet a cat named Diamonds who would provide him with firearms and the means to make the rest of his journey. His brief stay in Miami had been anything but a vacation, and he'd barely made it out with his life and his sanity, thanks to the twisted games that Diamonds liked to play. But even as twisted as Diamonds was, he kept his word and helped Animal, providing him with a piece of information that would prove invaluable for what he needed to do in New York.

Diamonds had offered Animal an entire arsenal, but he passed on the heavy firepower and opted only for a few handguns. They were easier to conceal in the small rental car than a bunch of machine guns. The last thing he needed was some overzealous state trooper to find them and create a whole new set of problems. There was no doubt in Animal's mind that he would hold court in the streets before he allowed anyone to cage him again, but he figured if he could save himself the headache he would.

The drive from Miami to New York was over twenty hours, but he didn't mind. After what had happened with Diamonds and his crew in Miami, he needed time to think and plan his next move. The plan had been for him to go directly to his safe house in New Jersey, but he had to see Gucci. Sonja had sent word to him about what hospital she was staying in and her condition. Thankfully, she was alive, but she wasn't doing well at all. It wasn't a smart move for Animal to go to the hospital, but he wasn't thinking with his head; he was thinking with his heart, and his heart longed to be reunited with his lover.

As soon as Animal crossed the George Washington Bridge, he rolled the windows down and inhaled deeply. His nose and lungs were filled with the familiar scents of exhaust fumes, rotting trash, and money. He had finally made it home, but he was still a fugitive and had to tread very carefully.

Slipping into the hospital proved to be easier than he'd thought. Security paid little to no attention to him. They had their hands full helping the doctors and paramedics deal with the heavy load of patients that were coming in from what Animal was able to pick up while ear hustling. There was some sort of drug war taking place on the streets of Harlem. Normally, he and his crew would've been on the streets doing recon to see how they could capitalize on the feud, but Animal had more pressing issues to deal with than street beefs.

Thinking back to his running partners, Brasco, Nefertiti,

and Ashanti, it filled him with great sadness. They had been all each other had when things were good, but the events leading up to Animal's arrest tore them apart. Secretly, he blamed himself for the decimation of their crew. Had he only listened to Gucci and left the streets alone everything would still be good, but his unwillingness to let go of old grudges had ruined everything. On more than one occasion, he had wanted to reach out to his comrades to let them know that he was okay, but he knew it was impossible. The police knew how close the four of them had been, so there was no doubt that they were being watched closely.

Animal had spent many sleepless nights worrying about his friends and how they were holding up. Nef had never really been cut out for the streets, so it wouldn't have surprised him at all if he'd squared up and gotten a job somewhere. Brasco was a warrior, so there was no need to fear about his fate. Whatever Brasco was up to it was probably centered on chasing a dollar. Those two were good, but it was little Ashanti that worried him.

Ashanti had been the runt of their crew. He was the smallest man but had the biggest heart and the most to prove. Much like Animal, Ashanti had lived a very hard life, which is probably why they took to each other the way they did. In Ashanti he saw what Tech must've seen in him and took the boy under his wing, protecting him and teaching him to defend himself. Ashanti was a very quick study and proved to have a knack for violence that you didn't see in the average teenager, but as he had proven time and again, Ashanti was anything but average. From an early age, hardship and the streets had turned his heart to stone, and he loved nothing or no one but his crew.

Thinking of his mischievous face made Animal smile, and he was going to make it a point to try to get word to him that he was okay.

Moving as quietly as possible, he entered the room. Sitting in a wooden chair next to the bed was Tionna. She was hunched over the bed sobbing. Knowing how close Tionna and Gucci were, he knew Tionna had to be taking it hard, just as hard as he was. He and Tionna had never really seen eye to eye, but they both loved Gucci so they tolerated each other. Looking past Tionna, he saw Gucci's sleeping form. Seeing her hooked up to all the machines monitoring her vitals almost made him cry, but he had to be strong for her.

Tionna must've felt his presence because she turned around and scanned the room nervously. Animal pressed himself further into the shadows behind the door and watched as she cautiously approached. She looked into the hallway before closing the door and turning to go back to Gucci's bedside. Animal thought about calling out to her, but he didn't want to startle her and risk drawing the attention of the hospital staff, so he moved behind her and clamped his hand over her mouth. Tionna struggled and tried to scream, but Animal had a firm grip on her.

"I'm going to remove my hand, and you are not going to scream, do we understand each other?" a familiar voice whispered in Tionna's ear. She nodded. "Good," he released his grip. As soon as he moved his hand she shrieked and broke for the door. Before she could get it open, she was grabbed roughly from behind and forced against the wall. "Damn it, Tionna, shut up before hospital security comes," Animal told her.

Tionna turned as white as a ghost when she saw Animal.

"But you're dead; everybody said you were dead," Tionna blinked, thinking her eyes were playing tricks on her.

"No, I'm very much alive, which is more than I can say for the men who did this to Gucci." He approached her bedside and stared down at her. She was just as beautiful as he remembered her, if not more so. "How long has she been like this?"

"For over a week now. The doctors say she had a mild stroke during the last surgery," Tionna explained.

Animal took her hand in his and kissed her cold fingers. "My poor baby." Tears fell from his eyes and splashed on her arm. "Look what they did to you. Don't worry. I'm here now, and I'm gonna make this right, I promise." Animal leaned in and kissed Gucci on the lips before turning to make his exit.

Tionna followed Animal to the door. "What are you going to do?"

He looked over his shoulder at her. "What do you think I'm going to do?"

Tionna nodded. "Can I ask a favor of you, Animal?"

"I'm all out of good will, T," he said seriously.

"It ain't for me; it's for Gucci . . . well, kinda. I know I might be wrong for saying this, but I don't care. When you find the ones who did this, punish them." Tears welled in Tionna's eyes. "Make them suffer for what they did to my girl."

"That I can do." Animal agreed. "Get word to your friends and loved ones, T. Tell them that they might wanna stay off the streets for a time. The sky is gonna rain blood over Harlem, and I don't care too much who gets wet."

Tionna nodded. "Animal, I'm not gonna ask where you've been or what happened because I'm sure it's a long story, but I'm glad you're alive, and I know Gucci will be too."

Animal cracked a half smile. "I hope so. I was afraid she wouldn't want to see me after all that's happened."

"Boy, you know Gucci loves you more than anything. No matter how much we all tried to get her to go on with her life, she never gave up the hope that you might come back to her one day."

Animal ripped a piece of paper off one of the hospital charts and scribbled down the number to one of the burn-out cell phones he had. "Here," he handed it to Tionna, "this is for your eyes only. Try to only use it in cases of emergencies. Keep me updated on her progress, and I know I don't have to tell you not to give it to anyone or tell anybody you've seen me."

"Animal, I'm not stupid." She put the piece of paper in her pocket. "I'll call you the minute there's a change in her condition. Now you better go before—" The words hadn't completely left her mouth when the door to the room opened.

"Oh my God," Ms. Ronnie gasped, her mouth falling agape. The bag of Chinese food she'd been carrying dropped to the floor. She had intended to surprise Tionna with the late-night meal, but she ended up being the one surprised to see her daughter's boyfriend who had risen from the grave.

"Hey, Ms. Ronnie," Animal said sheepishly.

There was an awkward silence, and then Ms. Ronnie moved cautiously toward him wearing a shocked expression. She touched his arms, then ran her hands along his baby face to make sure what she was seeing wasn't some warped dream. Ms. Ronnie's lips began to tremble, and she tried to speak but couldn't. She smiled at Animal, before slapping him viciously across his face twice. She raised her hand a third time, but instead of slapping him, she pulled him into an embrace and broke down into tears.

"Do you know how worried you had us?" she sobbed into his chest. "We all thought you were dead."

"I was for a time," Animal said honestly.

"Well, at least tell me where you've been."

Before Animal could answer Ms. Ronnie's question a portly, dark-skinned nurse came into the room. She was so focused on the clipboard in her hand that she literally walked into Animal. When she looked up at the wild-haired young man she took a cautionary step back. "What's going on in here? Visiting hours were over at 8 p.m." She was talking to all three of them, but her eyes were locked on Animal. He looked familiar to her, but she couldn't place him.

"Sorry, Nurse Jenkins." Ms. Ronnie stepped up. Nurse Jenkins had been Gucci's attending nurse over the last few weeks, so she knew Ms. Ronnie and Tionna and let them bend the rules from time to time. "I was just checking in on Gucci and bringing Tionna some food because she's been here half the night."

"That's fine, Ms. Ronnie, but you know we can only allow immediate family in here after a certain time." She cut her eyes at Animal.

"Oh, this is Gucci's—"

"Cousin Mike," Animal cut Ms. Ronnie off. He flashed his winning smile at Nurse Jenkins, and she softened a bit.

"Well, it's nice to meet you, Cousin Mike, but like I said, only immediate family can be here after visiting hours. I could get in trouble if one of the doctors finds all of y'all in here."

"We wouldn't want that, now would we? My apologies,

Nurse Jenkins, and thank you for letting me check on my cousin," Animal said.

"You're welcome, sugar, but you got to be going now. As a matter of fact, I need all of you to step out so I can check on Gucci and change her dressings."

Animal took one last look at Gucci and walked silently into the hallway, followed by Ms. Ronnie and Tionna. He could feel tears welling again, so he placed his head against the wall and closed his eyes to compose himself. A few seconds later he felt a soft hand on his shoulder. When he turned around and saw the sadness written across Ms. Ronnie's face he couldn't hold it back any longer, and the tears rolled freely down his cheeks. "I'm sorry," he whispered.

"It ain't your fault," Ms. Ronnie wiped the tears off Animal's face.

"But it is. If I had been here, then Gucci wouldn't have gotten shot. I could've stopped it," Animal said emotionally. "I gotta make 'em pay, Ms. Ronnie. My heart won't let me rest if I don't make this right."

Ms. Ronnie took Animal's hands in hers and spoke softly to him. "Tayshawn, I know you're hurting; we all are, but flying outta here mad at the world ain't gonna change nothing. Let go and let God."

Animal laughed menacingly and snatched his hands back. "God? Where was God when they hit my baby up?"

"Tayshawn, even when it seems so, God never abandons his children."

"Then I must be adopted because he sure left me for dead when I needed him most. Ms. Ronnie, I respect your faith in the higher power, but I'm gonna put my faith in *firepower*." He patted his waist. "I gotta go, but Tionna knows how to reach me if y'all need me." Animal redonned his hood and started for the exit.

"Tayshawn," Ms. Ronnie called after him. Animal stopped but didn't turn around. "I'm gonna pray for you."

Animal nodded. "Thank you, but I think the ones who done this are gonna need those prayers more than I will." And just as silently as he had come, Animal was gone and the wheels of murder were set into motion.

THREE

PRESENT DAY

THE CORNER OF 114TH AND BROADWAY WAS lit up like the Times Square strip. Expensive-looking cars were double-parked as far as the eye could see, while people dressed in their Sunday's best crowded the sidewalk in front of what had once been a small bistro until it had come under new ownership and undergone its grand transformation. The entire front was covered in a black tarp and guarded fiercely by rough-looking men in black suits. Drivers of passing cars rubbernecked, and residents of the neighborhood stood around talking about what was going on. The solemn look on the faces of the staff of the neighboring pubs and restaurants said it all. It was last call and all their asses were out.

Two cars pulled up to the curb, the first being a sleek black Benz and the other a black stretch limo. From the passenger's side of the Benz emerged a well built young man wearing black shades and a black silk shirt. Dangling from his neck was a white gold and diamond cross. He braced his cane on the ground and took a step onto the curb where he was immediately swarmed by paparazzi. The young man smiled and adjusted his collar as his picture was taken from all angles.

The second man to step from the Benz was older and slightly taller. He wore a smoke gray suit and simple gray fedora. From beneath the brim of his hat he scanned the crowd of people for familiar faces and old scores. When one of the cameramen snapped his picture he barked something that made him clear out so fast that he almost fell. Unlike the younger man, Holiday, Angelo did not crave the spotlight. He had lasted as long as he had in the game for flying under the radar and didn't intend to change it, no matter what the rest of his crew chose to do. Both Angelo and Holiday positioned themselves at opposite ends of the limo just as the valet was opening the back door.

Swann stepped out first, sporting a red Armani button up and a pair of shades. That night he wore his hair out and pulled into a ponytail as opposed to his signature braids. He gave a nod to his partners and extended his hand to help his lady Marisol out of the whip. She was dressed in a cute red strapless number and some mean heels that were killing her feet, but she endured for the sake of making a good show of it. Through her man she was a member of the royal court and had to be on her A-game at all times. Swann escorted Marisol to the front of the establishment, where security was posted up, before returning to the limo and taking up his position as the third guard. This was the inner circle, and all three of them had pledged to live and die for the man who was just climbing out of the limo.

To say that Shai Clark stepped onto the curb would've been an understatement. He moved with such fluidity that his body appeared to be missing bones when he walked. He wore a three-piece black suit that hugged his wiry form like a second skin. There were more people out that night than Shai had thought there would be, but Sol had told him as much and he didn't listen. No matter, the more that were on hand to witness it the better it was for his rapidly growing legacy. The streets knew what time it was with Shai, but he was still fighting tooth and nail to strengthen the Clarks' stronghold in the legitimate business world. The move he was making that night was a power one, and he wanted everyone to know it.

Making it a point to avoid the cameras he busied himself helping Honey from the limo. She was wearing a cute black dress that was trimmed in sequins along the shoulders and around the waist. As usual, her golden silk locks were flawlessly curled. Around her hairline was a handmade headband that was sprinkled with little yellow and white diamonds. Honey's face was so flawlessly made up that she looked like she had just stepped off a television set. The cameramen swooped in and started snapping pictures of her. From the crowd she heard someone shout, "Madam Queen," to which she just smiled.

As Shai pulled her through the wall of flashbulbs, she placed her hand protectively over her ever-growing stomach to try to sooth the child growing inside it, who was reacting to her nervousness. Honey knew how important this was to Shai, and she wanted to make sure she was the epitome of the perfect fiancée, supporting her man. Shai must've picked up on her nervousness because he squeezed her hand and gave her a little wink, letting her know everything would be fine.

Shai continued to ignore the cameras and walked Honey to the entrance, with Angelo, Swann, and Holiday in tow. Looking like a gray dot in the middle of the black-clad security guards was Sol Lansky, an old friend and business partner of the late Poppa. He had once sat at the table as Poppa Clark's advisor, and now he whispered into Shai's ear. The gray-haired old man gave Shai a proud smile, the tension immediately drained from Shai's chest, and he was ready to address the crowd. Shai raised his hands for silence and the clambering people quieted like the president was about to give the State of the Union address. He might not have been the president, but in Harlem, he had just as much power, because he was the boss.

"God is good all the time," Shai began in his silky voice.

"And all the time God is good," the crowd responded accordingly. Poppa Clark had always taught him that if he wanted to get a room full of people's attention, then start with something religious because if they tried to ignore you, that would feel like they were blaspheming. When Poppa had first said this to him, he thought that his old man was out of his mind, but over the years, he learned that Poppa was *right* more than he was *wrong*.

"I would like to take this time to welcome you all to the latest piece of the Clark empire." Shai waved his hand, and the tarp was snatched away to reveal the chic restaurant that had been hiding beneath. "Daddy's Kitchen!"

Shai was immediately met with applause and whistles. Daddy's Kitchen was a decent-sized establishment, but what it lacked in size it more than made up for in swag. There was a large two-way glass with the words Daddy's Kitchen scrawled across it in gold letters. The two-way glass is so that people who valued their privacy could enjoy a nice meal without worrying about prying eyes, while still enjoying the view of the neighborhood. The spot would surely attract the cream of the socialite and underworlds, but it was also open to the people of the neighborhood. Daddy's Kitchen was a place where regular folks could mingle with stars on a level playing field. All were welcome at Daddy's Kitchen.

"This has been a long time coming," Shai continued, "and it was no easy road we took to see it happen. When my father first brought the idea to the table of putting money into rebuilding Harlem, everybody thought that he was crazy. They said that the glory days of Harlem had come and gone and that it would be a waste of time and money to bother with it. As we stand here tonight on this special occasion in the midst of Internet cafés, less than two blocks from the prestigious Colombia University, I guess we see who was right in that debate."

The crowd laughed.

"Tonight is a special occasion, but it is only the first in a string of many occasions such as this because we're not gonna stop here. I intend to keep putting money into the neighborhoods that I grew up to love so much until we restore the glory of Harlem, where we looked out for each other and keep the money in our own neighborhoods. I intend to show the naysayers that the people who were born, raised, and live in these neighborhoods have just as much right to make their fortunes in them, if not more so, than the people who are only here to make money off it. After all, that is the American dream, isn't it?"

The crowd went crazy, as he had hoped they would after the well rehearsed speech. After a few more words of thanks to those who had helped to make it possible, Shai cut the ribbon and officially opened Daddy's Kitchen to the public.

"Bravo, sweet prince." Sol clapped his hands, coming over to congratulate Shai. Everyone else had gone inside except Shai and a few of his team. "Kid, you know if you ever decide to get outta the life, you'd have a bright future in politics."

Shai smirked. "Thanks, but no thanks. I do my best work out here among my people."

"Indeed you do," Sol agreed. "Shai, over the years I've seen you put legitimate dollars in quite a few pockets, and I'm proud of your progress, and you know without me saying that Poppa would've damn sure been proud of you."

"Thanks, Sol, that's big coming from you."

"Yo, I can't even front; this shit is fly!" Holiday cut in. "Man, I seen some bad bitches roll up in here that I need to get at."

"You will mind your manners and do your job. We're here to work and not chase *bitches,* as you love to call them," Angelo told him sternly.

Holiday twisted his lips. "Angelo, you need to loosen up and stop being so stiff."

"Better to be stiff in the streets than stiff in the dirt, and you'd do well to remember that, li'l nigga," Angelo shot back. He had served during the reign of three different bosses in the Clark family and was one of the few left from the original regime. He had seen some twisted things in his days, so Angelo was always waiting for the other shoe to drop.

"Whatever."

A brown Buick pulled up alongside Shai's limo, boxing it in. Before they even got out of the tinted bucket, Shai and his whole crew knew who they would see. Alvarez and Brown hopped out of the whip, walking with a swagger that said they owned the night, but everyone knew who it really belonged to, which was part of the reason the detectives hated Shai so much. The limo driver rolled his window down to let the detectives know he couldn't move out of the parking spot, but they ignored him and headed straight for Shai.

"Well, well, if it ain't Cagney and Lacey." Holiday stepped between Shai and the detectives. He gave them a look that said exactly how he felt about them.

Detective Alvarez smirked and shook his head.

"What the fuck is so funny?" Holiday asked.

"The fact that you're too stupid to be afraid of us," Alvarez told him seriously. "You know, one of these days they might find you slumped in an alley behind that big-ass mouth of yours."

"Yeah, but I'll bet when they find me they'll find at least three niggaz that I took with me too."

"You really wanna do this here?" Alvarez asked. His eyes said he was ready to go there, but so did Holiday's.

"We can do it anywhere you want," Holiday matched his tone.

Angelo stepped over and pulled Holiday away. "Know how to pick your battles," he whispered in Holiday's ear as he positioned himself between him and the detective. "How can we help you, gentlemen?"

"What's up, Angie? Been awhile since I last saw you," Brown said addressing Angelo by his nickname.

Angelo shrugged. "My lady thinks that police contact is bad for my health."

"Your lady is very wise," Brown told him. The detective didn't like Angelo, but he respected him. He was an old-school hustler and understood the unspoken rules of conduct between the law and the lawless. "We just need to have a few words with your boss." He looked over at Shai.

Angelo looked over his shoulder at Shai, who was making his way toward them with Sol and Swann in tow. Shai placed a hand on Angelo's shoulder letting him know that it was okay.

"What up?" Shai asked, not bothering to hide his irritation with the detectives.

"Not much. Just came to have a short chat with you," Detective Brown told him.

"I don't think that's a good idea without his legal representation present," Sol spoke up. He looked down at his watch. "Mr. Scott should be here shortly if you gentlemen care to wait." Sol was referring to Scotty, Poppa Clark's one-time protégé and current legal counsel and coconsigliore to the family.

"That won't be necessary. This is a social call, not business," Detective Brown said, tapping the manila envelope he was carrying against his leg. It made him smile to see how Shai's eyes kept cutting to the envelope, wondering what was in it.

"Speak and be gone. I got people waiting on me," Shai said shortly.

"So I see." Alvarez craned his neck to see inside of Daddy's Kitchen. "This your new spot, Shai?"

"Something like that. Does the grand opening have anything to do with why you're here?"

"Nah, man, I was just wondering how the pork chops were in this joint. I might wanna bring a couple of the fellas from the department here for dinner," Alvarez said sarcastically.

"This ain't your kinda spot. We don't serve or allow pork, but there's a Dunkin' Donuts not too far from here."

Detective Alvarez laughed. "You're a funny guy, almost as funny as Tommy Gunz. Speaking of big bro, how is he? I haven't seen him around much lately."

"Tommy is good."

"Glad to hear it. You know Tommy Gunz was one of the last *stand-up guys* out here, no pun intended," Alvarez said with a cunning smile. A few years earlier Tommy had been paralyzed in the shooting that claimed his father's life and had since been confined to a wheelchair. Alvarez knew he was hitting below the belt with that statement, and so did everyone else.

Shai took a step toward the detective, fist balled and ready to pop off. Sol placed a calming hand on his arm and gave him a slight squeeze. Shai didn't go any further, but he stared daggers at the detective.

"If you've got something to say, then say it; if not, get the fuck from around my establishment before I have you brought up on harassment charges," Shai said through clenched teeth.

Detective Brown chuckled. "That shit sounds good, but we know people like you don't talk to the police . . . at least not all of you." He let his eyes sweep Shai's soldiers accusingly. "Anyhow, we've had our fun, so now let's cut the bullshit and get to the point of why we're here. Word on the streets is that you've got a problem, Shai."

Now, it was Shai's turn to chuckle. "Nah, I ain't got no problems. Everybody loves the Clarks. I'm afraid you boys are getting bad information."

"Yeah, maybe if you paid your informants a li'l more for their souls they'd do their jobs properly," Swann added.

"If I were you, I wouldn't be so quick to make jokes, Swann. We hear your name is still on somebody's piece of paper for what you did to Tech. Word has it you're number one on the Blood Hit Parade," Brown said slyly.

Swann shrugged. "I don't know nothing about no Bloods, and I don't know anybody named Tech."

Detective Brown sneered. "So you say, but the hood is saying otherwise. We all know Tech was a piece of shit. Hell, that whole bastard clan from Jah down to Ashanti have all been rotten from the inside out, but the streets love a degenerate like that. Tech was a man of respect, and he got done dirty. Right now, the only thing that's keeping you off the front page of the *Daily News* is the fact that you're Shai's number-one hand job. If the Clarks ever decide to lift that veil of protection, it's over for you, *Blood*," Brown said sarcastically.

"Whatever, nigga. I told you I don't know nobody named Tech," Swann said, trying to keep his voice steady, but Detective Brown was getting under his skin.

Brown shrugged. "Just the same, I'd grow eyes in the back of my head if I were you. Now, back to what I was saying." He turned to Shai. "Shai, I think we all know that there is a laundry list of people who don't like the way you're running your father's organization and would love to see you crushed by the shadow you've been living in. They're saying that your reign as king is over, and it's time for some fresh blood," Brown taunted him.

Shai waved him off. "If all you've come here to do is tell me a bunch of shit that people are saying, then we ain't got nothing to talk about. You gentlemen have a good night." Shai turned to walk away, but the picture Detective Brown pulled from the envelope and tossed at his feet made him pause. He looked down at the picture of a man and woman in a car riddled with bullets and turned to look at Detective Brown.

"I thought that would get your attention." Brown pulled the rest of the pictures from the envelope. "That was Willie Jones and his girlfriend. They were murdered leaving a baby shower." He tossed another picture at Shai's feet. This one was of a young man who was missing one side of his face. "We found him in an abandoned drug house. His mama had to give him a closed casket funeral. And this is one of my personal favorites." Brown held up the picture of Slick's mutilated face. "Poor bastard left behind a child and a grieving mother. The killer left a little note for you too." He pointed out the word carved into Slick's forehead.

"Fuck does any of this have to do with me?" Shai turned away from the picture.

"It has *everything* to do with you, baby boy." Brown tapped Shai in the chest with the picture. "All of these stiffs lead back to you. At one point or another, all of these guys worked for the Clark family."

"Unless you've got a paycheck issued to one of these men from one of our companies you can't prove that," Shai said dismissively.

Detective Alvarez's cheek twitched at Shai's arrogance. He wanted to slap the young man, but he knew the game that he and his partner were playing was hurting Shai more than his hands could. "We may not be able to prove it, but we all know there's truth in what my partner is saying. Since being coy about it ain't getting us nowhere, let's be frank, shall we? Shai, I don't give a fuck about your ex-stripper girlfriend or the faggot with the ponytail standing at your side like he wanna do something." He jabbed his finger at Swann. "I ain't got a problem with a nigga putting two in ya head, because that's probably the only thing that is gonna knock some sense into it, but it becomes a problem when it happens on my streets and innocent people are placed in danger, all because you dickheads wanna make movies in the streets. We ain't having it, Shai, not from you or anybody else in this city. You wanna kill each other, take it to New Jersey. New York is off-limits, and I'm willing to go the extra mile to keep it that way, feel me?"

"Nah, I don't feel you," Shai said. "I don't feel you coming out here fucking with my groove, nor do I feel you fucking with my time over some murders that ain't got nothing to do with me. You talking fantasies right now, my nigga. If you wanna sell stories, get yourself a Facebook page and a graphic designer to put 'bestseller' on the cover," Shai mocked him. "Whoever did this is a slum nigga, and you know that ain't never been my style. I'm a businessman, and when I took over this family, all illicit dealings were shut down. Now do *you* feel *me*?"

"Shai, we didn't come here to argue or embarrass you on your special night, so let's not make it more than what it is. All we want is a name and a reason so we can shut this down before more blood is spilled." Detective Brown tried to sound sympathetic.

Shai looked him square in the eyes. "I'm afraid I can't help you. Good night, gentlemen."

"G-code, huh?" Alvarez asked Shai.

"Live by it, die by it," Swann answered for him.

"If y'all like it, we love it," Brown said, "but Shai, I'd like to leave you with a little something to think on, if I may." Shai's face remained unchanged, so Brown continued. "Whoever is going at you don't give too much of a fuck about what your last name is and is going out of their way to let you know as much. It's one thing to play war from a distance, but it becomes a whole different animal when the feud spills over into your neighborhood and eventually starts to soil your doormat. This is the part of the game that your daddy couldn't teach you, but I guarantee the streets will if you don't wise up. Y'all have a good night." Brown started back for the Buick. Alvarez gave Shai and his crew the once-over before following his partner.

"You gentlemen have forgotten your pictures," Sol called after them, referring to the graphic photos that were still lying on the ground in front of the restaurant.

Detective Alvarez ignored him and got back in the passenger seat, slamming the door firmly behind him. Detective Brown paused and addressed Sol. "Nah, you guys keep them. We've got plenty more at the station." He paused. "Mr. Lansky, you've been around the block a few times. If you love Shai like you profess to, then talk to him and let him know what time it really is before he makes it to our collection of photographs." Brown got behind the wheel of the Buick and peeled off.

Just as the detectives were pulling off, Scotty was hopping out of a taxi in front Daddy's Kitchen. He was wearing a simple black V-neck sweater under a cream-colored blazer. Chugging along behind him was a thick Spanish chick, who was wearing a dress that was so tight you didn't have to wonder what her intentions were for the night. Scotty was smiling from ear to ear because he couldn't wait to come through the event sporting the porn star, but the smile faded when he saw the Buick pulling off and the look on Shai's face. In less than three seconds his demeanor changed, and he went from homeboy to consigliore. He whispered for the porn star to meet him inside and walked over to see what was good with his friend.

"Was that who I think it was?" Scotty asked, giving Shai dap and nodding in salute to the others.

"Yeah," Shai said, still staring out into traffic. He was so mad that he felt one of his fillings shift when he flexed his jaw. Shai had worked his ass off to clean up the Clark image and gain the support of the people who made the world go round, and the detectives tried to throw a monkey wrench in it by showing up there. People with power generally had secrets, and seeing him being accosted by the police might make some of them skittish.

Scotty noticed the pictures on the floor at Shai's feet and frowned. He scooped the pictures up and flipped through them. "Take these shits somewhere and burn them," he told Holiday, passing him the pictures. "Shai, what did them two dicks want?"

Shai dismissed it. "They ain't want shit, just fishing as usual."

Scotty screwed his face. "My nigga, pictures of dead bodies at your feet on one of the biggest nights of your life don't look like fishing. Somebody tell me what the fuck is going on," he said, looking at all the men assembled.

"They're saying that somebody murked them cats in the pictures to send a message to Shai," Angelo spoke in a hushed tone.

"Did they say who?" Scotty asked.

"That's what they came to ask us."

Scotty ran his hand over his face in frustration. "Leave it to the police to be more clueless than most. Well, we ain't at war with anybody that I know of so my question is; who might've been holding a big enough grudge to risk getting wiped off the fucking map for disrespecting this thing of ours?" He looked at Shai.

"Someone with very little to lose," Sol answered for Shai.

FOUR

ANIMAL SLOUCHED IN THE CHEAP MOTEL CHAIR with his feet outstretched and crossed at the ankles. Playing softly in the motel's cheap CD player was the first mix tape he had released under Big Dawg. With his eyes half-closed, dreamily, he nodded and mouthed the lyrics. He had been sitting in that position almost the entire night, chain-smoking and replaying the night's events over and over again in his head like his favorite movie. The heady rush of the kill had him too wired to sleep.

Sleep hadn't come easy to Animal in a long time, and it became harder for him with every sin he committed. He was afraid of the things he would see when he closed his eyes. Sometimes he would stay awake until his body forced him into deep, dreamless sleep just to avoid the images that lived in his subconscious.

Old San Juan would forever be a stain on Animal's already splotched soul. The war between Poppito and Cruz had torn apart the very streets that they both claimed to love so much.

Poppito was a powerful drug baron who commanded a small army, but Cruz was a crooked police captain and had the government on his side. Poppito couldn't match Cruz's resources, and it looked as if he would lose the war when, in an act of desperation, he made a pact with the devil and in came Los Negro Muertes.

Los Negro Muertes was a crew of mercenaries known throughout the Caribbean and coastal U.S. as the Black Death, a title they had earned from the trail of dead bodies they left in every city they visited. Their numbers were made up of outlaws from different ports who had sold their souls to the ringmaster of the deadly circus, K-Dawg. Animal watched as K-Dawg twisted the wills of his followers to where they were loyal to him above all, including their families. Animal had seen this firsthand when he found himself in a fight to the death with his own brother.

When Animal fled the clutches of Los Negro Muertes in an attempt to get back to Gucci, it was Justice who K-Dawg sent after him. Animal couldn't believe his eyes when he came out of the church to find his brother waiting for him with some of K-Dawg's men and orders to bring him back dead or alive. Animal sought to reason with his brother, but when Justice pointed that M16 at him, he knew there was no more to be said between them. In the shadow of a church in Old San Juan, history repeated itself and pit Cain against Abel, but in this version, it was Abel who bested Cain. When Animal opened his brother up and saw the blood, the same blood that pumped in his veins, he couldn't bring himself to do it. He spared Justice's life, but left him with a scar letting him know he wouldn't be as merciful the next time they met.

The first rays of the sun crept through the motel window and kissed Animal's eyelids, bringing him back to the here and now. Animal stood and stretched the kinks out of his body from sitting in one position for so many hours. He stiffly pulled his hoodie over his head, then went about the hassle of stuffing his hair into the wool Rasta cap. With his disguise in place, Animal armed himself and headed for the door. As an afterthought, he went back and grabbed the CD from the player and took it with him.

Traffic was light at that hour of the morning. Animal rolled through the drive-through to grab two breakfast wraps and two coffees. He mashed both breakfast wraps and guzzled one of the coffees by the time he was pulling out of the McDonald's parking lot and hung a left for the West Side Highway. He steered the rental with one hand and used the other to pour the last bit of liquor from the pint into the other coffee cup. It was way too early for him to be drinking and far too late for him to care.

Animal shot north on the West Side and merged with the morning commuters into the traffic leading toward the George Washington Bridge, heading into New Jersey. The ride to Jersey City was longer than it had to be because of the route that Animal had chosen to take. Going through the Holland would've put him in Jersey City in less than five minutes, but he took the G.W.B. because it was a less secure route. The last thing he needed was to be a victim of a random checkpoint and have some overzealous cop lose his life for trying to stand between Animal and fate.

He pushed the rental through the streets of Jersey City, navigating more by instinct than the directions of the GPS on his lap. He wasn't too familiar with Jersey, but he knew the place where he was going like the back of his hand. He turned into the driveway of the park and coasted through the parking area but didn't see the car he had been tailing for the past few weekends. Since he didn't see it, he pulled to the far end of the lot and decided to wait. One thing he had learned was patience. After checking to make sure his gun was loaded and a round chambered, he turned his attention to the basketball court a few feet away.

Teenagers crowded the court wearing either black or white basketball jerseys, playing ball, while an older white man in a warm-up suit barked instructions at them. Animal ignored most of the teens and searched for one in particular. It took a few minutes, but he finally spotted him at the other end of the court practicing his free throws. Animal studied his youthful brown face and couldn't help but to marvel at how strongly all the men in that family resembled one another. Seeing the boy's face took Animal to a place of pain and rage. His heart beat so hard in his chest that he feared people could hear it outside the car, so he turned up the volume on the CD spinning in the system. Something about the sound of his own voice soothed him, and he was able to calm down a bit, though not much. He was always on edge just before a kill.

Animal watched the boy as he and the rest of the teens performed a series of drills, then separated into two teams and played a game of full court basketball. The young boy was impressive as he moved fluidly up and down the court, scoring on the other kids with ease. He was a natural, and it was apparent to anyone watching. If the boy managed to fly straight he would have a promising future, but if he was anything like the others, he would throw his future out the window once he got his first good whiff of the streets.

"Such a waste," Animal said to no one in particular.

Animal had been so engrossed in watching the boy that he almost missed the SUV he had been waiting for turn into the parking area. It was a money green Yukon with tinted windows and a chrome grill to match the rims. As luck would have it, the hulking truck pulled to a stop directly behind the rental, boxing Animal in. Animal adjusted his rearview mirror so he could try to see who was inside. The tints made it almost impossible to make a positive ID on the driver, but it didn't matter. They were dead. Shoving his pistol into his pants, Animal slid from the car to step to his business.

"That joint go hard."

The voice startled Animal. He spun, ready to draw his weapon and cut down whoever had tried to get the drop on him, but caught himself when he realized it was the boy from the basketball court speaking to him. He hadn't even heard him approach, but there he was standing less than three feet away.

"You shouldn't sneak up on people like that, kid," Animal told the boy.

"My fault, I was just trying to hear the song." The kid took a cautionary step back. His eyes drifted from Animal's face to the bulge under his shirt.

Animal started to shoo him away, but thought better of it. If he played it right he could use the boy to draw his prey out and put him at a disadvantage.

"You good, shorty," Animal leaned against the rental. He positioned himself so that he could still see the Yukon in his side mirror. As soon as the driver stepped out to investigate, Animal intended to splatter him.

"What you know about that?" Animal asked the boy.

"Man, it ain't like nothing I ever hear round here," the kid said with a slight accent. Animal could tell he was a native of the South, but couldn't place exactly where.

"That's because your generation don't know much about real music."

"Who is that?" the boy asked, fascinated with the complex lyrics.

Animal paused. "Just some dude I used to know." He made small talk with the boy, while watching the Yukon the whole time. The driver finally got tired of waiting and made to get out of the car as Animal knew he would. "Go ahead and turn it up so you can really hear it." Animal opened the door for the boy so he could get in and adjust the volume. While the boy fumbled with the stereo Animal drew his gun, ready to bang out on his enemy, but when he caught a glimpse of the reflection in the window of the open door, it wasn't a man storming in his direction, but a female. In his haste for vengeance he had almost made a horrible mistake. Animal barely had time to throw the gun back in his pants before she was on them and furious.

"Boy, have you lost your damn mind?" The woman shoved Animal out of the way and snatched the boy from the vehicle. She was dark skinned and beefy with salt-and-pepper hair that she wore in feathered curls. "This ain't the South. Little naïve boys get kidnapped in New York City," she scolded him.

"Suge, I was only listening to the music," the boy tried to explain.

"I don't give a hoot what you were doing; it was danger-ous. You know how your cousin is over you and ain't no telling what he'd do if I let something happen to you," she said. Animal could pick up the genuine fear in her voice under all her gruff bravado.

"It was my fault, ma'am," Animal interjected. "He liked the song, so I was trying to let him hear it. I didn't mean any dis-respect."

Suge looked Animal up and down. "What you did or didn't mean is anyone's guess, but you look like you got sense enough to know you can get in a mess of trouble for inviting children into your car."

"You're right, and I'm sorry," Animal said sincerely.

Suge nodded, neither accepting nor rejecting his apology. "Let's go," she ordered the boy and stormed back toward the car. The boy gave Animal a sad wave, then made to follow Suge to the SUV.

"Hold on, kid," Animal called after him. He popped the CD from the player and placed it in the CD case. "Here you go." Animal presented the boy with the CD.

"I can have it?" The boy's eyes widened in excitement.

"Since you like it so much, run with it. I ain't got no more use for it," Animal told him.

"Thanks a lot, man!"

"What's your name, kid?" Animal asked, though he wasn't sure why. There was something about the way the boy carried himself that made him intriguing.

"Nicholas, but everybody calls me Nickels."

"Nicholas Clark, if I gotta call you again we're gonna have a problem!" Suge shouted through the window.

"I gotta go, but thanks again," Nickels told Animal and hurried to the truck.

Animal had spent the entire ride from New Jersey back to Harlem fuming over the cancelled hit. This wasn't just some street punk he was after; it was Angelo, one of Shai's capos and closest friends. Angelo was a cagey street vet who kept with no set routine except taking Nickels to basketball practice on weekends. Animal wanted to chalk Angelo's absence up to shitty luck, but something about it didn't feel right. The fact that Angelo wasn't there meant that Shai and his crew had gotten the message and were gearing up for battle. The fact that they were now aware of the threat did little to take away from Animal's element of surprise because he was pretty sure none of them knew how to defend themselves against a ghost.

Animal jumped off the highway and took the streets. He rode down Broadway, looking at the General Grant Houses looming to his left. He had had some wild times in the hallways in his days as a street punk. The last he'd heard, King James had Grant in a headlock and was gobbling up more and more territory by the day. Animal knew firsthand that King had been groomed by one of the greatest criminal minds of the underworld to be the next heir to the throne of Harlem. Much like his mentor, he quickly established himself as a force in the streets, but unlike his mentor, he was a novice at the arts of manipulation and diplomacy. King James had built a reputation as a bull on the streets, and Animal respected his gangsta for taking the hood the way he did, but wondered if he possessed the qualities it would take to hold onto what he had taken.

Animal sat waiting for the red light to turn green at the intersection of Broadway and LaSalle. He was admiring the renovations they had done to some of the stores when he spotted a familiar face coming out of the bodega. When he realized who he was looking at, his heart leaped into his throat, and he almost cried out. He started to hit the horn, but caught himself. He wasn't in New York on a social call and had to keep his focus on his mission.

Ashanti had gotten taller since the last time Animal had seen him, but he still had the same baby face and wore the same mischievous scowl. His jeans were sagging off his ass so you could see his boxers and he was *flamed up,* with a red bandana tied around his neck and one hanging from his back pocket. His whole appearance screamed gang related, and he wore it like a badge of honor. Animal used to always warn Ashanti about making himself a target for rivals or the police, but big brother wasn't around to scold him anymore so the youngster was marching to his own beat.

On Ashanti's heels was a young girl. She was short with a pretty face and curves so nice that you couldn't help but to take a second look. From the way she moved Animal could tell she was too young for him to ever consider going in on, but she was just Ashanti's speed. Animal smiled like a proud father as his young boy handled the girl with the poise of an old head. In all the years Animal had known Ashanti, this was his first time ever seeing him interact with a girl, outside of trying to avoid getting slapped for something he said or did. It was an emotional and proud moment for Animal, and he had no one he could share it with because he was supposed to be a ghost. Ashanti and the young girl ended the conversation, and he sent her on her way in the direction of 3150, while he, himself, climbed back on his mountain bike and went his way.

Seeing Ashanti made Animal think of young Nickels Clark and how what he planned to do would affect the grand scheme of Nickels's life. He wondered how little Nickels would make it in the world if he was left to raise himself. Would he still chase his hoop dreams or become like the rest of them—another bastard child of the ghetto?

FIVE

THE PROJECT APARTMENT WAS A WHIRL OF noise and activity. In the kitchen, a crackhead named Patty stood over the stove, shuffling pots and adjusting the level of the flame as needed like a master chef. She took a pot off the stove and eyeballed it, making sure the cookielike object was in the bottom of it. Once the cookie began to coagulate, Patty removed the pot from the stove and placed it on the table, where two chicks sat chopping up the cookies that had hardened already and placed small pieces into baggies to be sold on the street. Welcome to the trap house.

King James stood near the window staring out intently, stroking his goatee occasionally. He wore a red and white Nike tracksuit with the matching red and white Nikes. Hanging from his neck was a thick cable chain with a large medallion dangling at the end of it. The medallion was black onyx with a diamond-filled number seven nestled in a crescent moon. For all who saw it, the piece was a symbol of his faith and his ruthlessness.

The sound of raised voices drew his attention from the window to the middle of the living room. Two young men, Dee and Meek, sat on the couch in front of a big-screen television engaged in a heated game of NBA 2K12. Dee was getting the better of Meek, and Meek wasn't happy about it, cursing every time he missed a shot. King James had tried ignoring them, but their bickering had finally gotten on his last nerves.

"Fuck is y'all making all that noise for?" King snapped.

"This nigga is mad because I'm getting in that ass," Dee laughed.

"Fuck you! The only reason you're winning is because you got the Heat and I'm playing with these bum-ass Hawks," Meek shot back.

Dee flicked his thumb on the controller and nailed a three-pointer with Mario Chalmers. "My nigga, you could have the Dream Team and I'd *still* be busting your ass because you're garbage!"

King walked over and snatched the cord from the wall, abruptly ending their game. "I'm glad y'all got time to play video games instead of doing what the fuck I'm paying you to do."

"C'mon, King, we had money on that game," Dee whined.

"Nigga, fuck the money on that game. We got money on the streets, and y'all need to be worried about that instead of that fucking game."

"It's slow right now. Ain't nothing going on outside," Meek said, propping his feet on the coffee table and lighting the weed clip he and Dee had been smoking.

King James slapped Meek's feet off the coffee table and snatched him up roughly by his shirt. "Ain't nothing going on, huh?" He dragged Meek to the window and pressed his face to the glass. "What is that?" King pointed to a Direct TV van that was parked near the bus stop.

"It's a cable van, B. Somebody is probably getting their cable hooked up. Why you acting all paranoid?" Meek babbled.

"This is the projects. You're not allowed to have those dishes, so why would they be here, you dumb muthafucka?" King released him. "Keep your eyes on that fucking van. If they're still there in fifteen minutes close shop for the day. And you," he turned to Dee, "since you ain't got nothing to do, grab a razor and help these bitches finish chopping and bagging my shit."

"I ain't no bitch," one of the girls at the table spoke up.

"For as much as I pay you I can call you what the fuck I want. If you don't like it, get yo monkey ass out, and I'll get somebody to replace you," he told her. King crossed the living room and saw that the apartment door was open, which angered him more. Everybody in the spot knew that unless you were coming and going, the doors were to be closed and locked at all times. "Who the fuck is that?" He snatched the door open, startling Fatima, the girl who had been holding the door ajar.

When King first went away, Fatima was a kid playing jump rope in the park, but when he came home, she was a young woman and had hung up her jump rope for grown folk's games. If you had to describe Fatima in one word, it would be BAD. She was a young redbone piece who stood just a hair over five-five, with more curves than a roller coaster. More than a few people were waiting for Fatima to turn eighteen that year so they could officially make their bids for the beauty. She had offered herself to King and for as much as he wanted to hit it, he passed. He had known Fatima all her life and trusted her like a sister, so bringing sex into the equation would've complicated things.

"That ain't nobody but Beans." Fatima nodded at the addict standing outside the door holding two shopping bags. "He's selling bottles of champagne half price," she explained.

"I don't care who is selling what. If he ain't here to buy drugs, then get the fuck away from the door." King slammed the door in Bean's face. "Fatima, how many times do I have to tell your hardheaded ass not to open this door for nobody who ain't a part of this team? That kinda stupid shit gets niggaz' cribs ran up in."

"A'ight, I heard you," Fatima said with an attitude.

"If you heard me, then I wouldn't have to repeat myself. Get ya shit together Fatima, or your ass is outta here, feel me?"

Fatima's eyes narrowed to slits. She had always been King's favorite, so for him to talk to her like that in front of the other workers threw her off. "You got it," she said slyly and left the apartment, slamming the door on her way out.

"What good is having a team if you gotta do everything yourself? Word to mine, if y'all don't get ya shit together, you will all be looking for somebody else's operation to fuck up!" King shouted.

"Fuck is going on out here?" Lakim came rushing from one of the bedrooms with his gun at the ready and the flap of his do-rag blowing behind him. Lakim was a short, stocky dude, with a slight overbite that he capped with gold teeth. He was King James's right hand and best friend. "Damn, fuck is ya problem, God?" Lakim asked King.

"My problem is that we're at war, and everybody around this bitch is acting like this is Sesame Street!"

Lakim saw the worry etched across King James's face that no one else noticed. "Yo, give me this walk to the store right quick."

"Nah, I gotta make sure the rest of this shit gets packaged up and outta here."

"King, the soldiers got it. Take a walk with me." Lakim undid the locks and held the door open for King. King was hesitant, but he eventually walked through the door and allowed Lakim to lead him outside the apartment.

The hall was empty save for a young boy named Biz, who hustled for King. Biz was leaning against a wall talking to a fiend, shuffling through the drugs in his hand to show her his wares. King's nostrils flared, and he made hurried steps toward Biz. Biz smiled when he saw King coming his way, but that smile faded when King grabbed him roughly by the collar and shoved him against the wall. Lakim ushered the fiend out of the building and came to stand beside King.

"What are you doing?" King pressed Biz, who looked like he was about to piss his pants.

"I'm making a sale. What's the problem?" Biz asked confused.

"The problem is y'all niggaz can't follow directions. I told you that when you sling, make the sale outside! If you ain't always violating the lobbies and stairwells, scaring the shit out of the old heads that live in the building, they're less likely to call the police on you. We give respect to receive it, do you understand?" King released Biz and smoothed his clothes where he had wrinkled them when he grabbed him.

"Yeah, man, my fault," Biz said sheepishly.

"Don't worry about it, my nigga. Just be more tactful with

how you get ya money, fam." King patted him on the back letting him know all was well, then exited the lobby.

The minute King stepped out of the building he scoped the Direct TV truck. There was a Spanish dude sitting in the passenger's seat watching King and Lakim, but acting like he was reading his clipboard. Instead of going to the store on the corner they decided to cut through the projects and hit Amsterdam. The block was just beginning to come back to life. It had been raining all morning, which kept most people indoors, and even though it had stopped by that point, everything outside was still damp. Meek hadn't been lying about it being slow because there wasn't a fiend in sight besides the one Lakim had chased out of the lobby.

"What up with you, God? It seems like any li'l thing is setting you off lately. Speak on it," Lakim said.

"Ain't shit, man. I'm just dealing with a lot right now," King told him.

"You stressing over shit with sun and them talking to them people? I told you I already put the wheels in motion, and that faggot will be dust before the sun sets," Lakim assured him.

King saw the look on Lakim's face and immediately began to question his decision to let Lakim handle it at his discretion. Recently they had found out a youngster that King had handpicked had betrayed them. Apparently his eyes had gotten bigger than his belly, and he was stealing work from King James and selling it in the Bronx. The punch line was that he was doing it with the blessings of the police. The kid was a confidential informant who had helped the police take down the same cats he was selling the drugs to. This kept his furry rat pockets stuffed with money, and the police were able to make their quotas every week. To their knowledge, he had never given up any of King's people, but they weren't about to sit around and wait for it to happen, so they laid a trap for the rat.

"These niggaz confuse me, La," King began. "It seems like no matter how much you give them freely they still want to take more."

Lakim shrugged. "They're criminals, what the fuck you expect?"

King laughed. "True indeed." When the laugh had faded King's face became serious. "I was thinking about sun, but that ain't what's weighing heaviest on me. I'm still tripping off this nigga, Shai."

Lakim sucked his gold teeth. "You still off that shit?"

"Shouldn't I be?" King asked honestly. "All I was trying to do was get a sit-down with the kid and look where we're at with it now." King patted his chest, and you could hear the heavy thud of the bulletproof vest under his track jacket.

"I feel you, but some shit just can't be avoided. You came at sun like a man, but the nigga Shai is arrogant, so he felt like he had to make a movie, and now it's on and popping." Lakim raised his shirt and showed King the butt of his gun.

"True indeed, God. You know I'm 'bout my business from the womb to the tomb, but Shai is the boss of bosses with an army behind him, so the deck is stacked against us off the muscle."

Lakim sucked his teeth. "Let me break something down to you, B. I respect all that Shai is, a boss with his li'l army and all that, but we still holding the best hand."

"How you figure?"

"Simple. They got it all, and we ain't got shit, so we ain't got no problem dying in the streets for what we believe in. Why the fuck should we? I mean, who's gonna miss us when we're gone besides us? Shai's people got families they wanna go home to, and the millisecond they hesitate while they're thinking about those families is all the time I need to blow one of their faces the fuck off!"

King nodded, reflecting on what had brought them to that point. In the beginning, the plan had been to simply try to set up a meeting with Shai to talk business. King James, being the new hustler in town, thought it would be looked on as a sign of respect by approaching Shai with tact and grace, but it didn't go down like that. Alcohol, egos, and the tempers of their entourages turned it into something else. Any chance of reconciliation went out the window when Shai sent his young boys to try to murder King. The die had been cast, and it was game on.

"Yo, how ya shoulder, kid?" Lakim changed the subject, seeing King didn't really wanna talk about the beef with Shai.

"Ain't about shit." King rotated his shoulder in a half circle, wincing a bit. "The bullet took a nasty chunk outta my arm, but it didn't stick around. I'm probably gonna have a scar for life though."

"Better a chunk outta ya arm than a chunk outta ya head," Lakim quipped. "While I'm thinking about it, I dropped that bread off to Dump's BM."

This made King perk up a bit. "Yeah? How's the god doing?"

"You know that nigga is tougher than leather. They patched his ass up at Bellevue Hospital, and soon as he's up to it they're gonna arraign him. I asked the nigga did he need anything, and he told me to bring him two strippers and a Viagra pill!"

King laughed. "Same old Dump."

Dump had been the muscle of their crew. When it went down in the club with Shai's people, his hammer had definitely barked. Unfortunately for Dump, he got hit with a bullet and a charge. He was currently in the hospital recovering from the surgery and awaiting transport to Rikers Island. Dump was already on parole and now looking at two bodies, and being that he was found at the scene of the crime, shot, it didn't look good for him. Word on the street was that they offered to let Dump skate on a three to six if he rolled over on his people, but Dump told them to *eat a dick,* as King James knew he would. King had hired the best team of lawyers crack money could buy to defend his friend, and if, God forbid, Dump had to do time, King would take care of him for the rest of his days. Dump was one of the few dudes who understood the rules of the game, and he played it accordingly.

"The nigga asked me to tell you to come *hoffa* at him when he touch the island," Lakim continued.

King's brow furrowed. "I'll write him, but I don't know if I'm gonna make that trip just yet. I'm hot with them people because of the thing with Shai, so I don't need them crackers playing connect the dots by having me on Dump's visiting list. Give the homie my love the next time you're up though."

Lakim's cell going off took them off the subject of Dump and his bid. "Peace," Lakim said into the phone. He listened for a few seconds and nodded. "True," he said, then hung up.

"Who was that?" King asked.

Lakim smirked. "Let's just say you got one less headache to deal with."

SIX

OF ALL THE PLACES ALONZO COULD BE at that moment, standing in front of the Root Spot on 123rd and Seventh wasn't one of them. He was tired, musty, and wanted nothing more than to go home and take it down, but he needed money more than he needed rest, which is what brought him to the Root Spot.

Alonzo had been young and wild in the days when he was known as Zo-Pound. They called him this because of his fetishes for .45s and .357s. Five was his lucky number, so he stuck to it. From a young age, Zo-Pound was on the fast track to becoming a hood legend until a state bid gave him some time to reflect on his life. When he was released, his attitude was different so he finally managed to put Zo-Pound to bed and began to be comfortable being Alonzo again. With a nice job as an assistant manager at a supermarket and a girl in his sights, all was right in Alonzo's world. This all changed the night he agreed to take a ride with his brother Lakim. Alonzo found his life changed dramatically in the blink of an eye. A series of events had cost him his job, the girl he loved, and almost his sanity. He'd slipped and let Zo-Pound out and was now having trouble getting him back in the box.

After what seemed like forever, the green Acura he had been waiting for finally pulled up. Alonzo slipped back inside the doorway of the Root Spot and waited. The driver of the Acura got out and made his way to the entrance of the Root Spot. He was a short kid with a big head that he wore cut low. His name was Sean, and he had been a low-level street dealer until King James put him on and gave him status. Up until recently, he had been a good and reliable worker who King James spoke very highly of, but somewhere along the line, things had changed so Zo-Pound was sent to pay a call on him.

When Sean reached for the door, Alonzo stepped out and they collided. Sean looked up, ready to bark, but his face softened when he saw a familiar face. "Oh shit, what's good, my G?" He gave Alonzo dap. He only knew Alonzo as a cat from the hood who worked at the supermarket so he was at ease around him.

"Not too much, just stopped through to get a shot." Alonzo raised the bag he had purchased an hour before.

"Yeah? I fuck with those root-shots heavy! A shot and a good blunt will have you hit," Sean said.

"That's what I'm about to do now, hit these shots and burn an L. You know I got that fire on deck, right?" Alonzo said in a hushed tone. He showed Sean the bag of pretty green Kush he had palmed.

"You selling weed now, Alonzo? I thought you was on some working shit?" Sean frowned.

"Nah, I'm still working my gig. This is my li'l side hustle, ya dig? This weed been leaving niggaz stretched all over the projects, kid," Alonzo told him.

Sean faked disbelief. "Say word?"

"Word!" Alonzo insisted. "Check it out. Let's get in the whip and blow one down, and if you like it, you spend something with me. If you don't like it, then fuck it; you just got high on me."

Sean, being the moocher he was, saw the opportunity for a free buzz. "A'ight, that's a bet. Let me just grab my shots and let's spin."

Sean got his shots, then he and Alonzo got in the whip and spun off. They rode around Harlem, shooting the breeze while Alonzo twisted two blunts. After smoking the first one, Sean was so high that he suggested that they pull over and burn the last blunt. They found a secluded block on Ninety-something Street and parked the Acura and sparked the weed.

"Man, you wasn't lying about this weed being good, bro." Sean smirked goofily. His eyes were glassy, and his speech was beginning to slow.

"I told you." Alonzo took two tokes and blew them back out without inhaling. "I been making some decent money off this weed thing because the job market is slow. Shit, I got bills and a new a baby on the way, so I gotta make it happen any way I can. It's crunch time for me, my nigga," Alonzo said, his tone sincere.

Sean's brain began to whirl. From what he knew of Alonzo, he had always been a good and loyal cat. With the way some of the circles he was moving in he could use a soldier like Alonzo to watch his back. Knowing that money was the root and salvation of most problems, that's how he came at him.

"Check it out, my dude," Sean began. "I been seeing ya li'l movements around the hood, man. I can respect your grind."

"Thanks, Sean. That means a lot coming from a cat who's where you're at with it." Alonzo stroked his ego.

"All good, my nigga. I'm just calling it like I see it. But, yo, you know I'm making some moves, power moves of my own, right?"

Alonzo nodded. "I see you out here getting it."

"Yeah, I'm getting it, but I'm trying to share it too, feel me? Yo, if you ever feel like you tired of nickel and diming, you need to come holla at me."

"That's love, Sean, real talk. But, yo, don't you work for that dude King James?" Alonzo asked.

Sean made a dismissive gesture. "I don't work for nobody, nigga! I work with King James and that's a temporary arrangement." Sean took another hit of the blunt and his eyes dipped a little lower. The weed had him feeling arrogant, and he wanted to impress Alonzo. "I got it on good authority that King's reign on the top is gonna be shorter than leprechauns."

Alonzo twisted his lips. "Nah, the way I hear it is, King James got the streets in a headlock that ain't nobody been able to break. None of the crews want it with that cat."

"That's because they crews ain't big enough." Sean laughed at his own inside joke.

"What you mean by that?"

Sean thought on it for a minute. "Let's just say that the biggest gang in the world is about to knock the King off his throne, and as soon as that happens, I'm gonna snatch it!"

"Wow, that's crazy. But I thought you and King were close."

Sean frowned. "Fuck him; that nigga ain't good to nobody

but himself. I can't wait on no man to feed me. I gotta get it how I get it, feel me?"

"Nah, I don't feel you," someone said from the driver-side window. Sean turned and saw a kid perched on a mountain bike, wearing a black hoodie and black shorts. A red bandana was tied around his face, but you could see his eyes. They were the eyes of someone who had lost all faith in the world. "In fact, you sound like a bitch-ass nigga to me." He pulled a long silver gun.

Sean opened his mouth to say something, but the kid shoved the barrel of the gun into his mouth, breaking two of Sean's teeth on its way to his throat. "This will teach you to keep your big-ass mouth closed." He pulled the trigger. Alonzo barely had time to jump out of the passenger's side before the back of Sean's head sprayed all over the inside of the Acura.

"Why the fuck didn't you let me get out of the car before you shot him?" Alonzo barked, getting to his feet. He had scraped his hands and knees while diving out of the car.

Ashanti pulled the mask down so that Alonzo could see his grinning teenage face. "Sorry, dawg, I guess I just got caught up in the moment."

"You be on some bullshit," Alonzo said, climbing on the back of the bike.

"Shut up and handle your business so we can dip," Ashanti said, passing Alonzo the gun.

Alonzo looked in the car at the mess that had once been Sean. His throat and the back of his head were sitting in the cup holder, and there was smoke still coming out of what was left of his mouth. King James had been good to Sean, and Sean snaked him. He was a traitor and a rat who had been feeding the police information. That offense was unforgivable, and the sentence was death.

Alonzo shook his head, saddened by what the game had been reduced to. "Alpo-ass nigga," he said and fired two shots into Sean.

Ashanti and Alonzo peddled from the scene and left it to God to sort out the rest of Sean's affairs.

Ashanti rode with Alonzo on the back of the bike until they got to 116th Street and Lenox, where they left the bike leaning against a store and headed for the avenue.

Alonzo pulled out a cheap cell phone he had purchased that morning and punched in a number. When the person on the other end picked up, he simply said, "Dead men tell no tales," and ended the call. He then removed the SIM card, which he placed in his pocket, then shattered the phone in the street and kicked the pieces into a gutter.

"That it for the day?" Ashanti asked.

"Yeah, we done, at least for now. The next move is on them," Alonzo told him.

"All this chess shit is getting on my nerves, Zo. I say rush homie's spot and wipe them niggaz out once and for all," Ashanti said heatedly.

Alonzo shook his head and smiled at Ashanti's anxiousness to spill blood. "That's because you're still too young and too inexperienced to understand the value of life. You don't rush into a lion's den and put yourself at a disadvantage; you draw him out and give yourself a fighting chance."

"Whatever, Zo," Ashanti said dismissing his wisdom. "What you getting into for the rest of the day?"

Alonzo shrugged. "Not too much. I'm headed to the crib now to blow it down and freshen up. I got a date later. Bumped into this chick I used to fuck with awhile back, and we're supposed to hook up later. I'm trying to crack that."

"Damn, it seems like you rocking with a different shorty every night. What're you trying to do, break Wilt Chamberlain's record?" Ashanti teased him.

"More like finding a needle in a haystack. It seems like it's easier to get a job than finding a good chick out here these days," Alonzo said sadly.

"Then why keep looking? I say to hell with it. Be single and mingle."

"True, but it gets old after awhile. Sometimes it's nice to have somebody in your corner who rocks with you for who you are and not what you got or can do for them. I'm just looking for somebody who I can smile with after a long day of frowning out here on these streets. And it can't be just anybody; she has to be special."

"I think I understand," Ashanti weighed his words. He gave Alonzo grief but secretly looked forward to his words of wisdom. "So what happened with shorty from the projects? I didn't know her too good, but I can tell you thought she was special."

"Who, Porsha?" Alonzo smiled thinking of the young lady who had stolen his heart not so long ago. "Yeah, she was special in her own way. In a perfect world, I'd have loved to see where things could've gone with Porsha, but it wouldn't have worked, and I think deep down, we both knew it."

"Why? Because she was a stripper?" Ashanti asked innocently.

Alonzo laughed. "Nah, li'l homie. Her being a stripper

didn't have anything to do with it. I've never too much cared what people said or thought, especially when it comes to my heart. I think Porsha and me were a case of both of us bringing too much baggage to the table."

"You ever think about following up with her?"

"No," Alonzo said, but there was uncertainty in his voice. "Anyway, I'm about to bust a move," he changed the subject. "You wanna come through for a minute?"

"Nah, I gotta go see a nigga about some change, but I might push through later on," Ashanti told him and started for the train station.

"You need me to roll with you?" Alonzo called after him.

"For these niggaz?" Ashanti laughed. "I doubt it. Niggaz know how I give it up; give me mine or pose for that white line," he patted his waist where his gun was tucked. "I'm out," he saluted Alonzo and disappeared down the train station stairs.

SEVEN

BEFORE TAKING CARE OF HIS BUSINESS ASHANTI stopped by his small apartment to change his clothes. His chest swelled with pride when he put the key into his front door. It was a small kitchenette furnished with only a futon, writing desk, and television, but it was more than he'd ever had in the past. Every place he ever laid his head was always someone else's place and he was at their mercy, but this apartment was his. It was the first time he had ever owned anything, and he had King James to thank for it.

After seeing him in action, King James took Ashanti under his wing and made him a part of the organization. There was too much traffic going in and out of the apartment where Ashanti was renting a room, so King hooked him up with an apartment of his own to hold down. The gesture meant the world to Ashanti, but to King, it was just his way of looking out for his family. He knew Ashanti's twisted story, a story not too unlike his own, so he understood his pain. In addition, Ashanti was a loyal soldier and would bust his gun without having to be told to, which was something King both loved and hated about Ashanti. He was a child of the streets and wore it on his arm like a badge of honor. Sometimes King and Lakim would get frustrated with Ashanti, but never Alonzo. He was patient with him, teaching Ashanti the tricks of the trade as he knew it.

Alonzo was one of the coolest dudes Ashanti had ever met, but there was also a dark side to him that Ashanti had seen firsthand. Ashanti silently watched the battle between Alonzo and Zo-Pound, and it had saddened him because he knew the eventual outcome. He watched the same internal struggle tear his best friend Animal to pieces before eventually becoming his undoing. Though Ashanti never fully bought into the rumors of Animal's demise, a part of him was eased to hear it. The demons that rode Animal's soul could no longer haunt him.

After taking a quick shower to wash off any leftover gunpowder residue, Ashanti dressed in blue jeans, a white thermal, and Yankee fitted, which he wore pulled low. After checking himself in the mirror he headed for the door. As an afterthought, he grabbed his gun and tucked it into the front of his pants. He doubted he would need it where he was going, but it was better to have it and not need it than to need it and not have it, so he wasn't taking any chances. On the way out, he stopped and looked at the picture of him, Animal, Brasco, and Nef, sitting on a project bench. Animal was holding up the magazine cover with him on it. It had been one of the last times they'd all been together before all the bullshit that had torn them apart.

"Protect me from my enemies, seen and unseen," Ashanti placed his hand over the picture and left the apartment.

The train ride to Brooklyn was relatively quick. Ashanti came out of the train station and got his bearings before starting out in search of the address scribbled on the back of the business card he was holding.

The building wasn't too hard to find because you could smell the weed smoke as soon as you turned into the block. Ashanti let himself in the gate and rang the doorbell. For as loud as the music was playing on the other side of the door he wasn't sure if they could hear him so he banged on the door with his fist. A few seconds later the door was snatched open and Ashanti found himself confronted by a dangerous-looking cat whose face appeared to be locked into a permanent scowl.

"What it do, Blood?" the man scowled down at the shorter Ashanti.

"All is well. What's popping, Devil?" Ashanti extended his hand.

The man called Devil stared down at Ashanti's outstretched hand for a few seconds before letting what passed as a smile spread across his face. He engulfed Ashanti's hand in his much-larger mitt and pumped it vigorously. "I can't call it, Young Blood. I'm hanging in like everybody else."

"Looks like you're doing better than most," Ashanti admired the brownstone.

"Yeah, this shit looking real sexy; too bad ain't none of it mines. I'm on the payroll like everybody else."

"Better a payroll than a bedroll," Ashanti said.

"I know that's right." Devil gave him dap again.

"Is ya man around?"

"Yeah, he in the back in the studio. Go ahead in, but you know I gotta pat you down," Devil told Ashanti.

Ashanti just looked at him. "Do we really need to dance this dance, D? You already know what you're gonna find if you look, so why not just let me handle my business and skate? I ain't tripping today."

Devil weighed it. He knew that there was no way Ashanti was going to part with his gun and trying to get him to do so would've been more of a headache than it was worth. If Ashanti said he wasn't tripping, then Devil would take him at his word. Everyone who knew Ashanti knew he respected little in the world except a man's word. "A'ight, but I got my eye on you, li'l nigga."

"Fair enough, big homie," Ashanti said sarcastically. He made to step inside, but Devil stopped him.

"Ashanti, we ain't seen each other in awhile so I didn't get a chance to say this to you face to face; I'm sorry to hear what happened to Animal. I know a lot of niggaz say it, but I mean it, feel me?"

Ashanti knew who he meant without him having to say. "Thanks, Devil."

Devil stepped aside to let Ashanti enter the brownstone, whose eyes and nose were immediately assaulted with the smells of weed and sweat. The brownstone was a zoo. "Welcome to hell, Young Blood," Devil laughed before closing the door behind him.

After the many fiascoes at his main office in the Empire State Building, it became a hot spot for unwanted attention, so Don B. had started spending more time at the studio/office in downtown Brooklyn. It was at the ground level of a brownstone he owned in a relatively busy block. He had picked that location so that the comings and goings of some of his less-than-savory associates wouldn't stick out so much. His offices and one of his apartments were on the top floor of the brownstone and off-limits to all but The Don and the occasional admirer, but the ground floor was for the Big Dawg family. It boasted a large studio that took up most of the floor and a separate one in what was once a bedroom. The sitting area and kitchen had been turned into a lounge with a fully stocked bar, where the Big Dawg family gathered. Normally it would be packed with artists hanging or grinding it out with projects, under Don B.'s watchful eye, but this night was special, as Don B. was trying to woo a new artist.

There were so many blunts and cigarettes burning that it was difficult to see your hand in front of your face, let alone breathe. The newest Big Dawg mix tape banged through the speakers, receiving positive feedback from everyone who wasn't too preoccupied to pay attention. At least a dozen women were walking around the main area either half-dressed or wearing nothing at all. Seductive vixens sat on the laps of rappers and ballers whispering evil things into their ears. It was a circus, and standing in the center of it was the ringmaster, Don B.

The lord of the manor moved around the room with an air of royalty that was heightened by the silk bathrobe and matching slippers he was wearing. To make a good show of it, he had thrown on most of his jewelry, so his arms, neck, and hands looked like ice sculptures and cast funny patterns on the floors and walls when the light hit them. A World Series Yankee cap sat ace-duce on his head with the brim covering one side of his sunglasses. A female guest made the mistake of asking him why he was wearing his sunglasses inside, and he simply responded, "Because I'm The Don, bitch," before having security remove her. No one questioned the king in his castle, and Don B. enforced this with an iron fist.

Don B. shuffled across the room, pinching asses and hitting Ls in search of his latest conquest, and it wasn't long before he found him, sitting on the sofa wedged between two big booty stallions that were thumb wrestling in his pants. He looked over at Don B. and smiled. Big Dawg took care of their own . . . at least according to Don B. when he started chasing Dance.

Young Dance was a slick, young, light-skinned dude from Harlem that had a hustler's swag and a Mark Zuckerberg mind. Everyone who came in contact with Young Dance recognized that he had a personality that was bigger than life and had stardom written all over him, which is why Don B. tried to sink his claws into him. Dance was talented, but he was also very smart, which made the task of snaring him a bit more complicated than Don B. had expected, but The Don always got what he wanted.

"You good, my nigga?" Don B. gave Young Dance dap.

"I'm better than good; I'm great," Young Dance tugged at the brim of his Kansas City Royals fitted.

"I told you we show our peoples nothing but love on this side," Don B. said.

"And so I see," Dance smiled at something one of the girls had just whispered in his ear.

"Well, if seeing is believing, then believe Big Dawg is where you need to be."

"Come on, Don, I thought we wasn't gonna talk about business tonight," Dance reminded him.

"It's always about business," Don B. said and dismissed the two girls, then sat on the sofa next to Dance. "Check this out, my nigga; I see you working ya li'l thing on the streets, and I respect it. You are one hell of a hustler, Dance. Can't nobody but the Lord take that from you, but the key to any successful hustle is finding the right connect, and Big Dawg is the main-line to your wildest dreams."

"Yeah? What you know about my dreams, Don B.?" Dance challenged.

Don B. removed his glasses and looked Dance square in the eye. "I know you're tired of your grandmother living in them projects. I know you're tired of hiding your car in garages at night because you owe the city money for tickets, and most important, I know you're tired of being a local celebrity when the world could be your playground. Don't test me, young boy. I made my fortune of knowing what people dream about."

"I hear you talking, Don, but I been doing okay on my inde-pendent grind, so who's to say I won't make it on my own?"

"I'm to say. You know why? Because I'm like God in this game. He who holds the gold holds the crown, and right now, my company is smashing the competition. Dance, you ain't new to this, so you know what's popping, and I challenge you to name one Big Dawg artist that didn't go platinum."

Dance couldn't.

"Exactly," Don B. continued. "You know what we do over here."

Devil came over and whispered something into Don B.'s ear. Don B. peered around his bodyguard and spotted Ashanti standing across the room watching him like a hawk. He motioned to give him a second and turned his attention back to Young Dance.

"Dance, I ain't in the way of twisting nobody's arm; I'm just trying to give you a little direction. Now, I'm about to go holla at my man right quick and give you a few ticks to ponder that." Don B. got up and left Dance alone with his thoughts.

EIGHT

ASHANTI WATCHED DON B. AMBLE ACROSS THE room, greeting people and kissing the cheeks of women. The way he carried himself you'd have thought he was the prince of Harlem. It took all of Ashanti's resolve not to throw up. He hated Hollywood types like Don B.; the ones who were nobodies until they came into a few dollars, then they started acting like they had status in the hood. On more than one occasion he had warned Animal about trusting Don B., but they were getting money together, so Animal let him live. Now Animal was gone, leaving his musical legacy to Don B. and Ashanti unanswered questions. A few times he'd thought about getting at Don B. on some extortion shit, but he learned that you could catch more flies with honey than you could with vinegar, so he played the game.

"What's goodie, my nigga?" Don B. greeted Ashanti with a warm smile.

Ashanti's face remained unchanged. "I took care of that thing for you." He pulled an envelope from his back pocket and handed it to Don B.

Don B. opened the envelope and reviewed the papers stuffed inside. It was a waiver signed by a popular music producer. He was suing Don B. for illegally using his beats on mix tapes. Don B. had tried everything from throwing money at him to threatening him, but the producer wouldn't budge . . . until Ashanti paid him a visit.

"Damn, I been trying to get this for months. How did you get him to sign off on it?" Don B. asked.

Ashanti gave him a look. "Do you really wanna know?"

"Nah, I guess I don't. I just hope you left him whole enough to still work."

"His hands are good money, but his jaw is another story."

"Fuck it, he ain't no vocalist; he's just a producer. His hands are the only things that matter anyway, right?"

Ashanti didn't answer.

"Anyhow," Don B. continued, "I appreciate you taking care of that for me. I keep telling these dudes they don't make cats like you and Animal anymore. If I had ten of y'all on my squad I'd be good. What do you think about coming to work for Big Dawg?"

"Nah, I'm a street nigga. I ain't off punching no clock, and to keep it one hundred, I don't too much care for rappers."

"You like bitches, don't you? At Big Dawg, we specialize in three things: good music, money, and pussy."

"So I'm told," Ashanti said unenthusiastically.

"Why don't you kick back for a minute and enjoy the party? We gonna get into some gangsta shit with some of these hoes, then roll out to get some food in Brooklyn before we hit the club. Hang with us tonight, my nigga," Don B. urged him.

"If it's all the same, I'll take what you owe me and bounce," Ashanti told him.

"Right. I got some paper for you, don't I? Check, why don't you come by tomorrow and pick it up from the office? I don't know if I got that kinda paper on me right now."

Ashanti's face soured. "Blood, don't even try to play me. Services rendered, services paid for. Now, if you ain't got my bread, then I'd be more than happy to take it in trade." Ashanti let his eyes roam over Don B.'s jewelry.

Don B. smiled. "My nigga, you know I was just playing with you. Come with me to the back room. I got you." He draped his arm around Ashanti and led him across the room.

"This is quite the party you got going on," Ashanti said.

"Every day is a party at Big Dawg, my nigga. It's the life of the young and rich. You need to get up on it," Don B. boasted.

"I'm working my way up. But check, since you getting it like that, I'm gonna need you to put something on top of that paper you owe me. I wanna drop it on Gucci's people."

Don B. frowned. "Gucci's people? Animal's royalties go into an account, and I know for a fact his lawyer breaks her off every so often so I know the broad ain't hurting for no cheese."

Ashanti wanted to slap Don B. in the mouth for his reckless talk, but he kept it cool. "Blood, it ain't for Gucci. It's for her peoples. You know she all twisted up in the hospital, and her moms and Tionna been taking off work and shit to hold her down, so I know things gotta be a li'l tight. They ain't asked me for nothing, but I figure they could use it."

"Tionna? Man, fuck that bitch! She could be sitting at Jesus' bedside, and I wouldn't put a dollar in that tramp's hand," Don B. spat.

A few years ago he and Tionna had a thing that went sour. Tionna thought she had a come-up in Don B. and tried to play him like a trick, but she soon found out there was a dark side to The Don that she wasn't ready for when he released a tape of them having sex that spread on the net like wildfire. The sex tape scandal rocked Tionna's life to the core and proved to be the straw that broke the camel's back in her already shaky relationship with her baby daddy, Duhan.

To get back at Don B., Tionna threatened to go to the police and scream rape. Shortly after making the threat, she came home from work one day and found that her apartment had mysteriously burned down, leaving her and her children homeless once again. The message was clear, so Tionna wisely backed up off Don B., but the bad blood between them still lingered.

"Blood, you still off that shit?" Ashanti asked as if it had been a simple argument.

"Muthafucking right. That bitch tried to break me, then ruin me, and I'm supposed to let it go? Nah, B. I ain't doing shit for Tionna," Don B. said finally.

"Then don't do it for Tionna. Do it because I'm *asking* you to."

Don B. looked at Ashanti. His face was emotionless, and his eyes had that same predatory look that Animal's did when Don B. had first met him. "Because I got love for you, I'm gonna do it. But don't make this shit no habit, B. Is twenty-five hundred enough?"

"For now," Ashanti said with a devilish smirk.

"This nigga here." Don B. half-laughed and continued leading the way through the spot.

Don B. was saying something to Ashanti, but he was only half-listening. His attention was focused on the kid in the blue Kansas City cap staring at him from across the room. Ashanti thought he recognized his face, but couldn't place it right off.

The two young men drew nearer to each other, and it dawned on them both at the same time. Ashanti hadn't seen him in years, but Dance looked the same as he did when they attended middle school together. Ashanti and Dance had been friends back then, but after awhile, Dance had started doing music, and Ashanti got caught up in the streets so they went their separate ways. Though Dance was a Crip and Ashanti claimed Blood, they had remained cordial the few times they did bump into each other.

"Damn, you're one of the last people I'd have expected to bump into here. What up, Ashanti?" Dance shook Ashanti's hand, then pulled him in for a hug.

"Chilling, baby boy. Been a long time," Ashanti smiled. It was the first time in a long time that he had smiled, and it was genuine. "What's good with you, Dance?"

"I was about to ask you the same thing. I ain't seen you in a minute, but I hear your name ringing all through these streets though. They say you grew up to be a menace to society," Dance told him.

"And they told me you grew up to be a pop star, so I guess we can't believe everything *they* say, huh?" Ashanti replied.

"True," Dance nodded, "but what you been up to otherwise? It's like once you stopped going to school you vanished off the face of the earth."

"I always been here. You just had to know which rock to look under to find me," Ashanti half-joked. "But enough about my tragic-ass life; I hear you're doing your thing with the music. I'm proud to see cats from the trap make it, real talk."

"Thanks, Ashanti. It's been hard, but we're hanging in there trying to do what we do."

"And everything you do is gonna be *big* for as long as you're fucking with *Big* Dawg," Don B. cut in. "I didn't know y'all knew each other." He looked from Ashanti to Dance.

"Man, me and Ashanti go back to free lunch," Dance told him.

"Oh yeah?" Don B. raised his eyebrow behind his shades. "Then I gotta ask, has this li'l nigga always been this vicious?"

"Ashanti been about his business since he was yay high to a mailbox. But being that y'all know each other, I guess I ain't gotta tell you that, huh, Don?" Dance said slyly.

"Cut that out, Dance. This my li'l man right here." Don B. tried to drape his arm around Ashanti affectionately, but Ashanti stepped out of his reach. When he did so, he accidentally bumped into a kid who had been passing by. He was wearing a red T-shirt and flannel shirt and denim Capris.

"My fault," Ashanti said. Little did he know, the kid and Dance had been trading evil looks all night as their respective crews were from different sides of the color line.

"Yo, watch that shit, Blood," the kid snapped. Seeing Ashanti talking to Dance the kid assumed he was a part of Dance's crew.

"I said sorry, fuck you. Want a cookie, homie?" Ashanti barked back.

By now, the kid's crew came to flank him. Dance stood with Ashanti, ready to put in work if it went that far. The kid Ashanti had bumped lifted his shirt exposing the butt of his gun. "Nigga, I think you need to recognize where you at."

"I know just where we at, now ask me if I give a fuck," Ashanti said, drawing his gun. "You wanna bang, nigga? Stop bumping ya gums and draw," Ashanti challenged. Everyone looked on in surprise as the frail little boy stood fearlessly against the goons.

"Y'all niggaz chill the fuck out." Lord Scientific stepped to the forefront. His long dreads swung back and forth when he moved.

His lanky frame seemed to tower over the rest of his homies. Lord Scientific was another artist Don B. had recently signed who hailed from Newark, N.J. He lived the life most rapped about and wore it on his sleeve like a badge of honor. He was street poisoned with no care for an antidote. Don B. had seen firsthand the kind of mayhem Lord Scientific could bring to a venue so he quickly signed him to a record deal, as well as purchasing the rights to his mix tape, which was about to be rereleased under Big Dawg Entertainment.

Lord Scientific stood before Ashanti. "Blood, you really wanna go there with it?"

Ashanti looked him up and down. "Not really, but I ain't in the way of being carried either. A man respects a man, and I'm a man."

Lord Scientific nodded in approval. "A man of simple philosophies and strong principles."

"The only philosophy I know is survival of the fittest. Anything besides that," Ashanti paused, "I guess I'll leave it to God to sort out."

"I hear you, shorty. Ain't no problems here, right?" Lord Scientific looked at the kid who started it. He hesitated, but finally nodded. "Cool," Lord Scientific extended his fist to Ashanti.

Ashanti studied the fist as if it might have been booby-trapped before giving Lord Scientific dap. "Cool." Ashanti was about to leave, but Lord Scientific wasn't done.

"What's your name, shorty?" Lord Scientific asked.

"My name isn't shorty; it's Ashanti."

"Ashanti," Lord Scientific stored the name in his head. "I'll remember it."

"You'd do well to, as I'm sure you'll be hearing it again," Ashanti told him with a knowing grin.

NINE

"Ashanti? I don't know about that one," Pam said, refilling her plastic cup with coconut Círoc. Pam was older than Fatima and loved her like a little sister. The two girls did almost everything together. For the last hour or so, she and Fatima had been sitting on the benches, sipping and talking shit when the conversation switched to guys in the hood that they would sleep with.

"What's wrong with Ashanti?" Fatima asked defensively. This was her first time ever confessing her crush on the young shooter to anyone, and she didn't like Pam's reaction.

Pam paused, trying to find the words to articulate what she wanted to say without being offensive. Eventually she shrugged and said, "Because he's Ashanti!" she saw anger flash in Fatima's eyes so she softened her approach. "Fatima, all I'm trying to say is with all the *boss dick* that would love to have you, why get hung up on a soldier?"

"It ain't always about what somebody can do for you, Pam," Fatima told her.

Pam reared her head back. "Why isn't it? Listen, my sister used to always tell me that if a man couldn't do anything for you, then he wasn't worth keeping around for more than the occasional nut."

"I guess that's why ya sister got four kids by four dudes," Fatima capped.

"Bitch, don't go there with all the brothers and sisters you got floating around. No disrespect, Fatima, but I heard when your dad was running the streets, him and his crew was knocking everything down with a pulse," Pam laughed, but Fatima didn't.

"Fuck that nigga," Fatima said.

"Wow, y'all still beefing?" Pam shook her head. She knew the history between Fatima and her father. "When you gonna let that shit go?"

"When that nigga is in the ground," Fatima said seriously. "Don't get ghost and then come back in the ninth inning and expect us to be the Cosbys. I ain't trying to hear that shit."

Her father was a touchy subject. Her mother had been little more than another conquest to a hustler named Cutty whose name used to ring off, and he made it apparent by not bothering to take an active role in Fatima's life. Cutty would drop money off every so often, but other than that, the only time Fatima saw him was when he came through to smash her mother. When she was about six, Cutty went to prison for murder, among a slew of other charges, and was supposed to never see the light of day. Due to a technicality, he was released after serving just over ten years. By then, Fatima was already a young woman and set in her ways so when Cutty finally came around to play daddy she rejected his efforts. As far as she was concerned, she didn't have a father.

Pam knew enough not to press Fatima so she switched back to their original topic. "So let's talk about you and Ashanti . . ."

"Ain't no me and Ashanti," Fatima cut her off. "All I said was that he could get it!"

"It ain't *what* you said, but *how* you said it. I know you, Fatima. I know that look," Pam told her.

"What look is that?"

"The love-struck schoolgirl look."

"Get outta here," Fatima waved her off. She picked up her drink and took a sip so that Pam wouldn't see the *busted* look that had just spread across her face. "And let's say if I did have designs on Ashanti, why would that be wrong, because his paper ain't up?"

"That and the fact that that li'l nigga is dangerous," Pam became serious. "Fatima, I got mad love for Ashanti, probably more than most because that li'l nigga got heart! But at the same time, I know a rabid dog when I see one."

Fatima rolled her eyes. "Ashanti ain't even that bad. I know he does dirt, but who doesn't?"

Pam shook her head. "You have no idea where I'm coming from, do you? Fatima, you on it like that because you're just meeting Ashanti since he's been fucking with King, but do you *really* know the nature of the animal you're dealing with?"

Fatima was silent.

"A'ight," Pam continued, "dude is younger than me but we ran in some of the same circles. I was fucking with his man Brasco."

"Why does that name sound so familiar?" Fatima racked her brain.

"Because he was Animal's best friend," Pam helped her along.

82

"Animal, the rapper?"

"No, Animal the mass murderer. Now stop cutting me off so I can finish my story. Like I was saying, me and Brasco had a thing, and it looked like it was gonna get serious so he introduced me to his brothers, Animal, Nef, and Ashanti. I knew they wasn't real brothers, but it still felt special that he was introducing me to people close to him. Brasco treated me better than any guy I've ever dated, but I had to back up off him."

"Why?" Fatima asked, now caught up in Pam's story.

"Because when they let me into their inner circle, I found out that I wasn't dealing with men. They were monsters, and some of the shit I've seen still gives me nightmares. They were killers with baby faces, and the most ruthless of their crew was Animal. That was the first man I've ever met whose eyes were just empty. It was like somebody had just cut the lights out in his soul. All y'all li'l chicks know the rapper, but I know the demon who lives where a young man's soul used to reside. And when I look at Ashanti, I see that same dead look in his eyes. That boy has been molded in Animal's image. When I saw that King had put Ashanti down with his crew, I knew that it was about to be all bad."

"You act like Ashanti is evil or something," Fatima said, reflecting on what her friend was telling her.

"Not evil, baby, just broken," Pam said. "Ashanti is the last of a dying breed. Most dudes talk about how gangsta they are, but kids like Ashanti are willing to die to prove it. He's street poisoned."

"Maybe all he needs is to find the right antidote," Fatima tried to reason.

Pam snorted. "Boo-boo, no matter how good of a chick you

try to be to a kid like Ashanti, you'll always be in competition with that other bitch."

"What other bitch?"

"Death, ma. Death is his mistress, and despite your best efforts, she'll always be waiting in the wings for him."

Before the conversation could go any further, Fatima's cell phone went off. She looked at the number, hit ignore, and put it back in her pocket.

"Who that you looping?" Pam asked.

"That ain't nobody but King James. He been blowing my phone up since I left earlier," Fatima told her.

"He's probably mad that you didn't come back to finish your shift," Pam said.

Fatima rolled her eyes. "Like I give a fuck. He should've thought about that before he tried to style on me. That nigga was trying to talk to me like I was one of his workers."

"Technically, you are," Pam pointed out.

Fatima cut her eyes at Pam.

"Hey, don't shoot the messenger. I'm only keeping it tall with you, Fatima. There are a lot of people eating out of King's hand right now, and to keep them in line, he has to be stern with everybody, including his fake baby sis," she nodded at Fatima. "You know this game is all about appearances, and if you let one person slide, then you'll have everybody testing your authority."

"But I ain't everybody, Pam. Me and King go back to when he was James King, running around trying to get a dollar like everybody else. We got history!"

"If y'all got history, then you of all people should know what it took to put him where he is and respect the things he has to do to hold that position. Everybody has to be held accountable. Playing favorites in this game can get you murdered, ma."

"Whatever," Fatima waved her off. But she digested everything Pam was telling her, and even agreed with her to an extent, but wouldn't give her the satisfaction of saying so.

"Speaking of paper chasers," Pam changed the subject, "I knew I had some fresh gossip to tell you. You'll never guess who I'm hooking up with tonight."

"Well, don't keep an asshole in suspense; spill it!" Fatima said excitedly.

"Girl, Young Dance!" Pam confessed excited.

"Young who?" Fatima was confused.

Pam slapped her hand against her forehead in frustration. "Young Dance, the rapper."

"The cutie from Fifty-third? Bitch, you lying!" Fatima squealed.

"I put that on my kids," Pam declared. "Me and my homegirls went out one night to celebrate her birthday, and Young Dance happened to be performing that night. He took one look at me in that tight red dress and caught the vapors. He tried to slide with me that night, but I put him on pause so he didn't think I was a ho or nothing."

"I am *so* sure," Fatima said sarcastically.

"Shut up and let me finish," Pam scolded. "Anyway, we exchanged numbers and been playing phone tag for the past week or two, and he asked me to come hang out with him tomorrow night. I think Big Dawg got something going on downtown so you know there's gonna be money in the room."

"Money and killers," Fatima scoffed.

"I know you ain't passing judgment when you've got a crush on a junior serial killer," Pam teased her.

"Fuck you, Pam," Fatima laughed.

"But on the real, come out with me, Fatima."

"I dunno, Pam. My bread ain't really right," Fatima said.

"C'mon, ma, you don't need no bread. All we gotta worry about is getting to the spot. Once we in the building, everything is on Dance. You know how I do."

Fatima was still hesitant. "Maybe I'll just play the block, and we can hook up when you come back."

Pam looked at Fatima as if she had lost her mind. "Play the block? Fatima, you *always* play the block. Yo, for as long as I've known you I can't ever recall you ever traveling outside of Manhattan. The world is gonna pass you by if you keep thinking like that."

Fatima rolled her eyes. "Pam, don't even go there because you spend as much time in this hood as me, if not more. You been in this hood all your life."

"And look how my life turned out because of it. I got baby daddy drama, my kids drive me up the wall, and I can't get a decent job to save my life, because I spent all my good years on the block accepting what life gave me instead of seeing what else it had to offer."

"I know, but sometimes I just feel like I'm gonna miss out on something when I leave the hood," Fatima admitted.

Pam reached out and touched Fatima's hand. "Fatima, I don't wanna see you as just another washed up broad out here like the rest of us bitches. The only thing you're gonna miss out on by traveling outside the hood is the same bullshit that goes on every day; somebody getting locked up or murdered."

As if on cue, a commotion broke out a few feet away from where the girls were sitting. Biz, the young dealer who King had been chastising earlier, had just made a sale to a random fiend on the avenue. As soon as he did, the doors to the Direct TV truck King had been warning them about all day flew open and out jumped several undercover police officers who swooped in on Biz. The youngster put up a good fight, but the police eventually swarmed him and tossed him, kicking and screaming, into a paddy wagon.

Fatima looked from the throng of police to Pam and shook her head. "You might be right; maybe it is time for me to get outta the hood for a minute."

Pam smiled. "Now you're talking, baby girl. Now you're talking."

"FRANKIE ANGELS, YOU HEAR ME TALKING TO you?" Cutty nudged her. He clutched the steering wheel of his black Excursion in one hand and a blunt of sour in the other. His cold eyes constantly scanned the slow-moving afternoon traffic on the 1&9 North, headed for the Holland Tunnel.

"My bad, I was daydreaming," Frankie told him. Her attention had been fixed on the skyline of Jersey City. She admired the waterfront buildings in the distance and wondered if she would ever have a place that nice to call her own.

"See, that's your problem. Your head is always in the damn clouds instead of on this money," he scolded her. It seemed like every time Cutty spoke he was scolding her, even when he wasn't. That was just his way. Cutty was an old-school cat who had recently been sprung from prison, but he still had a mess hall mentality.

"Nigga, you tripping. My mind is always on my paper." Frankie rolled her pretty brown eyes. She was a pretty cinnamon-complexioned girl with beautiful long black hair, which she, that day, wore pulled back into a tight bun showing off her attractive features. "Now pass the weed with your stingy ass." She plucked the blunt from his hand, accidentally dropping ashes on the jumpsuit she was wearing. It was a skintight number that gave you a rare glimpse of Frankie's well proportioned frame.

They were making their way back from an all-night caper they had pulled out in Union, N.J. For the last few weeks, Frankie had been making time with a young Greek gentleman who was the manager of a car dealership out that way. She wasn't really into foreigners, but he had long paper and was dashingly handsome. He was olive skinned with wavy black hair and movie star good looks. For all his good looks, he had the personality of a rock. The Greek felt because he had money women should worship him to be rewarded, so she did, and he fell hard for her. What the Greek didn't know was that he was just a means to an end. Frankie had fleeced him for a copy of the keys to the car lot, and while he was out spending his money on her, Cutty and a few of his boys were making off with his cars. Cutty already had buyers for them at different chop shops in Newark and Elizabeth, so the flip would come back almost immediately. It was a sweet lick. Frankie felt kind of bad for stringing him along like that, but at the end of the day it was business. It was always business when it came to getting money with Cutty.

"You speak to Jada?" Frankie picked up. "I know she's probably worried or *suspicious* being that we've been gone all night."

"Nah, but Jada cool," Cutty said as if it was nothing.

Frankie twisted her lips. "Cutty, you been out all night with another woman and you ain't bothered to call your lady. Don't you think she's gonna be a little pissed? Hell, I'd be waiting for your ass with a pot of hot grits when you came in."

Cutty looked at her. "Let me tell you something, li'l one. Jada is a soldier, so she's gonna be okay. I taught her to be as cold as ice and put nothing above this money, which is what I'm trying to instill in yo' young ass." He snatched the blunt back.

"I still think you're wrong for not calling." Frankie folded her arms over her nice-sized breasts.

"Well, I guess it's a good thing I don't give a damn what you think. You know, Frankie, you've been getting pretty damn lippy lately, and I don't know how I feel about it. We been getting a nice piece of change together so I fuck with you hard-body, but let's not forget that your ass is still in my debt," he reminded her.

Frankie looked down at her lap. "Nah, I didn't forget," she said barely above a whisper.

Not so long ago, Cutty had fronted Frankie some drugs to make money when she and her roommates were in danger of getting evicted. Frankie had never been a drug dealer, but in her desperation she had no choice but to adapt and make the best out of it, which she did. In almost no time, she had not only made Cutty's money back but had a nice piece of change for herself. Things looked good for her until a dude from her hood named Scar and a few of his goons kicked her door in and attempted to rob her. They beat Frankie to within an inch of her life, but she didn't go down without a fight. She managed to shoot two of them before she blacked out, but when she woke up she was in the hospital and being charged with double homicide.

The legal aid she had been assigned was an imbecile, and

Frankie was looking at quite a bit of time whether she took the plea bargain or not. Things were looking bleak for her when Cutty had thrown her a lifeline in the way of a high-powered lawyer and posting her bail. The lawyer had gotten the charges reduced to involuntary manslaughter, but they still wanted her to do time so they took it to trial. The lawyer had promised to drag the trial out for as long as possible, but to do so, he would need money, which she didn't have. Cutty agreed to foot the bill for her legal expenses, but in return, she had to go to work for him. Granted, Frankie was making money in the streets with Cutty and doing better than she had been, but he never let her forget that he owned her until she could repay her debt.

"C'mon, I didn't mean it like that." His voice was softer now. "I'm just trying to keep you focused, ma. I like ya style, Frankie, and debt owed or not, I think we can win together. Even though you got a twat between your legs, you've got bigger balls than most niggaz out here. The stakes we're about to be playing for are too high for mistakes, baby girl. One fuck up could mean the end of both of us, ya dig?"

"I hear you talking," she rolled her eyes.

Cutty laughed. "There's that funky-ass attitude. You know, sometimes you remind me of my daughter. She's another young broad who's got her ass on her shoulders and thinks that she's got the world all figured out."

"Fatima is seventeen; I'm grown," Frankie pointed out.

"Don't matter. The both of y'all still wet behind the ears when you measure it against what a vet like me knows."

"You couldn't have known that much or else your ass wouldn't have winded up in prison for all those years," Frankie rolled her eyes.

"Don't get fucking cute, Frankie. I did what I did for the team, shorty. Loyalty above all else is how me, Rio, and Shamel lived, and I'm trying to see if some of your cousin's blood actually flows through you or if all y'all share is a last name."

"You know I'm built, Cutty, so you ain't gotta question my character," Frankie assured him.

"I ain't questioning your character; I'm questioning what's going on in your head. Your mind is supposed to be on money at all times and not whether I called my bitch or not to check in."

Frankie's eyes narrowed to slits. "See, that's the bullshit with men. In one breath you claim to love us, and in the next breath, you're calling us all kinds of bitches. How would you feel if somebody was always calling Fatima a bitch like you do Jada?"

"Nigga call my baby girl a bitch and I'm gonna put his fucking lights out," Cutty said seriously.

"Exactly, because it's disrespectful and you'd hurt a nigga who disrespected someone you love, so why does that make it okay for *you* to do it?"

"Damn, you going through all this because I didn't call Jada to let her know I was staying out?" Cutty was confused. He knew Frankie could be a firecracker, but he'd never seen her that irritable.

"It ain't just that; it's a bunch of shit. Look, just forget it. It ain't my business, and I shouldn't have said anything," Frankie said.

Cutty looked over at Frankie, who had her arms folded and was staring intently out the window. Her face was as hard and uncaring as it always was, but there was a wavering in her eyes that said something was going on with her. Cutty knew from his championship bouts with Jada that there was no wining an argument against a stubborn woman so he offered a truce. "I'll call Jada in a few if it will appease that woman code thing nagging at your conscious."

"Thank you," Frankie said sarcastically, then went back to looking out the window.

Cutty coasted through the Holland Tunnel, cutting across Canal Street, and eventually crossing the Manhattan Bridge into Brooklyn, where Frankie was currently resting her head. After getting evicted from the project apartment she and her roommates had been subleasing, Frankie found herself in quite a bind. In the beginning, she bounced around from place to place until she could think of what to do, and it was Cutty who came to her rescue . . . again. Cutty hooked her up with a Jewish cat he knew that owned a building in Bed-Stuy and was looking for a tenant to fill a recently vacated apartment. Because he owed Cutty a *favor,* the dude agreed to give it to Frankie for half the normal rent for the first three months. It was a small one bedroom, but it was perfect for Frankie. She was just happy to have a crib she could call her own without having to share it with roommates, at least not permanent ones.

Creeping up Marcus Garvey, Cutty drove past the Blood Orchid, which was a small social club and current mystery to the people from the neighborhood. Since it had been erected it had never been officially open for business, but you could catch people sliding in and out at all times of the night. There was plenty of speculation about what the real deal with Blood Orchid was, but only a select few knew for sure.

Cutty turned onto Jefferson and pulled up in front of Frankie's building. It was a nice day, so, of course, everybody was outside. In front of her building two grills were set up on either side of the stoop and a card table was erected along the side of the building, where several familiar faces were engaged in a game of Spades. The front steps were occupied by two girls Frankie really didn't rock with named Vashaun and Bess, who were smoking a blunt and speaking in hushed tones. From the way they kept cutting their eyes at Cutty's truck Frankie figured they were probably talking about her, but that was nothing new. They were a messy pair so Frankie did her best to avoid them, but with all the time they spent on the block it was hard to miss them.

Working one of the grills was a thick chick named Monique, who Frankie didn't know that well, but they spoke when they saw each other. Monique tipped the scales at two and some change easily, but she carried herself like she was one hundred and fifty pounds, always wearing revealing clothing. Monique was big, proud, and didn't give a shit what anybody thought about it. She was real, and that was one of the main reasons why Frankie respected her gangster.

Working the other grill was Dena, a pretty brown-skinned chick with an around-the-way swagger and Harvard ambition. She was a few years younger than Frankie, but the things she had gone through weighed her down with an old soul, so hardships acted like a magnet bringing the two girls together. Dena was born and raised on that strip so everyone knew her and she knew everybody, but she had only recently moved into that building. Before that, she shared an apartment with her mother, siblings, nieces, and nephews up the block near Throop. When Frankie first moved in, she acted like sort of a welcoming committee, hipping Frankie to little things, like the easiest way to the train station, who had the best weed, and who was bad

94

news. Frankie always appreciated the jewels Dena dropped on her because living in Brooklyn was like living on Mars to her.

"These muthafuckas," Frankie sighed, reaching for the door handle.

Cutty peered out the window and noticed the neighborhood dudes were clocking the whip. He reached in the center console and took out his gun which he placed on his lap. "You want me to get out with you?"

"Please, them niggaz are harmless, but it's nice to know you care." Frankie winked at Cutty before climbing out of the truck.

"I'm just protecting my investment," he called after her.

The moment Frankie hit the curb all eyes turned to her. Her neighbors were used to seeing her dressed down in jeans or sweats, so to see her in the tight jumpsuit and heels were welcomed surprises, and their faces said as much. Their stares made Frankie a little uncomfortable, but she played it off and greeted them with a smile. "Hey, y'all," she greeted Dena and Monique.

"Looking sharp, girl. Where you just coming from, a job interview?" Dena smiled, admiring Frankie's outfit.

"Nah, had a li'l date," Frankie said as if it was nothing.

Dena looked at her in surprise. "Not Ms. Antisocial?"

"Cut it out, Dena. I'm not antisocial," Frankie protested.

"Could've fooled me. You don't speak unless somebody speaks to you first," Vashaun said, finger combing her nappy blond weave.

"That's because I don't rock with just anybody; that ain't my style," Frankie told her.

"Harlem to the heart, huh?" Bess said with a smirk. Her eyes narrowed to slits from the blunt pinched between her fingers.

"You better know it," Frankie rolled her eyes. She didn't care for Vashaun or Bess, but at least she could tolerate Vashaun's simpleminded ass. Bess, on the other hand, made Frankie's ass itch with her sneaky and meddling ways. She always had something slick to say.

"So who was the lucky guy?" Dena asked.

"Nobody special, just a dude I been talking to." Frankie downplayed it.

"He must've been special enough for you to squeeze into that jumpsuit. Damn, I didn't know you had ass like that, Frankie," Monique teased her, reaching out as if she was gonna pinch Frankie's butt.

"You know I don't even play those games, ma." Frankie warned. "What's up with the mural?" Frankie nodded at the candles and empty liquor bottles sitting at the foot of the tree near the card table.

"This dude from the neighborhood got killed," Dena told her.

"Oh, I'm so sorry to hear that," Frankie said sincerely.

"That's some sad shit; people always dying in the hood," Vashaun shook her head. "They killed him right over there on Fulton in front of McDonald's. I heard it was because he was wearing a blue coat in the wrong neighborhood. These li'l niggaz kill me with this gang shit."

"Vashaun, you sound stupid right now. That kid didn't get killed over no gang beef. He robbed a muthafucka last week, and the boy he robbed caught him slipping," Bess corrected her.

"Well, it's still somebody dying over something stupid!" Vashaun snapped.

"Listen to Mother Theresa," Bess laughed, showing off the

gold crowns on her two front teeth. "This is coming from the same chick that told a lie and almost got an innocent man killed because he fucked her and didn't call back!"

"That was different," Vashaun rolled her eyes.

"Different how? Somebody got shot in both scenarios," Bess retorted.

"Why don't both of y'all be easy? The front porch ain't really the place to be airing your dirty laundry, especially when the streets are always watching," Dena said, cutting her eyes at one of the dudes by the card table who had been eavesdropping on their conversation.

"You're one hundred percent right, D," Bess said, "but my thing is, keep it one hundred. This shit is fucked up, and we all contribute to it in one way or another, and I accept that, but I get tight when people do foul shit, then boo-hoo about shit like they don't know what's up out here."

"Fuck you, Bess," Vashaun spat.

"Maybe after I've had a few, but not right now," Bess said with a sly grin.

"Y'all are a trip," Frankie laughed, trying to ease the tension. She peered over at the coolers laid out next to the grills that were packed with meats and drinks. "Damn, look like y'all ready to kick off a block party with all that shit."

Dena wiped her hands on her apron and retrieved two Coronas from the cooler. She cracked one for herself and handed the other to Frankie. "Vashaun got her stamps so we was just gonna throw a li'l something-something together, but you know how niggaz is when they smell barbecue," she nodded to the dudes at the table. "Everybody kicked in a li'l something so we gonna do it how we do it until all the food is gone."

"At this rate, we gonna be out here all night," Monique said, placing some more chicken on the grill.

"Oh, while I'm thinking about it, did you ever look into that *thing* for me?" Dena asked Frankie.

"You know I did. I got it the other day but haven't had a chance to holla at you. That shit is gonna look *right* on you, Dena," Frankie assured her.

"See, that's the bullshit in your life, Frankie. You never get nothing for us shapely chicks. Big girls like to get fly too!" Monique complained.

"All you gotta do is hit me with your measurements and it's a done deal, ma," Frankie winked and walked into the building.

"I might as well take care of that now." Dena took off her apron and hung it on the rail of the stoop. "Mo, I'll be back in a sec," she told her friend and followed Frankie into the building.

ELEVEN

FRANKIE TURNED THE KEY AND STEPPED INTO the place she now called home. The apartment was cute and cozy but boasted high ceilings and railroad apartment style long hallways. The small living room was decorated simply with a couch, coffee table, and small entertainment system that held a 32 inch flat and stereo system. Off to the right was the kitchen which was sectioned off by a counter. It wasn't much, but it was hers, and Frankie loved it.

"Park yourself on the couch. I gotta grab your stuff outta the back," Frankie told Dena, tossing her keys on the counter and disappearing into the bedroom. She came back a few minutes later to find that Dena had made herself comfortable. A half bottle of Mascato that Frankie had in the cut was now on the coffee table flanked by two glasses. On the couch, Dena was just putting the finishing touches on a blunt she was rolling. "Make yourself at home," Frankie said sarcastically.

Dena looked up at her and rolled her eyes. "Girl, please. You looked like you could use a stress reliever."

"I'm that transparent, huh?" Frankie took a seat on the couch beside Dena and traded the bag of goods for the blunt.

"Yup, as transparent as glass. I know that look because I've worn it more often than not, and trust me when I say I know what comes with it. Take my advice and stop letting that nigga drag you down."

Frankie took a deep pull of the blunt and released the smoke through her nose. "Listen to you trying to sound like you know what's going on in my life."

"I know enough to know if you keep going at this rate, it ain't gonna be too much of a life to reflect on by the time you turn thirty. Frankie, I don't know what your ties are to ol' boy, but I do know you always seem more stressed when you're around him than when you're not. The dick can't be that good, ma," Dena pointed out.

Frankie rolled her eyes. "I've told you before that me and Cutty ain't fucking. This is just a business arrangement."

"I wonder what kinda arrangement that is, where it brings you out in the streets in the wee hours of the mornings," Dena said. Frankie raised her eyebrow. "Oh, don't look so surprised. My window is in the front so I can see when ya ass is creeping in and out."

"You're so fucking nosey." Frankie stood up to walk into the kitchen.

Dena stood up and blocked her path. "I'm not nosey, I'm concerned, ma. I know Cutty's type, and niggaz like him don't mean you no good."

"Dena, I'm a big girl, and I can take care of myself." Frankie sucked her teeth and tried to step around Dena. "Move, Dena," Frankie demanded.

"Not until you listen to what I have to say." Dena folded her arms. Frankie's nostrils flared. "What, you plan on moving me?"

In answer to her question Frankie gave Dena a shove, catching her off guard and causing her to stumble backward. Dena rushed Frankie, and they both stumbled over the coffee table and ended up crashing onto the floor. They tussled around through the living room with Frankie eventually ending up on top of Dena with her hands around her throat, but Dena held two fists full of Frankie's hair. They glared at each other, neither willing to release their grips. Just as the ball of violent energy between them threatened to pop, Frankie leaned in and kissed Dena.

The kiss was rough and feral, with Frankie's teeth nicking Dena's soft lips. Dena didn't back down, kissing Frankie just as deeply and pinching her tongue between her teeth and applying pressure. They rolled again and this time Dena was on top, rubbing Frankie's breasts through her shirt and suckling her bottom lip. They tore at each other like animals until they were both nude and wrestling around on Frankie's throw rug. Dena planted passionate kisses all over Frankie's body, going from her chin to her navel, leaving a trail of moisture down Dena's torso. Dena kissed both of Frankie's inner thighs, dancing around from one to the other, grazing Frankie's pussy with her lips each time she crossed it. Slowly and deliberately, Dena used the tip of her tongue to part Frankie's pussy lips and toyed with her clit.

Frankie grabbed the back of Dena's head and forced her face deeper into her crotch, grinding on her nimble tongue. Dena ate Frankie like a starving child from a third world country, jacking her finger in and out of Frankie's pussy as she did so. Waves of toe-curling pleasure shot up through Frankie's body making her meow like a cat in heat. With a spasm Frankie came, spraying Dena's face with her juices. When she was done, she pulled Dena up by the hair so that they were face to face and they began kissing, Frankie tasting the fluids on Dena's chin and lips and licking them away until she was clean.

"Your turn," Frankie purred, wiggling from under Dena and laying her on her stomach. She placed a throw pillow under Dena's stomach so that her butt was hiked up and began to knead her ass cheeks like she was about to bake a loaf of bread. For a petite girl she had very strong hands. Frankie kissed one butt cheek, then the other, and let her tongue dance along the crack of Dena's ass. Dena braced herself when she felt Frankie's lips graze her pussy, but Frankie changed direction and went back to kissing her ass cheeks.

"Stop playing and get this shit," Dena panted. She reached back trying to grab Frankie's head, but Frankie moved out of her reach.

Frankie slapped Dena on the ass, then bit the cheek. "Shut up and let me do this." Frankie finally stopped teasing and got down to business. She spread Dena's ass cheeks wide and laid her face softly in the center of her, slurping like she was trying to remove a clam from its shell. Frankie touched every corner of Dena's pussy with tongue and lips, even treating her asshole to some attention. Frankie had initially been a novice at pleasuring a woman, but through practice and time she had gotten quite good at it.

Dena clawed at the carpet and cursed while Frankie made her climax over and over. The last nut swelled like a balloon in the pit of Dena's gut, and her leg began to shake violently. Just when Dena couldn't take it anymore, she exploded, soaking the carpet as well as the lower half of Frankie's face. When it was all over, the two spent lovers lay side by side, staring into each other's eyes and lost in their own thoughts.

When Frankie met Dena you would've never in a million years thought that they would become lovers. Frankie had experimented with girls when she was young, but it wasn't her cup of tea, at least it hadn't been back then, but then she met Dena and everything changed . . . including her.

From their first conversation it was obvious that Dena and Frankie were kindred spirits, having both had very rough lives where they had been taken advantage of by men they had trusted. Though Frankie had been in the streets and knew that there were always consequences, the men who had invaded her home had no right to violate her the way they did. They'd left Frankie for dead and through the grace of God she had survived, even managing to take two of them with her, but her survival came with a price, and the devil holding the receipt for her soul was named Cutty. He had a hold over Frankie, and when it suited him, made her dance like a puppet on a string. The way he toyed with Frankie infuriated Dena because it was a grim reminder that she too had once danced on a string, but it had cost her far more.

Dena had been young, dumb, and looking for life's next big thrill, and she had found it in the form of a pimp named Black Ice. Ice came into Dena's world and turned it upside down, introducing her to big money and high society. People warned her about what type of person Black Ice really was, but the naïve young girl chalked it up to them hating on her and her new *man*. Dena ignored the warnings and continued to ride the roller coaster with Ice until it slammed her headfirst into a wall at a party hosted by the notorious Don B. That was the first time she saw her knight in silk armor for what he really was—a wolf in sheep's clothing.

The man who she thought she loved saw her as little more than a new addition to his stable. When Dena balked at the idea of selling her body for money, Black Ice drugged her and set her out to the wolves. Of that day she still had no idea how many of them there were, nor did she care to remember. One by one they took turns violating every hole on the young girl's body and humiliating her in a room full of people. For what he'd done, Black Ice was rewarded a ruthless and very public death at the hands of Dena's brother Shannon. Shannon sacrificed his freedom, and eventually his life, in the name of his sister, but it couldn't stop the slow slide into hell that the rape had sent Dena on.

After the rape, Dena woke up in the hospital, barely alive and broken from the inside out. Fate would mock her once again when she was notified that traces of the HIV virus had been found in one of the semen samples they had collected from inside her. She had tested negative, but it was the beginning of the worst five years of her life. Every six months she would have to go back to the hospital to get tested, living in constant fear that she would find out she had a death sentence. Years later, Dena still hadn't come up positive, but the damage to her psyche was already done. After what had happened at the Big Dawg party, she swore she would never again let a man touch her.

Frankie's cell phone rang from somewhere in the jumble of

clothes strewn around the living room. She tossed aside shirts and bras until she finally found the BlackBerry. "Hello," she blurted into the phone.

"Damn, did I interrupt something?" a familiar voice said on the other end.

"No, simple ass. What's good, Porsha?" Frankie greeted her friend and former roommate.

"Ain't too much. Calling to check in on my favorite evictee," Porsha joked on the other end. She was one of the two other girls that shared the apartment in the projects with Frankie until they had all gotten kicked out on their asses. They had all gone their separate ways, but Porsha and Frankie kept in contact.

"Shit, just getting back to BK."

"Just getting back? Where the hell are you just coming from?" Porsha asked suspiciously. She knew Frankie was a homebody who rarely got out.

"Nowhere special, just taking care of something," Frankie said in a tone that said it wasn't up for discussion.

"I hear that hot shit. Anyhow, what you getting into tonight?" Porsha asked.

"Not much. I was gonna watch some movies and chill out," Frankie told her. Dena crawled over to her and started kissing Frankie's breasts. Frankie giggled and pushed her away. "Why, what's up?"

"Let's go out tonight and get white-girl-wasted!" Porsha yelled in Frankie's ear.

"Here you go. Porsha, it's the middle of the week," Frankie pointed out.

"And what is that supposed to mean to me? Every day is Friday when you're self-employed," Porsha boasted.

"I know you ain't back in the clubs," Frankie said seriously.

"Bitch, you must've fallen and bumped your head if you think times have gotten that hard for me. You see where that shit got me, so why would you even ask?" At one time, Porsha had been on the fast track, stripping in some of the tristate's most notorious clubs. She made lots of money doing it, but in the end, she learned that all that glittered wasn't gold and became another one of Don B.'s unsuspecting victims. That, coupled with everything else that was going wrong in Porsha's life, weighed heavily on her and when they got evicted that was the breaking point. Porsha had hung up her stilettos and applied herself more to school and the greener pastures of a regular nine-to-five.

"I didn't mean it like that, Porsha, and you know it," Frankie said sincerely.

"Yes, you did, and you know it," Porsha laughed. Her mood had softened. "Well, if you must know, I got my first check from that modeling gig."

"What modeling gig?"

"Frankie, are you serious? Remember, I told you I uploaded some pictures to a couple of the modeling sites to try to get some extra paper while I'm working my day job? Damn, we're supposed to be girls, and you don't listen when I talk."

"I'm sorry, P. But I do remember you saying something about a website. So it worked out for you?"

"Sure did. About two months ago one of the agencies called me in to do some test shots. They liked what they saw and got me some work. It was a just a little spot modeling jeans in a catalog, but I got a nice check out of it. They say they'll probably be calling me in to do some more stuff soon."

"Congratulations, Porsha, I'm so proud of you!" Frankie screamed.

"Yeah, right, when you were just accusing me of going back to stripping five minutes ago," Porsha teased. "But on some real shit, thanks, Frankie. I'm really trying to go hard with this modeling because I can't see myself punching a clock every morning for the next thirty years. Something gotta give."

"I know that's right, but until such time, we gotta do what we gotta do to get by."

"I totally agree, and I say that in honor of bitches busting their asses day in and day out. Let's go get fall-down-drunk tonight. I got a few dollars, Frankie, so let's go spend them before I blow them on clothes."

Frankie thought about it. She looked over at Dena who was teasing her pussy with her finger and staring up at Frankie with pleading eyes. "A'ight, Porsha, but can I bring a friend?"

OMENS

TWELVE

SHAI STOOD ON THE FREE THROW LINE of his indoor basketball court, focused on nothing but the rim. The state-of-the-art replica NBA court had been his birthday gift to himself when he turned twenty-one. It was equipped with four rows of cushioned benches on both sides of the gym and two regulation height rims at either end. The entire gym, including the rims and lines on the court, were painted blue and orange in homage to his favorite team, the New York Knicks. When he had been a promising college prospect his dream had always been to play for his hometown team, but that dream seemed like a lifetime ago.

Shai took a deep breath, aimed at the rim, released the ball . . . and missed. On any given day he could come in the gym and knock down one hundred free throws straight without a miss, but that day he couldn't seem to sink two in a row. He started to jog after the ball but decided against it. He was tired, so very tired.

Shai had been barely out of his teens when he was literally

handed the keys to the city. With his father dead and his brother fighting his own demons, Shai became the boss by default and had to wear all the bullshit that came with a criminal enterprise. For the most part, he had managed to limit himself to the legitimate side of the Clark Empire while Swann, Angelo, and Big Doc handled the business on the streets, but the smooth ride was a short one. Swann and the others came up under Poppa and were used to the craziness, but Shai wasn't. He just wanted to be a good man to his family and honor his father's memory, but it was near impossible to do from the sidelines. Shai soon learned that the king had to not only speak, but be seen. The crown he had been cursed with proved heavier to wear than he ever imagined, and sometimes he wondered how long he would be able to carry it.

"Shai," Honey called from the doorway, startling him, "everything okay?" She approached with a worried look on her face.

"Right as rain, baby." He kissed her on the lips. "Why do you ask?"

"Because," she picked up the discarded basketball and dribbled it awkwardly, "in all the time I've known you, I've only seen you miss a free throw on a few occasions, and each time there was something on your mind." She shot the ball, and it fell soundlessly through the rim.

Shai shook his head and laughed. "Nice shot, nosey ass."

"I learned a thing or three from being around you these last few years," she winked, "now quit changing the subject. What's bothering you, Shai?"

Shai picked up the basketball and began dribbling it through his legs. "Honey, don't go jumping to conclusions over a missed free throw." He shot the ball and made the basket this time.

"Normally, I wouldn't. But when Swann shows up unannounced, that generally means something is up. He's waiting for you upstairs in the kitchen," she informed him. Shai tried to keep his poker face, but his eyes confirmed her suspicions.

"Thanks, baby." Shai patted her on the ass as he passed her on his way to the stairs that lead to the main house.

"Shai, what is it that you're not telling me?" Honey was right on his heels.

He downplayed it. "Nothing for you to worry about, ma."

"Shai," she grabbed his arm and spun him to face her, "don't talk to me like I'm some random chick off the streets that doesn't know what time it is. You don't think I didn't peep those two detectives show up at the grand opening? Every time those two crooked muthafuckas show up, something bad is about to go down, and if that's the case, then I need to know."

Shai stopped short of the door leading to the kitchen. "Honey, all I will say and should have to say is that it's *family business*." He left it at that and went up into the kitchen where Swann was waiting for him.

Big Suge made her way around the kitchen, rattling pots and pans as she prepared dinner for the Clarks. Perched on two stools around the kitchen's island were Swann and little cousin Nicky, whom they all called Nickels. Swann had given him that nickname because the youngster was always asking him for change. Nickels was only fourteen, but had the soul of a man who had *been here before* and was far wiser than he should've been at that age. He was well read, polite, and soft spoken, but had hustler in his blood, which was apparent from all the mischief he'd managed to get into during the short time he had been living with the Clarks. He was every bit of his father's child, and Gator was probably smiling from the grave.

Gator had been Shai's cousin and the man who had stood the tallest on the front lines when the streets moved on Shai to take what Poppa had left him. In the end, his young life was cut short in a gun battle with the police outside a seedy motel where they had just executed one of Shai's rivals. He sacrificed himself so that his comrades could escape, and Shai would be forever in his debt for the selfless act. Years later when Nickels and his mother Janette showed up on Shai's doorstep with a story of hard times and poverty, he would have a chance to pay it forward.

Shai had heard Gator speak of the shorty he had left back in Florida but never of fathering a child with her so her sudden appearance was suspect, but when Shai laid eyes on the boy, he knew Nickels was a Clark. Sol called in some favors and managed to get a sample of Gator's DNA, which was on record with the Dade County Department of Corrections, and to everyone's shock, Janette was telling the truth and there was a new addition to the Clark family.

Janette and Nickels stayed with Shai and Honey at the compound for two weeks while Shai got to know the little boy that his cousin had abandoned. Nicky was a little rough around the edges, but he was a good kid who had been through some real grown-up things. When Janette announced that she was ready to head back to Florida, Shai found himself reluctant to toss his little cousin back to what was waiting for him, so he set Nickels and his mother up in the guest house while she tried to get herself together.

Shai enrolled Nickels in a private school in New Jersey, and his abilities on the court and engaging personality quickly made him popular in school and the transition that much easier. It wasn't long before Janette fell back into her old routine of partying. She fit right into the New Jersey underworld society and spent more time with hustlers than she did with Nickels. Though he never said anything, Shai and Honey knew it bothered the boy, so they went out of their way to make sure Nickels always knew that he was loved under their roof. A little over a month ago, Janette said she was going to Florida to take care of some business and would only be gone a week. That was the last time anyone saw her alive. Shortly after she left, Janette was found murdered in the home of a notorious Miami drug dealer. They had both been shot, execution style. Social Services wanted to take Nicky, but Shai wasn't trying to hear it. Nicky was one of the few people who carried Clark blood in their veins, and his place was with his family.

"What it do?" Shai came into the kitchen and gave Swann dap. He leaned in to hug him, but Swann held him at arm's length.

"Chill, my nigga; you too sweaty to be all up on me. You might fuck up my white tee." Then he brushed imaginary dirt from the white T-shirt he was wearing.

"My dude, that's a five-dollar T-shirt not Versace." Shai leaned on Swann, getting sweat on his T-shirt. "What's goodie though, my G? I know you ain't burn up that high-ass New York gas just to come over here and shoot the shit."

"Fuck you, Shai," Swann laughed. What Shai said wasn't

that funny, but the way that he said it reminded Swann of Tommy Gunz.

"Watch your mouth." Shai nodded at Nickels, who was looking back and forth between them, grinning.

"Who this li'l nigga?" Swann mussed Nickels's hair. "Shorty got a worse mouth than mine."

"He better not let me catch him cussing," Suge said over her shoulder. They had all almost forgotten she was standing there.

"But on the real, Shai," Swann continued, "you ever had a conversation with this li'l dude? I mean a *real* conversation?"

"I know just how deep the rabbit hole goes with this li'l one, don't I, Nickels?" Shai smirked at his little cousin.

"Yeah, cuz," Nickels said, smiling back mischievously.

"So as long as you know that I know, then we're all good." Shai bumped fists with Nickels. "Now, go watch TV in the other room so I can rap with your uncle Swann right quick."

"A'ight." Nickels slid off the stool with a saddened look on his face. He gave Swann dap before disappearing into the living room.

Swann waited until he was sure they were alone before he addressed Shai in a hushed tone. "I got some scuttle on that shit them two dicks was talking about the other night . . ." he began, but Shai cut him off with a raised finger.

"Let's go outside and talk." Shai led the way through the glass doors from the kitchen into the sprawling green acres of land that was his backyard. They walked down the cobblestone path to the duck pond, where they posted up on a wooden bench. There Shai nodded, letting Swann know it was okay to talk.

"Like I was saying, I got word back on one of them bodies them bitch-ass detectives came at us about," Swann said.

"Well, don't keep an asshole in suspense," Shai said sarcastically.

"The boy's name was Slick. He was one of our lieutenants who had it clicking on the Westside," Swann explained.

Shai searched his memory bank and shrugged. "I don't know that nigga."

"Of course you don't, because you got a nigga like me to keep you insulated from the soldiers," Swann said proudly. "Anyhow, I managed to track down the broad who had been with Slick that night and got the *E! True Hollywood Story* of what happened, and it ain't good."

"Swann, please stop setting the scene and tell me what the fuck *is* good." Shai was agitated.

"Slick had just dropped off the package and picked up the bread for the night when some nigga wearing a Halloween mask got the drop on them. He roughed the broad up but let her go, then he murdered a cat in front of one hundred people before he bounced with Slick and the car."

"So what happened to the bread?" Shai asked, more concerned about the money than the life lost.

"That's the thing. When the police found Slick's car, all the money was still there, the whole twenty-five thousand," Swann said.

Shai was shocked. "Get the fuck outta here."

"On my li'l ones, that money is sitting in a police evidence locker as we speak. To keep it one hundred, that's the thing that's fucking with me the most. Why go through all that trouble and risk having those kinds of problems and not take a dime for your trouble?" Swann wondered.

"War," Shai said, remembering the photograph.

"Huh?" Swann was lost.

"War. It was the word carved into homie's forehead. Whoever did that was an attention whore and wanted to be seen, so we're gonna make sure we see them." Shai nodded in anticipation of retaliation.

"I'm with you on that. There are a few cats who'd like to see us knocked outta the box, but if I had to place a bet, then my money would be on them cats from Grant Projects we got into it with at Brick City. I had my ear to the streets, and the word is that nigga King James been selling wolf tickets about how it's over for us."

Shai's mind flashed back to the altercation in the VIP. "You talking about the bum-ass nigga with the big chain? Them dudes is bottom-feeders; they ain't got the balls or the resources to get it popping with us. On our long list of enemies he falls at the bottom," he boasted.

"Maybe, maybe not. I'm just trying to make sure we cross all *t*'s and dot all *i*'s going into this," Swann told him.

"You right, my nigga, so instead of focusing on one, we'll make our rounds and touch 'em all. We gonna pat these niggaz on the asses right quick to let 'em know that the Clark name still rings bells in Harlem!"

Honey sat on the living-room couch with her arms folded and her leg bobbing up and down. Shai and Swann came through the living room on their way out to only God knew where. She said good-bye to Swann, but rolled her eyes at Shai. When he leaned in to kiss her, she made sure to nick his bottom lip with her teeth. When he told her he loved her, she just rolled her eyes and let him leave without giving him a second look. She was heated and wanted him to know it.

The conversation she and Shai had on the stairs a few hours prior was still fresh in her mind, and she got angrier the more she thought about it. She understood that he kept certain things from her for her own protection, but the way that he had dismissed her, stating that it was *family business,* stung her. She had known Shai since he was still a screwed up teenager playing gangster in the streets. She was wearing his ring and about to welcome his child into the world, so in Honey's mind, she was a Clark and part of the family, but the way that he'd carried her showed Honey that there was still an imaginary line in the sand that she wasn't allowed to cross.

"You okay?" Nickels asked, coming to sit on the couch beside Honey. He had a pair of oversized headphones on his head and a portable CD player in his hand.

"Yeah, I'm good. Thanks, Nicky." Honey patted his leg. "What you listen to?"

"Oh, this new CD I got. This joint is cold!" he said excitedly.

"I thought when you liked something you said it was fire?" Honey said.

"Nah, y'all say fire up North; down South, we say cold."

Honey laughed. "Okay, so what is this cold CD?"

"I ain't never heard of him before, but he's pretty tight." He handed Honey the CD case.

When Honey looked down at the artwork on the CD case and saw the diamond and gold grill sneering back at her she dropped the CD to the carpet and clutched her chest. As cautiously as if it was a snake, she picked up the CD case and stared at it in horror. When she saw the signature on the cover she felt a sharp pain shoot through her side. Without realizing what she was doing Honey grabbed Nickels and began shaking him. "Where did you get that CD?" she asked.

"Honey, why you tripping?" Nickels was getting nervous. The look in her eyes was the same one he would see in his mother's eyes right before she hit him.

"Where the hell did you get this?" she repeated.

"I got it from a guy at the park where we have basketball practice on Saturdays. The dude was blasting it from his car, and when I told him how much I liked the song he gave me the CD. Did I do something wrong?" Nickels's eyes were pleading and frightened.

"No, I'm sorry, Nicky." Honey hugged him to her. "You didn't do anything wrong," she consoled him. She continued to reassure Nickels that he wasn't in trouble, but she couldn't take her eyes off of the CD. Was someone giving Nickels the CD a coincidence or an omen?

THIRTEEN

ANIMAL TRIED TO GET SOME REST BEFORE he initiated the next phase of his plan that night, but it was futile. He had too much weighing on him to sleep, so he decided to go out for a walk. It was risky considering he was a hunted man, but between his long voyage and being holed up in a motel room the whole time he had been back was starting to make him feel caged. Besides, it had been far too long since he'd taken a stroll through Harlem.

Much had changed since last time he strolled the streets of Harlem. Where tenements and bodegas had once stood there were now high-rise buildings and fancy cafés. The changes to Harlem weren't limited to the construction; the people had changed too. The once-predominantly black neighborhoods were now occupied by different ethnic groups of people who had migrated uptown to get their pieces of what was now considered prime real estate. It was as if they were the natives and he was now the outsider. Just about everyone he'd known was either dead or in jail, and he didn't recognize any of the new faces hugging the blocks he once claimed as his domain.

He reached in his pocket for his pack of cigarettes and found it empty. With a sigh, he crumbled the empty pack and tossed it on the ground before heading into the store on the corner. The first thing he noticed when he entered the store was the pungent odor of weed. Several young men lingered inside the bodega trying to act as if it wasn't a front for whatever they were up to. Animal kept his head down as he approached the counter, but he could feel all their eyes on him.

"Let me get a pack of Newports and two Dutch Masters," Animal told the cat behind the counter. He was an older Spanish dude, rocking a do-rag and a chain that was supposed to pass for real, but clearly fake to someone who knew fine jewelry.

"Eleven eighty-five," the Spanish cat told him.

Animal was caught off guard by the price hike. "Damn, shit really has changed in Harlem." Reluctantly, he pulled out his bankroll and peeled off some bills to pay for his items. On his way out of the store, he noticed one of the boys tap his friend and nod in his direction. He knew they were sizing him up, weighing their options. There was no doubt in his mind about him being able to take the youngsters, but a confrontation with the street punks was something he didn't need. He had much bigger fish to fry.

After making it almost a block away from the store, Animal felt the hairs on his neck stand. He knew the feeling well from his years of being both predator and prey in the streets. He veered to cut across the street and looked down the block as if he was watching for traffic and spotted two of the boys from the store at the end of the block, trying as best they could to be stealthy. They were amateurs and stuck out like sore thumbs. He had hoped to avoid a confrontation, but it didn't seem like they were going to give him a choice.

Animal made a left on 126th and Seventh Avenue and headed west on a block that he knew was a less-traveled one. In the back of one of the buildings there was a dip that led to a small loading area that you couldn't see from either end of the block until you were right on top of it. He stepped into a corner of the nook and undid his belt like he was about to relieve himself. His back was to the street, but he could see behind him via a small dirty mirror that sat above the loading bay door. Just as he had predicted, the two knuckleheads rounded the corner a few seconds later. Animal let out a sigh. They were little boys who were trying to play grown men's games but would learn that Animal didn't play well with others.

There were only two of them, one wearing a hoodie and the other only a T-shirt. It was simple to figure out which of them, if either, was armed. After some debate, the one with the hoodie was designated the point man on the caper. With his heart halfway in his throat and a knife in his hand, he approached his intended victim with his partner in crime on his heels.

"Yo, you know what this is. Give up before I—" That was as far as the kid in the hoodie got.

Animal spun, snatching his belt off as he did, and went on the offensive. The thick leather belt struck as quickly as lightning, snapping twice across the kid's face and ruining his whole game plan. Before he could even consider swinging the knife, Animal had looped the belt around his wrist and slung him face-first into the loading bay door. The impact of the kid's face hitting the door set off a thunderous boom, but it was nothing compared to the scream the kid let out when Animal broke his wrist with the belt.

The second kid tried to run, but Animal tripped him and he fell, face-first, to the ground. Before he could get up to scramble away, Animal was on him. He looped the belt around the kid's neck and dragged him into the corner, where his partner was rolling around on the ground blubbering about his broken wrist. Animal let his attention slip for a second while trying to decide what to do and that was all it took. The kid with the belt around his neck swung blindly and managed to pop Animal in the mouth, busting his top lip. Animal licked away the trickle of blood and gave the kid a nod of respect before he stomped on his ankle and broke it. The kid in the T-shirt lost his balance, and Animal swung him headfirst into a brick wall, opening a nasty gash on his forehead. With a quick jerk of his belt, Animal spilled him on the floor next to his partner.

Animal looked down at the two crippled would-be robbers. "Everybody wants to be a tough guy." He shook his head and walked off.

An hour after dealing with the two knuckleheads, Animal found that he was more wound up than when he had initially set out. The two kids were little more than a warm-up, but their screams had stirred the monster that lived inside him. The beast demanded to be fed, but the meal was not yet ready.

Animal continued to walk, lost deep in his thoughts. He didn't have a particular destination; he just knew he needed to walk to burn off some of his anger. Twenty minutes into his walk he was passing a church and stopped abruptly. The church was old and looked like it had seen better days but was still beautiful in its design. Staring at the church, there was something familiar about it that tugged at his brain. He couldn't recall ever having been to the church, but something about it was familiar to him. He started to walk away, but curiosity made him go inside.

The interior of the church wasn't as dilapidated as the exterior, but it needed serious work. A rat scampering across Animal's foot drew his attention to the wooden floors; at least he assumed they were wooden. All of the varnish was stripped away, turning the floor a very pale shade of brown. The purple cushions that padded the benches were faded and stained on the few seats where they hadn't fallen or been ripped off of. It was obvious that there hadn't been any worshiping within those walls in quite some time.

Animal quietly made his way down the aisle, eyes fixed on a stained glass mural that depicted Jesus Christ which hung over the podium at the front of the church. It was the only thing in the entire place that didn't seem to have been touched by time and neglect. The ruby eyes seemed to bore into the killer accusingly, as if the mural could see his sin-laden soul.

Animal sneered at the mural. "Who the fuck are you to judge me?"

"Have you no respect for the church?" a feminine voice startled Animal. He spun, expecting to find an enemy, but was surprised when he was confronted by a young woman dressed in leather pants and a white shirt, sitting on one of the benches. She was a beautiful girl with olive skin and long, jet-black hair. From her features he knew she was from somewhere in the Middle East, but her thick lips and hips indicated that she may have been mixed with something else too. Her fierce black eyes stared at Animal accusingly.

"Sorry, I didn't realize anyone else was here," Animal said sincerely.

"It shouldn't matter if you were here alone or not. This is still a house of worship, and you'd be wise to leave all that street mess at the door when you enter these walls," she scolded him.

"Damn, who are you? The freaking church hall monitor? Look, I said I'm sorry. What more you want, shorty?" he challenged.

She stood and approached Animal. "My name isn't shorty. It's Khallah, and you will address me by my name or not speak to me at all." She got in his face.

"Baby girl, you better back up. You're a little too close for comfort right now," he warned.

Khallah laughed. "Little boy, you have a sharp tongue. Maybe we should see what we can do about dulling it a bit."

"Ma, back up before one of us gets hurt and ends up having to apologize for clowning in this church."

"And I would gladly accept your apology, as soon as you're released from the hospital," Khallah said in a deadly tone. Her hands hung at her sides, but her fingers were rigid and pointed like spears.

"That will be quite enough, Khallah," a male voice called from the podium at the front of the church.

Animal had been so focused on the girl called Khallah that he didn't even see the bald man in the army jacket standing a few feet away.

"If I were you, I'd listen to him, shorty," Animal taunted her.

Khallah took a menacing step forward, but the man's voice

boomed again. This time it was more of a command than a suggestion. "Khallah." He stepped from the podium, his shiny black combat boots clanking heavily on the wooden steps. "Please do not make me repeat myself."

It was apparent from the look on Khallah's face that she wanted to tear into Animal, but the man's words outweighed her rage, and she reluctantly let it go. "Yes, Father." She lowered her head and turned away. "Pompous jackass," she mumbled as she headed for a door leading to the church office.

"Love you too, boo," Animal called after her.

"It's not smart to taunt her like that. Khallah can be a real spitfire when pushed," the bald man told Animal as he approached. He was tall with a clean shaven head and thick goatee that was sprinkled salt and pepper. He wore a black army jacket and blue jeans tucked into a pair of black combat boots. A black leather patch covered his right eye, but you could see the scar beneath that stretched from just above his brow to his cheek. A silver rosary swayed slightly in his left hand.

"I think I could've taken her," Animal said sarcastically.

The man thought about it. "Hand-to-hand, I doubt it, but if you'd pulled that hammer, it might've tipped the scales in your favor." He nodded at Animal's waistline.

Animal looked down to see if the gun was noticeable, but it wasn't, so how the hell did the man know it was there? "Fuck is you the police or something?" Animal drew the gun, looking frantically from side to side as if at any minute the church would be swarmed with law enforcement.

"Easy," the man said, holding his hands so that they were visible. The rosary rattled in his trembling left hand while he reached for the collar of his jacket with his right. Carefully, he pulled his jacket open so that Animal could see the white priest's collar that snaked around his neck. "There's no need for that."

"So says you. I'd rather have it and not need it than to need it and not have it." Animal tucked the gun.

"Or you can remove yourself from situations that leave you such limited choices," the priest countered.

"News flash for you, old-timer, in the ghetto, you play the hand you're dealt, and you play to win. Being a man of the cloth I wouldn't expect you to know too much about hood politics." Animal flopped on the tattered bench and cast his eyes back to the mural.

The priest sat down next to him, but kept a safe distance. "I think I know a thing or three about hood politics."

Animal looked over at the priest. "What? You gonna tell me how you, an ex-dope boy, found religion?"

"Nah, I never really had the patience to stand around selling drugs. My lane was a little faster, if you know what I mean." The priest shaped his fingers like a gun. "Gained some, lost more." He pointed to the patch over his eye.

Animal reflected on Gucci. "I know all about losses."

"Money or a woman?"

"What?" Animal asked confused.

"It's either money or a woman that's got you sitting in a church with a gun looking like you're planning on doing something you're probably gonna regret."

"I'm planning on doing a lot, Padre, but I highly doubt if I'll regret any of it. Sometimes the principles of a thing outweigh the repercussions."

The priest nodded. "Talking like that, I'm guessing it's a

woman. Only a lady can send a man on a kamikaze mission and have him convince himself that it actually makes sense. Love comes and goes, kid, but you won't be able to be there to catch it the second time if you throw your life away over some broad."

"What the fuck does a priest know about love? Ain't all you muthafuckas virgins or something?" Animal said mockingly.

The priest smirked. "It's like I told you; I haven't always been a priest, and even my long walk with the Lord hasn't been without its detours. Love is a double-edged sword. It can be a gift from God or a curse from the devil, all depending on how you chose to wield it. When in doubt," he shrugged, "leave it in God's hands."

Animal snorted. "That's a fucking laugh. So far, leaving things in God's hands hasn't done much for me but making sure that I'm on the short end of the shit stick every time. God don't give a fuck about kids from the ghetto."

"God loves us all," the priest assured him.

"Then how come he don't love me?" Animal looked up at the priest. His eyes were moist, but he wouldn't let the tears fall in front of the stranger.

"Young man, I assure you—" the priest began but Animal cut him off.

"Assure me *what*? That God loved me when my family abandoned me to the streets and I had to eat trash to survive? Did he love me when he let my stepfather beat me until I shitted blood for a week? Or maybe he was just showing me love when he tried to take away the only thing I ever cared about?" Animal's sadness was replaced by rage.

"I'm sorry," the priest said sincerely. His heart truly went out to Animal.

"Not as sorry as my enemies will be when they're choking on their own blood." Animal stood to leave. The priest stood to block his path. "Stand aside, old man. I'd hate to hurt a servant of the Lord, but don't think I won't if you try to get between me and my due."

The priest ignored Animal's threat. "Revenge is not the answer."

"Maybe not, but it's all I got left. Thanks for the chat, Padre." Animal stepped past him and headed for the church exit. When he was halfway there the priest called after him.

"Vengeance is mine, sayeth the Lord."

Animal looked up at the mural. "Not this time, Padre." He patted the gun on his hip. "Not this time."

Long after Animal had gone, the priest still stood in the aisle, looking toward the door as if he expected Animal to change his mind and come back. Deep down, the priest knew that he wouldn't. From the moment the young man had walked into the church the priest could smell it on him, the stink of death. The tormented soul had his feet firmly planted on the ground and would not be deterred from his path of vengeance, and there was nothing that the priest or anyone else would be able to say to sway him.

"I don't like him," Khallah said from just behind the priest. She moved so silently that he hadn't even heard her approach. She was learning.

"The boy is in pain. Don't be so judgmental, my child," he told her.

"And his pain is going to get him killed," she said.

"Or show him the light," the priest countered.

130

"Only those who acknowledge the higher power are fit to receive his light. He's just like the men who turned their backs on you. He does not believe!" she said heatedly.

"And neither did you at one time," the priest reminded her. "It was the Lord's divine will to interweave these particular strands of fate, and like good servants, we will watch what is to come and reap the rewards of the faithful. No matter how either of us feels, the boy has already started his walk down the lonely road and nothing short of death or victory will stray him from his path. It's in his blood."

"Do you think he'll succeed?"

The priest measured the odds. "Honestly, no. But with faith, anything is possible." He smiled knowingly.

FOURTEEN

ASHANTI WALKED INTO THE HOSPITAL LOBBY, CHATTING away on his cell phone, trying to put some things in motion for the night. The day had been a trying, yet prosperous, one that left him with a pocket full of cash, and Ashanti intended to celebrate the spoils. As he was passing the security desk en route to the elevators he noticed one of the security guards giving him a dirty look, so he returned the favor and mugged him back.

"No cell phones," the portly guard said with way too much attitude.

"My fault," Ashanti said, ending the call and slipping the phone into his pocket.

"Where are you going?" the guard pressed him.

"Upstairs to visit somebody," Ashanti said as if it should have been obvious.

"All visitors must be at least eighteen or accompanied by an adult. How old are you?" the security guard asked, looking at Ashanti suspiciously.

"Nineteen," Ashanti lied.

"You got some ID that says so?"

Ashanti rolled his eyes. "C'mon, Blood, you seen me come in and outta here twice this week already. What you need to see my ID for?"

The security guard stood up and pointed his finger accusingly at Ashanti. "First of all, I ain't ya Blood, son. Second of all, you gotta show ID because I *say* so."

"Man, I ain't got time for this shit." Ashanti turned to walk away.

The security guard came from behind his desk and grabbed him by the arm. "Boy, don't you walk off while I'm talking to you!" he barked.

Ashanti looked at the hand gripping his arm, then glared up at the security guard. "My nigga, if you don't get yo' slimy-ass claw off me, we gonna have a problem."

The security guard's nostrils flared, and his eyes narrowed to slits. "What? You gonna do something, boy? You got some frog in you? Come on and try me. Come on!"

Ashanti slapped the security guard's hand away, shocking and enraging him. The security guard drew his pepper spray, but Ashanti knocked his hand away and shoved him roughly against the desk. At the same time the security guard was reaching for his nightstick Ashanti was reaching for his gun. A hand landed on Ashanti's shoulder, and he spun, ready to do battle, but froze when he saw Ms. Ronnie's angry face.

"What in the hell is going on down here!" Ms. Ronnie shouted. By then, two more security guards had arrived on the scene and managed to separate Ashanti and his antagonizer.

"This little bastard is going to jail!" the security guard screamed.

"Jail? For what?" Ms. Ronnie looked rapidly from Ashanti to the security guard.

"Assaulting an officer."

"Officer?" Ashanti laughed. "Nigga, you got your badge in the mail. Ain't no power behind that."

"We'll see how much laughing you do when the police get here," the security guard fumed, picking up the phone behind the security desk.

"If that's the case, then I might as well earn the bogus charge you're trying to put on me." Ashanti took a step toward him, but Ms. Ronnie blocked his path.

"Wait a second, everybody, just calm down," Ms. Ronnie told both of them. "Officer, may I speak to you for a minute?" she said, addressing the security guard. Reluctantly, he let Ms. Ronnie pull him to the side for a private conversation. They exchanged a few words, and eventually he calmed down. Ms. Ronnie shook his hand and gave him her thanks before turning her attention back to Ashanti. "Fool boy, are you trying to get yourself locked up?"

Ashanti sucked his teeth. "Ms. Ronnie, I ain't stunting that toy cop."

"And that 'toy cop,' as you call him, could've called some real ones in here to straighten your little ass out, and I think it's safe to say that you getting searched right now would yield some very interesting findings." She looked down at his waistline, knowing the little boy was strapped.

"You're right, Ms. Ronnie," Ashanti said sheepishly.

"I know I am. Now, I've gotten him to agree not to press charges if you apologize," she told him.

Ashanti frowned. "Ms. Ronnie, he touched me first. I ain't

apologizing to him. He's lucky I didn't fold him for what he tried to pull."

"Ashanti, you better tuck that pride and do what you gotta do to stay your mischievous ass outta jail. Now, go over there and make nice before you and me end up having a misunderstanding." Ms. Ronnie folded her arms and gave Ashanti a no-nonsense look.

"A'ight," Ashanti sighed, knowing Ms. Ronnie wasn't going to back down. He shuffled over to the security desk.

The guard stood there with a smug expression on his face and his arms folded. "You got something you wanna say to me, boy?"

"I apologize," Ashanti mumbled.

"*Excuse* me?" the security guard said as if he couldn't hear him.

"I said I'm sorry!" Ashanti said loud enough for everyone to hear him.

"And you should be. I don't know what's wrong you young kids today. You got no respect for your elders. Maybe them skinny jeans y'all have taken to wearing has cut off the circulation to your brain." The security guard laughed at his own joke.

"Whatever." Ashanti fought the urge to punch the security guard in his face but, instead, walked back over to Ms. Ronnie. "Satisfied?"

"No, but it'll do for now," she said. "Ashanti, why is it that you can't seem to stay out of trouble?"

He shrugged. "I don't know, Ms. Ronnie. Trouble seems to just have a way of finding me."

"Then do a better job of hiding from it! Ashanti, day in and day out I see kids like you who have so much promise but throw their lives away for little to nothing; somebody said something to you or you didn't like the way that they were looking at you. My God, when are you kids gonna wise up? After what happened to Gucci, then this craziness with Animal, and this stupid vendetta—" She paused, but the damage was already done.

"Animal? What's he got to do with any of this and what vendetta?" Ashanti asked suspiciously.

"Nothing. I meant the vendetta he carried that was eventually his undoing," Ms. Ronnie lied. "Ashanti, I've come to know and love all y'all little misfits like my adopted children, and I just don't know what I'd do if I lost another one of y'all."

"Don't worry, Ms. Ronnie, I ain't going nowhere. I'm gonna be here for you and Gucci when she wakes up," he vowed.

Ms. Ronnie cupped his face lovingly. "Please don't make me promises you can't keep," she said thinking of when Animal had said the same thing. "Boy, you got me down here getting all emotional." She dabbed the corners of her eyes with a napkin. "I gotta go check on a few things at the house so you can go on up and visit with Gucci while I'm gone. Tionna is up there too."

"Cool, but before I forget, I have something for you." He pulled a wad of money from his pocket and peeled off two thousand dollars of the money Don B. had given him which he extended to her.

"Ashanti, I can't take your money," she said.

"It ain't all mine. We took up a collection in the hood," he lied with a smile.

Humbly, Ms. Ronnie took the money and put it in her purse. "Thank you, Ashanti, and please tell your friends I said the same." She hugged him tightly.

"I will, and no thanks needed. Since Animal is gone, you

and Gucci are among the few people left who I look at like family, and I would do *anything* for you."

"I know, and that's what frightens me the most." She patted the back of his hand. "Now, go ahead and visit with your friends."

Ashanti silently entered Gucci's hospital room. Gucci was as she had been every other time he visited, sleeping soundlessly while the machines measured her vitals. He still had a hard time seeing her that way so he focused on Tionna, who was sitting in the corner with her head buried in a book, giggling to herself.

"What's up, Tionna?"

Tionna leaped from the chair and dropped her book on the floor. "Boy, you scared the shit out of me! Why don't you make some noise when you walk?"

"I did, but you're so caught up in that damn book that you didn't hear me. What are you reading anyhow?" He picked the book up and looked at the cover and the title. "*The Last Outlaw*? What is this? Some kinda western or something?"

"No, it's not a western." She snatched the book from him. "It's an urban fiction novel."

Ashanti frowned. "I've heard of fiction and nonfiction. What the fuck is urban fiction supposed to be?"

"It's like rap music, but on paper instead of CDs," she explained. "You should try checking some of these out. I know you'd like them."

"I'm cool on that reading shit. Don't none of them books talk about where I'm from so I ain't got time to be reading no white man's fantasy," Ashanti said in a disinterested tone.

"For your information, most of these books are written by

blacks and Latinos who come from the same thing we come from, and a lot of the stories are very good. Stop being so closed minded about everything."

"Anyhow." He twisted his lips.

"So, what brings you this way three times in one week?"

"Nothing. I just wanted to check in on Gucci and drop something off to you." He took out the remaining five hundred from the money Don B. had given him and handed it to Tionna.

"What's this for?" she asked suspiciously.

Ashanti shrugged. "I dunno. Just because. I know you've been taking off from work to sit with Gucci, so I thought you could use a few dollars."

"Well, I ain't never one to turn down no paper." She started to put the money in her purse but hesitated. "You ain't kill nobody for this, did you?"

"No, I didn't kill anybody for the money, Tionna. Look, if you don't want it, you can give it back and I can spend it on weed and strippers." Ashanti reached for the money, but Tionna snatched it back.

"The hell you will." She quickly stuffed the money in her purse. "With your little ass I can never be sure if the money has blood on it or not, and I don't need your kinda trouble, Ashanti."

"Whatever." He waved her off. "How's Gucci?"

"Better, thank God." Tionna went to stand at Gucci's bedside. "They removed her breathing tube a few days ago, and there haven't been any more complications from the surgeries, but she's still in a coma and the doctors can't seem to figure out why. It's like she just won't wake up."

"Is there anything we can do?"

"Wait and pray that someone turns the lights back on in

those eyes of hers." Tionna brushed Gucci's hair out of her face. "You gonna be a'ight, ma." She kissed her on the forehead.

"You're talking to her like she can hear you," Ashanti said.

"She can, she just can't answer. You know Gucci's nosey ass ain't never missed a beat," Tionna joked.

Ashanti came to stand beside her, and this time he couldn't help but to look down at Gucci. It was almost as if she was in a deep slumber. With the breathing tube gone she didn't look as tragic, but it was still hard for him to look at her. In his mind he saw her scrambling eggs for him when he had come down to visit her and Animal in Texas and trying to get him to abandon his criminal life and resume his schooling down there. Every time she brought it up, Ashanti would laugh and say they'd talk about it later, and to his despair, later may never come.

"I'll never get used to seeing her like this," Tionna began. "This shit is so fucked up because Gucci ain't never did nothing but try to help people, even when they didn't deserve to be helped. This wasn't supposed to happen to her." Tionna's voice cracked, but she didn't cry. She had cried so much since Gucci had been in the hospital that she didn't think she had any tears left.

"It's gonna be okay, T." Ashanti gave her a gentle hug.

"I know." She composed herself. "A lot of people had love for Gucci, and this ain't just gonna go away. Somebody gonna feel this shit," Tionna spat.

"Listen to you trying to sound all gangsta." Ashanti nudged her playfully to try to lighten her mood.

"Nah, I ain't no gangsta, but I know a few." She gave Ashanti a knowing wink.

Ashanti turned his attention back to Gucci. He felt awkward

just standing there. He needed to say something, but he wasn't sure what, so he took her hand and spoke from his heart. "Baby girl, I know you and the big homie always urged me to do the right thing, but you know I've never been good at doing the right thing, so it is what it is. You take all the time you need to get well, but just know that while you're in here recovering, I'm gonna be in the streets banging for you. That's on the homie Animal," he vowed. Ashanti squeezed Gucci's hand, then something happened that left him speechless . . . she squeezed his hand back.

FIFTEEN

ANIMAL GASPED LIKE A DROWNING MAN WHO had just cracked the surface of the water. His brain was still heavy with sleep, and his eyes blurry, but from instinct he snatched up his gun and swept the room for enemies. Slowly the sleep rolled back and his vision cleared. He sighed and lowered his gun. He was safe . . . at least for the moment.

His heart was working overtime in his chest, and the burst of adrenaline made his head hurt, but he was getting used to it. The dreams were always intense. Since Animal had returned to New York he'd started having nightmares that felt more like intense hallucinations. Some of the murders he had committed began to replay themselves in his head while he slept. Animal had an extensive résumé of bodies, but the nightmares were of the brutal ones. The one he had just awakened from was always one of the worst. Not because of how he killed his victims, but because of how cruel he had been in the deed.

_____

The road Animal traveled trying to escape Puerto Rico to sneak back into New York was a rough one and mostly done by water. Even with Sonja using her father's resources to help Animal, his face was too notorious to dare risk getting on an airplane, so he would have to go the long way. He traveled by ship from Puerto Rico, to the Dominican Republic, and eventually, Florida. During his travels, he had visited many ports and came in contact with people from all walks of life, but none stuck with him like the New Orleans refugees that he had met in Miami.

Sonja had hooked Animal up with some cats from New Orleans who had set up shop in Miami. Diamonds was a slick-talking Creole cat, who, along with his crew, had escaped to Florida during Hurricane Katrina. Rumor had it that Diamonds had executed a big-time dealer from New Orleans and robbed him of all his product before fleeing, which was how he was able to establish himself so quickly as a power player in the Sunshine State. Diamonds was supposed to be the man to provide Animal with guns and safe passage to New York from Miami for a fee that neither he nor Sonja had ever revealed to Animal. She seemed to trust Diamonds, but Animal never really did. There was something sinister about the young Cajun that Animal couldn't put his finger on.

Diamonds and his team welcomed Animal as if he was one of their own while he was in Miami and as Sonja had promised, Diamonds provided him with the things he would need to get to New York and handle his business once he made it, including his choice from an arsenal of firearms. The whole time leading up to Animal's departure Diamonds had been trying to sway Animal to get down with his crew, but Animal declined. His business was in New York, not Miami. For all Diamonds's best efforts, he couldn't sway Animal, but on the night before Animal was to depart, Diamonds made a statement that would change everything.

"The tongue of my enemy will speak the name of your enemy. I think we can help each other, *mon ami,*" Diamonds had whispered to him. When he had Animal's full attention, he went on to offer Animal what he would think back on as the devil's bargain.

There was a prominent dealer in the area named Flames who held sway over some territory that Diamonds was looking to take over. Flames was well connected in the Florida under-world, and for Diamonds or one of his crew to touch Flames would've been an immediate death sentence, so he turned to Animal to do the deed. In exchange for murdering Flames, Diamonds would give Animal the one thing he desired most: the name of the ones responsible for shooting Gucci.

Animal's voice was hard and cold when he replied. "When I kill a man you can always expect it to be clean, but for the name of the dude who tried to waste my old lady, I'll see to it that your enemy's mama is gonna have to lay him to rest in a sippy cup, cuz it ain't gonna be enough left of him for a coffin." And with that, the bargain was struck.

Normally Animal would've stalked the victim for at least a week before moving on him, but he didn't have that kind of time. He needed to get back to Gucci ASAP, so he kept it to three days; two to get a feel for his movements and one to push him off the planet. Flames was easier to find than most because everybody who was anybody in South Florida knew him. Finding him was one thing, but getting to him would be another. He moved carefully and rolled with a ruthless gang of young boys under him that loved to murder niggaz. Animal knew that staying one step behind Flames wouldn't get the job done so he moved a step ahead of him.

Flames had homes all throughout Florida, but his primary residence was a townhouse in a gated community that sat just outside Cocoa Beach, Florida. It was the one place that was off-limits to his crew and where Animal would spring his trap.

One night after Flames had been clubbing he returned to his townhouse, as he did most nights, with a chick on his arm. This one was a curvaceous chick wearing a dress so tight that it left little to the imagination. Flames and the girl staggered through the front door and into the living room, pawing, kissing, and trying to tear each other's clothes off. They were so caught up in each other that neither of them initially noticed the man sitting on the couch, cloaked in the shadows of the moonlight shining through the window, but they both paused when they heard the familiar sound of a gun being cocked.

Animal's voice cut the darkness. "Had I known you were bringing company home, I'd have set an extra place at the table."

If Animal had expected Flames to show fear, he would've been disappointed. The gangster poked his chest out defiantly. "From yo' accent I can tell you ain't from round here, so you can't possibly know who it is you trying to rob, dawg."

"I'm holding the biggest bag in this whole city."

"And what's that?" Flames asked and immediately regretted the question.

"Revenge."

Animal tapped the trigger twice. The first shot snapped Flames's head back so violently that you could hear his neck crack. The second shot hit him high in the chest, taking him off his feet. Flames landed at the feet of the terrified girl, and she looked upon what was left of him in horror. The skin of Flames's left cheek, as well as his upper lip, had been completely blown off, leaving behind exposed bone and muscle. What was left of his ruined mouth flapped open and closed like a beached fish as he whimpered something that was too distorted for her to make out.

The girl opened her mouth to scream, but Animal's hand wrapped around her neck, trapping the scream in her throat. "You'll get your chance to scream." He kissed her on the lips softly. "But you'll have to wait your turn." He slapped her viciously across the face, knocking her out.

The girl was awakened by what felt like someone licking her face. She turned her head in the direction of the tongue and began to suckle it gently between her lips. Slowly the fog began to roll back from her brain and remembering where she was, her eyes suddenly snapped open with a start. She was greeted by Animal's grinning face hovering over hers. Pinched between his fingers playfully was a severed tongue. It didn't take a rocket scientist to know whose it was.

"Oh my God," she recoiled and scrambled into the corner.

Animal stood and stalked slowly toward her. "Nah, not God, more like the rebellious little brother who they kicked outta heaven. I think you know who I mean." He drew his gun and chambered a round.

"Please don't kill me," she pleaded.

"No loose ends, baby. It's one of the first lessons I learned and a rule I live by." Animal pointed the gun at her.

"But I got a kid," she said, tears pouring down her cheeks.

"Good," Animal nodded. "That means they'll be somebody to mourn your passing," he told her before blowing her brains out.

Revisiting that particular murder always made him ill. It was necessary to murder Flames because he was a means to an end, but he could've spared the girl. He tried to convince himself that he had killed her to keep her from identifying him, but it was a weak lie. The chances of the girl going to the police and admitting to being at the scene of a murder of a known drug dealer was about as likely as him turning himself in for committing the murder. In all truthfulness, he had killed the girl more out of spite than anything else. He wanted to spite God as God had sought to spite him when Gucci was taken away. They were all casualties in his personal holy war.

This made him think back on the conversation he had had with the priest at the church. The priest's words were like searing needles in his skull that he desperately wanted out. The priest thought that by challenging Animal's faith he could reason with him, but Animal would not be swayed. First blood had been on them, and the last would be his to draw.

Shrugging off the ghosts that were trying to ride him into insanity, Animal got out of bed and prepared for the night's work. He took a weed clip from the ashtray and lit it on his way to the kitchen, where he began rummaging through the cabinets until he found what he was looking for: a half-empty bottle of Jack Daniels. Animal turned the bottle upside down and took several hardy gulps before slamming it on the counter. The burn was good; it woke up his senses and stirred the evil lurking in his heart. With the bottle dangling from his hand and the blunt hanging from his lips, he shuffled out of the kitchen.

Even in the dark, Animal navigated the apartment with ease. Before hanging up his guns for a microphone, it had been the only home he knew and one of the few places he always felt safe. Since he'd been back, he'd been staying at a safe house in New Jersey, but after seeing the condition they had left Gucci in, he knew that he needed to be in the center of the hornet's nest, but to set up in New York he needed someplace where he could be at ease, so he went home.

Most would've called Animal crazy for hiding out in his double apartment, in a city where he was wanted for multiple counts of murder and a prison break, but there was always a method to Animal's madness. Sometimes the best place to hide was in plain sight, and he was right under their noses. During his trial, the police had gotten warrants for the apartment he and Gucci shared in New York as well as their house in Texas, but the apartment had never been mentioned because the police didn't know about it. When Animal had taken over the apartment from his aunt and uncle, he'd left all the paperwork in their names and gave them money every month to pay off household bills. At the time he'd done it that way because he was irresponsible and knew they'd make sure everything was up to date, but years later, the decision had proved to be one of the smartest he'd ever made. Since his name wasn't on anything involving the apartment there was no paper trail back to him.

Animal stepped into his bathroom and flicked on the fluorescent light over the mirror. The reflection staring back at him was startling and frightening. His hair was more of a mess than usual as it hadn't seen a comb in Lord knew how long. Heavy bags hung under his eyes from sleepless nights, and the stress had stripped him of at least ten pounds. He was starting to resemble the shadow of death that he had been so long compared to. Between the drugs and the sleepless nights, Animal was putting a hell of a beating on his body, and it was starting to show in his appearance. Disgusted with the sight of himself Animal put his fist through the bathroom mirror in an attempt to destroy the monster staring back at him, but the monster simply multiplied in the broken shards of glass. In each split image he saw the faces of his victims laughing at him mockingly.

By the time he finished the Jack Daniels, Animal was halfway dressed. He pulled on a black thermal and a pair of black fatigue pants, stuffing a red bandana deep into the back-right pocket. He strapped on a lightweight bulletproof vest and pulled on a thick hoodie to conceal it. Animal stood in front of the mirror tugging at the straps of the vest. The Kevlar would help, but he would need to retrieve his armor before he was truly ready to do battle, and for that, he needed to pay a visit to an old friend.

Animal set out on his mission with visions of his enemies begging for their lives at the wrong end of his smoking guns, but little did he know, he wasn't the only one with murder on his mind.

SIXTEEN

AFTER MAKING SURE HE TOOK CARE OF everybody he needed to see for the day, Ashanti was finally able to focus on the person most important to him . . . . himself.

When he'd left the hospital Gucci was still heavy on his mind. He was used to her fussing and chasing after him about this or that, so seeing her still and silent stabbed him in his gut with guilt. Ashanti had singlehandedly turned the tide against Shai Clark's assassins and managed to save everybody except the person he should've been protecting: Gucci. His wasn't the bullet that had struck Gucci, but he felt responsible because he had initiated the shooting. Ashanti had replayed the night at the club over and over in his head, wondering if things could've been done differently, but he kept coming to the same conclusion. It was either stand by and say nothing or watch his homies die.

After some effort, he was able to push the tragic night out of his mind and turned his thoughts to what he would get into that night. Zo-Pound was off chasing pussy like he always did so that pretty much left Ashanti to his own devices. He figured he would hit the liquor store, then roll through the hood to see who was out. With any luck he might be able to bump into one of the project rats and see about getting her to do something strange for a piece of change. Ashanti had become quite popular with the chicks in the hood since he started running with King James, which was something he wasn't used to. He wasn't a virgin, but his experience with women had been somewhat limited. The only person he had confided this in was Zo-Pound. He expected Zo to laugh, but instead, he gave him some words of wisdom. "You're a young man, so you don't have to rush and try to eat the whole meal at one time. Sample each dish and see which one appeals to your palate."

When he'd first made the statement, Ashanti had been clueless of what he was talking about, but the more chicks he dealt with, the more sense it made. Ashanti was enjoying the spoils of being with a made crew, but no matter how many women he slept with, he still felt like something was missing. The chicks were cool to fuck and get high with, but after the bottle had been drained and his nut had been busted, he quickly lost interest. He didn't see the same spark in his conquests that Animal saw in Gucci or Alonzo saw in Porsha when he was chasing her. There was one girl in the hood who he did enjoy talking to and wanted to push up on her, but he doubted that Fatima even knew he was alive. Chicks like her didn't date the help; they dated the boss, and Ashanti wasn't quite there yet.

Ashanti contemplated walking back to the hood from the hospital because it was a nice night, but he didn't feel like it. He wanted to be alone with his thoughts so he called a Harlem cab and requested a driver he was cool with to come scoop him up. Fifteen minutes later, a big white Suburban pulled up in front of his building. Ashanti jumped in the back and greeted the driver, who he called Nine-Five, which was his cab number. Nine-Five was a young Senegalese cat who Ashanti had met through Brasco.

"What's good, little brother?" Nine-Five bumped Ashanti's fist. He was rocking a Yankee fitted, pulled low on his head, and an iced out cross dangling from his neck on the end of a chain. Nine-Five had only been living in the States for just a little over ten years, but from the way he spoke and dressed, you would've thought he was born in America.

"Chilling, Nine-Five. What's good with you? I called the base a couple of times for you but you weren't working," Ashanti told him.

"Yeah, I had to go home and check on some shit," Nine-Five replied, referring to his native Senegal.

"Everything good?" Ashanti asked, recalling some of the horror stories Nine-Five had mentioned of his childhood growing up in Africa.

"Yeah, man. Had to oversee some work on one of my properties on the coast," Nine-Five explained.

"One of your properties?" Ashanti asked surprised.

"Yeah, little brother. I own like six properties back home, and I just opened a second bed and breakfast. I make a killing off the hospitality business during tourist season," Nine-Five said proudly.

Ashanti looked dumbstruck. "My nigga, if you got all that going on in Africa, then why the hell are you over here driving a cab?"

"Because I'm a hustler," Nine-Five boasted. "Driving this cab is one of many things I do to get money. I take what I make here, send it home, and quadruple it."

"If I was caking like that, I'd just kick back," Ashanti said.

"That's because you are an American," Nine-Five shot back.

"Let me tell you something, little brother. Y'all Americans are lazy, and I mean that with no disrespect. The people out here in the United States have everything so they appreciate nothing. In my country, we are born into nothing and don't even have the lands we are entitled to by birth, so we have to work five times as hard for what little we have. My family gave everything they had so I could come to America and have a shot at a better life, and I would not dishonor their memories by wasting the opportunity I have been given. From the first time I saw the bright lights of Manhattan, the seeds were planted in my mind that I would become wealthy one day and be able to take my little brothers and sisters out of squalor."

"Good luck with that," Ashanti said sincerely.

"You don't need luck when you have ambition, little brother," Nine-Five told him. Before Ashanti could press him further, Nine-Five's cell phone ringing stole his attention away. He turned the music up slightly and began speaking to whoever was on the other end in a language that Ashanti didn't understand.

Fifteen minutes later, Nine-Five was pulling up across the street from the projects, in front of the liquor store on Broadway. "Good looking." Ashanti slipped Nine-Five a twenty. The ride didn't cost that much, but Ashanti liked to tip the driver.

"No problem, li'l brother. I'ma catch you later." Nine-Five gave Ashanti dap before he slid from the truck.

Nine-Five was about to pull off, but Ashanti stopped him with a question. "So where are your brothers and sisters now?" Ashanti asked curiously.

Nine-Five smiled. "My oldest sister is my partner in Harlem Cab. The one behind her is in her third year at Howard, and my two youngest brothers attend a private school in North Carolina where they play on the basketball team."

"Damn!" Ashanti was impressed.

"Ambition, little brother." Nine-Five winked and pulled off with his music blasting.

Ashanti was impressed by Nine-Five's story, and it gave him plenty of food for thought. If a poor boy from the slums of Senegal could make something of himself, why couldn't a poor boy that was born here?

Still reflecting on Nine-Five's words, Ashanti went into the liquor store. Tapping on the counter to get the old man's attention, he requested a fifth of Hennessey and some plastic cups. The old man gave the young boy a suspicious look, but gave him the liquor anyhow. Anyone with eyes could see that Ashanti was hardly twenty-one, but he was connected, and when you were connected, you were denied nothing in your hood.

Ashanti was barely out of the store when he cracked the bottle and took a long sip. The fire that spread through his body empowered him and burned away all his worries. With a confident stride, he crossed the street and headed to the projects. Biz getting locked up the night before had slowed the traffic, but it didn't stop it. Fiends still shuffled through the projects looking for a blast, and the little dealers were out to make sure they got it.

At the same time Ashanti arrived at the ramp entrance that led to the front of 3150, a gray Mercedes was slow-creeping through the block. The windows were heavily tinted, but rolled down partially so although Ashanti couldn't see who was in the car, he knew there was more than one of them. Immediately he felt his heart start racing, sending a numbing chill through the tips of his fingers. Before Ashanti was even conscious of what he was doing, he had drawn his weapon and had it dangling at his side. He tilted his head and gave the Mercedes an inviting nod. He was ready to bang. Fortunately, the occupants of the Mercedes weren't, and they wisely pulled off. Ashanti stood there, watching the car until it turned the corner and was out of sight before he continued toward the building.

Two young knuckleheads named Dee and Meek were in front of the building, making it hot as usual. Dee was the opportunist, and Meek was the good soldier, so they worked well as a team. Handling the direct sales was an older cat named No-Good. He'd come aboard to replace Biz who was in the slammer. No-Good was well into his thirties and still tried to carry himself like he was in his early twenties. Every time you turned around he was planting greasy ideas into the heads of the young and impressionable. Ashanti never understood why King let the troublemaker get money with the team, but it wasn't his place to question the decision. Ashanti tolerated No-Good, but he didn't like him.

Ashanti was about to salute the homies from deep and make a detour to avoid interacting with No-Good when Fatima, coming out of the lobby, gave him pause. She had on a white blouse that she wore slightly unbuttoned at the top. Freshly painted toes peeked out from the fronts of her sandals, with a nice-sized heel that accented her well-defined calves beneath the black leggings. The homies were on her like flies on shit, but No-Good was extra aggressive in his approach. It was clear that Fatima wasn't feeling his advances, but No-Good didn't seem to be taking rejection well. When Ashanti saw No-Good grab Fatima by the arm, he knew it was about to get ugly. The rational side of Ashanti told him to leave it alone because it wasn't his problem, but the Hennessey told him to step to his business.

SEVENTEEN

DEE POSTED UP IN FRONT OF 3150, leaning against the building like he was posing for a *GQ* spread. With him were his best friend Meek and a cat named No-Good, who was making hand-to-hand sales a few feet away. Dee was anxious for No-Good to finish up so he and Meek could get with the night's entertainment. The entertainment was two sisters from the neighboring projects, Manhattanville, who Meek and Dee had been trying to freak off with for over a week. After seeing the way Dee and Meek were handling the complex drug operation that night, it was looking like their efforts would pay off. Everyone loved a boss, and they were no different.

"Baby, how much longer we gotta be out here?" Keisha toyed with the gold chain hanging around Dee's neck. She was the oldest of the two sisters and the thickest, with plump breasts and a shapely ass.

Dee coolly exhaled the smoke from the L. "As soon as my homie is finished." He nodded at the dude on the bench who had just served a fiend. "You know it's business before pleasure."

"A'ight, but the drinks are gone, and I'm getting hungry," Keisha told him.

"Me too," Karen chimed in. She was the younger of the two and slightly prettier than Keisha. They were both dark skinned, but Karen's skin was smooth and tender while Keisha's was splotched and bore faint signs of her many street fights over the years.

Meek picked up on the fact that the girls looked like they were ready to bounce so he tried to speed up the process. "What we looking like, homie?" he called out to No-Good.

"We looking like new money." No-Good bopped from the playground to the front of the building where everybody else was standing.

"You been at it for a minute. That G-pack ain't gone yet?" Dee asked. Meek had the situation under control, but Dee wanted to flex his muscle.

"Slow motion beats no motion. I got this, baby boy," No-Good told him with a slight attitude. He resented the fact that he was under the supervision of a cat that was younger than he.

The door to the lobby opened up when Fatima and Pam stepped out, bringing the debate to an abrupt end as all eyes went to them. Pam was stunning in a tight-fitting black dress and a pair of sling-back shoes, with heels so high it was amazing that she was even able to walk in them. Fatima had aged five years with a flawlessly made up face and laced hairdo. The black stretch pants she wore looked painted on, and if you looked close enough, you could see that she wasn't wearing any panties. All of the young men in front of the building ogled her, but it was No-Good who went the extra mile.

"Damn, Fatima, you thicker than a Snicker!" No-Good invaded her personal space.

Pam stepped between them. "Back up, R. Kelly. Ain't you like thirty-six?"

"Age ain't nothing but a number," No-Good shot back. "Where y'all going all dolled up?"

"Out," Pam said flatly.

"Don't hurt 'em too bad." Meek gave Fatima dap.

"You know how I do," Fatima smiled. She and Meek were cooler than the rest of the youngsters because he wasn't always trying to sleep with her.

"Anybody with eyes can see how you do, redbone," No-Good added. "Fatima, when you gonna stop treating me like a step-child and give a nigga some time?"

"When hell freezes over." Fatima rolled her eyes.

This drew a laugh from the two sisters who were with Dee and Meek and No-Good didn't like to be laughed at. "I don't know what the fuck y'all smuts is laughing at, when all you're waiting around for is a meal and some stiff dick," he said venomously.

"Fuck you, old thirsty nigga." Keisha snaked her neck.

"Better an old thirsty nigga than a young dumb bitch," No-Good snickered.

"Ya mouth is off the fucking hook," Fatima said. She had a low tolerance for disrespectful guys, and No-Good was about as disrespectful as they came.

"Shorty, my mouth is good for a whole lot more than talking slick. Why don't we hook up later, and I might be able to teach you a few things." No-Good took Fatima by the wrist.

"Nigga, if you don't get off me I'm gonna teach you how to sell crack with one hand when I cut this cruddy muthafucka off," Fatima said seriously.

"Yo, why don't you stop acting like your pussy is made outta gold?" He applied pressure to her wrist.

Fatima winced in pain as No-Good's grip began to cut off her circulation. "Ow, get off me!"

"Let her go, No-Good." Pam grabbed at his arm, but he pushed her away.

"Mind your fucking business," No-Good snarled. "This li'l bitch is always running around like she's better than everybody else, but she ain't nothing but another hood rat."

"Get off!" Pam grabbed for him again, but No-Good's grip held fast. "Y'all ain't gonna check this nigga?" she addressed Dee and Meek who both looked like they were confused about what to do.

"Homie, why don't you be easy?" Ashanti appeared seemingly out of thin air. His eyes were glassy, and there was a scowl plastered across his face. The block seemed to grow deathly quiet. Among the youngsters Ashanti was something of a folk hero for his legendary exploits in the streets. He had been like them, a kid from the bottom, and had successfully clawed his way up the ladder into a position of power in King James's organization.

"What's good, Ashanti?" Meek extended his hand to give Ashanti dap. Ashanti ignored him and kept his eyes on No-Good.

"You hear me talking to you?" Ashanti asked No-Good, noticing that he was still holding onto Fatima.

"Fall back, my nigga. Ain't nobody trying to hear that captain-save-a-ho shit you kicking," No-Good barked.

"Ho? I don't see ya mama out here," Fatima said defiantly.

No-Good turned his attention to her with rage in his eyes. "I got something to close that smart-ass mouth of yours." He drew his hand back to slap her, but his arm was stopped midswing.

158

"I said, be easy," Ashanti warned, holding No-Good's arm.

No-Good shoved Fatima roughly and gave Ashanti his undivided attention. "Shorty, what the fuck is good with you? You looking for a problem?"

"No, but I got one for you if you want it, Blood," Ashanti told him.

"I ain't your muthafucking blood, nigga, so miss me with that five-star shit. Y'all know what I rep," No-Good boasted. Word on the streets was that he had joined the Crips for protection during his last prison visit.

"Yeah, I know what you rep, and you know how I give it up," Ashanti said coldly. The tone of his voice made everyone except No-Good take a cautionary step back.

No-Good laughed in Ashanti's face. "What the fuck is that supposed to mean to me? You got these li'l cats spooked of you, but I know what it is. The only reason you ever got respect in the hood was because of Animal and Brasco, but now both them niggaz is out the box."

"Why don't you cut that shit out?" Dee suggested to No-Good. He saw the look on Ashanti's face. It made him nervous. Unlike the rest of them, he'd seen firsthand what Ashanti was capable of.

No-Good spun on Dee. "Fuck you mean cut it out? Dee, I know you ain't scared of this li'l pint-sized criminal too?" He shook his head. "I gotta speak to King about bumping me up to management because y'all ain't built. This li'l pussy," he thumbed Ashanti, "ain't killing nothing and ain't letting nothing die. Fuck him and the bitch who pushed him outta her rank-ass pussy!" No-Good laughed.

Ashanti stood there glaring at No-Good. His ears were filled with No-Good's mocking laughter. In his mind he was transported back to when his mother would let her boyfriends humiliate him, then they would sit back and laugh at Ashanti while he cried in the corner, wishing for God to put him out of his misery. The slow-burning fuse that had been lit inside him from the moment No-Good laid hands on Fatima ate up the last bit of the wick and Ashanti exploded.

He swung with so much force that when his fist connected with No-Good's jaw, it sent a painful shockwave up his arm. No-Good stumbled backward and bounced off the building. He tried to get his wits about him, but before he could, Ashanti was on his ass again, raining rights and lefts to his head and face. No-Good managed to retrieve the razor that was stashed in his pocket, but by the time he brought the blade out, Ashanti had already drawn his gun.

"Never bring a knife to a gunfight, Blood," Ashanti taunted him.

"Be easy, fam," No-Good urged. Seeing the big gun stole all of his bravado.

Ashanti slapped fire out of No-Good with the gun. "You wasn't talking all that easy shit when you called yaself playing me like a sucka. Who the li'l nigga now, homie?"

"You got it," No-Good said, barely above a whisper.

"What? I didn't hear you, muthafucka." Ashanti shoved him against the building.

"I said you got it," No-Good repeated.

Ashanti cocked the gun and pointed it at No-Good's forehead. "Ain't no surrender in war, Blood. Night-night, nigga."

"Ashanti, don't!" Fatima rushed over.

"Back up, Fatima. I don't want ol' boy's brains getting on your pretty shoes," Ashanti told her.

Fatima leaned in and whispered so that only Ashanti could hear her. "And if you blast him in front of all these people, how long do you think it'll be before somebody sends the police to your doorstep? Let it go, Ashanti." She tugged at his arm. Reluctantly, Ashanti let Fatima pull him away from No-Good, who was leaning against the building staring daggers at them.

A taxi had just pulled up on the avenue and beeped its horn.

"Fatima, our ride is here. Let's go," Pam told her.

Fatima looked at Ashanti who looked like he could still snap at any second. "Nah, go ahead. I'll meet you down there."

Pam sucked her teeth. "Fatima, I know you didn't get all dressed up for nothing. Don't pull this shit on me."

"I said I'll meet you down there," Fatima repeated.

"I can't believe this shit. You're gonna get enough of this block and the bullshit that comes with it." Pam flipped her hair and sashayed to the waiting taxi.

"Go ahead with your friend, ma. I'm good." Ashanti was talking to Fatima but still staring at No-Good, trying to decide if he would kill him anyway.

"Nah, she'll be okay. You need to cool off. Take a walk with me," Fatima held out her hand.

Ashanti stared at her hand for a few seconds like he was trying to figure out if it was a trick or not. Finally, he took her hand and allowed her to lead him deeper into the projects and away from No-Good. Only when the young killer was out of sight did everyone breathe a collective sigh of relief. Things were quiet again, but little did any of them know, this was only the calm before the storm.

EIGHTEEN

THE GRAY BENZ WENT UP AMSTERDAM AND made a left on LaSalle, then crept slowly up the block. Holiday sat on the passenger side, watching the heavy drug traffic moving in and out of the projects and shook his head. There had always been money in Grant, but what Holiday saw that night impressed him. Fiends went in and out like zombies, all wearing the same dumbfounded expressions on their faces. Grant was a gold mine, but Shai wasn't being given his taste of the proceeds from the new outlaws who had set up shop on the Westside, which is why Holiday had come to pay a call on them.

"Papi, how many times are we gonna drive around this block?" Marisol asked from behind wheel. She was an older Spanish chick who was still cute enough to get a second look, but her secret crack habit had decimated the picture of perfection she used to be.

"We gonna keep driving around until I say otherwise. That was that nigga Ashanti we rode past earlier. If I murder that cat, Shai is sure to give me a promotion. Now stop asking so many fucking questions and drive." Holiday lit his cigarette. He had kept Marisol out all day driving him around while he took care of business and hadn't let her take a blast in hours, so he knew she was jonesing, which is how he had planned it. The more desperate Marisol became to get high the more of a slave to Holiday she would be because she knew he was the man holding the bag. He could've set her on fire, and she probably wouldn't have cared as long as she burned up with a pipe between her lips. The thirstier she was, the more susceptible she would be to go along with the crazy shit he had planned.

"Chill, sis, let me handle what I gotta handle so we can get this paper," Jesus said from the backseat. He was Marisol's little brother, a local hardhead with a chip on his shoulder and something to prove. "Yo, bro, why don't I just hop out and let that nigga have it?"

Holiday gave him a dumb look. "Be my guest, if you want Ashanti to blow your fucking brains out. I seen that cat in action. He might be small, but he's a vicious li'l bastard."

"Man, fuck him and his whole crew. I'll smoke any one of them niggaz. I don't give a fuck!" Jesus declared.

Holiday spun on Jesus and glared at him. "Look, shut the fuck up with all that cowboy shit because I'm tired of hearing it. You can't just get out and *smoke 'em* because these buildings all have cameras on them, or would you like to go to prison, you dumb muthafucka?"

Jesus was silent.

"That's just what the fuck I thought." Holiday continued. "Now fall the fuck back and be ready to get it in when I tell you to."

Marisol and Jesus were getting on his last nerves. As tired as they were of driving around, so was he. It was only a few days to his birthday, and instead of getting ready for his party, he was riding around on a mission. He was irritated, but there was nothing he could do about it. He had to handle Shai's business before he attended to his own.

After chastising Jesus, Holiday went back to surveying the hood. Up ahead he saw four people come down the path that spilled out onto LaSalle, the same four people that Holiday had been watching for the past two hours. Unfortunately, Ashanti wasn't among them. Holiday saw one of the dudes break off from the group and start walking toward Broadway. He told Jesus what the plan was and had Marisol slow the car down when they passed the trio who were standing around the mailbox. The dude with the two girls tried to stare Holiday down like he was tough, but Holiday smelled the bitch in him. The kid was so focused on Holiday that he paid no attention to Jesus, who was poised to let the TEC ring from the backseat. The kid's theatrical performance of a real nigga gave Holiday a wicked idea.

"Let Mr. Tough Guy watch while his man get dropped. You ready?" Holiday asked over his shoulder.

Jesus chambered a round into the beat-up TEC-9 he had for the mission. "Yeah, yeah, let's put a hole in that nigga."

After a while things died down in front of 3150 and it was back to business. No-Good was still mad and ranting about what he was going to do to Ashanti, but after smoking a blunt he calmed down enough to get back to moving the drugs.

"So what's up? When we going to eat?" Karen asked for what seemed like the hundredth time.

Dee sucked his teeth in irritation. "I told you, when the package is gone."

Karen rolled her eyes. "We'll probably have died from starvation by the time he finishes knocking off all that work. How about you give me some money so me and Karen can go get something to eat while y'all handle your business? We can all hook back up later."

Dee suddenly felt a tinge of panic in his chest. He knew if he gave them any money he wouldn't see them for the rest of the night and he had worked too hard for the pussy to wait another week. "A'ight, I'll let Meek shoot across the street to grab y'all some snacks to hold you down for now, and as soon as No-Good is finished, we can go to Red Lobster and eat real good."

Both Keisha and Karen's eyes lit up at the prospect of a lobster dinner. It sounded far more promising than the Chinese food they were going to settle for when they skipped off with Dee's money. "A'ight," Karen agreed.

"I don't know, Dee. La said we supposed to stay two up and one down at all times." Meek reminded him of Lakim's decree before he left the block. He wanted them to work in threes, one man to hold the drugs, one man to hold the money, and one man to hold the gun. He didn't elaborate on why they had changed things up, and they didn't question him; they just nodded and said, "Okay."

"C'mon, son, you just running across the street. What the fuck could possibly happen in five minutes? Stop acting like a li'l nigga," Dee teased him, and Keisha and Karen laughed.

"Fuck outta here, I'm a boss too!" Meek poked his chest out. Dee always knew the right things to say to put a battery in Meek's back, and it had been like that since they were kids. Outside of his mother, who he hardly saw because she was strung out, Dee was the only family Meek had in the world. He looked up to Dee like a big brother and valued his opinion of him above anyone's.

"Then *boss* yo' ass to the store so we can finish this shit up and bounce. I got something I wanna show Keisha," Dee said slyly, looking at her. The look she gave him back let him know it was going down that night.

"A'ight, well, hold this for me." Meek handed him the .25 he had in his pocket. He didn't want to walk to the store with it in case he became the victim of a random police stop and search.

"A'ight and hurry yo' ass up." Dee tucked the gun in his jacket pocket. "We gonna wait for you by the mailbox," he told Meek as they walked down the narrow path to the mailbox on LaSalle. Dee leaned against the mailbox and watched Meek make hurried steps toward the store across the underpass.

"So it's just y'all two that run this whole shit?" Karen asked unexpectedly.

"Nah, it's a few of us, but me and Meek are the brains of the operation," Dee lied.

"We heard it was some dudes in Grant getting big money, but we had no idea it was y'all," Keisha said.

"Yeah, we them niggaz." Dee was feeling himself. Then he noticed a gray Mercedes riding slowly up the block and dipped his hand into his pocket where the .25 was stashed.

There was a Puerto Rican girl behind the wheel, and he could make out a figure in the backseat, but couldn't really see who it was because of the heavy tint on the back windows. On the passenger's side was a brown-skinned dude who had his arm dangling out the window smoking a cigarette. He looked up at Dee, and when their eyes met, a chill ran down Dee's spine, causing his palm to sweat and making the gun in his pocket slippery in his grip. There was something about his face that rang familiar with Dee, but his fear had his heart and brain out of sync. Smelling Dee's fear, the brown-skinned dude smiled at Dee, raised his fingers in the shape of a gun, and pointed it toward the corner. The Puerto Rican girl mashed on the gas, and the car sped toward Broadway.

Dee was confused at first, but when he looked in the direction the car was traveling and saw Meek walking across the street he realized what was about to go down.

"MEEK!!!!!!" Dee screamed, but it was already too late.

For a long while Ashanti and Fatima walked in silence. He had his hands shoved deep into his pockets and his eyes on the ground. Every so often he would look at Fatima, but whenever their eyes met he would quickly turn away. Ashanti was as brave as they came when it came to battle, but around Fatima he felt like a coward.

"You okay?" Fatima asked, startling him.

"Yeah, I'm cool. Why do you ask?"

"I dunno, you're just real quiet," she said.

"I'm always quiet," Ashanti replied.

Fatima raised her eyebrow. "Knock it off, because you know I've seen you cut up something fierce when you're with Lakim and the rest of those ignorant fools," she laughed.

"Yeah, I guess we do get a li'l wild sometimes, but no wilder than you and your homegirls," Ashanti half-smiled.

Fatima rolled her eyes playfully. "We are ladies."

"You might be a lady, but I think Pam is part dude. I seen her throw hands before. Not for nothing, if it had gone down between her and No-Good, my money was on Pam."

"Speaking of that, I never got a chance to thank you. You know, for what you did," Fatima told him.

Ashanti shrugged. "It wasn't about nothing. No-Good is a bitch-ass nigga for being out here trying to hit on a girl. It was only right that I stepped up."

"God knows none of them other cats out there were gonna step up," Fatima shook her head.

"Them niggaz ain't built. Dee and them out here playing gangsta, while the rest of us are living it."

"You're definitely about your business," Fatima said with a smile. "Could I ask you something?"

"Sure," Ashanti said, slightly nervous as to what she might ask.

"Would you really have shot No-Good over me?"

Ashanti thought on it for a minute. "I would've shot No-Good for the principle of it; defending your honor would've just been a bonus."

Fatima smiled. "I've never had a man defend my honor before."

"I find that hard to believe. I know some cats that would kill and die for a chick like you, Fatima."

"Well, please introduce me to them because these scumbags I keep running into ain't about nothing but themselves."

"Maybe you're running in the wrong circles."

"It's possible. Any suggestions which circles I should be running in?"

"I can think of a few."

Before their flirting could go any further there was the sound of a scream somewhere in the projects.

"What the hell was that?" Fatima asked.

"I don't know, but it can't be good. Come on." Ashanti took Fatima by the hand, and they hurried back in the direction of the building.

When Meek started out for the store he was still feeling salty about how Dee had talked to him in front of Keisha and Karen. He could take a good joke just like the next guy, but because of the fact that he looked up to Dee it always stung when he did it.

Dee had been looking out for Meek since he found him on the receiving end of an ass whipping in the fifth grade. Meek had always been smaller than the other kids and because his mother was on drugs, he never had clean clothes so he was an easy target for bullies. It was Dee who taught Meek how to defend himself and eventually get money selling drugs. Meek had never really had the heart for the hustle, but it was the only thing he was good at and it kept him from going back to nothing. Meek just wanted to make enough money to where he could bounce down south to Atlanta and start his life over. Unlike Dee, Meek had no desire to retire in the streets, but sometimes the streets stole the choice from you.

Just as Meek was about to go into the store he heard some-one calling his name. He turned around just as a gray Benz whipped around the corner and skidded to a stop a few feet away from him. It only took Meek a few seconds to figure out what was going down but that was more than enough time for Jesus to roll the window down and aim the TEC at him.

"Say good night," Jesus told him and pulled the trigger.

Instinctively, Meek closed his eyes and prepared for the end but several heartbeats later he was still alive. He opened his eyes and saw Jesus fumbling with the bullet that had jammed in the gun. God had thrown him a lifeline, and he had no intentions on squandering it. He dipped his hand in his pocket, looking for the .25 Lakim had told him to carry at all times . . . and came up with lint. His last thoughts before his brains sprayed all over the bodega window is that he wished he'd listened to Lakim.

When Ashanti and Fatima rounded the corner of the building the first thing they noticed was that the courtyard was now empty. All of the workers had unexpectedly abandoned their posts, which was a sure sign of trouble. He heard the scream again and looked up in time to see Dee dashing down the block in the direction of the corner store. Directly across the street he saw a gray Mercedes screech to a halt. He recognized it as the same Mercedes he had seen earlier.

"Stay here," he ordered Fatima, drawing his gun.

"Wait, what's going on?" Fatima asked in a panicked tone.

"Just stay here!" he shouted and ran down the block.

Ashanti made it to the corner just as the first shot rang out. He saw Meek's head snap back right before he hit the ground. From the stain on the bodega window there was no question of whether he was dead or not. When the man who had shot Meek turned his gun on Dee, who was fumbling with the .25, Ashanti got a good look at his face, and it was familiar. When he realized where he had seen him before his heart filled with rage. It was the same man who had shot Gucci in the club. He had promised if they saw each other, one of them was going to die and the moment was at hand.

"Remember me, muthafucka?" Ashanti shouted before the flash of his cannon turned night to day. The shooter ducked back into the Mercedes, narrowly missing having his head blown off. "Don't run now!" Ashanti kept firing until his clip was empty and the car had disappeared into the night. His enemy had escaped but only temporarily. The shooter owed Ashanti a debt that could only be paid in blood, and even if it took the rest of his life, he would not be denied his due.

The girls and No-Good had disappeared as soon as the shooting started, which was expected. No matter how big they talked, none of them were really built for war. A few feet away, Dee knelt over the body of his childhood friend. Dee's sobs were so heavy that Ashanti felt them in his own chest. Meek was just a kid, but he had chosen to play a very adult game and ended up losing.

Soon the police would arrive and start interviewing witnesses to see what had happened. Ashanti wasn't worried about what anyone would say because everybody knew King James ran the hood and to snitch on him was a death sentence. What troubled him more was having to break the news to Meek's mother that the streets had claimed her baby.

NINETEEN

HOLIDAY SAT WITH THE SMOKING GUN ON his lap, while Marisol sped down Broadway. Every so often he would nervously look out the shattered back window, fearing that he would see the police hot on their heels. So far, they had made it eight blocks and all seemed clear, but it still didn't make him feel any better about the botched hit. He sighed heavily because he knew he had nobody but himself to blame.

The plan was a simple one: roll through the projects, lay down whomever they saw that was affiliated with King James, and get ghost, but the plan went horribly wrong and almost cost Holiday his life. When Jesus tried to pop off, the TEC jammed and he was so zooted that he couldn't clear the bullet. Murder was a time-sensitive thing and every second they wasted put them one step closer to a prison cell, so Holiday had to get his hands dirty. The first shot was a head shot, which killed the kid instantly, but Holiday dumped two more in his body to be sure. He was about to finish off the boy's partner when *he* showed up.

172

Ashanti seemed to appear from nowhere, like some ghetto-avenging angel who was determined to drag Holiday directly to hell. Holiday had barely escaped with his life, but he knew that luck would only get him so far when dealing with a character like Ashanti. He would keep coming until one of them was dead. Holiday would have to take Ashanti out sooner than later, but first he needed to deal with the matter at hand.

He gave Marisol directions to an underground parking garage off the West Side Highway, where they would abandon that car and pick up another one before going back through the hood. Marisol was so nervous that Holiday prayed she didn't crash the car on the way down. When they got inside the garage he gave her a G-pack for her troubles and her nerves immediately calmed. All that was left was for him to compensate his accomplices, and they would all go their separate ways.

"You mind if I get right real quick?" Marisol asked when they had parked the Benz. She was rubbing her hands up and down the thighs of her jeans nervously.

"Damn, you can't wait to do that shit on your own time?" Holiday barked.

"I'm sorry, baby, but my nerves are bad. That shit you did fucked me up, that's all."

"Listen, don't worry about that, ma. Anybody that could've identified us is dead. You know I wouldn't put you in harm's way." Holiday tried to ease her fears.

"I know, I know . . . it's just that . . . ." Between her craving and her fear Marisol was having difficulty putting her words together.

The chick was starting to come unraveled, and Holiday

had to regain control of the situation by any means necessary. "Marisol, go ahead and take a blast while I settle up with your brother. Just roll the fucking window down."

"For what? We ain't even got a window in the back," Jesus laughed.

"Shut up. Get right, Marisol," Holiday told her.

"Thanks, Holiday, thank you so much," Marisol said as if he had just given her a presidential pardon. She reached into her purse and pulled out her Demo, which she proceeded to pack with one of the chunky white rocks Holiday had given her. The moment the flame touched the rock the car was immediately filled with the smell of burning plastic. Marisol took a deep hit and lolled her head back against the headrest of the Benz with a dreamy smile on her face.

"Let me take care of y'all muthafuckas so I can get outta this bitch before my clothes start stinking," Holiday fanned the smoke. "Jesus," he turned to the backseat, "you know I can't hit you with those five stacks since technically you didn't do what I hired you to do."

"C'mon, my G, I would've laid that kid if this funky-ass gun didn't jam. Don't do me like that," Jesus almost pleaded. He had that same yearning in his voice that his sister had, and it would only be a matter of time before he walked a mile in her shoes.

"A'ight, because I'ma fair nigga, I'm gonna break you off something for your troubles." Holiday counted out a bunch of bills and handed them over his shoulder to Jesus.

Jesus quickly counted the money. It was one thousand dollars. He had plans for the five thousand he had been promised and had considered trying to rob Holiday but decided against it, after remembering how he had remorselessly laid the kid out in front of the bodega. "Good looking out."

"Don't worry about it, fam. I know it wasn't ya fault that the gun jammed. Them TECs ain't good for shit," Holiday said in disgust.

"Word up, my nigga. The only reason I brought this was because it was the only thing I could get my hands on right away." Jesus hoisted the TEC for Holiday to see.

"Let me check that piece of shit out." Holiday reached for the TEC.

When Jesus went to hand it to him, Holiday closed his hand around Jesus', locking his finger on the trigger. The two struggled while Holiday turned the TEC toward Marisol. She came out of her nod just as Holiday squeezed Jesus' finger and discharged the TEC. Her entire face came off, taking part of the driver's window with it. With his free hand, Holiday brought his 9 mm around and fired two shots into Jesus' chest, knocking him into the backseat. He was twisted but still alive. Holiday then placed the 9 mm in Marisol's dead hand and held it up so that it was level with Jesus' face. Jesus let out a gurgled plea for his life, but it was drowned out by the bang of the 9 mm.

Holiday didn't bother to wipe anything down because he'd been wearing gloves the whole time he was in the car with Marisol and Jesus. Had they not been so blinded by their greed, then they might've noticed that he was wearing gloves in the summer and suspected that they would never make it back from the fool's errand. Marisol and Jesus had been doomed from the moment they got into that car with Holiday. When the police found them in the car with the money and the drugs they would chalk it up to a deal gone wrong.

Holiday got out of the Benz and hobbled four cars down in the lot, where Angelo was waiting for him in a white Escalade. Holiday jumped in the passenger side, and they exited the garage as if nothing had happened.

"I trust all went well?" Angelo asked when they had made it a few blocks from the parking garage.

"Yeah, I slumped that nigga something proper," Holiday said proudly.

Angelo gave Holiday an angry look. "The plan was for you to *pay* somebody to do it."

"Sometimes plans change, fam. In the end, I ended up saving us four stacks on the job," Holiday pointed out.

Angelo just shook his head. "Anyway, do you think we made our point?"

"Absolutely," Holiday said with pride. "After this shit, ain't nobody in they right minds gonna come at Shai's neck."

TWENTY

ANIMAL MADE THE TRIP FROM HARLEM TO Brooklyn in less than twenty minutes. Traffic was light on the FDR so before he knew it he was sailing across the Brooklyn Bridge and into downtown Brooklyn. Taking Atlantic Avenue would've saved him some time, but he didn't want to run the risk of getting pulled over on the busy street so he took Park Avenue into Bed-Stuy.

He crept slowly through the seedy Brooklyn blocks in his rental, drawing the occasional stare but otherwise going unnoticed. Passing the grim brown buildings of Marcy Projects, Animal was taken back to his youth when he and Tech used to put in work for a local cat named Shine. Shine had been a good dude who always took care of the people in the neighborhood, but he was also a beast who many feared. They feared him so much, in fact, that some cats gunned him down in front of his girlfriend and infant child. When Shine died, he took a piece of Animal with him, because they had become very close. The police never found his killers, and they never would because

Animal and Tech had burned their bodies and scattered the ashes to the four winds after they tortured them to death.

Animal took Tompkins Avenue deeper into Bed-Stuy and made a left on Jefferson, where the landscape changed from project buildings to renovated tenements and brownstones with freshly paved driveways. To the unsuspecting, the strip looked like a nice block to raise your kids in, but Animal knew the truth behind the new construction and skyrocketing property rates. For as nice as Bed-Stuy might've looked on the outside, the bowels of it were still defiled with killers and miscreants, and these were the people who really controlled everything that moved in the hood.

When he crossed Throop he turned his eyes to the corner bodega, and it tugged at his memory. Tech had always told him stories about a thorough young soldier named Spooky who had met his end on that corner. The exploits of Spooky and Jah were the gospel Tech always preached when Animal was coming up, and it was the deadly duo who he and Tech had always aspired to be like. Tech wanted them to walk a mile in their shoes, and in a sense they had since Jah, Spooky, and Tech had all died violently. Animal had often wondered what his end would be like, or if he would even care when it happened.

Across the street a group of young men glared at the rental as it passed, trying to see who was behind the wheel. Animal sank a little lower in his seat and slipped his burner on his lap. He kept his eyes on the kids but didn't mug them to force a confrontation. One of the kids brazenly threw up the gang sign for his hood, and Animal simply nodded and kept it moving. They couldn't have been more than teenagers with mischief written across their faces, but these days, the killers were getting younger and younger, and Animal was living proof of that.

The parking gods were kind, and Animal was able to find a spot on Jefferson between Marcus Garvey and Lewis so he wouldn't have far to walk to his destination. Slipping his burner back into his pants, he got out of the car and headed up the street. Passing a building near the corner he noticed a group of young girls on the stoop. All eyes were on him. Animal heard one of the girls hiss at him, trying to get his attention, but he ignored her, watching her friend out of his peripheral. She was brown skinned, wearing a powder blue sweater dress and white boots with matching white earrings. She was a very attractive girl, but Animal was watching her because he thought he knew her. Her face was familiar, though he couldn't think where he'd seen it. The look that she was giving him said that she recognized him from somewhere too. Remembering the incident with the maid in North Carolina recognizing him, he pulled his hoodie up tighter over his head and sped up. As he was turning the corner he heard one of the girls say, "He looks like that rapper."

Animal ignored the girls and walked across the street to a spot called Blood Orchid. The sign on the front gate of the basement stairs said closed, but that was only for nonmembers, and Animal was a member. Fishing a key from his pocket, he undid the front door lock and stepped inside. The place was empty, or so it seemed. Animal made his way across the room, past the wooden tables that looked like they had seen better days. The horseshoe bar was abandoned, but a half-empty glass sat on the glass top. Behind the bar was a door marked private, which Animal pushed through and descended the dark stairs.

At the bottom of the stairwell was another door, this one was thick and had no visible locks. Animal stood in front of the door and looked up at the right corner of the hinge. There was a round bolt securing the corner of the door that doubled as a camera. He looked into the lens, flashed his gold-toothed smile, and waited. After a few seconds, there was a click and the door came open a crack. Animal could immediately smell the weed seeping from the room and hear music playing in the background. He stepped through the doorway and into a cloud of thick weed smoke. Behind him he heard two familiar clicks; one being the door locking after he entered and the other being the sound of a bullet being chambered. Animal made to turn his head, but a threatening voice gave him pause.

"You move that pretty little head one more inch and I promise you I'm gonna fuck up that perm of yours," a voice said in a raspy whisper. "Who you be and why you here?"

"Came to holla at a loved one," Animal said, still with his back to the woman.

"Impossible. Love don't live in this place and ain't lived here in a long time. Come better than that or prepare to read your own thoughts on that wall," she told him.

"If you got designs on killing me, then at least give me a soldier's death," he said.

The words staggered her. *Death before dishonor, and when I die give me a soldier's death so I can look into the eyes of my killer.* Her mind ticked off the words they had all spoken on that drunken night after one of the homie's wakes many years ago. Very few had taken the oath and fewer still were alive to recite it.

"Turn around and do it slowly," she ordered. Her voice was shaky.

Slowly, Animal turned, keeping his hands in sight and his palms out. Under the dim light of the basement he faced his adversary. She looked a bit older than he had expected, but still held her youthful glow. Her hair was now black with red streaks and woven into tight boxed braids that were pulled back into a tight ponytail that drew attention to her weed-slanted eyes. She was slim, with a pecan complexion, rocking tight jeans that hugged her slight curves and Timberlands that she wore untied. A red bandana was tied neatly around her neck like a choker to hide the scar beneath. A blunt dangled from her Mac chocolate lips, taking the smoke in on one side and expelling it on the other. She stood wide legged not three feet away from Animal holding a big .45 level with his head. When the light of recognition went off in her head she loosened her grip on the gun and her eyes began to mist up.

"What's up, Kastro?" Animal smirked, flashing the diamonds on his teeth.

Kastro backpedaled until she was pressed firmly against the door and as far away from Animal as possible. He made to take a step toward her, but she quickly raised the gun and pointed it at his heart. "I seen a lot in my life, but I ain't never seen the dead walk. If you're Satan, then I'll leave it to you and this four-five to negotiate the terms of the deal."

"Baby girl, this ain't no figment of your imagination. It's me, Tayshawn, live in the flesh, ma." Animal patted his chest. Carefully he moved toward her with his hand out. Keeping his eyes locked with hers, he slowly reached for the gun. Kastro tensed, but she eventually let him move the gun harmlessly away. Animal's other hand took Kastro about the wrist and placed her hand on his chest. "It's me."

Kastro ran her hands up his chest, over the groves in the breast plate of the bulletproof vest. Her fingers traced a line from his chin up to the temples of his head and tangled themselves in his mane of curly hair. She buried her face in his chest and at that moment, the floodgate that had been holding Kastro's tears back burst and she broke down.

Kastro spent all of ninety seconds as an emotional wreck before she was back in G-mode, scowling and angry. "You dirty muthafucka! You had everybody thinking you were dead and buried." She punched him in the arm.

Animal shrugged. "The circumstances were beyond my control."

Kastro folded her arms and glared at him. "God, you were the centerpiece in one of the biggest hood stories since Larry Davis, then you pop up almost three years later talking about *circumstances*? This is me, so you know you gotta come better than that."

"Where I've been is a long story; why I'm back is a shorter one."

Kastro shrugged. "I ain't got nowhere to be. Come on in the back. I'll pour us a drink while you bring me up to speed. I gotta hear this one."

TWENTY-ONE

TWO DRINKS AND A BLUNT OF KUSH later, Animal had recounted the events of his life from his disappearance to the moment he showed up on Kastro's doorstep. Kastro listened intently and watched with saddened eyes as Animal fought to keep from breaking down when he spoke of Gucci and what had befallen her. It pained her to see someone she had always known to be so strong seem so vulnerable, but she knew Animal well enough to know that it was only the calm before the storm.

"Damn, baby boy. You been through some shit these last few years, huh?" she said, pouring him another shot of cognac.

"Indeed." He accepted the shot and downed it without flinching. "But as they say, what does not kill me will kill them."

"I don't think that's quite how the saying goes," she said.

"I know, but that's how it's gonna play out. The gauntlet has been laid, and I've already picked it up."

Kastro studied his face. "So, you mean to say you've gone through all this, only to throw your life away in a battle that you don't stand a snowball's chance in hell of winning?"

Animal pondered her question. "At this point, it ain't about winning or losing with me, Kastro. It's about settling the score. If I'm to die righting a wrong for someone I love, then so be it. Let the chips fall where they may. As long as I can drag a few of their souls to hell with me, it'll be worth it. I know you of all people can understand what it feels like to have someone you love stumble into harm's way and be powerless to do anything about it."

The statement took Kastro to a dark place in her mind, the day she had lost her niece Mimi. Kastro had never been blessed with children of her own, but she had helped her sister raise little Mimi as if she were her own. Even when Justice came into the picture and helped her sister with some of the parental burdens, Kastro remained a fixture in Mimi's life. Kastro was a street person and had always tried her best to steer Mimi down a different path, but the blood that pumped through the young girl's veins drove her to the streets and footsteps of her aunts and uncles. When Kastro saw that she couldn't sway Mimi from the streets, she figured she could at least instill the survival skills Mimi would need to have a shot at winning the game she chose to play. Mimi was a natural and quickly went from hustling under her aunt Kastro to hustling with her.

Mimi became the darling of the hood because of her unyielding loyalty and resourcefulness when it came to getting money. Mimi was a jack-of-all-trades and excelled at being a criminal. The young girl was on track to becoming a ghetto star, but fate had double-crossed her into an early grave instead. They had come for Animal, but the bullets found Mimi, and she traded her life for his. The men responsible had only lived sixty seconds longer than Mimi, but it did nothing to lift the yoke of guilt that had been placed around Animal's neck when Mimi closed her eyes. It was one of the darkest days in Animal's life, and the relationship between him and Kastro had never been the same.

"You know I hated you for a long time after Mimi was killed," Kastro admitted.

"I know," Animal said softly, "and I can't say that I blame you. Mimi should've never been there, and I should've died that night."

"Mimi *shouldn't* have been there and *wouldn't* have been there if I had been there for her like I was supposed to. I didn't turn her onto the streets, but I turned her out to them. It takes a village to raise a child; instead, we helped put her in the ground. The damned are we . . ."

". . . for we are the damned and will never know peace," Animal finished the quote. It was from the story of a fantasy author Animal had introduced Kastro to, named Kris Greene. Animal had always been big on supernatural books and eventually turned a few of his friends onto them too. "Ironic how true that rings in the real world, huh?"

"You ain't never lied. So what now?" Kastro asked.

"I keep trying to right the wrongs I've caused," Animal said standing up. He had a mean buzz going and was borderline tipsy, but it was nothing some fresh air wouldn't clear up.

"Once The Animal has been sent for you, he doesn't stop until he gets you."

Kastro shook her head sadly, knowing there was no deterring her friend from the suicide mission.

"Ain't nothing changed with me, Kastro."

"So I see. Fuck it; if you're gonna go on this ride to hell I might as well keep you company." Kastro drew her pistol. "You might've beat me to the punch with killing the men who murdered Mimi, but at least I can blast on a few muthafuckas in her name."

Animal smiled. "Kastro, I'll take your wild ass into a firefight before any ten dudes I know, but not this time. I gotta take this ride on my own, ma."

"You would deny me a chance at glory?" Kastro's jaw tightened. She lowered her head sadly.

Animal tenderly lifted her chin and looked her in the eyes. "I ain't denying you glory. I'm giving you your life."

"I know, but I just feel so helpless. I can't sit on my hands and do nothing, not again."

"I got a-plenty for you to do to help the war effort without getting your head blown off, baby, and you can start by giving me what I came for so I can do what I gotta do."

"It's like that?" Kastro surprised.

"Straight like that. Go grab my armor, ma, so I can ride on these niggaz properly."

Kastro disappeared into a room in the back. A few minutes later she came back carrying a wooden box which she placed on the table in front of Animal. It had been several years since he'd given it to her, and his heart beat with anticipation as she undid the clamps and slid the box across the table for him to open.

Animal peeled the lid back and smiled at the contents, which were resting on a bed of soft velvet. There were two rose-tinted chrome Glocks with red grips that Animal had gotten as a birthday gift one year. He called them his Pretty Bitches and loved them dearly. He had only fired them once, and that was when he had tracked and murdered the stepfather who had abused him and his mother when he was a kid. The next round he was saving for when he finally bumped heads with the biological father who had abandoned him without so much as a look back, but his turn on the receiving end of the Pretty Bitches would have to wait until the immediate business was handled.

The last item in the box stole Animal's breath when he touched it. It was a link chain with a jeweled figurine hanging from the end of it. It was his namesake and favorite character, Animal. The fourteen karat gold and diamond piece was the first custom chain he'd ever bought himself. When he got his weight up he retired the smaller chain for the gaudy Animal bust that had become his calling card, but he had always kept the original chain. It represented an era in his life when he was young, hungry, and dangerous, and it was about time he got back to that.

"Ain't you gonna try it on?" Kastro snapped him out of his zone.

Animal lifted the chain and hesitated. Staring at the little Muppet swinging back and forth taunted him to take the next step. Animal slipped the chain around his neck and a chill swept through him when its coolness touched his skin. It was heavier than he remembered, but then again, so were the burdens he was carrying. He smoothed the chain out over his chest, and for a few fleeting seconds, all was right with the world.

Kastro smiled. "Now, *that's* the Animal I know."

"Feels good." Animal adjusted the chain. "Real good. They niggaz ain't gonna see me coming."

"They will unless you do something about this." Kastro ran

her fingers through his tangled hair. "Baby boy, it's a crying shame how you're letting this beautiful hair go to shit."

"I ain't had too much time for grooming, Kastro."

"Obviously," she snickered. "Grab them scissors, comb, and hair grease off that cabinet over there." She nodded toward a rickety dresser in the corner.

"Kastro, you're outta your rabid-ass mind if you think I'm cutting my hair." Like Samson, he believed his strength came from his hair.

"Tayshawn, I would never disrespect you like that. Just bring me the stuff and let me take care of this," Kastro ordered him.

She gave Animal's hair a good washing before greasing and combing it. When she was done, it was a bit shorter because she had to cut out some of the knots, but when it was done, she had restored it to the rich, beautiful black mop that had made all the ladies fall in love with Animal, including her. With a proud smile, she handed Animal a mirror to admire her handiwork.

"Ain't seen that dude in a while." Animal spoke of his reflection in the mirror.

Kastro stood behind him, placing her chin on his shoulder. She looked at their cheek to cheek reflection and smiled. "Glad to have you back." She kissed him on the cheek. Then Kastro turned Animal around to face her. She zipped up his hoodie for him as if he were a child and brushed his shoulders off. As a parting gift, she kissed Animal on his forehead. "Go out into those streets and remind them who you are, Animal. Show them that real niggaz don't die."

TWENTY-TWO

"*Real Niggaz Don't Die*," PUMPED FROM THE iPod mounted on the pink dock in Frankie's bathroom while she mouthed the words without missing a beat. She loved N.W.A., and the song was one of her favorites to bump when she was *feeling herself,* and that night she was in rare form. Her last few nights on the town had been about business, but this night it would be just her and her girls having a good time.

Frankie was just applying the finishing touches to her hair when she heard a knock at her door. She removed the towel that she had wrapped around her shoulders to keep from getting makeup on her white shirt and used it to wipe the excess oil sheen off her hands before heading for the door. It seemed like the closer she got to the door the more intense the knocking grew.

"Hold on, damn it!" Frankie shouted down the hall. She crossed the living room fuming as the knocking increased. She snatched the door open, lips pursed to go off, and saw Dena on the other side. Though Frankie was now holding the door open, Dena was still knocking on it, smiling mischievously.

"You're such an ass," Frankie laughed, and stepped back for Dena to enter.

"Takes one to know one," Dena capped as she passed her.

"Somebody is stepping out ready to play." Frankie admired Dena's outfit. She was wearing a blue sweater dress with white Go-Go boots and big plastic white earrings. She'd even ratted her hair to a high puff to kick off the retro look.

"This ain't about nothing. I've had this outfit for a while, but I just haven't had a reason to wear it." Dena tugged at the dress. "I see you ain't pulling a lot of punches tonight either." She checked out Frankie's outfit, consisting of a fitted white blouse, skintight black jeans, and a cute purple peep-toe heel. She had done her eyes in shades of purple and white to match the blazer she'd laid across the couch to go with the outfit.

"Porsha is my girl, but we ain't seen each other in a hot minute. I can't show up having her think I fell off," Frankie explained.

"Wow, this Porsha chick must be something else if Ms. I-don't-give-a-fuck is going out of her way to get all dolled up to see her," Dena said sarcastically.

"Stop it, five." Frankie raised her hand. "It ain't even that type of party with me and Porsha. We like sisters; that's my dawg." Frankie patted her chest for emphasis.

"Damn, I was just playing with you, Frankie. Let me find out." Dena looked at her suspiciously.

"Whatever, heifer." Frankie rolled her eyes. "Why don't you twist something up while I finish getting ready?"

"And who says I'm holding?" Dena asked.

"I say, that's who. I saw you when you met Rasta on the corner." Frankie laughed.

"Nosey bitch," Dena said, pulling a bag of weed from her purse and a Dutch. "But on some G shit, what's up with ya peoples that we about to get up with? You know I'm funny about allowing new people in my circle, Frankie, especially them stuck-up Harlem bitches, no offense."

"*Harlem on the rise and you don't want no problems with us guys,*" Frankie sang. "Nah, but on the real, Porsha is good peoples. You know I wouldn't have you around anybody that wasn't good peoples."

"And how do I know that when this will be my first time ever meeting anybody from your past?" Dena questioned.

Frankie looked at Dena and frowned. "You say it like you're the new thing about to get introduced to the new boo. It ain't that serious, ma."

"*Us* or *this*?" Dena shot back.

"Neither, Dena. We're having a girls' night out with an old friend. It ain't too much more to it," Frankie said coolly.

"If you say so," Dena said.

Frankie didn't like the way Dena said it. She had noticed that since they had been kicking it a little more frequently Dena had showed signs of possessiveness. Frankie enjoyed her romps with Dena because she gave her something she was hard-pressed to find in guys, compassion, but that was about as deep as the rabbit hole went. Frankie dabbled in pussy soup, but she wouldn't have called herself a lesbian. More like lost in translation and trying to make sense of it all. Dena had designs on what she wanted to do with her future, which was commendable, but Frankie wasn't thinking that far ahead. She was just worried about getting through one day to the next and letting everything else fall into place.

"So where are we going to hang out, *Harlem*?" Dena asked with a hint of sarcasm in her voice.

"Actually, Porsha is coming to *Brooklyn*. We're meeting downtown at BBQ's, smart-ass." Frankie checked her. Finally tiring of Dena's shit she decided to check her. "Yo, you've been talking real sideways since you walked in here. What's good with you tonight?"

"I'm a'ight," Dena said as if it was nothing.

Frankie gave her a disbelieving look. "Dena, don't lie about it, and then spend the whole night talking out the side of ya neck. If something is going on with you, then let's get it out in the open now so it doesn't fuck up our night. I wanna have a good time, and I'm not really up for attitude from you or anybody else."

Dena hesitated. "It's nothing, Frankie. I'm just going through some shit with my moms and them."

"Is everything okay? You know we peoples, and you can talk to me about anything, D," Frankie said sincerely.

"Well, you know when my brother got killed, she took it harder than any of us," Dena began. "Shannon was on the run for years from a body he caught, and the next time any of us would ever see him is when we took Moms to identify his body. Shannon was a straight-up gangsta, but he was still Mama's only son."

"Damn, I'm sorry, Dena," Frankie told her.

"The fucked-up part is that my sister keeps trying to put it in her head that all this was my fault," Dena said.

"That shit is foul! How she gonna put it out there like you had something to do with your brother getting killed?" Frankie was hot. She knew what it felt like to be surrounded by family and still be the outsider.

"The most hurtful thing about it is that, in a way, she's right," Dena continued. "Shannon always warned me to stay away from these street niggaz, but I was too stuck on myself to listen." Her eyes misted up. "When I told Shannon what had happened to me, he cried like a baby. Until that point I didn't know my brother *could* cry. When the tears finally dried and I saw the look in his eyes, there was no doubt in my mind what Shannon would do."

"Did you try to stop him?" Frankie asked. She didn't know where the question came from, but it was out there now.

Dena looked at her with sad eyes. "I thought about it, but I didn't. I mean, why should I have? Those men raped and humiliated me, Frankie, and all I could think about was revenge. Shannon was my avenging angel. My big brother would still be here if I'd kept my legs and my mouth closed."

Frankie had heard the ghost stories the neighborhood told about Dena's older brother Shannon, and how he gave it up. Word was that he was a stone killer and would give it to anybody who felt like they wanted it. Frankie had always pictured him as some super-thug, but hearing Dena fill in the blanks changed her perception. He was just a young man trying to take care of his family. She couldn't do much but respect that.

"Dena, you can't carry that one. You were young and naïve, and those guys had no right to do what they did to you. Shannon did what any big brother, or real nigga, period, would've done, and that's go all out to protect his little sister. There's not a jury in the land that would've convicted him on that one."

"I guess you're right. Too bad his conviction came in the streets instead of a courtroom or I might still have a big brother." Dena gave a sad smirk. "Enough of this sad shit. Let's hit the streets and get this party started."

"Amen to that." Frankie grabbed her blazer and keys. "Tonight, we ain't two broke hoes living in an overpriced tenement; we're divas out to paint the town."

"Say that shit." Dena gave Frankie a high five.

The two girls exited the apartment, leaving their troubles on the kitchen counter, and set out to see what the night had in store for them.

When Dena and Frankie came out of the building they were greeted by Vashaun and Bess, who were sitting in the exact same spots they had left them in hours prior, in almost the exact same poses. The only things that had changed were their eyes were a little more slanted from the weed and the pungent odor of alcohol was a bit heavier. No matter what went on, the party never stopped with those two.

"Look at these bitches, all gussied up and shit," Bess said snidely.

"If you think this is *gussied,* you need to see me when I *really* throw it on." Frankie smoothed back a strand of her hair that slipped out of place.

"How y'all rolling to a party and didn't invite us?" Vashaun asked.

"We're not going to a party. We're going to hook up with one of Frankie's peeps from Harlem and kick it downtown," Dena explained.

"Let me find out you on some Harlem shit now, Dena," Bess said accusingly.

"Bitch, don't play yaself. You know I'm Bed-Stuy until I die, but unlike y'all stoop rats, I realize that the world is bigger than Brooklyn," Dena shot back.

Their word exchange was interrupted when a car pulled up and parked across the street from their building. A young man hopped out and looked around suspiciously, before locking his car and heading in their direction. He was dressed in dark clothes and moving with extreme caution, which most likely meant he was up to no good, but that was nothing unusual for that neighborhood. He was a handsome dude, with girlish lips and long hair that he kept brushing out of his face. He was very easy on the eyes and all the girls took notice, but it was Vashaun who made a move.

"Pssst," Vashaun catcalled at him. He spared her a brief glance, but kept it moving. "Word, it's like that, shorty?" she called after him. "That nigga probably gay," she said scornfully.

"Or somebody hipped him to all them miles you got on your pussy," Bess teased her.

"Fuck you, Bess." Vashaun gave her the finger.

"He looks mad familiar." Dena stared at his face as he passed. She had seen him somewhere before but couldn't place him right off. He must've felt her eyes on him because he adjusted his hoodie and put a little pep in his step.

"He looks like that rapper." Bess observed him approaching the entrance of the Blood Orchid.

"What rapper?" Vashaun asked. She considered herself an authority on celebrities due to her extensive research in the quest of trying to land one.

"You know the one." Bess racked her brain trying to place a name with his face. "The kid from Harlem. Frankie you're from Harlem so I know you know who I'm talking about."

"Bess, just because Harlem is small doesn't mean we all

know each other," Frankie said. "Besides, he can't be no rapper rolling up in there." She nodded at his fleeting form as he disappeared inside Blood Orchid.

"Word up, because don't nothing but killers hang in that spot," Dena agreed.

The girls debated what they thought went on inside the Blood Orchid for a time, then the taxi Frankie had called pulled to the curb and beeped the horn.

"Our chariot awaits." Frankie nudged Dena and made her way toward the waiting taxi.

"A'ight, we'll see y'all chicks later," Dena told Bess and Vashaun before falling in step with Frankie.

"Maybe me and Bess can meet up with y'all. Where you gonna be?" Vashaun called after them.

Frankie stopped short and gave Vashaun a warm smile. "Wherever the wind blows us," she said and ducked into the cab with Dena, leaving Vashaun and Bess feeling like the odd chicks out.

"I can't stand them uppity bitches." Bess spat on the ground.

Vashaun snorted. "Word, they think they better than somebody, like we ain't got no class."

"Fuck them and their girls' night," Bess snarled. "I got five on the next bottle, what's good?"

"I got enough to put with that and get a pint of something to get us going, and I know I can game scrams down the street for a free bag of weed. That's enough to start our own little party right here on the block," Vashaun said enthusiastically.

"See how easy that came together," Bess smiled. "Let them bitches have their fun. I'd rather chill on the stoop than go downtown with them anyway."

"Me too," Vashaun agreed.

Neither of the girls sounded very convincing. For all the shit Vashaun and Bess talked about other people, they couldn't even get enough money together to start a proper party, but to them, a *little* was better than *nothing*, so they were still winning. While Vashaun and Bess plotted on their next buzz, Frankie and Dena were on their way to downtown Brooklyn to meet up with Porsha to start a night that none of them would soon forget.

TWENTY-THREE

ALONZO SAT WITH HIS ELBOWS ON THE table and his hands steepled. In front of him was a half-eaten plate of Sticky Wings and a corn on the cob he had barely touched. Outside of the heavy dent in his Texas-sized Hennessey Colada, his meal was only slightly picked over. His head was cocked slightly to the side, and the faintest hint of a smile touched the corners of his lips as he occasionally nodded like he was actually interested in what the chick sitting across from him was blabbing about.

Veronica was a chocolate honey with love-me eyes and fuck-me from the back hips that he knew from back when he was running in the streets heavy, who he happened to bump into again during a chance meeting on the Triborough Bridge. Alonzo had been driving out to Queens with Lakim to pick some bread up, and when they went through the toll, Veronica happened to be the booth attendant. Back when Alonzo was still in the streets heavy she had been his main chick. Veronica was seriously into dope boys, and Alonzo was a star on the rise. The two chopped it up at the toll booth for a minute, holding up traffic, before exchanging numbers and promising to keep in contact.

Between both their hectic schedules it was hard to keep that promise, but they finally set a date nearly a month after the exchange. Veronica was living in Brooklyn, so Alonzo suggested they do something out there to make it convenient for her, but in all truthfulness, he was protecting his own best interests. North of Canal Street he was guilty by blood and association and didn't want to play the odds. The war brewing between King James and Shai Clark had ripped Harlem right down the middle, with the young outlaws riding with King James and the old regime standing behind the Clarks. King James had heart, but Shai had an army. Tensions ran high in the hood because everybody knew the storm was coming; they just weren't sure when it would start raining.

In a stroke of luck, King had broken down and let Alonzo hold his wheels. He looked like new money when he pulled up in front of Lafayette Gardens to scoop Veronica up in the sleek black SUV sitting on bulky rims. He turned quite a few heads, but Veronica turned even more when she came out of her building rocking a form-fitting purple dress that showed off every last one of her curves. Her thick hips and ass looked like rolling hills as she sauntered down the walkway toward the car. Alonzo couldn't help but smile at the thought of peeling Veronica out of the dress before the night was over.

The date was off to a great start but would hit a few rough patches on the way to dinner. The plan was dinner and a movie, in no particular order. There was a movie theater on Court Street, which was around the corner from BBQ's, so Alonzo figured he could kill two birds with one stone without doing too much moving around. He and Veronica smoked the other half of the blunt clip while reminiscing about old times on their way to the theater.

Alonzo had his heart set on seeing DMX's new action flick that had just come out, but there was also a new romantic comedy in theaters starring Kate Hudson. Taking Veronica into consideration, he bought tickets to the romantic comedy, thinking she would enjoy that more than the bloody action flick. Fifteen minutes into the movie, however, Veronica made him regret his decision. She hemmed and hawed all through the movie about everything from the lack of designer names in the character's wardrobe to the fact that there weren't enough black people in the movie. When a couple sitting behind them politely asked Veronica to keep it down she got belligerent and threatened to slap the girl. Alonzo was able to calm the situation, and he and Veronica moved to different seats where they watched what was left of the movie in tense silence.

Dinner started out a little better, but it didn't last. Veronica took forever to decide what she wanted off the basic menu before settling on Surf and Turf. When they brought the meal out, she complained about the steak being undercooked and the shrimp being fried when she thought they would be steamed. Had Alonzo not slipped the waitress an extra twenty on the side, along with his apologies, he was sure she would've spat in their food. Noticing that Alonzo was getting irritated, Veronica apologized more than once. Alonzo smiled like it was all good, but the damage was already done. By the time they had made it halfway through their meals Alonzo was just ready for the date to be over.

"Zo, did you hear what I asked you?" Veronica spoke up to get his attention.

Alonzo blinked twice as if he was coming out of a daze. "I'm sorry, baby. What did you say?"

"I was asking if you remember the time when all of us went out to the Tunnel back in the days." Veronica repeated the question.

"Oh yeah, right before they closed down." Alonzo smirked, remembering that night. He and a bunch of his crew had taken their ladies out to the popular nightclub one winter night. They were all underage, but for fifty dollars a head, the bouncer turned a blind eye to the youths. By then, the Tunnel had lost most of its luster, but to the high school kids it was like being at the Roof Top in eighty-nine. After the impression the Tunnel left on him Alonzo vowed that he was going to get big money in the streets or die trying. Luckily for him, prison derailed his delusional plan and brought him back to his senses, at least for a time.

"We were having major fun until those cats from the Bronx started acting up, but you laid it down, baby!" Veronica squealed excitedly as if it had just happened last night. Some older cats who were getting money in the Bronx tried to disrespect Alonzo and his young crew by stepping to their girls, but they soon found out that the teenagers were as vicious as a pack of wild dogs. Alonzo pistol-whipped one of the older dudes so bad that he never regained the sight in his right eye. "After that, everybody knew not to fuck with Zo-Pound. You really showed them."

"I sure did," Alonzo said with a sigh.

What Veronica was omitting from the story was how when the shit hit the fan about assault and the police came around asking questions, it was one of her girlfriends who got spooked

201

and sent the police in Alonzo's direction. He ended up catching a case behind the incident, but because of his age and the dude's criminal history, Alonzo managed to escape with five years probation.

"You know, I always knew you were going to be a ghetto star in the hood, even after you went away," Veronica told him.

Alonzo raised an eyebrow. "Is that right? And what makes you say that?"

Veronica looked at him as if it were a stupid question. "Because you're Zo-Pound, baby. In high school, we used to talk about who was gonna blow up and who was just fronting, and all the girls knew you were serious about your hustle. You stayed fly, and you kept me fly, and that's why we were the king and queen."

Alonzo hadn't meant to, but he laughed. "Veronica, you got jokes. You ended up working for the city, and they threw my black ass in prison, and ten years later, we're both still living in the projects. So what exactly are we the king and queen of besides hard times?"

Veronica frowned. "Don't be a dick, Zo-Pound. Of course, I know a lot has changed over the last few years, but I'm still me, and you're still you, and the fact that we're even sitting her entertaining this conversation is proof that there's still chemistry."

"Yeah, ma, I was digging on you when we bumped heads at the toll booth," Alonzo admitted.

"A'ight, then, so stop playing and act like you know," she told him.

They talked a bit more for a while, and Alonzo even found himself trying to have a good time, in spite of the rocky start to the date. Between the shots he was taking and the big-ass drink on the table, he started to loosen up, and Veronica didn't seem to be feeling any pain either. Every so often she would reach over and touch his thigh under the table and cause his penis to become erect. Staring at Veronica's cleavage, Alonzo began to change his mind about ditching her early. He figured if nothing else came of it, he could at least get some pussy so that the night wouldn't be a total loss.

Three-quarters to the bottom of the Texas-sized drink Alonzo's bladder was good and full. He excused himself from the table and headed for the restroom. On his way there, he remembered that he had turned his phone off when they went into the movie theater and never turned it back on. When he powered the phone on he saw that he had several text messages and a few voice mails. He checked the texts and didn't see anything that required his immediate attention so he decided to let the voice mails wait until the end of the night before he checked them. He had just about made it to the bathroom when he heard a familiar laugh coming from one of the booths. Out of curiosity, Alonzo peeked around the corner and spied on the occupants of the booth. There were three nice-looking chicks, eating and sipping colorful drinks. When his eyes landed on the chick sitting in the corner with a french fry pinched between her fingers and a smile on her lips, his heart felt like it had skipped a beat. He threw a glance over his shoulder to make sure Veronica wasn't paying attention before approaching the booth.

TWENTY-FOUR

PORSHA CHECKED HER WATCH AND WONDERED FOR the twentieth time in as many minutes what the hell was keeping Frankie. After she had spoken to Frankie earlier to arrange a time and meeting place, she still dragged her feet around town getting her nails done and her hair touched up before finally jumping on the A train to Brooklyn. Because of a track fire at West Fourth, Porsha ended up ten minutes late and Frankie *still* hadn't arrived, which was unusual because Frankie was big on punctuality.

BBQ's was crowded that night so Porsha had put their names on the waiting list for a table and went outside to wait for Frankie. It was a nice night, thank goodness, but she was still irritated at the fact that Frankie hadn't made it yet. She only hoped that Frankie would make it by the time they were called to be seated. She was getting hungry and wanted to get her drink on after having a rough day at work. Porsha's primary source of income was from the office building where she worked as one of the receptionists. The bosses were evil, the job was stressful, and the pay was shitty, but it beat shaking her ass for singles or being homeless. She had dabbled in both and was a fan of neither, so she thugged it out at her gig.

Porsha longed for the day that she would be able to free herself from the plantation and model full time, but modeling was slow motion at the moment, especially trying to break in at the age Porsha was. She was still in her early twenties, but in the modeling world, she might as well have been on the cusp of retiring. A lot of the girls she found herself competing against for the good jobs were younger, taller, and thinner than she was.

Porsha was a beautiful girl, standing at around five-foot-something, depending on the shoe, with a beautiful smile and well-defined curves. She was becoming very popular with some of the hipper, more urban magazines who catered to the around-the-way chick, but the bigger brands she was shooting for kept passing her over. They wanted rail-thin girls who were still in high school or fresh out, who were willing to starve and abuse themselves in the name of perfection. Porsha couldn't get with that program, so she had to take work where she could get it. She had done a few bathing suit spreads and had been offered some nice cash to do partial nudes, but she didn't want to taint her brand. She knew one day her ship would come in so she held fast to that and kept grinding.

Porsha was leaning against the wall outside BBQ's texting Frankie to see where she was when she felt a presence looming over her. She looked up and found herself staring at a dude who looked like he had just walked off the set of *New Jack City*. His Fila sweat suit was two sizes too big, and all ten of the thin gold chains he was wearing looked like he copped them fresh from the kiosk in the mall. Adjusting the brim of his white

Kangol, he flashed a single gold tooth among several rotten ones at Porsha.

He said, "What's up, baby? Can I talk to you for a minute?"

"Not unless it's to tell me that you apologize for coming out dressed like that. Have a good night." Porsha shooed him away with a flick of her hand.

"Fuck you, bitch," the dude said in disgust and stormed away.

"Ya mammy is a bitch, *bitch!*" Porsha shouted after him. Since she stepped out of the house they had been on her like stink on shit, with corny lines and promises of ice-cream dreams, but Porsha wasn't on that. She had enough going on in her life than to add training a man to her list of things to do. No matter how old or young, they all needed a little training, at least that's what she reasoned. When she looked at her reflection in the restaurant window, she smiled and couldn't say that she blamed them for pressing her because she was looking quite tasty that night.

Porsha had her homegirl at the shop give her hair a subtle blue-black rinse that you would only notice in the right light and press it up into a high Mohawk. She dug out her tightest blue jeans, which looked painted on over her plump ass, and accented them with a length of chain and padlock instead of a belt. The final pieces to the puzzle were an ode to her stripper days in the form of a pair of thigh-high black leather boots that stood on chrome-wedged heels that added at least three inches to her height. She drew more than a few stares for her appearance, but Porsha didn't care. Her style was her style, and that's what set her apart from the rest.

She was just about to hit send on her text message to Frankie when she saw a Livery Cab come to an abrupt halt two cars down from where she was standing. She saw Frankie spill out of the cab first, followed by a girl she didn't know wearing a cute sweater dress. Both of them were exchanging words with the cabdriver. The cabdriver shouted something back at them in a language that Porsha didn't understand, but she was able to make out the word "*Bitch*," and she saw Frankie's head rear back in shock. Porsha knew what would come next; she had seen it on more than one occasion. She headed in their direction as fast as she could in the tall shoes. The high wedges made her feel like she was on ice skates, trying to get to Frankie before her hand made it into her purse.

By the time the taxi carrying Frankie and Dena had crossed into downtown Brooklyn, the two women were thoroughly irritated. The taxi didn't have air-conditioning, and the windows were broken so they didn't roll down. To top it off, the stuffy car smelled like so much funk that the girls feared the smell would linger in their clothes. From the route that he took, it was obvious that he wasn't familiar with Brooklyn, but when they tried to give him directions, he ignored them. The fifteen-minute ride ended up taking forty minutes, and they were pissed about that.

"About fucking time," Frankie cursed when they finally hit Livingston Street and spotted BBQ's in the distance.

"Thank God, now please let me out of this cab before I faint." Dena fanned herself.

The driver slid the divider back and stuck his coal-black face through it. "You pay now," he ordered in clipped English.

"Ain't nobody trying to skip out on your li'l bum-ass fare," Frankie barked and tossed two balled up bills through the partition.

The driver uncrumpled the bills, which were a ten and a five. "No, no . . . it's no fifteen dollars . . . twenty-five-dollar ride."

"*Twenty-five dollars* to come from the Stuy to downtown? You bugging," Dena told him.

"I not bugging, you bugging!" he shot back. "It take almost one hour to come here so you pay me twenty-five dollars."

"Nigga, first of all, I don't see no meter in this cab. Second of all, it took us an hour to get here because you didn't know where the fuck you were going and wouldn't listen when we tried to tell you." Frankie was getting heated.

"You pay me or I call the police," the driver threatened.

"Call whoever you want, but best believe that when they get here, you'll *still* be sitting on that same fifteen dollars because I ain't giving you shit else," Frankie stated, throwing the door to the taxi open and stepping out. Dena was right behind her.

"You owe me money!" the driver screamed out the window at the girls, waggling his fist.

"We don't owe you shit. As a matter of fact, I need to send your nasty ass a bill because your cab funked up my dress," Dena replied.

The driver said some things that neither of them understood, but from the tone of his voice, they could tell they weren't compliments. The girls kept walking until they made out the word "*bitches*," and then Frankie came to an abrupt stop. She had never been fond of the word *bitch*, even when it was said in jest among her girlfriends, but it was a definite no-no when it came out of the mouth of a man. When Scar and his crew robbed her, the word took on a whole new meaning. While they were beating her within an inch of her life, all Frankie could remember was hearing them call her a *bitch* over and over. Whenever she heard a man say the word now, it took her to a dark place.

"*What* did you call us?" Frankie turned back to the cab.

"You heard me. I call you thieving bitches," the driver repeated, daring Frankie to do something.

A sinister smirk crossed Frankie's face. "That's what I thought you said." As cool as the other side of the pillow, Frankie slipped her hand into her purse. She was drawing her .22, ready to pop a hole in the cabdriver for disrespecting her, when a firm hand grabbed her about the wrist before the gun could clear the purse. Frankie's head snapped around, but some of the fight drained from her eyes when she saw that it was Porsha.

"Francine, I know you're smart enough to know doing what you were about to do ain't a good look in downtown Brooklyn, especially since we're just a hop and a skip away from the precinct," Porsha whispered in her ear. Porsha's words brought Frankie back to her senses. "Frankie, let it go, ma." Porsha began slowly pulling Frankie away from the altercation.

The realization of what almost happened made the cabdriver realize that the extra ten dollars he was trying to beat the girls for wasn't worth a bullet, so he wisely pulled off.

"Asshole!" Dena said to the taxi's fleeting taillights. "You know, for a minute, I thought you were really going to shoot him," she told Frankie, expecting her to laugh off.

Frankie didn't.

"She was," Porsha said seriously. "That's Frankie for you. Ready to set it off at the drop of a hat."

"So I'm finding out," Dena said. "Well, since Frankie's mind obviously isn't on etiquette, I'm Dena, and you must be Porsha." She extended her hand.

"Indeed I am." Porsha shook Dena's hand. "Now, if you girls are done playing gangsta, let's go up in here and get something to eat. I'm starving."

A half hour later, the girls were seated, munching on appetizers and throwing back shots of tequila. It had been a little tense at first after what had happened with the cabdriver, but by the time they reached the third round of shots, everything was all good. Even Frankie managed to snap out of her dark-ass mood and started having fun.

Porsha had initially been a bit apprehensive about the girls' night because she didn't know Dena and was always skeptical about allowing new people into her circle. After going through what she had gone through over the last few years, Porsha had major trust issues. To her surprise, Dena ended up being a really cool and down-to-earth chick, and they were more alike than either of them cared to admit. To someone on the outside looking in, you would've thought that Dena and Porsha were the old friends and Frankie was the new chick.

The waitress came back over, bringing them round number four of shots and their main courses. Frankie tore into her chicken and rib combo like a starved woman, which made all of them laugh heartily. The laughter abruptly ended, and Porsha noticed that Frankie and Dena were both smiling like they knew a secret that they were dying to tell. She was about to ask them what was up when she felt a presence looming over her. When she looked up, she was both surprised and pleased when she saw the handsome brown face smiling down at her.

"Long time no see," Alonzo said with an easy smile.

TWENTY-FIVE

FRANKIE SPOTTED ALONZO BEFORE ANYONE ELSE. DENA was in the middle of telling a funny-ass story and had all their attention when she saw him come around the bend. He gave Frankie a light nod, then turned his full attention to Porsha. She was so caught up in the story and ketchup-soaked french fry that she didn't even notice him. When everybody suddenly got quiet Porsha sensed something was wrong and looked over her shoulder. When her eyes landed on Alonzo you could almost see the spark in the air.

Porsha had to do a double take to make sure her eyes weren't playing tricks on her. It had been a minute since she had seen Alonzo, but she would know that smile anywhere. It was the same warm smile that greeted her every morning when she went into her local supermarket, where he had been the assistant manager. The last she'd heard, he had abruptly quit one day, and from the looks of things, he had found a noticeably more lucrative source of income.

Alonzo's hair was freshly cut, and his waves were spinning like a Caribbean sea during a tropical storm. He was wearing a

211

simple black V-neck sweater and black jeans, cuffed over a crispy pair of black Vasque boots. She did a quick inventory of his ears, wrists, and neck and confirmed that everything was shining and sparkling. Alonzo stood there with his head cocked and thumbs hooked into his belt loop, staring at Porsha. She returned his stare. There was an uncomfortable silence before he finally broke it.

"Long time no see," Alonzo said with an easy smile.

Porsha's mouth was suddenly very dry. She searched for a witty response but draw a blank and mustered a weak, "Hey."

"What it do, Zo?" Frankie smiled.

"It *do* whatever is necessary to make tomorrow better than yesterday," he said to Frankie but kept his eyes on Porsha. He could tell seeing him had thrown her off, so he threw something extra in his stare and watched her squirm like a deer in headlights. She was about to say something to him, but he purposely snubbed her and turned his attention back to Frankie. "What's up, Frankie Angels? How you been, love?"

Frankie shrugged. "I'm here, so I can't complain. You're looking good, ain't he, Porsha?"

Porsha didn't reply. She just rolled her eyes.

"Well, is somebody gonna introduce me, or am I gonna keep wondering who the elephant in the room is?" Dena spoke up. For a minute they had forgotten she was there.

"Dena, this is Alonzo; Zo, this is Dena, my homegirl from my building." Frankie made the introductions.

"Zo like Zo-Pound?" Dena asked. The moniker tugged at her brain.

"They called me that once upon a time," Alonzo confirmed.

"I think you knew my older brother Shannon, from Jefferson." Dena finally put the pieces together. Her mind went back to the day Shannon and Spooky let Dena tag on one of their shady adventures into Harlem. The dude they went to meet had his little brother with him, who he called Zo-Pound. He was way younger than Shannon and Spooky, but the two seemed to have a great deal of admiration for the young cat. Dena would never see Zo-Pound again until that night in BBQ's, but she would hear his name a time or two over the years, and it was always associated with mayhem.

Alonzo's eyes lit up. "Yeah, that was my old head. He was wild as fuck, but one of the most genuine niggaz I ever met. We lost contact when I went up north, but I'd love to get up with my nigga and see what's good with him. You got a number or an address for your brother?"

"Yeah, Rose Hill Cemetery. That's where we buried him after he was murdered." Dena gave him the short version of what had happened to her mother's oldest son.

"Shit, I'm sorry to hear that. My condolences to you, sis," Alonzo said sincerely.

"Thanks," Dena said with a smile. "So, how do you know Frankie and Porsha?" she asked, changing the subject.

"He and Porsha used to date," Frankie answered for him.

Dena raised an eyebrow. "Really?" She gave Porsha a nod of approval. Though Dena wasn't into dudes anymore, she was still a female and couldn't deny the fact that Alonzo was fine as hell.

"I see you got jokes, trick." Porsha rolled her eyes at Frankie. "No," she addressed Dena, "Alonzo and I didn't date."

"Y'all should have. Everybody knew that y'all were crushing on each other so I don't know why y'all didn't just make it official," Frankie laughed.

"Porsha never felt like I was quite in her league," Alonzo explained.

Dena looked from Alonzo to Porsha. "You must set your standards *way* high," she laughed.

Porsha ignored Dena and addressed Alonzo. "You know you wrong for spreading that lie. Don't act like that, Zo."

"I'm just teasing you, ma," Alonzo assured her. "In all truthfulness, I owe you a debt."

"For what?" Porsha asked suspiciously.

"Because you gave me some advice that changed my life," he said seriously. "You once told me that I was stuck where I was at because I was afraid to fly beyond it, so I sprouted some wings," he said, brushing imaginary lint from the sleeves of his sweater.

"So no more supermarkets, huh?" Porsha asked playfully.

Alonzo's lips twisted in disapproval. "Baby, I know your brain has already processed what your eyes told it, so why even play it like that?"

Porsha was taken aback. "I'm scared of you, Mr. Man." She looked him up and down.

"Don't be scared, ma, be open to the idea," Alonzo shot back. "And for the record, my name ain't Man, it's Alonzo. Zo-Pound if you know me like that." He leaned in and whispered to Porsha, "I told you a long time ago that you were gonna stop sleeping on me."

"Whatever," Porsha waved him off as if it was nothing. Truthfully, the way Zo was coming at her was turning her on. The person standing before her wasn't the cocky young dude stacking boxes in the supermarket, but a confident young cat who was about his business.

Their little moment was interrupted when a fifth party joined their group. Veronica stood there, wide legged in her tight purple dress, nostrils flaring slightly, and eyes sweeping the gorgeous girls at the table. She looked Porsha up and down but didn't stare. "I guess you got lost on your way to the bathroom," she said to Alonzo.

"Nah, just bumped into a few of my peeps and popped over to say hello," Alonzo said as if it hadn't been about to go down between him and Porsha. "Ladies," he addressed the girls, "this is my *friend*, Veronica."

Frankie and Dena nodded and waved, but Porsha let her voice be heard. "Charmed, I'm sure," she said with a crooked grin. She knew Veronica was trying to mark her territory. Porsha had to admit that Veronica had a banging body, but her whole swag screamed *hood rat*. She couldn't fuck with Porsha.

"Damn, I'm over here going down memory lane and neglecting the young lady I rolled in here with. Please forgive me for being a poor date." He kissed Veronica's hand, looking up at Porsha. She gave him a knowing look. *Checkmate,* he thought to himself. "It was good seeing you again, ladies." Alonzo saluted them and threw his arm around Veronica, leading her back to their table.

"Hey, Alonzo," Porsha called after him, stopping him short. When he turned around she raised her shot glass and said, "Here's to sound advice." She downed the shot and slammed the glass, upside down, on the table.

Alonzo smiled. "To sound advice." He continued to his table with Veronica.

Porsha watched Alonzo walk away, not really caring who saw the look she was giving him. She saw Veronica say something to him and Alonzo brush her off, which made her smile. Veronica could have Alonzo's dick, but Porsha would forever have his heart.

TWENTY-SIX

"WHAT WAS THAT ALL ABOUT?" VERONICA ASKED when they were back at their table.

"What was what about?" Alonzo seemed oblivious to what she was talking about.

"The chicks you were over there talking to. Did you used to see one of them or something?" she asked.

"Nah, I just know them from the neighborhood," he told her.

"Seemed like a li'l more than you just know them from the neighborhood. The chick with the Mohawk kept shooting me dirty looks like she had something she wanted to say."

"I doubt it. Porsha ain't the type of chick to bite her tongue if she has something to say," Alonzo stated. Without even realizing he was doing it, he let his eyes drift back to Porsha. She was staring in his direction too, but when they made eye contact she turned away.

"So you *do* know her like that," Veronica pressed.

"I told you, I know them from the hood," Alonzo said in an irritated tone.

216

"Look, I'm sorry, Zo." She reached under the table and rubbed his thigh, purposely letting her hand brush his penis. "I don't wanna come off as a crazy, jealous bitch on our first date and turn you off, but we had a good li'l vibe going and the detour kinda threw it off, ya know?"

"Indeed, and that was my fault. I shouldn't have left you hanging. That was rude," he conceded.

"See? That was painless." Veronica rubbed her hands together, then spread them apart as if she was crushing something, then releasing it to the wind. "How about we pick up where we left off?"

"Works for me," Alonzo agreed.

They ordered another round of drinks and dessert while trying to get their date back on track. Every so often, Alonzo's eyes would drift back to Porsha, but for the most part, he stayed focused on Veronica. Soon, there was a commotion at the front door of the restaurant that caused both of them to look that way. A group of young girls, including several of the waitresses, crowded around the entrance squealing like high school kids while trying to get camera phone shots of whomever it was coming in. When the restaurant manager and a few of the bus boys managed to thin out the crowd Alonzo saw that the person who had caused the commotion was none other than Don B.

Don B. pulled to a screeching halt in front of BBQ's and threw the candy red Benz in park and put the hazards on. Two seconds later, a white Benz identical to the red one pulled up behind it. Don B. hopped out, wearing black shades, baggy blue jeans, and a white V-neck T-shirt with a blue Yankee fitted cocked to one side. Pinched between his lips was a smoldering blunt, which bobbed every time he said something. He hit the alarm and stepped on the curb with every intention on leaving the car where it was while he ate. It was in a bus lane and sure to get a ticket or worse, but he didn't give a shit. He was The Don, and all that mattered to him that night was that he was hungry.

Young Dance got out of the passenger's side of the red Benz, trying his best to light his blunt with a lighter that was obviously out of fuel. He too was wearing a fitted cap and white T-shirt with blue jeans. For summertime in Harlem having a plethora of white tees and a few fitted hats was a must, and Young Dance was Harlem to the heart. He and Don B. had been kicking it heavy all day, and The Don was showing Dance the time of his life. The Big Dawg crew was showing him major love, and he soaked it all up.

A cat named Tone jumped out of the white Benz and brushed himself off. Unlike Don B. and Dance, Tone had slightly different tastes when it came to dressing. He wore a crispy blue Polo shirt with a white fisherman's cap, white linen pants, and a pair of white Nike Airs. Tone had been running with Don B. for years, but while Don B. was in the streets, Tone was away at school. When Don B. started getting big in the music industry, Tone left college to help his friend and applied what he had learned to helping his friend grow his record label. Don B. had always been a natural hustler, but with Tone's book smarts and cutthroat nature, Big Dawg blew up!

"Damn, I didn't realize how hungry I was until we got here," Tone said, rubbing his stomach and looking inside the window of BBQ's hungrily.

"Me too." Dance licked his lips, which were now extremely dry from the weed. "Are we gonna wait for Devil and them to get here before we go in and eat?"

"Nah, Devil and them niggaz went ahead to the club. We're gonna meet them down there when we bust this food down," Don B. explained.

Young Dance looked shocked. "Son, for as big of a star as you are I thought you would roll everywhere with security."

Don B. gave Dance a queer look. "My nigga, I ain't no gangsta rapper; I'm a gangsta-turned-rapper. I keep security with me when it's necessary, like doing clubs and appearances, but when I'm in the streets, I like to move how I move, smell me?"

"I guess," Dance said.

"Besides, Tone would never let anything happen to me, would you, Tone?" Don B. said playfully.

"Never," Tone answered with a serious face.

"Come on, let's go eat so we can make moves to the spot." Don B. led the way toward the entrance. It was quiet when he first walked in, but all it took was for one person to recognize him, then out came the groupies. Chicks were even trying to throw themselves at Dance because he was with Don B. "Feels good to be a rock star, doesn't it?" Don B. whispered in Dance's ear as he signed an autograph for one of the waitresses.

Once the manager and a few of the bus boys broke up the crowd, he asked Don B. to follow him to a secluded booth in the back where he could eat in peace. Don B. moved through the restaurant with a heavy dip in his walk so his big chain would swing harder. At one table a girl made the mistake of staring at him for too long and the dude she was with threw a glass of water in her face before getting up to leave. All eyes were on

Don B., as he preferred it. He wanted everybody in the joint to know that a *real* nigga was in the building.

As they crossed the dining room en route to the section the manager was seating them in, Young Dance made an offhanded comment about a cute dark-skinned chick who was sitting with two of her friends in a corner booth. When Don B. looked to see who he was talking about, he doubled over in laughter. He tapped Tone, who laughed too, and when they let Dance in on the joke, they laughed as a trio. Don B. could see rage flash across the girl's face, and it only made him laugh harder. She barked something at him, trying to cause a scene, so he decided to feed into it and have a little fun at her expense.

Alonzo felt his stomach twist into knots when he saw Don B. and his crew approach the booth where Porsha and her friends were sitting. The thought of Don B. trying to holla at Porsha infuriated Alonzo, because he knew his type. People like Don B. thought that because they had money it entitled them to anything they wanted, while people like Alonzo had to jump through hoops for what little they had. Well, if somebody like Don B. was who Porsha wanted, then fuck her, he was gonna make the best out of his night with Veronica.

"You know them cats or something?" Veronica asked, noticing how Alonzo was looking at Don B.

Alonzo downplayed it. "Something like that."

"Damn, you rolling heavier than I thought," Veronica said, impressed that Alonzo knew such important people.

"Don't believe the hype, ma. Me and scrams go back a bit, that's all." Alonzo waved his hand dismissively.

Veronica leaned back in her chair and folded her arms while

looking at Alonzo. "Zo, you kill me with this too cool for school attitude of yours."

"How do you mean?" he asked curiously.

"I mean how you carry yourself like nothing fazes you. Zo, we come from the same thing, which is nothing, but here you are moving around with boss niggaz. Most muthafuckas would've lost their composure having those kinds of connections, but not you."

"Well, I ain't most muthafuckas," Alonzo shrugged. His eyes cut back in Porsha's direction. Don B. was smiling and kicking what he assumed to be some weak-ass lines to Porsha.

"That's obvious to a duck," Veronica continued. "A girl could probably spend most of her life trying to figure out what makes you tick."

"I wouldn't argue with you on that count. I'm like an onion, baby; there's layers to me, so it may take you a minute to get to the center of who I really am," he told her.

"I'm trying to get to know you, but your ass is like a puzzle that I can't quite figure out."

"Well, while you're busy trying to figure me out, let me pick your brain a li'l bit. One thing I gotta ask is, how come a sexy broad like you ain't got no man?" he asked.

"Why I gotta be a *broad*?" Veronica threw a napkin at him playfully. "To answer your question, it's because most of the dudes I meet don't have the same ambitions that I do."

"I know that's right." Alonzo raised his drink, and they clicked glasses. He was waiting for Veronica to drop some more wisdom, and that's when the conversation went to the left.

"True story, Zo," she continued. "Most of these dudes just wanna get paroled to your crib or have you take care of them, but I ain't off that. If I'm bringing something to the table, then you gotta be bringing something to the table too. Shit, I got three kids, and it ain't easy raising them on my own."

"You got what, where, who?" Alonzo's brain hit the air brakes.

"That's why I fucks wit' you, Alonzo." She ignored the bewildered expression on his face and kept talking. "You're about your business, daddy. I think that we can do big things together."

"You're coming at me with a lot right now. Give me a minute to digest all this." He tried to derail her, but it was not to be.

"Ain't too much to digest, Zo. I'm a girl who doesn't believe in beating around the bush. When I see something I want, I go for it, and I want you!" Veronica told him.

"Baby, you don't even know me," he pointed out.

"Boy, please, we've known each other since high school. I had a soft spot for you then, and I got one for you now, Zo. You gotta admit that we were good together."

"I hear you, V, but shit is different now than when we were in high school. I fucks wit' you heavy, but I ain't looking for no girl, at least right now. I'm just trying to make it through from one day to the next. As it stands, my life is a li'l complicated at the moment."

"And I ain't trying to complicate it further, Zo, I just want a chance to earn my spot in your heart."

"The heart is a complicated thing," Alonzo said honestly.

Veronica reached over and turned his head so that they were eye to eye. "Only as complicated as you make it. Boo, I was always the Bonnie to your Clyde, and we can be that way again, but on another level. With a bitch like me at your side, you can go all the way to the top!"

Alonzo was totally lost. "To the top of what?"

"Of the *game*. What else?" she asked as if he should've known. "Zo, I know you, boo. You can fool some of these muthafuckas with that 'working nigga' shit, but my ears are always to the streets, so I know what it is."

"And what is it?" he asked, still in total disbelief at how Veronica was coming at him.

"The streets are buzzing about how Zo-Pound is back. I didn't believe it at first, but when I saw you with your brother Lakim that day, I knew it was true. Boo, I can show you better than I can tell you why a bitch like me would be such an asset to your team."

Alonzo was waiting for her to hit him with the punch line so they could both have a good laugh, but the broad was serious. "You mean to tell me all this was about a job interview?" He laughed. "Baby, you shot-out, and that's real talk. I don't know who you think I am, but I ain't *that* nigga, and I thought you weren't *that* bitch, but obviously we were both wrong about each other." He waved the waitress over so he could get the check. "I think it's time for me to drop you off."

"Wait a second, Zo. Did I do something wrong?" Veronica asked, confused and slightly panicked as she felt her hold on Zo slipping.

"Nah, baby, it ain't you. This is all on me," he told her, handing the waitress some bills and telling her to keep the change. Veronica kept trying to explain herself, but Alonzo was only half-listening, steering her toward the front door with his hand in the small of her back.

Passing the table where the girls were sitting he noticed that Porsha was on her feet, slinging obscenities at a million miles per minute. Don B. said something to Porsha, and whatever it was must've been foul because Frankie sprang to her feet and got into the argument. It looked like it was about to get real ugly. Alonzo turned away and continued walking toward the door with Veronica but stopped short. Every ounce of his good sense told him to keep walking and to mind his business, but he just couldn't.

"Give me a second, Veronica." Alonzo excused himself and started in the direction of the altercation.

"Zo, where you going?" she asked, but he never answered.

TWENTY-SEVEN

IT WAS SAFE TO SAY THAT FRANKIE was thoroughly drunk. She and the girls had drunk, eaten, and talked shit well into the night and everyone was feeling good, especially Porsha. Frankie didn't miss the sly looks Porsha and Alonzo were giving each other from across the room. She had watched Alonzo and Porsha dance around their feelings for years, but anybody with eyes could see their chemistry. Randomly bumping into Alonzo that night after all that time was an act of fate, and Frankie just hoped that they would get it right this time around. She was looking around for the waitress to ask for the check and a dessert to go when she saw a face that soured her whole mood.

He stormed into the place like he owned it, flanked by two of his cronies. His Yankee fitted was cocked deep to one side, with the brim stopping just short of the frames of his black sunglasses. The icy chains hanging around his neck looked like Fruit Loops with their multicolored diamonds. The people eating at the restaurant threw themselves at the feet of the superstar rapper treating him like a god, but Frankie knew better than most that

225

he was the devil incarnate wearing a man's skin. She had hoped that her friends hadn't noticed him, but the looks on their faces said that they had. Both Dena and Porsha, on separate occasions, had confided in Frankie, so she alone knew the dark secrets that bound the two girls from two walks of life to one notorious man.

If looks could kill, then Don B. would've surely dropped dead from the murderous daggers Porsha was shooting at him. Porsha had been warned about Don B. and his antics, but the love and gifts he showered her with blinded her to his wicked ways. She actually thought she had a shot at being Don B.'s main lady, but soon learned the ugly truth when he drugged her and she woke up in a bed full of strange men and women.

When Porsha sobered up enough to make heads or tails of what had happened, she went off on Don B. and threatened to go to the police about the rape. He laughed it off and assured her that by the time his high-powered lawyers got done dragging her checkered past through the mud and media she would end up on the receiving end of a charge for trying to extort him. It was the lowest moment of her life and also a turning point.

Dena had been the youngest and the most innocent when she fell into Don B.'s clutches. She had been a young girl in love with a fast-talking pimp who pawned her off to a den of wolves, with Don B. as the Alpha of the pack. They broke Dena's body and spirit, and though her brother had sacrificed his life in the process of eradicating her assailants, Don B. remained as a constant reminder of how the grown men had snatched her young innocence.

"Come on, y'all, let's get outta here," Frankie suggested.

"I think that's a good idea," Dena agreed, collecting her purse from the seat next to her to put up her portion for the bill. Her hands were trembling so bad that she had trouble getting her money out. It had been her first time seeing Don B. since that horrific night so many years ago, and it broke down all the mental blocks she had erected in her mind. She could almost smell Don B.'s sweat on her as if the rape had only happened moments prior. It was all she could do to keep from screaming hysterically.

"We don't have to go nowhere." Porsha placed her right hand over Dena's to reassure her. She knew from the look on the younger girl's face that something had happened between her and Don B. too, and being in the presence of another of his victims only infuriated Porsha more. "Fuck that clown," Porsha said loud enough for Don B. to hear.

Don B. spotted Porsha and Dena sitting at the table and tapped Tone. He whispered something to his crime partner, and they both started laughing. Young Dance was ignorant of the joke, but when they let him in on it, he started laughing too.

"If you got something to say, don't whisper it, bitch nigga. Say it loud enough for everybody to hear it," Porsha snapped. Don B. had her seeing red and she couldn't control herself. The Don accepted her challenge and began making his way over to the booth. Everyone appeared uneasy except for Porsha. The fire in her eyes said that she was ready for war.

"Be easy, Porsha," Frankie whispered, noticing Porsha's left hand was wrapped around a steak knife on the table. She saw murder flickering in her eyes and was afraid of what Porsha might do.

"Since you asked so nicely, I'll tell you exactly what I said." Don B. glared down at Porsha. "My li'l man commented on how beautiful you girls were, and I explained to him that the both of y'all bitches would do something strange for a small piece of change." Don B. laughed, and so did Dance. Tone remained neutral.

"Nigga, please, all the money in the world wouldn't make a bitch fuck with your little, dirty-dick ass, and that's why you gotta drug bitches before you sleep with them," Porsha barked.

"You got a big mouth, li'l girl," Don B. told her. His voice had taken on a deadly edge.

"If my mouth is so big, then why don't you close it for me, you rapist faggot?" Porsha challenged. Don B. took a step toward Porsha, but a voice behind him gave him pause.

"Don't do it like that, homie."

Alonzo's heart was beating a million miles per minute as he approached the altercation. He kept telling himself to turn around and walk away, but with each additional step he committed himself deeper. By the time he reached them, Don B. was advancing on Porsha with his fists balled up like he meant to do her harm and that sealed the deal for Alonzo.

"Don't do it like that, homie," he spoke up, startling everyone at the booth.

"Chill, Zo, everything is all good over here," Tone assured him. He and Alonzo knew each other from the streets and had a mutual respect for each other.

"It don't look like it." Alonzo's eyes drifted from Don B. to Porsha.

"I got this, Zo. It's okay," Porsha told him. She tried to sound confident and tough, but her eyes said that she was glad he showed up.

"Who the fuck is you supposed to be?" Don B. looked Alonzo up and down like he was a peasant.

"Be cool, Don, you remember Zo-Pound. I introduced you to him at Brick City," Tone said jogging his memory.

Don B. had remembered that night. Zo-Pound had rolled up into Brick City with some gorilla niggaz from Grant Projects. Their whole vibe screamed goon, and they proved that accurate when he saw them stand off against Shai Clark's people. Zo's homies were said to be hardened killers who feared nothing, but their reputations meant nothing to Don B. In his mind, he was royalty and was untouchable by the thugs.

"Is this your bitch or something?" Don B. asked hostilely.

Alonzo chuckled to mask his mounting anger. "Nah, that ain't my *bitch,* but these *ladies* are friends of mine."

"Well, if it ain't your bitch then it ain't your problem. I'm about to start giving out lessons in respect, and unless you wanna learn one too, then I suggest you get the fuck up outta Dodge."

By this time Veronica had come over and was watching the altercation nervously. "C'mon, baby. Let's just go." She tugged at Alonzo's sleeve, but he acted as if he didn't even notice her.

"Man, listen to your girl and get up outta here." Don B. waved Alonzo off dismissively.

"You know," Alonzo began in an even tone, "I came over here and got at you like a man, but I'm feeling kinda disrespected by the way you're talking right now."

"If you think that's disrespectful, then check this fly shit out—suck my dick!" Don B. screamed in Alonzo's face, raining spittle on him.

Don B. had no idea he had even been hit until he staggered backward and bumped his pack against the corner of the booth where Frankie and her girls were sitting. The second slap was even more vicious than the first, lifting Don B. off his feet and sending him sprawling onto the table between Porsha and Dena, where Dena's drink *accidentally* spilled on his head. Alonzo felt someone behind him and spun, gun drawn, and pointed at Young Dance's chest. Tone tried to ease up on Alonzo from his blindside, but Alonzo's words froze him.

"Tone, I'll bet you all the money in your pocket that I can knock this li'l nigga out his shoes and still peel yo cap before you clear that gun. If you draw, nigga, you better be Picasso," Alonzo warned. Tone wisely dropped his hands to his sides.

Don B. had just come to his senses and was furious that he had been embarrassed in public in such a way. Seeing that Alonzo was preoccupied he tried to ease off the table and make his move but decided against it when Porsha pressed the steak knife she had been gripping to his neck.

"Please do something crazy so I can cut your throat," she hissed in Don B.'s ear. When he saw the maddened look in her eyes he knew without a doubt that she would make good on her threat, so he relaxed.

"Zo, don't do nothing stupid," Tone said.

"I think it's a little late for that," Alonzo said, eyes sweeping the faces of the terrified people in the restaurant.

"My dude, you know you dead for this shit, right?" Don B. threatened from the table where he was still lying with the steak knife to his throat.

"I don't know shit except that if you keep bumping your gums, both of us are gonna make the front page of the *Daily News*," Alonzo told him. Tone moved closer to him so his attention shifted. "Tone, I don't want to, so don't make me, fam."

"Zo, you know I can't let you violate the homie," Tone said. He was fond of Alonzo, but Don B. was his brother.

"I know that, and I know there wouldn't be too much you could do to stop me if I decided to off this fag," he nodded at Don B. "Don't worry, Tone, neither one of us wants that kinda trouble. Ladies," he addressed Porsha and her crew, "get your shit and let's roll."

Frankie slid from the booth, then pulled Dena out. Porsha lingered for a few seconds more savoring the feeling of having Don B. at her mercy. "I don't think you'll ever know how hard it was for me to not open you up tonight, you rapist," she hissed.

A broad grin spread across Don B.'s lips. "You're gonna wish you had. The next time I see you, I'm gonna show you what it truly means to violate a bitch." He laughed in her face.

"We'll see about that." Porsha nicked his neck with the knife as she got up from the booth.

"Dirty bitch!" Don B. yelped, grabbing his neck where she'd cut him. It was only a scratch, but it hurt like hell.

When all four of the girls had exited the restaurant, Alonzo started backing toward the exit, with his gun still on Don B. The rapper's shades had been knocked off during the scuffle, and Alonzo was allowed a rare glimpse at Don B.'s eyes. They were heavily slanted and red from all the weed he smoked and about as warm as a viper's. Don B. kept his eyes on Alonzo the whole time. Alonzo knew that look. It was a look that said this is far from over. Alonzo knew leaving Don B. alive was a mistake, but he just didn't have it in him. His mind raced through the wasted childhood he had spent in various prisons over the years, and he decided it wasn't worth it. The way Don B. operated it would only be a matter of time before someone killed him over something, but it wouldn't be Alonzo . . . at least not tonight.

TWENTY-EIGHT

AFTER THE ALTERCATION AT BBQ'S EVERYBODY WAS rattled. They all held their breaths in fear that the police would jump out and arrest them before they made it to safety. Thankfully, they were able to reach Alonzo's ride without incident.

Veronica was pissed when Alonzo offered to drop everybody off, especially since she lived the closest and would be the first one to go. Every so often she would glance up in the rearview at Porsha, who was sitting in the back with Frankie and Dena. Veronica had planned to fuck and suck Alonzo so good that night that he would have no choice but to make her his shorty, but that plan was ruined thanks to Porsha. She knew from the moment she saw the pretty dark-skinned girl with the Mohawk that she was going to be trouble, and the fact that she got dropped off in front of her building with a mumbled promise from Alonzo about calling her later confirmed it. Watching Alonzo's taillights disappear into the night Veronica vowed to whip Porsha's ass for ruining her night if they ever bumped into each other again.

Frankie and Dena were dropped off next in Bed-Stuy. Alonzo barely lingered long enough to make sure they got in their building before he peeled off. He wanted to put some distance between him and the County Of Kings before something else happened and he wound up going to jail that night. Both he and Porsha rode in silence until they were across the bridge and back in Manhattan.

Porsha broke the silence. "You didn't have to do that, you know."

"I think the correct thing to say would be *thank you.*" Alonzo cut his eyes at her.

"I said thank you a hundred times already."

"Then say it one hundred and one. I never get tired of hearing it, especially coming from you," he shot back.

"Stop being funny, Alonzo. You could've gone to jail or worse for pulling out a gun in front of all those people," she pointed out.

"What was I supposed to do? Just stand by and do nothing while that nigga disrespected you?" he asked. "The shit coming outta his mouth was foul."

"How much did you hear?" Porsha asked, not sure she really wanted to know the answer.

"Enough," he said. "Porsha, I don't know what happened with you and that cat, and it ain't really none of my business. All I know is that I wasn't gonna let him put his hands on you."

Porsha downplayed it. "They were just words, Alonzo; they couldn't hurt me."

"Looked to me like homie was planning on doing a little more than just talking," Alonzo said. "Porsha, I don't get you, ma."

"What do you mean by that?" she asked defensively.

"What I mean is, why do you keep settling on fucking with these bum-ass niggaz who ain't bringing nothing to the table but problems?"

Porsha rolled her eyes. "*Excuse* you? Alonzo, knock it off because it ain't even that type of party. A lot has changed since the last time we saw each other."

"A person can change their ways, but not their heart," Alonzo capped.

"And what the fuck do you know about my heart?" Porsha folded her arms.

"More than you give me credit for," he said sincerely. "Porsha, I ain't trying to argue with you, ma, I just wanna make sure you good out here in the world."

"Thanks, but I've been taking care of myself for a long time now and have been doing a pretty good job." She turned her back to him and stared out the window. Alonzo had struck a nerve, but she wouldn't give him the satisfaction of letting him know it. He had always been able to see through her façades, and it irked her that he knew her so well, especially when she had put so much effort into keeping him at a distance. It wasn't that she wasn't attracted to Alonzo; in fact, she was feeling him more than she cared to admit, but the old wounds from her past were still fresh, and she was afraid to let him get close. Alonzo was a good dude with a heart of gold and a magnetic personality that drew you helplessly to him. Porsha knew that if she crossed that line she would belong to him, body and soul, and the thought of being in love scared her more than the thought of being alone.

When the car came to an abrupt stop, Porsha snapped out

234

of her daze. She looked up and was surprised to see that they were in front of her building. "How did you know where I lived when I didn't give you the address?"

Alonzo placed his hand on his chest. "The heart is better than a GPS." He winked.

"Yo, if you only knew how stalker-ish you sounded just now." She laughed and shoved him playfully. Porsha's eyes landed on Alonzo's cell phone in the cup holder. She hesitated briefly before picking it up and fumbling with the keys.

"What you doing with my phone, Porsha?" Alonzo reached for it defensively, but she snatched it away.

"Relax." She finished typing on his phone and handed it to him. "I locked my number in there so we can keep in contact. Regardless, you know you still my nigga."

Alonzo looked down at the number and nodded in approval. "I guess being your *nigga* beats being your *nothing,* huh?"

"There you go with that bullshit." She shoved him playfully again. "And don't have none of them dirty skanks you deal with crank calling me on some jealous shit either."

"Watch that. All my skanks wash their asses at least once per day," he joked.

Porsha laughed. "You're a dick. But for real, Alonzo, let your li'l friends know what time it is if they ask about my number being in your phone."

"And what time is it?" Alonzo asked, drinking her in with his eyes. He saw the telltale glint that let him know he was making progress. Alonzo was inching toward her so subtly that she didn't even realize it until they were almost nose to nose.

Porsha sat there like a deer in headlights while Alonzo advanced on her slowly. He was so close that she could taste the faint traces of liquor on his breath from the restaurant. Right before their lips connected, she placed her finger on his lips and backed away. "It's time to say good night, Alonzo."

"That's cold," he said with a grin that let her know he wasn't done trying. His cell phone suddenly rang in his hand. He was going to ignore it until he saw the number on the screen. "What's hood?" Alonzo listened for a few seconds, then frowned. "Hold on, who got dropped? Shit, I'll be there as soon as I can." He ended the call.

"Everything okay?" Porsha asked with concern in her voice. The sudden change in his facial expression made her fear the worst.

"Yeah, everything is cool," he lied. "I just gotta go scoop my peoples up right quick. But I'm gonna call you, ma."

"Run off to scoop ol' girl. Looks like y'all had some unfinished business earlier anyhow," Porsha said with a tinge of attitude in her voice. She reached for the door handle, but Alonzo grabbed her by the arm.

"Don't even carry it like that, sis. Porsha, you know what it is with me, so you know I don't do games. I got a million ponies, but I'm still trying to tame that stallion, ya hear?" He looked her up and down.

His comeback made Porsha smile. "I hear you talking. Just make sure you call me, Zo." She got out of the whip.

"Bet on it." He nodded and peeled off.

When Alonzo was out of sight a broad smile crossed Porsha's lips. "Baby boy has definitely grown up," she said to no one in particular before heading into her building.

TWENTY-NINE

AFTER WHAT HAD HAPPENED IN BBQ'S, DON B. found himself in a foul mood. The girls had been minding their business, and he could've very well ignored them, but his ego and the fact that he wanted to impress Young Dance made him approach the girls and turn them into the night's entertainment. In the end, he ended up being the star of the show. Zo-Pound had violated when he stuck his nose where it didn't belong in trying to rescue the chicks, and what's worse, he had made Don B. look like a bitch in the process. He was The Don of all Dons and getting the shit slapped out of him in a room full of people wasn't a good look. If it was the last thing he did, he would make sure Zo-Pound and his bitches got what they deserved.

Don B. had a good mind to blow off the appearance he was supposed to make at the spot downtown, but he couldn't bring himself to walk away from the twenty-five stacks that he was being paid just to do a walk-through at the spot. Besides, he had to make up for what happened so as not to fall too far out of favor in Young Dance's eyes. Don B. had been chasing the MC for too long to let him slip away so easily.

The rapper and his entourage received a king's welcome when Don B. led them into the spot. It was more like a loft that had been converted into a lounge than the club it was billed to be. Don B. didn't care as long as they kept his glass and his pocket full. Devil greeted Don B. and Tone at the door and immediately picked up on the fact that something was wrong. Don B. downplayed it as nothing and promised to fill him in later on. He needed time to think up a lie because there was no way he was telling the big homie that he had let a young boy slap him in the mouth. He knew Tone wouldn't say anything, and if Young Dance was smart, he too would carry that secret to the grave. Don B. was proud of his reputation as a tough guy and was more than willing to shed blood to keep it from being besmirched, which is what Zo and the bitches would soon find out.

Tone signaled the DJ, and he immediately threw on Don B.'s latest song, officially announcing the arrival of the star. The small dance floor was instantly crowded and a floodgate of chickenheads burst open, with the ladies trying to get next to The Don. Don B. smiled, nodded, and received his praises like the arrogant bastard that he was, while Young Dance looked, smiling like a starstruck kid. Don B. was showing out, but the best was yet to come. When Don B.'s song was halfway over, they threw on a cut by Young Dance that no one had ever heard, including Dance. It was an old freestyle Young Dance had done on a mix tape when he was starting out, laid over a newly produced Big Dawg track. The verse was five years old, but it moved the crowd like it was brand-new. Young Dance stood there in bewilderment as he was suddenly surrounded by photographers and groupies, all courtesy of The Don.

Don B. stood next to Young Dance and posed for several pictures. He threw his arm around Dance and hugged him like a brother. "You feel that?" Don B. patted him on his chest. "That great big bubble that just formed in your chest is what success feels like."

"You don't play no games when you're recruiting a cat, do you?" Dance shook his head.

"None at all, my nigga. When I want something, I go full throttle to get it, ya hear?"

"Yeah, I hear. Yo, let me ask you something. Where the hell did you get that old verse of mine from?"

"The Don has his ways. Now stop asking so many questions and enjoy this good love the people are showing you. As a matter of fact, there's a chick over there who is staring at you like she would fuck you in the middle of the dance floor," Don B. nodded to a chick standing off to the side who had been clocking them since they walked in. Her face was nice, but her body was CRAZY.

Young Dance looked to see who Don B. was talking about and realized it was the chick Pam he had met a few weeks prior. "Oh shit, I know shorty. I met her a while back."

"Oh, that's you?" Don B. asked curiously.

"Nah, that ain't me, but I'm trying to fuck," Dance confessed.

"Well you sure as hell can't fuck her from way over here. Devil," Don B. turned to his bodyguard, "go get that bitch." Don B. watched as Devil lumbered over to Pam and whispered something in her ear. A few seconds later he was leading her by the hand to the circle where they were standing.

Young Dance hugged Pam. "What's good, ma?"

"Nothing, but I was starting to think you stood me up," Pam said with a playful attitude.

"Never that. We ran into a li'l situation on the way down here," Young Dance cut his eyes at Don B., "but we in the building now."

"In full effect," Don B. added, invading Dance and Pam's space. "Ain't you gonna introduce me to your friend?" Don B. asked Dance. Behind his shades he was looking at Pam like he wanted to eat her.

"My fault, yo. Pam, this is my nigga, Don B." Young Dance reluctantly made the introduction.

"Charmed, I'm sure." Don B. took her hand and brought it to his lips like he was going to kiss the back of it, then flipped it over and kissed the back of his own hand.

"I love your music," Pam said.

The statement was a simple one, but it spoke in volumes to Don B. It let him know all that he needed to about the girl and based on that, he marked her as food.

"Thank you, love." He gave her an easy smile. "So what's up, Pam? You in here dolo?"

"Yeah, my homegirl was supposed to come with me, but she flaked at the last minute."

"Well, that's her loss, now, isn't it?" Don B. put one arm around Pam and the other around Young Dance. "Don't worry, we gonna make sure you got a hell of a story for her the next time you see her. Any friend of Dance is family, because Dance *is* family. Ain't that right, Dance?"

240

"You know it," Dance cosigned.

"Say that," Don B. nodded. "Damn, where are my manners." Don B. grabbed a waitress that had been walking past. "Bottles and be quick about it." He released her. The girl looked like she wanted to curse Don B. out, but she needed her job so she let it go and went off to do as she was told.

Half an hour later, Young Dance and Pam were seated snuggly with the rest of the Big Dawg party on a velvet couch in the back of the loft. The table in front of them was crowded with bottles and wing platters, while L's were being passed around. Along the way they had picked up a few more chicks to join them, making an already lively situation livelier. The red-carpet treatment Dance got from being a part of the Big Dawg circle only made him look larger than life to Pam, and the way she kept pressing up on him showed it. She wanted to make sure the rest of the chicks in the spot knew that she had already claimed him as hers for the night. Young Dance was smiling like a kid on Christmas morning. He knew he was a dope MC and was well respected on the streets, but Don B. was showing him a whole different world of possibilities. Hanging with Don B. in his world was the first time Young Dance ever felt the kind of love that he felt he deserved.

"Should I take that look on your face as a hint to have a contract drawn up in the morning?" Don B. half-joked.

"I can't front, you've been very persuasive, but I still don't know, Don," Dance admitted.

"My nigga, this shit you seeing," he motioned to the bottles and the girls, "is light. This is a fucking Sunday afternoon for me. I respect you wanting to be your own man, Dance, but the bottom line is everybody needs a crutch when they're starting out, so don't let your pride make you slit your own throat."

"I feel what you're saying, Don, and I ain't too big to admit that I need a li'l push, but I need it to be the *right* push. Some of these labels have thrown some real nice offers at me, Don. I'm talking about enough scratch for me to finally pull my people out the trap."

Don B. laughed in Dance's face. "I been in this game too long for you to piss on my head and try to tell me it's raining. These record labels ain't trying to gamble no big money on real hip hop. They want gimmicks, and you ain't a gimmick rapper, Dance. My nigga, the only way you're gonna really get the support of a major label is if you dye your hair, throw on some white shades, and come up with a dance, and I can't see you doing that."

"So, Big Dawg would give me a major budget and still let me stay true to who I am as an artist, without trying to take over my project?" Young Dance asked suspiciously.

Don B. shook his head. "Man, ain't you been listening to nothing that I've been saying? I don't want to sign Young Dance as an artist, I want to bring your entire brand over to Big Dawg and put you on the map! Homie, we been playing this game long enough, and I think it's time you let me know what you wanna do." Don B. held out his hand and in his palm there were several colorful pills. "Green pill takes you back to your life and grind as unsigned hype, but the red pill erases all your troubles."

Young Dance stared at the pills for what seemed like an eternity. He weighed the world Don B. had shown him against what he would have to go back to when the night was over and the choice seemed like a clear one. Young Dance plucked a red pill from Don B.'s hand and popped it in his mouth. Don B. also popped a red pill, and they toasted with the glasses of champagne that they would use to wash the pills down. The bargain had been stuck, and Don B. had his prize.

"Any more seats left on this flight?" Pam interrupted their moment.

"But of course." Don B. extended the hand holding the pills and let Pam have her pick. Watching her pop the pill and wash it down he knew he had just killed two birds with one stone. It was good to be The Don.

Pam woke up the next morning to a splitting headache. When she tried to lift her head, needles of pain racked her skull. Cracking one eye she looked around and tried to get her bearings. From the thick curtains and large windows she deduced that she was in a hotel, but couldn't remember how she'd gotten there. The last thing she remembered was popping what she thought was ecstasy at the lounge with Don B. and Dance and everything else was like pieces of shattered glass that she couldn't quite put together.

Young Dance lay in on her shoulder, sleeping like a baby, with drool running from his mouth and down her collarbone. She vaguely remembered the two of them going at it like wild dogs at some point during the morning, but the details were sketchy. If her sore crotch was any indication of Dance's performance, he'd done his thing. Pam winced at the pressure on her bladder, letting her know she needed to pee out the liquor she had consumed throughout the night. She pushed Dance off her and went to get up but found that something was weighing her legs down. She pushed back the blanket that covered her body and realized that there was a chick sleeping with her face in Pam's crotch.

"What the fuck?" Pam tried to piece the events of the night back together. She wiggled from beneath the chick and climbed to her feet, using the blanket to cover her nudity. To her surprise, there were women strewn throughout the hotel room, nude and passed out. In the center of all the naked bodies was Don B. Seeing him sprawled out in the middle of the floor with a used condom hanging from the tip of his dick filled Pam with dread. She wasn't completely sure what had gone down, but it didn't take a rocket scientist to figure out that she had played herself.

Pam quietly pulled her dress back on and collected her shoes and purse. On her way to the hotel room door, she had an afterthought and went back. She ruffled through Don B.'s pockets, relieving him of all his cash before doing the same to Young Dance. "Fair exchange ain't no robbery," she said to no one in particular before making her exit.

PART III

YOU AIN'T NEVER HAD A FRIEND LIKE ME

THIRTY

No matter how many times Biz tried to reposition himself he couldn't seem to get comfortable. At least if he was in a holding cell he would've been able to stretch out on a bench or the floor, but he had no such luck. For the last fifteen hours he was locked in a windowless room, sitting in a hard-ass steel chair, handcuffed to a desk. The air conditioner was on high, and he was so cold that his nose seemed to run like a faucet. He was tired, hungry, and felt like he was going to piss himself, but there wasn't a soul who cared at that moment. He was fucked with a capital H and had only himself to blame for it.

All day long, King James had been on all their asses about being careful because the block was hot, but he didn't take heed. They sold drugs, which was illegal, so technically, the block was hot every day that they opened up shop. He chalked King's constant bitching up to him being stressed out over the beef with the Clarks. Biz didn't care about street politics. There was money to be made, and he was determined to make it regardless of the risks. He let his greed make him careless, and as a result, the police had caught him slipping.

Biz was lucky that he didn't have a lot of drugs on him at the time of his arrest, but with his record, they had enough on him to at least get his probation revoked, which would mean jail time, which he wasn't looking forward to but was prepared for it if it went that way. The most he could get was a one to three on the violation which wasn't too bad. The thing that had Biz unnerved was the fact that he hadn't been questioned yet. Ever since the night prior he had been alone in the little room with nothing but his imagination, and it was starting to play serious tricks on him.

The sound of a key being inserted in the lock turned Biz's attention to the door. A uniformed officer held it open for two men who were obviously detectives, no matter how unlike detectives they tried to dress. The black one was wearing jeans and a blazer over a black T-shirt. The Hispanic detective wore a sweat suit with a gold chain that had his badge dangling from the end of it. Biz recognized them as two dickhead cops who were always in his neighborhood harassing the homies. They were the scourge of the hood and known to step outside the law to get their convictions. When the uniformed officer left Biz alone in the room with the two detectives his mouth suddenly became very dry.

"What it do, homie?" Detective Alvarez greeted Biz, pulling up a chair across the table from him. Biz just nodded. "The strong, silent type, huh? That's cool, because at this point, all I really need you to do is listen." He dropped a manila folder on the table in front of Biz. "Do you know what this is?"

Biz shrugged.

"This is me fucking you with no Vaseline," Detective Alvarez smirked. "You recognize this kid?" Alvarez flipped the folder and slid a picture toward Biz. It was a snapshot of a kid with his brains blown out. Biz recognized Meek and turned his head in disgust. "From your reaction, I can tell that you do. This poor bastard got slumped on the same block you guys get money on."

"Man that ain't got nothing to do with me. Niggaz get murdered in the hood every day. I thought that was y'all mutha-fuckas' jobs to keep that from happening," Biz said sarcastically.

"Kinda hard to do when little fucks like you are running around offing each other on a nightly basis," Detective Brown spoke up. Unlike his partner, there wasn't a shred of humor in his voice.

Biz pushed the picture away. "I didn't kill that kid."

"Tell us something we don't already know, shit bird." Detective Brown picked the picture up and flicked it in Biz's face. "You ain't nothing but a two-bit hustler who wouldn't bust a grape in a fruit fight, so don't flatter yourself into think-ing we'd even suspect you for something like this, pussy."

"A'ight, well, since you know all this, why are you in here talking to me about a murder instead of booking me for the drugs you caught me with and sending me through the sys-tem?"

"You'll get your chance to play ass-tag soon enough, but how long you remain married to another man will depend on you," Detective Alvarez told him. "See, we know you're not behind this rash of killings that has broken out all over the city, but we also know that you can fill in the blanks about who is."

"Wish I could help you gentlemen, but I can't," Biz said try-ing to sound sincere.

"So that's how you wanna play it, huh?" Detective Brown

asked him.

Biz spread his empty hands. "Sorry."

Detective Brown reached across the table and grabbed Biz by the back of his neck. He slammed his head roughly against the table twice before punching him square in the chest, sending him flying back into the chair. The detective grabbed Biz by the front of his shirt and shook him violently. "You little scumbag fuck, you think people dying in the streets is a game?"

"Man, get yo' partner," Biz begged Detective Alvarez.

"What was that? You want me to go get you a soda? No problem. I'll be right back." He got up and left the room, leaving Detective Brown and Biz alone.

"Just me and you now, cupcake." Detective Brown smiled menacingly and stalked toward Biz.

"Why don't you cool the fuck out?" Biz tried to scramble away, but the chain that bound his right wrist to the table made sure he didn't get too far.

The detective grabbed Biz by his nuts and snatched him to his feet. "I'll cool out when you stop playing and tell me what I need to know."

"I keep telling you I don't know shit!" Biz's voice went up two octaves.

Detective Brown glared at Biz as if he wanted to kill him. "Okay." He released Biz and allowed him to fall back into the chair. "I see that's your story and you're sticking to it. I can respect the G-code. Let's see how much good that code does you when the judge hits your dumb ass with a football number."

Biz tried to hold his game face but couldn't help the nervous twitch in his eye. "You bluffing, duke. Y'all caught me with scraps. The most you can push for is a probation violation and maybe a li'l time on top of that."

Detective Brown laughed. It was a hearty laugh, and he slapped the table top for emphasis. "You simple bastard, you think I'm talking about drugs? Fuck them drugs. I'm trying to hang a few of these murders on you. Hell, I might even hang 'em *all* on you if we can get them to stick."

Biz felt his bowels shift. He looked at the detective to see if he was just trying to spook him, but the man's eyes said he was dead serious. "I didn't kill anybody. You said so yourself," he protested.

"I sure did," Detective Brown agreed, "but I ain't gotta prove you did it, Biz. All I gotta prove is that you had knowledge of it. If you have knowledge of a crime and do nothing to stop it or report it, that makes you coconspirator."

"Co-what?" Biz was confused.

Detective Brown shook his head at the man's ignorance. "It means that I can charge you with conspiracy and tie you into all this bullshit."

"You can't do that," Biz said nervously. For as many years as he had been on the streets hustling, he had the same Achilles heel that most young hustlers suffered from. They were unclear of the law and their rights.

"I can do whatever the fuck I want. Would you like to know why?" Detective Brown reached across the table and slapped fire out of Biz. "Because I'm the *po-lice,* and you ain't shit but a case number at the back of somebody's filing cabinet."

Biz looked at the detective with sad eyes. "You dirty, man. Stone dirty."

"Nah, I ain't dirty, but let me paint a picture of dirty for you, buddy. I can promise you that you'll get at least a dime with the violation of probation and the conspiracy charge, but I'm gonna whisper in the DA's ear and see if I can get it knocked down to five or so. Then I'm gonna get in the streets and start raising questions about how a piece of shit like you managed to get such a sweet deal. Word is already out that you got pinched with product on you, so you can bet your sweet ass that there's somebody having a conversation about whether you'll stand tall on this charge and what to do if you don't, so this will be an easy sell, Biz. You're fucked either way, and I'm offering you a way to make it consensual instead of rape." He leaned in to whisper to Biz. "You can either sing," he slid him a sheet of paper and a pencil, "or swing." He slid him the manila folder with the pictures in it. "Pick your poison."

"I can't believe you gonna do me like this over some drugs, man," Biz said in a defeated tone.

"Biz, I could care less about the drugs. I wanna stop these murders. We know there's a war going on between the Clarks and a new player on the chessboard. Now, we've got an idea of who the new player is but we just need somebody to connect the dots. All I need is a name and you can walk outta here tonight like none of this ever happened."

Biz looked back and forth between the folder and the blank sheet of paper. The more he thought about it the more he began to understand how dire his situation was. He could chuck it up and take his chances with the charges, but he figured, why gamble if he didn't have to. "King James," Biz blurted out before he could change his mind.

THIRTY-ONE

THE MOMENT KING JAMES STEPPED OUT OF the taxi in front of the projects he felt the butterflies in his stomach. It was the same queasy feeling he'd gotten when he first came home from his bid and laid eyes on the tall brown buildings for the first time after so many years. Those butterflies were stirred by joy, but these were stirred by guilt.

Standing in the walkway were Ashanti and Fatima. She was clearly upset and Ashanti consoled her as best he could. King felt a tinge of jealously watching Ashanti brush the tears from Fatima's cheeks gently. It wasn't that Ashanti was stepping on toes because King and Fatima weren't an item; it was just that he was used to her always fawning over him so to see her giving her attentions to one of his underlings bruised his ego. Ashanti nodded when he saw King approaching, but Fatima's mood only seemed to darken at the sight of him. She said something to Ashanti before walking off toward the building, leaving him standing there with a bewildered expression on his face. King knew she was still tight over the argument, but the things going on in the organization at the time were bigger than their argument. She would either get over it or get gone. He didn't have time to worry about it.

As instructed, the most trusted members of King James's crew gathered in the courtyard for the emergency meeting he had called. Their eyes lit up when they saw him, and he could see expressions of grief and anger painted on their faces. He would address them soon enough, but there was someone else he needed to speak with first. Moving up the walkway he could see Lakim standing near the entrance to the park speaking in hushed tones with Zo-Pound and Dee. All of the men's faces were solemn, but they tried to look alive when they saw King James.

"Peace to the God." Lakim embraced his friend.

"Peace Allah," King replied. He gave Alonzo dap, then turned his attention to Dee, who looked an emotional wreck. "How you?"

Dee shrugged. "I'm alive, so I can't complain too much, which is more than I can say for Meek."

"This shit is twisted." King ran his hand over his beard and sighed.

"Word-life, my nigga. I can't believe they laid Meek to rest," Lakim said. "That's a'ight, though, cuz we about to roll on them niggaz like Tonka trucks. As soon as you give the word, niggaz is dead!"

"We'll speak of retaliation later," he told Lakim. "She home, Dee?"

"Yeah, she up there, but she ain't doing too good. You sure you wanna do this now?" Dee asked.

"Stalling ain't gonna make it no easier. Might as well get

it out of the way now," King told him and walked toward the building. Lakim, Alonzo, and Dee fell in step behind him.

There was a small crowd gathered in front of the building and everyone looked sad. In the corner was a homemade mural that sat inside a cardboard box to protect it from the weather. People from the neighborhood were huddled around the mural, speaking of what had happened the night before and what would surely come of it. When they saw the quartet approach, they moved out of the way so they could pass. King stopped briefly and looked at the picture of Meek that sat among the candles in the mural. His heart always felt heavy when he lost a member of the team, but losing Meek hit him especially hard because he was so young.

"Rest easy, my nigga," King whispered to the picture before disappearing inside the building.

When King and his team got off the elevator on the third floor they were greeted by a sea of faces, some familiar and some not. King, Lakim, and Zo played the background and let Dee lead the way through the crowd to the apartment down the hall. The door was open, but Dee knocked anyway. A rough-looking dude wearing a white T-shirt and baggy jeans snatched the door open. It was an uncle of Meek's named Rodney, who had recently come home from a bid. Rodney scowled at King and the rest, but his face softened when he noticed Dee. The two men embraced each other, and Dee whispered something to him. Rodney was animatedly opposed to what Dee was proposing, but after some convincing he stepped aside and allowed Dee and his friends to enter.

Meek's mother sat behind the dining-room table, surrounded by some of her relatives. She was a known smoker in the hood, but that day she looked surprisingly sober. She was dressed only in a housecoat wearing a head scarf and a pair of furry slippers. A cigarette burned in the ashtray amid dozens of pictures that were spread out across the table. They were photos of Meek at different points in his short life. She looked up from her reminiscing and her red-rimmed eyes landed on King. She continued to glare at him until Dee came and placed a hand on her shoulder. He kissed her cheek and whispered something in her ear that made her eye twitch. After some prodding by Dee, Meek's mother got up and came to stand before King.

"Ma'am, I'm sorry for your loss," King began in a sincere tone. "Meek was like my little brother, so you don't have to worry about anything, I'm going to take care of whatever the funeral expenses are."

Instead of thanking him, Meek's mother hauled off and slapped fire out of King. "There is no amount of money that you could offer me that would compensate for what you took from me."

"Chill, sis, you bugging." Lakim stepped forward and was immediately met by Rodney. In his hand was a long black gun.

"Back the fuck up," Rodney barked, standing between Meek's mother and King's crew.

Meek's mother patted Rodney's arm, letting him know everything was okay, then moved to stand before King James. "James," she addressed him by his government name, "I've known your family since y'all was kids. Your mother was one of the sweetest people I've ever met, so I could never figure out

256

how her kids turned out so rotten. I thought when they took you off to prison it would scare you into making something of your life, but all it did was steal what little bit of good you had left in you. The worst part about it is that now you're out here corrupting other people's kids with that bullshit."

King had finally had enough of her insults. "Sis, I'm sorry for your loss . . . I truly am, but don't stand on your soapbox wagging your finger at me when you spend as much time as anyone in the streets."

His words stung, and it was clear in her eyes.

"You're right. If I had spent as much time being a mother as I have being a crackhead, then Meek might still be here. I'll wear that, *King* James, but that don't excuse you from being the reason my son is dead."

"I didn't kill Meek," he pointed out.

"You may not have shot him, but you put him on that corner. They say the worst pain in the world is a mother laying their child to rest, and I would like to thank you, King James, for letting me know just what that feels like." She broke down.

"Maybe we should go," Alonzo suggested.

"I think that would be best," Meek's mother agreed. She walked back over to the table and allowed Rodney help her back into her chair. "And Dee," she addressed the other young man, "if you ever bring him here again, then you will no longer be welcomed either, do you understand?"

Dee lowered his head. "Yes, ma'am."

"You heard her, nigga. Get the fuck out!" Rodney shouted.

King felt his fists instinctively tighten. He caught himself in time to keep from knocking all Rodney's teeth down his throat. There was a time and a place for everything, and this was neither the time nor the place. "Again, you have my condolences." He tossed a brick of money on the table and left the apartment.

King pushed open the lobby doors and welcomed the rush of warm air that washed over his face. Though he would never admit it, Meek's mother's accusations had cut him terribly deep. Every member of King's crew came into the fold of their own free will. He didn't force any of them to hustle or break the law, but he showed them how to do it and not get caught. He showed his team love by letting them get money with him, but his love was also putting them in harm's way. He would have to wear Meek's death, that went without saying, but he vowed that he wouldn't be the only one with a heavy heart that night. With this in mind he addressed his crew in the courtyard.

"Peace, peace, peace," King greeted his soldiers. "Y'all already know what it is so we gonna keep it short and to the point. Niggaz came through last night and laid the homie Meek out so now it's time to make that right. Word to me, niggaz is gonna feel it behind this one. Yo, Dee," he called the young man forward. "You sure about what you told me, as far as who the shooter was?"

"Yeah, man. I told you that I was so why you keep asking me?" Dee said with attitude.

King grabbed Dee by the shoulders and turned him around to face him. "Because I need to be one thousand percent before I make this move. Once we cross that line, we can't come back."

"He ain't bullshitting." Ashanti stepped up in Dee's defense. "It was Shai's boy Holiday. I saw him with my own eyes. I tried to tear his head off, but the bitch-ass nigga ran."

King believed Dee when he first told him, but hearing it out of Ashanti's mouth sealed the deal. An icy ball formed in his stomach as he thought about the corner he had been painted into. "That's what it is then." King nodded. "Blood will prevail where words failed. I want Holiday dead by the end of the week. Anybody else gets clipped in the process is a bonus."

"You know this will be considered an act of war, right?" Alonzo asked him.

King James looked at the young man who he had known since he was in Pampers, and his glare was as if they were meeting for the first time. "That still don't change what I said. Holiday dies. Period. I got fifty stacks for the nigga who brings me his kufi."

"I could use that bread." Lakim rubbed his hands together greedily.

"This ain't for you, God. Yo, Ashanti," King called out. Ashanti stepped up and looked King James in the eyes. King searched for traces of fear but found none. "You ready to earn ya stripes, li'l nigga?"

THIRTY-TWO

As expected, Holiday's birthday bash was something like a gangsta party. Hustlers from all over the city came out to help him celebrate his born day. The location he picked was a strip club in the Bronx called Sin City, where he was a regular. All the managers knew Holiday was a big spender and would attract more ballers, so they pretty much gave him the run of the club. There was food, drinks, and plenty of strippers to entertain Holiday and his guests.

Shai, Angelo, and Swann decided not to attend, but the rest of the team came out. Even Baby Doc, who was underage, was up in the spot making it rain on the girls. Swann and Angelo tried to get Holiday to cancel the party because of everything that was going on in the streets, but he wasn't trying to hear it. He had been planning the party for months and nothing was going to stop his fun, even an impending war. Holiday couldn't understand the thinking of Shai and his inner circle. They were the most powerful crew in the city, but at the first signs of trouble, everyone went to ground like gophers, but not Holiday.

He reasoned that everyone bled the same and any man could be killed, so long as he saw his enemies before they saw him he would always have the upper hand.

"What's up, li'l nigga? You having a good time or what?" Holiday pulled up a seat next to Baby Doc, who was sitting in front of the stage with his eyes transfixed on a girl's gyrating crotch. A half-empty bottle of Moët was clutched in his hand.

"Hell, yeah, I'm having a blast," Baby Doc said excitedly, never taking his eyes off the girl.

"See, I tried to tell Swann and them to come out, but them niggaz was fronting like they scared," Holiday said, slightly slurring his words. He was borderline drunk and trying his best to get all the way there.

"I don't think it's about being scared. I think it's more about them wanting to maintain low profiles with all this stuff going on with King James. I heard somebody killed one of their young boys the other night and them cats are screaming for blood," Baby Doc told him. He had no idea that Holiday had been the one who killed one of King James's soldiers.

Holiday laughed. "Yeah, somebody pushed their young boy's shit back pretty damn good." He recalled the look of fear in Meek's eyes before he put a bullet between them. "Man, fuck all that low-profile shit. A nigga would have to be out of his mind to get at a member of the Clark family. We're untouchable, B."

"My dad always told me that nobody is untouchable and to assume so could get you killed," Baby Doc repeated one of the lessons his father Big Doc had taught him.

"Big Doc is a wise old dude, but he still thinks this is 1988. Him, Shai, and the rest of the old heads need to step into the millennium. This is a new age we live in, and strong crews can't be maintained with outdated rules," Holiday said.

"I dunno, Holiday. Those rules were put in place for a reason. Shai says—"

"Shai says, Shai says," Holiday cut him off. "That's all Shai ever does is say. We out here in the streets getting it in while he's safe in his big house giving orders. Shai is the boss of this thing in name, but it's the niggaz who are in the streets who really run shit. Niggaz like me and you."

"Me?" Baby Doc asked curiously.

"Yes, you. Baby Doc, you still young, but you my li'l man and one of the few niggaz who I trust completely. You're the voice of reason when I be off my dumb shit."

"I never knew that, Holiday. Most times you treat me like a kid and act like you don't wanna be bothered," Baby Doc admitted.

"Nah, dawg. That's just me giving you a hard time so you'll be tough enough to handle it when it's your turn to start calling shots," Holiday told him.

"I can't see myself calling no shots. My dad says he wants me to finish school and live a normal life."

"That's what he says, but if he really meant it, why would he have you around us so much?" Holiday asked. "Big Doc ain't gonna come out and tell you to take it to the streets. He wants you to be man enough to choose your own destiny."

"You think so?" Baby Doc weighed Holiday's words.

"I know so. This life is in your blood, and when it's your turn to step up, there's no doubt in my mind that you're gonna be a solid capo, maybe even more solid than Swann."

"That means a lot coming from you, Holiday." Baby Doc

blushed. He looked up to Holiday, so hearing him sing his praises filled his heart with pride.

"I'm only keeping it one hundred with you, my G." Holiday took a long swig from the bottle and handed it to Baby Doc. Baby Doc took an awkward swing, spilling some of the champagne on his shirt. "Don't hurt yourself, li'l fella," Holiday teased him.

"That shit is like juice, you know. Yak is my thing," Baby Doc boasted.

Holiday laughed. "Li'l nigga, the last time we gave you some yak you threw up all in the back of Swann's truck."

Baby Doc laughed too. "I remember. He was mad as hell!"

The stripper who Baby Doc had been watching strutted over to the end of the stage he was sitting at. She was a pretty light-skinned chick with nice boobs but not much ass to speak of. She leaned over and shook her breasts in Baby Doc's face while he peeled off singles and timidly shoved them into her bikini top.

"You like her, do ya?" Holiday asked Baby Doc of the girl.

"Yeah, shorty bad than a muthafucka," Baby Doc replied.

Holiday stood up and waved the girl over to him. When she bent down he whispered something in her ear and handed her a stack of singles. The girl looked over at Baby Doc, smiled, and nodded. The next thing Baby Doc knew, the girl had climbed off the stage and was pulling him by the hand from his seat.

"What's going on?" Baby Doc looked back and forth from the girl to Holiday nervously.

"Don't ask obvious questions, youngster. Just go with her. She's gonna take care of you. And don't worry, it's on me," Holiday told him. He smiled as the girl led Baby Doc to a dark corner of the club to give the young man a cheap thrill. Holiday had the waitress bring him another bottle of champagne while he enjoyed the stage show. Halfway through the bottle, he found himself drunk and in dire need to relieve himself. Telling one of the homies to watch his bottle, he got up and went to the bathroom. On his way, he never noticed the two sets of eyes watching him from two different sides of the club.

Animal sat nursing a drink and acting like he was enjoying himself. He was wearing a fitted cap, pulled down tightly over his long hair and dark sunglasses. He had little to fear of being recognized because everyone in the joint was more focused on ass and titties instead of faces. The table he chose to sit at was in the corner of the spot, furthest from the bar. It had the worst view of the stage, but the best view of everything else.

He'd made it a point to arrive early that night, before the Saturday rush, and lay on his mark. Finding the perfect spot to see him slipping proved to be simpler than he would've ever expected. Holiday made sure that the whole world knew about his party, even going as far as running a radio promo for it. Hearing the young boy's voice was like nails on a chalkboard, but seeing his face before Animal put his lights out would be like the sweetest nectar. There were many men marked for death on Animal's mental checklist, but Holiday was at the top of it.

When he first saw Holiday enter the club, it made his pulse quicken. He watched disgustedly as the young thug diddy-bopped through the club, shaking hands and pinching the asses of the strippers like he owned the place. When Diamonds had given him the rundown on the man who was supposed to have shot Gucci, Animal had expected a bit more. Holiday definitely had the demeanor of a dangerous man, but he had yet to reach the stage where he could be called "killer." Animal was unimpressed and felt disrespected that such a nobody in the grand scheme of things had the audacity to touch something he held so dear. It took everything he had not to run up on Holiday and blow his brains out for all to see.

Animal just played the cut watching Holiday for the first hour. He was looking for Shai or one of his capos to show, but as the night wore on, he figured they'd decided to sit the party out. He wasn't sure why they'd decided not to attend Holiday's event, but when they saw how filthy he was going to do Holiday, they would mark it as one of the best decisions they'd ever made. He watched Holiday amble over to the stage and sit next to a young man who was clearly too young to be in a strip club but no one seemed to notice or care. The young man seemed to hang on Holiday's every word as if what he was saying was the gospel. After a few minutes, the young man departed with one of the strippers, and Holiday got up and headed to the bathroom.

"This one is for you, Gucci." Animal slid from his table and headed for the bathroom.

Ashanti played the end of the bar, tossing back shots of Patrón and sipping a Corona. He tried to keep his mind on business, but it was hard with all the grade-A flesh floating back and forth. Ashanti had been to Sin City before, but for some reason, that night, it seemed especially packed and had twice as many girls.

As if the whore gods had plucked the thought from his

mind, a short, brown-skinned chick with an ass shaped like a planet invaded his space. "What's good, big time? You want a dance?"

"Gangstas don't dance, ma." Ashanti tried to brush her off, but she was persistent.

"For twenty bucks, I can show you some shit you ain't never seen," she promised him.

Ashanti twisted his lips in disbelief. "If you say so."

"I *know* so." She threw one leg across his lap and plucked his beer from his hand. She took a sip to wet her whistle before wrapping her lips around the bottle and slowly pushing the entire neck of it to the back of her throat. Just as easily as she slipped it in, she slipped it out and handed the bottle back to Ashanti. Then she reached down and began tugging at his dick through his jeans, getting it rock-hard. "You sure you don't wanna spend the twenty with me?"

Ashanti thought on it for a split second. "Fuck it, I got a dub to blow. Where we at?"

The girl led Ashanti to a chair near the railing that overlooked the lower level, where the stage and single tables were. She shoved him down roughly in the chair and mounted him like a jockey who was about to race for it all. "All this for me?" she ran her hand down his waist and over his crotch.

Ashanti removed the gun he'd been concealing and tucked it in the cushion of the chair he was sitting in. "Not all of it, baby."

She placed his hands on her ass and began to rock back and forth on his lap. The warmth of her snatch grinding on his manhood superheated it and increased the already intense throbbing in his muscle. She pulled one of her breasts from her bikini top and shoved it in Ashanti's face. The girl's body smelled like sweat and cheap perfume, but Ashanti had smelled worse and still dove in.

He was so caught up in his lust for the girl that he didn't even notice Holiday walk into the club until he was standing a few feet away from him. If it had gone down that moment, Ashanti would've been shot, because it was damn near impossible for him to draw his gun fast enough to defend himself with the girl on his lap. Luckily for him, the big booty chick was as much a gift as she was a curse, because Holiday couldn't see Ashanti sitting under her. Ashanti placed his gun where he could get to it if he needed to and watched Holiday discreetly while the girl continued to dance on his lap.

He had expected Holiday to come out crew deep, but it was just him and a few of his goons. There weren't many of them, but they still outnumbered Ashanti, so getting to Holiday would be tricky. Ashanti felt something wet spill down the front of his pants causing him to jump and turn angrily on the girl. She was pouring water down the front of herself trying to be enticing but wetting Ashanti's clothes in the process. Ashanti started to bark on her, but the spilling water gave him a brilliant idea. He knew he wouldn't be able to get a clean shot at Holiday in such closed quarters so he figured he would draw him out.

THIRTY-THREE

HOLIDAY'S HEAD WAS SPINNING WHEN HE STAGGERED into the bathroom. He hadn't realized how drunk he was until he stood up and tried to walk. He had barely made it into the bathroom when he felt the telltale moisture build up in his mouth and knew he was going to be sick. Holiday kicked in one of the stall doors and threw up the turkey sandwich he'd eaten on the way to the strip club.

Taking a momentary pause before the next round of vomiting, he heard the bathroom door open. A kid wearing a fitted hat and sunglasses walked in. He glanced at Holiday and quickly turned away and went to the urinal. Holiday laughed to himself thinking how the dude looked like a girl with his long hair spilling from beneath his fitted cap. "Homo thug," he mumbled drunkenly before throwing up again. Once he'd gotten it all out his attention went back to his overflowing bladder. He'd made a mess of the stall so he went to the urinal to pee. As he was pissing, he looked up to find that the kid with the long hair was looking over at him. When he noticed Holiday look up, he quickly turned away. Holiday's lips drew back into a sneer as he zipped his pants and went to confront the kid.

"What are you, some type of fag or some shit?" Holiday barked.

"What you talking about, homie?" Animal turned to face him.

"You think I didn't see you looking at my dick?" Holiday shoved him.

"Oh, that? Nah, I ain't no fag, man. It's just that I ain't never seen a bitch with a dick," Animal laughed mockingly.

"Fuck you say to me?" Holiday retorted with his fist balled and ready to box, but Animal had other plans.

"I said you're a bitch." Animal drew one of his Pretty Bitches and pointed it at Holiday's face.

"Be easy, fam." Holiday raised his hands and began to back up slowly.

"I ain't your fam, I'm your judge. You should've never touched what belonged to me, Holiday," Animal hissed.

"Dawg, I don't even know what you're talking about. I ain't never seen you a day in my life," Holiday tried to explain.

"No, we ain't never met, but I'm sure you've heard of me." Animal took the fitted cap off and shook out his wild hair. "They call me Animal."

Hearing that name stole whatever was left of Holiday's buzz, and he was now as sober as a pastor on Sunday morning. "My G, if this is about Tech, I want you to know that my hands are clean of that man's blood. I never agreed with Swann killing him and—"

Animal grabbed Holiday by the front of his shirt and brought the gun down across the bridge of his nose, breaking it. Blood flew all over Animal as well as the white tiled floors. "If you're dumb enough to think that I don't know who killed my homie, then it's a wonder you ain't been murdered before tonight. Me and Swann will dance soon enough, but tonight, it for us, baby."

"Animal, I don't know what you think I did to you, but you got it all wrong. I ain't did shit," Holiday tried to explain.

Animal slapped him in the face with the gun again. This time, Holiday's lip opened up. "More lies spilled from the lips of a snake. Since your memory's so short, let me refresh it for you. Awhile back, you and your boys ran up in a spot uptown and turned it into the Old West, and my lady got hit by a stray bullet . . . *your* bullet, Holiday."

Holiday's mind raced back. He remembered the shoot-out with King James and his crew. It was the same night he took the bullet to the leg that put him on a cane. The same night he had accidentally shot the girl in the green dress. He dipped his head. "Fam, on everything I love, I didn't shoot that girl on purpose. We were at war, and she was an unfortunate casualty," he said sincerely.

"And so shall you be, at least that's how the newspapers will write it up," Animal told him.

"So you gonna shoot me because I accidentally shot your lady?"

"No." Animal put the gun away and pulled out a meat cleaver. "I'm gonna cut you first." He stalked toward Holiday with the hatchet.

Suddenly the sounds of the fire alarm filled the club. Outside, they could hear people screaming and glass breaking. Something or someone had sent the club into a panic. Animal needed to finish Holiday off quickly and get out of there. He grabbed Holiday by the neck and pressed him against the wall with the cleaver raised. Before he could execute him, the door to the bathroom swung open and a young man rushed in.

"Yo, Holiday, we gotta dip. Somebody pulled the fire alarm or some shit and they're—" Baby Doc began, but his words got stuck in his throat when he saw Holiday hemmed up in the corner. "What the fuck?" Baby Doc blurted out and reached for his gun.

Holiday used the distraction to make a last-ditch attempt to save his skin. He kneed Animal in the stomach, doubling him over and forcing him to lose his grip. Holiday jerked free of his grasp and tried to bolt for the door on his injured leg. Animal swung the cleaver for Holiday's head, but missed and ended up slashing him across the back. Holiday stumbled but kept moving for the door, leaving Baby Doc still standing there fumbling with his gun.

By the time Baby Doc managed to chamber a round, Animal was already on him. He brought the back of the cleaver down across Baby Doc's wrist, causing him to drop the gun into the sink. Animal socked Baby Doc in the jaw twice, dazing him, and tossed him headfirst into the bathroom mirror. Animal then grabbed him from behind in a chokehold and placed his gun to the side of Baby Doc's head. His finger caressed the trigger, but when he looked up and saw his reflection in the mirror, he abruptly stopped. His face was stained with blood, and there was a feral look in his eyes. The boy he held in his arm had gone rigid with fear and tears fell silently down his face.

"Please, man," Baby Doc croaked.

Animal pressed Baby Doc against the mirror and leveled the gun with his face. "Nothing in life is without consequences," he told him before pulling the trigger.

Baby Doc's eyes snapped close as he prepared for the end. He knew he was screaming because he could feel his vocal cords vibrating but couldn't hear anything but the intense ringing in his ear from the gun being fired. The fact that he was even able to hear that meant that he was alive. Slowly, Baby Doc opened his eyes, expecting to see the killer, but he was alone. He kissed the ground and thanked God for his life. It was at that moment that he understood that Big Doc was right and Holiday was wrong.

Ashanti hit the fire alarm and watched in amusement as all hell broke loose. Hearing the loud sirens immediately sent the club into a panic without anyone actually bothering to check to see if and where the fire had actually broken out. The bouncers tried to get people to leave in an orderly fashion, but they couldn't do much with the mob that was rushing the front door to avoid being burned up.

Ashanti watched the goons that had come in with Holiday leave the spot, but there were no signs of the birthday boy. A few minutes later, he spotted Holiday coming from the bathroom area. He was making hurried steps like he had the devil on his heels. He expected Holiday to exit through the front with the rest, but he made for a door in the back of the club. Ashanti knew the door led to a deserted block in back of the club, which was perfect. He made a mad dash for the front door. If he hurried, he could be there to greet Holiday when he came out.

Less than a minute after Ashanti had left to cut Holiday off, Animal came out of the bathroom holding a smoking gun and a bloodied hatchet.

Animal wanted to, he knew that he should have, but he couldn't bring himself to kill the little boy. Contrary to what people thought of him, he was a killer, but he was no monster. He had spared the boy's life, but Holiday would get no such mercy.

He stepped out of the bathroom into pure pandemonium. A wave of panicked drunks and half-naked women rushed the front door trying to make a speedy exit. Animal scanned the faces and noticed Holiday wasn't among them. He had almost thought that he lost him until he noticed a trail of blood on the ground, leading in the other direction. He looked up just in time to see Holiday escaping through one of the doors in the back.

"You won't escape me that easily," Animal said and headed after him.

Holiday came crashing through the back door so quickly that he lost his balance and fell, skinning his hands and knees on the cold concrete. Ignoring the pain in his back, he got to his feet and kept moving. He had been having some rotten luck lately, but managing to run afoul of someone as notorious as Animal topped everything else. Animal was dead, at least that's what the streets said, but the wound across Holiday's back said different. He needed to get word of Animal's resurrection to Shai ASAP. Holiday felt like shit for leaving Baby Doc back there, but he reasoned that Animal had come for him specifically, so he wouldn't kill Baby Doc . . . or so he hoped. Holiday needed to get back around to the front of the club and alert his team of the danger. Once they had regrouped, they could roll in force to take on Animal.

Behind him, Holiday heard the door he'd just come through swing open again. He knew that he shouldn't have, but he glanced over his shoulder, afraid of what he might see. Sure enough, Animal was on his tail. Thankfully, the back street was dark, so Animal didn't see him right away, but that all changed when Holiday kicked over a bottle and drew Animal right to him. He had Animal by at least a block so there might've still been hope for him. All he had to do was make it around the corner to where there were people. Animal wouldn't dare kill him in front of witnesses. Holiday almost made it to the corner when his luck went from bad to worse.

"What up, Blood?" Ashanti stepped out of the darkness and opened fire.

Animal burst from the emergency exit with the scent of blood in his nose and murder in his heart. He looked up and down the dark block but didn't see Holiday. He thought he had lost Holiday somewhere in the corridor leading to the fire exit and was about to double back when he heard glass breaking. He looked toward the end of the block and saw Holiday trying to escape.

"Don't rush off just yet; we were just getting to know each other." Animal jogged after him. He had almost closed the distance when he saw someone step out from the shadows. It was too dark for him to see who it was, but he could make out the shape of a gun in his hand. He saw the man say something to Holiday before letting off a shot in Animal's direction. That answered the question as to which side he was on. Drawing his two Pretty Bitches, Animal brought the thunder.

Ashanti cursed as Holiday went down, not because of his bullet but because of the trash he had slipped on that helped him to avoid it. He was about to try for another shot when a bullet ricocheted off the fence a few inches from his face. Ashanti peered down the block and saw a man rushing toward him, blazing two guns.

Ashanti dove out of the way and landed on the ground behind a car and a few inches away from where Holiday lay. "I see you brought some friends to the party," he said to Holiday. "Don't matter, though. After I take care of captain save-a-ho, I'm gonna smoke your ass." He shot Holiday in his good leg. "Try not to rush off while I'm taking care of this." Ashanti disappeared around the other side of the car.

Staying as low as he could, he crept alongside of the car trying to get the drop on his opponent. He peered through the window of the car he was hiding beside and didn't see anything, but he knew the man was out there; he could feel him stalking him. Ashanti heard a crunch of gravel, which gave him an idea where the man was so he popped up and fired at the sound. Six cars down a windshield shattered and drove the man from his hiding place. Ashanti tried to gun the man down while he was exposed, but just as quickly as he appeared, he disappeared. He was fast, almost too fast. Ashanti moved to get into better position and immediately found himself dodging bullets. He scurried under a car on the opposite side of the street and came up blasting from the other side of it.

They went on like this for almost five minutes, exchanging fire but neither man hitting his target. Ashanti was getting low on bullets and frustrated. He knew if he kept it up at that rate he'd be in jail when the police finally showed up—if he didn't get blasted first. He needed to end it now and get ghost. The man on the other side of the street must've been thinking the same thing because they both popped out of their hiding places at the same time, guns drawn. There was a tense silence as the two killers sized each other up from opposite sides of the street. They gave each other a respectful nod before the shooting started again.

Ashanti and the man leapfrogged between cars, exchanging fire and closing the distance until a single car was the only thing that separated them. Ashanti sat with his back against the car and his gun clutched to his chest. On the other side of the car he could hear the man's labored breathing. He had to respect the man's skill because most wouldn't have lasted that long against him, but respect aside, they both knew that there was only one way to end this. They came up at the same time, aimed, and pulled the trigger—but all three guns clicked empty.

Before Ashanti could figure out his next move, the man leaped over the car and was on him. He and Ashanti both went spilling to the ground in a mess of flailing fists and feet. Ashanti was a good brawler, but the man was heavier than he and had him at a disadvantage. He wrestled Ashanti to the ground and climbed on top of him, pinning his arms at his side with his knees. Ashanti saw the man produce a hatchet from somewhere and raise it to finish him off. He thought of all the things that he had done and all the things he would never do. He thought of Fatima and how she would take him dying on her before they really got a chance to know each other.

The cleaver made a whistling sound as it cut through the air en route to Ashanti's neck. Rays from the lone streetlight on the block kissed off the blade and for the first time Ashanti saw the face of his attacker. "Animal?" he blurted out in shock, just before the cleaver made contact.

Animal knelt on the cold ground, resting on his knuckles and breathing like he had just run a marathon. His adrenaline had him so pumped that his head hurt and felt like he would pass out if he tried to stand up too quickly. Next to him on the ground was the bent hatchet. At the last minute, he had been able to redirect his strike and hit the ground instead of the soft flesh of Ashanti's neck. Even now, Ashanti sat against a car a few feet away from Animal with the look of a terrified child on his face. He knew better than anyone how close he had come to meeting his Maker.

"You could've killed me," Ashanti said, breaking the silence.

"I was trying to." Animal stood up. He walked over and extended his hand to Ashanti to help him up. Ashanti was hesitant at first, but he allowed Animal to lift him. The two just stood there for what felt like a lifetime, staring and trying to figure out what to say.

Without warning, Ashanti hugged Animal. "Tell me it's really you. Tell me this ain't some fucked-up dream and that my best friend is really alive and standing here with me," he rambled.

"Yeah, little one. It's really me." Animal returned Ashanti's hug.

Suddenly, Ashanti pushed Animal away and took a defensive boxing stance. "Good, because I owe you an ass whipping.

How the fuck could you just disappear like that and let everybody write you off for dead?"

"It's a long story, Ashanti, one that we ain't got time to go over right now. Police will be here any minute, and I got some unfinished business to wrap up. Where's Holiday?"

"Probably still lying on the sidewalk bleeding where I left him." He pointed to the spot where Holiday had been, and the only thing left was a bloody smear leading around the corner. "Where the fuck did he go?"

"Escaped . . . again," Animal said in a defeated tone.

"With one bum leg and the other one shot to hell, I doubt he got very far. If we hurry we can catch him." Ashanti started for the corner. He had made it a few feet before he realized that Animal wasn't following him. "C'mon, my nigga. Let's go finish this fag."

"He's gone, li'l one. The only thing we're gonna get if we go around there after him is locked up. Holiday will keep for another day," Animal told him.

"That's the second time in less than a week that slimy muthafucka has slipped through my fingers. The next time I see him, that's on the hood, I'm gonna body him," Ashanti declared.

"Nah, that life is spoken for," Animal patted his Pretty Bitches. "When his blood runs, it'll be me who turns on the faucet. I owe him for what he did to Gucci."

"Say no more, big homie," Ashanti conceded. "Now that we've got that out of the way, let's deal with the elephant in the room; where the fuck you been?"

Before Animal could answer, his cell phone vibrated in his pocket. Only one person had that number so he didn't have to look at the caller ID to see who it was. "What up?" Animal's face immediately turned as white as a ghost as he listened to the caller chatter away. "Say no more, I'll be right there." He ended the call. Without saying anything he turned and started walking up the street to where he had stashed his rental car.

"Where you going?" Ashanti went after him. He caught up with Animal just as he was getting in the rental car. "I got a million and one questions that I need answered, and I ain't gonna give you the chance to vanish again before you do."

Animal sighed. "Since it's obvious that you're not going to let this go, get in and I'll tell you on the way."

Ashanti hopped in the passenger seat. "Where we going?"

"To the hospital," Animal told him and fired the engine.

THIRTY-FOUR

ANIMAL SCREECHED TO A HALT IN FRONT of Harlem Hospital and illegally parked the car in a bus lane. He was sure to have a ticket waiting for him when he came out, but the threat of one hundred tickets couldn't keep him from this moment. He had wasted enough time already.

He hopped out of the car with Ashanti on his heels, still firing questions about his disappearance. Animal had already given him the short version of what had happened, but Ashanti wanted him to fill in the blanks. They passed through the lobby, and the security guard who Ashanti had beefed with before was on duty again. He stood up like he wanted to say something, but the look on Animal's face told him to hold his tongue. Ashanti gave him a mocking smirk as he followed Animal into the elevator.

The elevator seemed to be moving at a snail's pace getting them to their desired floor. Animal was visibly nervous, and he kept rubbing his sweaty hands on his pants. Ashanti was saying something to him, but Animal's mind was a million miles away.

Before the elevator doors could fully open, Animal squeezed through them. Ashanti opened his mouth to give him directions, but Animal knew the way by heart. At the end of the hall he spotted Ms. Ronnie and Tionna standing outside Gucci's hospital room door. Ms. Ronnie seemed upset, and Tionna was rubbing her back trying to console her. Dread filled his heart as he feared he might be too late . . . again.

When Tionna spotted Animal and Ashanti coming down the hallway, she told Ms. Ronnie she'd be right back and walked to meet them. Tionna's hair was a hot mess, and she looked like she hadn't slept in days. He stopped short, waiting for her to say something . . . He *needed* her to say something. When Animal saw the tears in her eyes he feared the worst. He felt his eyes moisten and prepared for the devastating blow that he knew was coming. To his surprise and relief, Tionna threw her arms around him and squealed joyfully.

"She's awake," she whispered in his ear.

The two words were the sweetest Animal had ever heard. Unable to contain his elation, he scooped Tionna in his arms and spun her around and around, laughing like he had just won the lotto and crying tears of joy. When Ashanti found out the good news, he joined them, and the three of them danced and shouted through the hospital hallway. They were making so much of a racket that they drew the attention of several nurses as well as the attending physician who had been in Gucci's room.

"Would somebody please tell me what all the noise is out here?" Doctor O'Hara stormed into the hallway. She was a fiery redhead who appeared to be in her early forties with pale green eyes and freckles on her cheeks.

"Sorry, Dr. O'Hara. Everybody is just a little excited about the good news." Ms. Ronnie apologized and cut her eyes at Tionna and the others.

"I'm all for a little excitement, but this is still a hospital, so please respect the other people being treated here or I'm going to have to ask you all to leave. Are we clear?" Dr. O'Hara looked at the hugging trio.

"Yes," all three of them answered at once.

"Good," the doctor said frowning. She turned to Ms. Ronnie and gave her a playful wink, letting her know that she wasn't as mad as she pretended to be. "Now, back to the patient."

"Yes, yes, how is she?" Ms. Ronnie asked excitedly. Without being invited, Animal, Tionna, and Ashanti huddled around to hear the update.

Dr. O'Hara paused, but Ms. Ronnie nodded that it was okay to speak in front of them. "As we were saying earlier, the worst is over, and Gucci is officially out of the woods. The worst of her physical wounds healed while she was in the coma, and the graft we did on her stomach from the original gunshot seems to be taking."

"Will it leave a scar?" Tionna asked, drawing a funny look from the doctor.

"More than likely, but I think a little scar is a small price to pay for her life, don't you?" Dr. O'Hara asked sarcastically. Without waiting for Tionna to answer she went back to addressing Ms. Ronnie. "All the tests we ran after her stroke came back positive, so there are no signs of long-term neurological damage, but she's going to need a few weeks of therapy to get her motor skills readjusted. Once we get her rolling with that, we'll be able to better judge how close to her old self she'll get back to, but I think she'll be okay."

"Praise the Lord," Ms. Ronnie cupped Dr. O'Hara's hand in hers. "Thank you so much for bringing my baby back to me."

"Don't thank me, thank your daughter. I can admit now that it didn't look good in the beginning, but that little girl fought like hell for her life every step of the way. She refused to let go."

"I guess God felt like there was still work here for Gucci to do." Ms. Ronnie looked over at Animal who was wiping his eyes with the backs of his hands.

Dr. O'Hara glanced at Animal, then turned back to Ms. Ronnie and smiled. "That sounds like an accurate prognosis. There is nothing in this life stronger than the human will. Ms. Ronnie, you can go in and sit with your daughter for a few minutes, but you can't stay long. She needs to rest."

"Thank you," Ms. Ronnie told her and went into the room.

"Can I see her?" Animal asked the doctor.

Dr. O'Hara was about to give him the speech about only allowing immediate family into the room, but she took one look at the pleading in his eyes and couldn't bring herself to do it to him. She knew a bleeding heart when she saw one. "Listen, I'll give you five minutes. The nurses will be coming in soon to give Gucci her medication, and if they catch all you guys in her room, I have no idea how you got in, understand?"

Animal nodded. "Fair enough." He started toward the room, but the doctor's voice stopped him short.

"Second chances are hard to come by and should be appreciated. I'm sure you and the rest of Gucci's family will see that she makes the best out of the second chance she's been given, right?"

Animal flashed his gold and diamond smile. "That bet is sure money all day, Doc."

Animal stepped into the room as quietly as he could for fear of disturbing Gucci, but found her having a conversation with her mother, who was at her bedside brushing her hair. He stood around the bend of the room to watch Gucci for a few moments before he would make himself known. Ms. Ronnie said something to Gucci while putting her hair in a ponytail, which made her smile. It was the first time Animal had seen Gucci smile in years, and the sight of it choked him up. For so many years he had to get by from day to day on just the memory of her smile, but here he was seeing it live and in the flesh. It was a moment that he never thought would come, and now that it was at hand, he wasn't sure what to do with it.

Gucci noticed her mother staring at something just beyond her line of vision. "Who is it, Mama?" she asked in a groggy voice.

"Maybe it's best he tell you himself." Ms. Ronnie motioned for Animal to approach.

Slowly, Animal stepped from his hiding place. The overhead light stung Gucci's eyes, making it hard for her to see at first. The closer Animal got, the more of his features she was able to make out. The flowing hair, the smooth dark skin, they stirred memories deep within Gucci's still-clouded mind. When she saw the glint of gold and diamonds behind his bowed lips, she broke down into tears.

"What's the matter, baby?" Ms. Ronnie asked.

"They lied to me," Gucci sobbed. "The doctors told me that I would be okay, but they lied."

"They didn't lie to you, Gucci. You're gonna make a full recovery," Ms. Ronnie assured her.

Gucci looked up at Animal who was now standing directly

over her. "That can't be true, Mama. I'm dying. If I wasn't dying, then I wouldn't be able to see no ghosts."

Animal took Gucci's hand in his and placed it on the side of his face. Her hand was dry and coarse against his skin, but in his mind, it felt like the softest silk. "No, I'm not ghost."

Gucci shook her head from side to side in disbelief as the tears flowed feely down her face. She had craved his touch for so long that it didn't feel real; it couldn't be. It had been years since they had last seen each other, but Gucci would know her soul mate anywhere. "It can't be." She placed her hand over her mouth to try to stop from hyperventilating.

"But it is." Animal kissed her fingertips.

"You know, if I wasn't so doped up to lift my arms, I'd take your life for running out on me like that," Gucci said half-jokingly.

"And my life would be yours for the taking if it would ease the pain I inflicted on your heart, Gucci. If I could've done it differently . . ."

"You didn't, so no need to dwell on what-ifs when there are so many what-nows," she said weakly. You could see the fatigue riding her, but she wouldn't give in to it until she had fully spoken her piece. "They all told me you died, but I never believed them. I knew there was no way you could've passed from this life without my heart telling me so. We might not have been married, but we exchanged vows, remember?"

"Yes, I remember. In this life or the next, we will always be together," he assured her.

"So have you come to throw yourself at my mercy and beg forgiveness for breaking your promise, Tayshawn?"

Animal said, "You're my rib and know me better than my

closest comrades, so I know that you know my name and *mercy* don't belong in the same sentence. What I will offer you are my apologies and my word that I will never leave your side again."

Gucci closed her eyes and turned her face from him. "There was a time when those pretty words of yours would've been taken as the gospel, but after all that's happened . . . I dunno. My head is all screwed up right now."

Animal turned her to face him and planted a gentle kiss on her lips. "Then don't think with your head; think with your heart. I'm not asking you to forgive me, Gucci. All I want is a chance to right some of the wrongs I've done."

"But what if—"

Animal placed a finger over her lips. "No more *what-ifs*, remember? All we need to focus on is what will be. We've been given a second chance at love, so let's run with it."

Gucci's face suddenly took on a worried expression. "Speaking of running, the last time I checked you were a fugitive before you died. Won't your sudden resurrection put you back on the most wanted list?"

"Probably," Animal admitted sadly.

"I won't lose you again, Animal, I won't! Look, I've still got the money you left me. We can leave here together, just you and me, and we don't have to ever come back."

"Sounds like a plan to me, but not now. You've got to get better, and I've got some unfinished business in the city."

"What unfinished business? I thought you came back here for me." Gucci was confused. Animal didn't answer; he simply looked down at the bandage covering her stomach. It was then that it all made sense. "You mean to kill the man who shot me, don't you?"

He didn't respond; he just looked at the floor.

"No, Animal. Let it go. Revenge tore us apart once, and my heart couldn't take losing you again. Please, let's just run away together and put all this madness behind us," she pleaded.

"Sweet baby, I would like nothing more than to vanish and spend the rest of my life with you in some remote place, but it isn't that simple. Even if I wanted to, I've come too far to turn back now. I have to finish the game," he said with a heavy heart.

Ashanti stuck his head in the hospital room. "Big homie, one-time on their way down the hall. We gotta dip."

"They're probably coming back to question Gucci about the shooting again," Tionna said.

"Don't matter why they're coming, me being here ain't a good look. Gucci, I gotta go, but I promise I'll be back to check on you," Animal told her.

Gucci grabbed Animal by the sleeve and held on for dear life. "I won't let you go. Mama, please make him stay."

"Gucci, he's gotta go. It's for the best." Ms. Ronnie pried her daughter's trembling hand loose.

Animal kissed her on the forehead. "I'll be back, baby," he promised and headed for the door. Gucci shrieked and pleaded for him to stay until she was exhausted. Even when Animal was away from the room and had slipped out of the hospital her cries still echoed in his head.

Animal walked from the hospital to his rental car in a daze. There was an orange ticket on the windshield, but he hardly seemed to notice. He braced himself against the car and breathed in and out as if he was on the verge of an asthma attack. Leaving Gucci in such an emotional state was one of the hardest things that he had to do, but it was a necessary evil. There was no way they could be together until he had finished what he had come to do, which was murder his enemies.

"So what now, big homie?" Ashanti asked. Animal had almost forgotten that he was with him.

"I finish what I started," Animal told him.

Ashanti was taken aback. "Dawg, Gucci is good now. You ain't gotta chase this suicide mission no more. Take your lady and bounce, my G. Ain't nobody gonna hold that against you."

Animal turned to his friend. "By now, Shai Clark knows that not only am I alive, but it's been me who has been whacking his people. You really think they're gonna let me just ride off into the sunset like that? I gotta ride this train to the end, li'l one."

Ashanti lowered his head. For as long as he'd known Animal, he had always been at war with something or someone, more often than not, himself. The only time he'd ever truly seen him at peace was when he was with Gucci. Now that they had been reunited once again, the ghosts of war threatened to tear them apart. There was no way that Ashanti could sit idle and watch it happen for a second time. "Then move over, because I'm riding with you."

Animal looked at Ashanti. It was a noble gesture, but a pointless one. "You know where this train is likely headed, and there's a good chance neither one of us will ever make it off."

"Let's worry about that when it arrives at the last stop. Animal, since I was a kid, I've seen you stand with others in the best and worst situations. It's time somebody stood with you. We ride together," Ashanti extended his fist.

"We die together." Animal pounded his fist. "All we're missing is Brasco, and this unholy union would be complete."

"Well, Brasco might not be here with us to ride off into hell, but I got a cat who is just as solid," Ashanti said with a knowing smirk.

THIRTY-FIVE

THE LAST FEW DAYS HAD BEEN TENSE for everybody, especially Alonzo. King James had declared war and dragged all of them into it by default. Alonzo didn't want any part of war; he just wanted to keep getting his little paper on the streets until a solid job came through, but he wasn't left with much of a choice. Lakim had pledged himself to King James and the war effort, and he had to stand by his brother, no matter how much of a bad idea he thought it was.

Another thing weighing heavy on his mind was his friend Ashanti. Ever since the failed attempt on Holiday's life, he had been acting strange. There was no doubt that he would war with them when called upon. Some would even say he looked forward to it, but the dynamics of his and Alonzo's relationship had changed slightly. If he wasn't out with Fatima, he was disappearing unexpectedly and could never account for his whereabouts. Since they had been friends, he and Ashanti had been joined at the hip, but lately, he could hardly catch up with him. Alonzo would never question Ashanti's loyalty, but there was something off about him that he couldn't put his finger on, and he intended to confront him about it the next time they were alone.

With all the madness going on in Alonzo's life he was in desperate need of some downtime and some normalcy. He thought about catching a movie, but seeing a movie alone was no fun so he called an old friend to see if she wanted to keep him company. As soon as he dialed the number he regretted it. He really wanted to see Porsha again, but didn't want to seem too thirsty. And what if she was still playing games and shot him down once he put himself out there? He started to hang up and forget the whole idea, but before he could, she picked up.

"Hello?" Porsha's voice came through the phone. Alonzo found himself at a loss for words. "Hello? Look, whoever this is, you need to stop playing on my phone, asshole!"

"Wait, don't hang up," Alonzo finally blurted out.

"Zo, is that you?" Porsha's tone lightened. "Now *this* is a pleasant surprise."

"Hey, how you, Porsha?"

"Good, just a little shocked to hear from you," she told him.

"You said use the number, so I did."

"True, but I didn't think it would take you days to get around to it. I was starting to think I was wrong in giving it to you."

"You know you don't mean that. You were probably sitting by the phone waiting for me to hit you up," he joked.

"Don't flatter yourself, youngster. Anyway, to what do I owe the pleasure of this call?"

"Nothing much. I was thinking about you and decided to hit you up to see what was good. You feel like coming to Harlem to hang out with me? I was thinking that maybe we could catch a movie and grab a bite to eat."

"Aww that's sweet, but I can't."

Alonzo felt the wind leave his sails. "It's all good, Porsha. Can't knock a nigga for trying. I guess I'll holla at you later."

"Well, damn, don't be so quick to give up on a girl." Porsha shook her head in disappointment as if he could see her through the phone. "The reason I can't come uptown to hang out is because I promised Frankie that I would come kick it with her in Brooklyn. See? And you were all ready to hang up on me because you thought I was spinning you."

"No, I wasn't," Alonzo lied.

"Whatever, Zo. You know I know that your ass is as sensitive as hell."

"Fuck you, Porsha," he said jokingly.

"If you play your cards right, you never know," she said slyly. "But if you aren't doing anything, why don't you come out to BK and hang with us. There's a big-ass block party in Frankie's hood. Free food and free liquor. You can't beat that."

"I dunno, Porsha. You know I don't fuck with Brooklyn niggaz like that," Alonzo said apprehensively.

"You ain't coming to hang out with Brooklyn niggaz, you're coming to hang out with me. Don't act like that, Zo. Come party with ya girl and you never know, we might end up having breakfast together in the morning."

"There you go with the games again, ma. You know you ain't trying to go there with me."

"I guess there's only one way to find out, huh?" she challenged.

It didn't take Alonzo long to make up his mind. "A'ight, give me the address."

The street was blocked off so Alonzo had to get out of the taxi a block away and walk, which was cool because he wanted to scout the territory before he got to them anyway. The block was packed with the young and old, as well as the savory and unsavory, and everybody seemed to be watching him. He knew they were most likely just sizing him up because he was a new face so there was no immediate threat, but if it did pop off, he had his trusty .357 on him.

He managed to bend the corner without incident and made his way deeper into the block. He spotted Frankie first. She was standing on a stoop across the street talking to Dena. From their body language they seemed to be having a heated argument. He looked around for Porsha but didn't see her until he was almost in front of the building. There was a long line of kids that stretched off the curb. At the front of the line, sitting on a crate, was Porsha. She was looking good enough to eat in a pair of fitting tan Capris, black wedges, with a black tank top under a fatigue blazer. Porsha was expertly painting colorful designs on the faces of the smiling children. This shocked Alonzo because he had no idea that Porsha was an artist. She must've felt his presence because she looked up at him and winked. She motioned for him to give her a second so he went to say hello to Frankie and Dena while he waited.

"'Sup, ladies?" Alonzo interrupted their conversation.

Dena spun on him with fire in her eyes, but she checked herself when she realized who it was. "Hey, Zo," she spoke dryly and walked over to the grill to check the meat.

"Damn, did I kick her dog or something?" Alonzo asked confused.

"Nah, she's just having a bad day," Frankie told him while watching Dena aggressively work the grill. "What wind blows you this far south?" she asked Alonzo with a raised eyebrow.

"Do you even need to ask?" He nodded toward Porsha.

Frankie shook her head. "Y'all two kill me with this on-and-off shit."

"I ain't never been on to get off, but I'm trying to change that," Alonzo said slyly. He looked out at the crowd dancing in the streets to Caribbean music. He was a long way from home. "Damn, Frankie Angels, what the fuck made you move so far out? You know you got Harlem in your heart."

"I got wherever there's a roof over my head in my heart," she said seriously. "Brooklyn is different than what I'm used to, but it beats sleeping on friends' couches any day."

"Tell me about it," he agreed. "The best thing I ever did was move outta my mom's crib."

"I'll bet. Now you can have your li'l harem of shorties run around naked all day and night."

"Stop it, five." He waved her off. "I'd be lying if I said I didn't keep my dick wet pretty regularly, but you know it's only one chick who'll ever have this." He placed his hand over his heart.

"And who is that?" Porsha came up behind him.

"Why don't you make some noise when you walk?" Alonzo turned to her.

"Don't try to change the subject. Finish what you were just telling Frankie," Porsha dared him.

Alonzo gave her the once-over and put on his best Harlem

face. "Baby, at this point of the game, if I still gotta say it out loud, then it ain't worth my breath, ya hear?"

"He got your ass," Frankie laughed and pointed her finger at Porsha, instigating the situation.

"Shut up, Frankie," Porsha pushed her playfully.

"Ain't you gonna introduce me to your friend?" Vashaun came over. She was dressed in a pair of shorts that rode up in her ass, too small mules, and a shirt that looked like it belonged to her little sister, but you couldn't tell her that she wasn't killing 'em.

"I hadn't planned on it," Frankie mumbled under her breath.

Alonzo cut his eyes at her comment. "Zo." He shook Vashaun's hand, and when he tried to pull it back she was reluctant to let it go.

"Nice to meet you, Zo. I'm Vashaun," she introduced herself. "So where you from, Zo?"

"I'm from Harlem, why? You interviewing me for a gig?" He said it with a smile, but his irritation with her questioning was clear in his tone.

Vashaun rocked back on her heels and looked Alonzo up and down. "Ain't no need to get defensive, cutie. I just know you ain't from around here, so I'm trying to figure out if you came to see somebody or if you're fair game."

"Actually, he came to see me." Porsha folded her arms.

"My fault. I wasn't trying to step on no toes," Vashaun said, but there wasn't much sincerity in her voice.

"Never that, boo. I just said he came to see me, not that I had papers on him," Porsha shot back.

"I'll take that as food for thought," Vashaun said with a chuckle.

"Why do I feel like I'm at a slave auction?" Alonzo asked sarcastically.

"You stupid." Frankie elbowed Alonzo playfully. "Hey, V, where's your other half? Bess was out there a minute ago, but she seems to have just up and disappeared."

"She went around the corner to meet our homegirl. She took the train out here from L.G. and got lost, so Bess went to walk her over," Vashaun said.

No sooner than Vashaun made the statement, Bess came walking over. She was wearing a pair of sweatpants and a white T-shirt with a scarf tied around her head. Trailing a few feet behind her was the friend she had gone to meet. The girl was dark skinned with a nice body that she showed off proudly in the tight-fitting denim skirt and white tank top. Porsha and Frankie stared at the girl, both knowing that they had seen her somewhere before but weren't quite sure where. When they saw the slack-jawed expression on Alonzo's face all doubt was removed. It was indeed the same girl from BBQ's. Veronica.

"Small world," Veronica said with an attitude. She looked from Frankie to Alonzo to Porsha.

"I was just about to say the same thing," Porsha said sarcastically. She purposely leaned against Alonzo intimately just to irk Veronica.

"What's up, Zo-Pound?" Veronica ignored Porsha and addressed Alonzo.

Alonzo shrugged. "Ain't too much."

"Looks like you took care of that business and had some free time after all, huh?" Veronica said. She had been trying to get with Alonzo for the last few days, but he kept putting her off telling her that he was tied up with business in Harlem.

295

"Took a short break to come holla at peoples," Alonzo said smoothly.

"Y'all know each other?" Bess asked confused, looking at the assembled faces trying to figure out what was going on.

"I met these other broads in passing, but me and Zo-Pound got history," Veronica said with a smirk.

"Do tell," Bess raised an eyebrow.

"Ain't too much to tell. We know each other from high school," Alonzo said. He didn't mean anything by it, but Veronica took offense.

"Damn, it's like that, Zo? I thought we meant a little more to each other than just being high school sweethearts."

Porsha snickered.

Veronica turned to Porsha. "Something funny?"

"Pay me no mind. I'm off my meds," Porsha downplayed it.

"If you knew like I knew you'd get back on them." Veronica rolled her eyes at Porsha, then turned back to Alonzo. "You know, it's funny that the other night when I asked you what the deal was, you played it off like you and shorty only knew each other from around the way, but y'all look real comfortable out here."

"Slow up, Veronica. Right now, you bugging and trying to make this shit bigger than what it is," Alonzo told her. He smelled the drama cooking and was trying to put the fire out early.

"Wow," Bess said, instigating from the sidelines.

"I ain't trying to make it bigger than nothing, Zo. I just thought that we respected each other enough to keep it tall. You didn't have to lie about it. If you was fucking her, you should've just said you fucked her." Veronica's voice seemed to get louder.

"Veronica, not that it's any of your business, but Porsha and I have never slept together," Alonzo told her.

"It's still early," Porsha staged-whispered to Frankie.

Veronica spun on Porsha. "You got a problem with me or something?"

"No love, I'm good. I know my position, but it seems like you're the one trying to figure out where *you* fit into all this," Porsha said confidently.

"Well, I fit in pretty good until you and your little hood rat friends ruined my date by begging Zo-Pound to save you from that ass whipping," Veronica shot back.

"Damn, and I remember you telling me how much you were looking forward to that date," Bess continued to pour gasoline on the smoldering fire.

Porsha cocked her head and looked at Veronica as if she had lost her mind. "Boo-boo, you got me fucked up. Didn't nobody ask Alonzo to rescue shit, and for the record, it looked like your date was going south long before we got there, or is it a regular thing for niggaz to leave you sitting there looking stupid while they slide off to holla at other chicks?"

"Ladies, why don't y'all just cool out," Alonzo suggested, but it was as if he wasn't even there.

"You li'l bum-ass Harlem bitch, you ain't got shit on me!" Veronica shouted at Porsha.

Porsha snorted. "I ain't never been a bum in my life, and I can think of something that I got on you, but I ain't gotta state the obvious," she looked from Alonzo to Veronica.

Porsha's statement, coupled with the fact that Alonzo was up under her and not Veronica, stung. Her eyes narrowed to slits. "You a long way from home to be popping shit."

"Bitch, I could be in Alaska, and my mouth still gonna go off. I ain't no punk. What's really good?" Porsha spat. If it was a fight Veronica was looking for she was more than willing to give her one.

Frankie had been standing off to the side remaining neutral until she saw Bess trying to creep around to Porsha's blindside. Frankie stepped in front of her. "Ma, you already know that ain't going down."

"It's like that, Frankie?" Bess asked her.

"Straight like that. If these bitches wanna thump, then that's on them, but please believe I ain't having my homegirl get jumped," Frankie let her know.

Bess was a warrior, but she knew that Frankie was too. Bess couldn't say for sure if she could take Frankie in a fight, so she figured, why bother if she didn't have to. "What's up, V? You wanna shoot the one-deep with this chick?"

Veronica was hesitant. The only reason she had pressed it as far as she did was because she knew Bess had her back if anything went down. For as long as she and Bess had been hanging, she had always been the pretty one who reeled the guys in and Bess had been the rough one who knocked the bitches out. Without having Bess as her security blanket, she was no longer sure how the fight would play out and really didn't want to chance it, but she had already put it out there and couldn't back down.

"Fuck it. I'll molly-wop this bitch right quick." Veronica came out of her shoes.

"We'll see." Porsha came out of her blazer.

"Porsha, chill. Don't fight this girl over me. Shit ain't worth it," Alonzo tried to reason with Porsha.

Porsha chuckled. "Once again you give yourself too much

credit, youngster. I'd never fight a chick over some dick. I'm gonna beat this bitch's ass off the principle." She took her earrings off and placed them in Alonzo's hand. "This shouldn't take too long."

Porsha turned around just in time to see Veronica swooping in for a sneak attack. Porsha weaved and avoided getting punched directly in her face, but her chin took the brunt of the blow. Her legs got tangled, throwing her balance off for a second, but she quickly recovered and came back at Veronica throwing rights and lefts. She stole Veronica in the eye, snapping her head back and opening up a small cut over her eyebrow. Porsha grinned when Veronica noticed the trickle of blood running down her face.

Veronica touched her hand to her head, and to her horror, it came away bloody. "Bitch, that's yo' ass now!" Then she charged Porsha like a bull.

Porsha tried to sidestep the charge, but the wedges on her feet made her movements awkward and slow. Veronica locked her arms around Porsha's lower body and tried to lift her up. Porsha knew that if Veronica got her off her feet it would be a wrap. She rained blows ferociously on Veronica's head and face every time she tried to lift her. When Veronica's grip slackened, Porsha kneed her in the face.

Veronica staggered to regroup. Blood leaked from her nose and dripped on the ground. She seemed dazed but was hardly done. With a grunt, she took a boxer's stance and advanced on Porsha, throwing punches from the hip. Porsha managed to protect her face from the onslaught, but every time Veronica's fist connected with her forearm, she felt her bones rattle. She had to admit that Veronica hit like a jackhammer, but her pride kept her standing. There was no way in hell that she would be remembered on that block as the chick who came from Harlem and got her ass whipped over a man, because that's surely how the story would end up spun whenever it was retold.

Porsha moved to put some space between her and Veronica and a dude in the crowd stuck his foot out, tripping her. Porsha landed hard on her hands and knees and before she could get back to her feet Veronica was on her, raining punches. Alonzo and Frankie moved at the exact same time, with Frankie moving to pull Veronica off Porsha and Alonzo creeping through the crowd toward the dude who had tripped Porsha.

"Don't jump in, Frankie. Let that bitch take her medicine!" Bess warned.

"I ain't jumping in. Your peoples tripped her. Let her get up and shoot the fair one." Frankie stood between the Brooklyn girls and Porsha who was slowly recovering.

While Frankie and the girls were arguing, the dude who had tripped Porsha stood off to the side, laughing with his friends about his shady move. He never saw Alonzo coming, but he felt the powerful strike to his jaw. The dude stumbled, and Alonzo delivered two more bone-crushing punches to the side of his head to make sure he stayed down. One of the dude's friends snuck up on Alonzo and hit him in the side of the head with a bottle. Alonzo stumbled, holding his head. The dudes from the block closed in, ready to finish the Harlem cat off, but they all backpedaled when he came up waving his .357.

"Back the fuck up!" Alonzo roared, sweeping the gun back and forth. One of young boys tried to inch up on him and almost lost his foot when Alonzo blasted the ground. "Li'l nigga, don't make me murder you," Alonzo barked. He found himself backed into a corner with Frankie and Porsha, with damn near everyone from the neighborhood trying to converge on them. It was about to go down, and it wasn't looking good for Alonzo. Even being armed, there were five times as many of them as he had bullets. He cursed himself, because if he'd stayed his black ass in Harlem, he might not have been in that situation.

Alonzo was about to try to blast his way out when he heard what sounded like thunder, but there wasn't a cloud in the sky. The thunder rolled a second time and the crowd parted like the Red Sea, making way for a chick, followed by several dudes. They all brandished guns like they were legal. She was a thick chick with red and black braided hair who walked with the authority normally reserved for a man. In her right hand, she held smoking Desert Eagle and in her left a smoldering blunt clip. She took two drags of the clip before tossing it into the streets and turning her weed-slanted eyes to Alonzo and the two girls. Alonzo was still holding the .357, but she didn't seem to notice it when she stepped in front of him.

"Who the fuck is y'all making all this noise in my hood? Don't y'all know that don't nobody do no gun-clapping on this block unless it's us?" the redhead sneered at Alonzo.

"That bitch came through here fronting, talking about I was fucking with her man so I put the pieces on her," Veronica lied.

The redhead turned to Veronica. "I don't believe I was talking to you, V, and if your ass was in the middle of it, I know there's more to the story than what you're telling. Every time you come around here you get into something. I told you about that shit before." She looked from the bloodied Veronica to Porsha, who looked ready to pop off at a moment's notice, and finally to Alonzo. Even outgunned, he still stood defiantly clutching his .357. "Young man, you must sling dick like a porn star to have these two hoes out here boxing over you. Who you be, soldier?"

"The name is Zo-Pound," Alonzo announced.

The redhead scratched her chin. "Zo-Pound? You the same Zo-Pound that runs around with little Ashanti?"

"That's my crime partner," Alonzo told her.

The redhead turned to her shooters. "Ain't about nothing. The young boy gets to keep his life." The shooters griped and reluctantly lowered their guns. "Zo," she turned back to him, "we getting money around the corner so all this drama ain't no good for business. Take your li'l girlfriend and head back uptown."

"You got that." Alonzo grabbed Porsha by the hand and began leading her away.

Porsha stopped short and turned to Frankie. "You good, ma?"

Frankie laughed. "Yeah, y'all go ahead. These bitches is scandalous, but they ain't stupid. They know what it is with Frankie Angels, right?" she looked from Veronica to Bess. Neither of them said a word.

"A'ight, I'm gonna call you later." Porsha waved at her friend. She was skeptical about leaving Frankie in Brooklyn, but she wasn't really in a position to argue the point.

"Zo," the redhead called after him, "when you see Ashanti, tell him Auntie Kastro says hello and that he could at least call from time to time to see how I'm doing. We still family."

"I'll do that," Alonzo promised before hot stepping off the block with his lady in tow.

"Who is that chick, and how does she know Ashanti?" Porsha asked when they had rounded the corner.

"I don't know, and I don't care. Just keep walking before she changes her mind." Alonzo didn't feel safe until he and Porsha were in a taxi and on their way out of Brooklyn. "How come every time I turn around I gotta get you outta some shit?" he asked Porsha as the taxi carried them across the bridge into Manhattan.

"Nigga, knock it off because you know I didn't start that shit. That was your crazy-ass girlfriend who was out there clowning," Porsha rolled her eyes.

"She ain't my girl," Alonzo said defensively.

"Well, that bitch must not have gotten the memo." Porsha pulled her compact mirror from her purse to assess the damage from the fight. There were three faint scratches on the side of her face, but nothing that a little makeup wouldn't cover. "Crazy ho."

"Yo, I didn't know you could throw hands like that, Porsha," Alonzo told her. He knew Veronica to be a bruiser since back in the days but was surprised at how Porsha had handled her.

"When you're this pretty you gotta know how to defend yourself against haters," she capped while fixing her hair. "This bitch done pulled me all outta my character."

"Don't worry about it. You still the finest muthafucka living." Alonzo pinched her chin playfully.

Before they knew it, the cab was slowing up in front of the projects. Alonzo spotted Ashanti walking up the block with Fatima. He was about to tell the cabdriver to drop them right there until he saw the familiar brown Buick pull up in the bus stop. He already knew who was in the car so he told the cabdriver to let them off on the next block. As the cab passed the Buick, Alonzo watched the black and Hispanic detectives get out of the car and head straight for Ashanti, wondering what the fuck they wanted.

THIRTY-SIX

ASHANTI AND FATIMA WALKED UP BROADWAY, LAUGHING as they recapped the funny moments in the movie they had just come from seeing at the Magic Johnson Theater. They were the picture of an urban Romeo and Juliet, walking shoulder to shoulder and sharing an order of chicken wings. Every so often, they would nod or say hello to the people they passed, but their attention was fixed solely on each other.

Since the night of Meek's unfortunate murder the two of them had been inseparable. Though they had never spoken of it since the night it happened, they found an unspoken comfort in each other to get through it. Ashanti had had a crush on Fatima for the longest, and it seemed that she had been sweet on him too, but neither wanted to make the first move. For as tragic as Meek's murder had been, it had been the thing that pushed Ashanti and Fatima together and sparked an unlikely romance.

"That movie was funny as hell. What made you pick that one, Ashanti?" Fatima asked, chomping on a piece of chicken, trying her best not to get grease on her clothes.

"Because Russell Brand is in it. He killed it in *Get Him To The Greek,* so I went back and checked out some of his other stuff. That English dude has got issues," Ashanti laughed.

"Yeah, he is mad funny. I gotta see some more movies with him in it."

"I got a bunch of his stuff on DVD if you wanna come by one day," Ashanti offered.

Fatima gave him a suspicious look. "What? You trying to get me to your crib so you can take advantage of me?"

"Never," he said defensively. "Fatima, I told you I ain't on it like that. Me and you—"

"I was just joking," she cut him off. "Loosen up, Ashanti. You're always so serious."

"Life is serious."

"I know, but all the time?" she countered. "Ashanti, I know what it is with you, and I know your position out here, but you gotta treat yourself to a good time every so often. You can't eat, sleep, and breathe the streets."

"Why not?" he asked. It sounded like he was being sarcastic, but he was seriously asking.

Fatima wasn't sure how to answer. "You just can't." She threw her hands up in frustration. "Look, we all got problems, Ashanti, but that doesn't mean we have to carry them around with us everywhere we go. Besides, I'm young, and I like to have a good time, so if you're gonna be my boo, then you gotta learn to loosen up."

"So, I'm your boo now?" Ashanti raised an eyebrow.

Fatima smiled and looped her arm in his. "Yes, you're my boo." When she'd initially said it she was kidding, but the more she thought about it, the more appealing the idea became. Ashanti was a thug, but he was a good dude. He was always on his best behavior around her, and he treated Fatima like a queen instead of a piece of ass. In him, she found the love and attention that she had been looking for in all the wrong places.

They continued walking up the block toward the project building when Ashanti spotted the brown Buick pull up the bus stop a few yards in front of him. He had seen the car enough times in his life to know who was riding in it. "Fuck," Ashanti cursed.

"What's the matter?" Fatima asked.

"These niggaz." Ashanti nodded toward the detectives who were now walking in his direction.

Fatima saw the detectives and immediately thought of the gun she knew Ashanti had on him. Without him having to ask, she went into action. Fatima stepped in front of Ashanti, temporarily blocking the detective's view of him. She kissed him long and deep on the lips, while removing the gun from his pants and slipping it into her purse. "Holla if you need me." She wiped a smudge of lipstick from his upper lip with her thumb, then made hurried steps toward the building.

Watching her walk away, Ashanti couldn't help but to beam. That one act let him know that he had a down-ass chick in his corner, and Fatima was a keeper.

"Where's your li'l girlfriend off to in such a hurry?" Detective Alvarez asked when they had finally reached Ashanti.

"I wonder what we'll find on her if we go stop her," Detective Brown chimed in.

"Ain't y'all got nothing better to do than harass innocent people?" Ashanti spat on the ground.

"I doubt anyone kissing your rancid mouth could be considered innocent, kid," Detective Alvarez shot back.

"Y'all come to trade insults or try to pin a bogus charge on me? Either way, I ain't got time," Ashanti said with an attitude.

"Now why would you think we had a reason to come over here and charge you with anything? You done something you wanna tell us about?" Detective Brown questioned.

Ashanti twisted his lips. "You know me better than that, fam. Steel don't break." He patted his chest.

Detective Alvarez laughed. "Yeah, but it'll sure as hell bend if you apply enough heat. I gotta admit, they don't make them like you anymore, Ashanti."

"And they never will again. Now, state your business so I can be on my way," Ashanti told him.

"A'ight, gangsta," Detective Brown said. "I could stand here and tell you about all the murders that have been committed recently, but somehow I don't think it would surprise you."

Ashanti's face remained blank.

"Exactly," Detective Brown continued. "Now, I'd bet my pension that your li'l ass is elbows deep in blood, but you're still just a puppet on a string. We want the puppet master. Where is King James?"

"Who?" Ashanti faked ignorance.

"You know who! The idiot who declared open war on Shai Clark in our streets," Detective Alvarez cut in.

"War? I thought the president brought all the troops home already," Ashanti laughed.

"You think you're real funny, don't you?" Detective Brown addressed him. "Well, let me tell you something that you might not find so funny. Word on the streets is that King James is trying to take the throne and calling Shai to task. Right now, none of you are enough of a threat to warrant his attention, but that's gonna change pretty soon. When it does, Shai is gonna send a death squad to take King James out and anyone with him is going along for the ride, including you."

"Maybe even his pretty girlfriend too," Detective Alvarez added.

"Man, I don't know no Clarks, no Kings, and no Queens, Detectives," Ashanti said with a straight face.

"So be it." Detective Brown shook his head sadly. "You might feel like dying, but let's hope your man King James is smarter than that." He shoved a business card down the front of Ashanti's shirt. "We expect to hear back sooner than later." He walked off with his partner closely behind.

Ashanti waited until the detectives had gone before tossing their business card on the ground and spitting on it. "Fuck outta here."

"What them niggaz wanted?" Alonzo appeared behind Ashanti as if by magic.

"Homie, you know better than to be creeping like that. You could've got blasted on." Ashanti gave him dap.

"I doubt it. I saw you pass your hammer to Fatima. Back to my question, what did those pigs want?" Alonzo pressed him.

Ashanti exhaled. "Chasing tall tales about King. Man, shit crazy right now."

"Asking about King? What the fuck for?" Alonzo asked surprised. For as long as he had been rolling with the team, King James had been like a ghost to the police, flying under their radar, so the fact that they were now asking about him was odd.

Ashanti hesitated. "I'll fill you in later," he told Alonzo

while cutting his eyes at Porsha, who was a new face but looked familiar.

Alonzo noticed his hesitation and made the introductions. "Porsha, this is Ashanti. Ashanti this is Porsha."

Porsha extended her hand, but Ashanti pulled her in for a hug. "Handshakes are for strangers. For as much as I've heard about you, I feel like we're family."

"I hope they were good things that you heard," Porsha smirked.

"All good." Ashanti winked at her. "Fuck happened to your head?" he asked Alonzo, noticing the knot on the side of his head from where he had been hit with the bottle during the scuffle.

"Long fucking story, but it'll keep." Alonzo touched the knot on his head and winced.

"Looks like we got some story swapping to do. But dig, I see you busy so I'ma let you do what you do with shorty, but we gotta talk later," Ashanti told Alonzo.

"Funny, because I was gonna say the same thing," Alonzo replied, thinking of how he wanted to confront Ashanti about his strange behavior.

"A'ight, so we'll meet back here at sundown," Ashanti gave him dap and headed toward the building.

"Yo, Ashanti," Alonzo called after him. "Who the fuck is Kastro?"

Ashanti smirked. "One more topic for tonight's conversation." He disappeared into the building.

"Everything okay?" Porsha asked once Ashanti was out of earshot.

"Yeah, everything is cool. Let's go get something to eat, then

I'll put you in a cab back to your hood." Alonzo threw his arm around Porsha and led her down the block. On the outside, he was cool and collected, but on the inside, he was filled with uncertainty. It didn't take a rocket scientist to know why the two detectives came through the hood, but the question was, who sent them? Somebody was talking, and there was only a handful of people who knew enough to bury them all, so the list of suspects was a short one. Alonzo had told himself a long time ago that before he let the words of another man put him back in prison he would make sure that the man could no longer speak . . . and it didn't matter who it was.

THIRTY-SEVEN

SHAI HAD JUST FINISHED DOING THE LAST-MINUTE walk-through and briefing his managers at Daddy's Kitchen before they opened for the night. They were all professionally trained young men and women and were more than capable of running the place without Shai looking over their shoulders, but it gave him something to take his mind off of everything else that was going on in his life.

Things were always crazy on the streets, but it was starting to spill over into his household. Lately, he noticed that Honey seemed increasingly paranoid and began to question him about his comings and goings, which wasn't something she had ever done in all the time they'd been together. Shai had been dismissing her fears as the baby growing inside of her playing with her emotions until she mentioned a name that he thought he would never hear again. Animal.

There had been no love lost between Shai Clark and Tech's protégé, and when Shai had ordered Swann to murder Tech, it drew an imaginary line in the sand and it would only be a mat-

311

ter of time before the upstart crossed it. Shai had contemplated having Animal killed, but somebody beat him to the punch. Word on the streets was that Animal had been abducted by someone off his laundry list of enemies en route to prison and put to death for his crimes against them.

Honey's sudden interest in a dead man was surprising, to say the least. When he pressed her about it, she came clean about the CD Nickels had been listening to. Shai felt a little better hearing this. For as much as a lowlife as Animal had been, he left a legacy of music that played in ghettos across America, so the CDs were everywhere. He assured Honey that Nickels coming across the CD was a coincidence and that Animal was dead and gone, but when she asked what made him so sure, he didn't have an honest answer for her. None of his sources had ever reported finding a body or any other traces of Animal after the jail break. It was like he had vanished off the face of the earth. As far as Shai was concerned, it was good riddance to the little nuisance, but the mention of Animal's name stirred old memories that he had long sought to put to bed.

Then there was the business with Holiday. Against Shai's advice, he'd gone through with his birthday bash, and to make matters worse, he took Baby Doc with him. As Shai had predicted, somebody showed out, and as a result, Baby Doc lost the hearing in one of his ears and Holiday had almost lost his life, which wouldn't be worth much when Big Doc caught up with him. Holiday was too hot for Shai to visit in the hospital or speak to on the phone, so Shai had to wait for Swann to come back to get the story of what had actually happened.

When Shai heard the front door of Daddy's House open, he looked up in anticipation expecting it to be Swann, but his face darkened when two detectives walked in. Angelo stood to block their path, but Shai waved him off.

Detective Brown looked from Angelo to Shai. "Wow, I'm impressed. Did you teach him how to roll over and play dead yet?"

"Fuck you, pig!" Angelo spat.

"Sorry, but you ain't pretty enough," Detective Brown winked at him. "Young prince of Harlem, what it do, player?" He extended his hand to Shai to give him dap.

Shai looked at Detective Brown's hand as if it had been dipped in shit. "What can I do for you, Officers?"

"That's *detectives*, and we actually came bearing gifts," Detective Alvarez told him.

"Sorry, my dad always told me never to take gifts from strangers," Shai said.

"Looks like your daddy taught you everything except the right things. But who am I to judge?" Detective Brown shrugged. "Getting back to why we came, I hear one of your young boys got done filthy a few nights ago."

Shai shrugged. "If you say so. I've been at home attending to my pregnant fiancée. She's been on bed rest, so I play it close these days."

"Yeah, you play it close, and it's getting closer by the day," Detective Alvarez lit a cigarette.

"This is a nonsmoking establishment," Shai told him.

Detective Alvarez took one last pull before throwing the cigarette on the restaurant floor and crushing it under his sneaker. "Shai, everybody knows that boy who got shot at the club is connected to you, and the fact that somebody tried to whack him means whoever you've pissed off is working his way up the food chain. First your soldiers, now your lieutenants. Soon, even your capos are gonna have to grow eyes in the backs of their heads." He looked at Angelo. "We know you feel that noose tightening around your neck, Shai."

Shai didn't take the bait. "Anyhow, you said you had something for me?"

"Oh yeah, we did, didn't we?" Detective Alvarez smirked. He was having a good time making Shai sweat. "I've got some good news and bad news for you. The good news is that the guy who tried to clip Holiday got away, so it gives your goons first crack at putting him in the dirt before we can put him in a cell. The bad news is that this wasn't just some schmuck trying to get a payday. Congratulations, seems like you've got a *real* gangster on your ass now," the detective announced proudly.

Shai tilted his head quizzically. "You know, if you guys have come down here to try to scare me, then you're doing a piss-poor job."

"We haven't come down here to scare you, Shai. We've come to warn you," Detective Brown told him in his no-nonsense voice. "You're a scumbag, but we're still officers of the law, and as such, we have an obligation to warn you that we have reason to believe your life is in serious danger."

Shai was unmoved. "And this is supposed to be the part when you tell me that you guys are the only ones who can save me, right?"

"You've got a knack for stating the obvious, my young friend," Detective Brown said. "This thing is getting out of hand, and we need to put it to bed. We know somebody is gunning for you, and we're ninety-nine percent sure of who it is, but we need confirmation from you. Give us a name so we can lock this bastard up, and you can go back to pretending you're Poppa Clark."

Shai said nothing for a long moment. He looked over at Angelo. "Did this muthafucka just ask me to rat?" When he turned back to the detectives his face was twisted into a mask of rage. "How fucking dare you disrespect me by asking me to help you put another man in prison! I'm a Clark, and if you don't know what that means, then I suggest you ask somebody. Now get the fuck outta my establishment before I forget y'all are cops." Shai turned his back on the detectives and leaned against the bar, where he motioned for the bartender to bring him a drink.

"Did you just threaten a police officer?" Detective Brown pushed his blazer back so that his gun was visible and accessible.

Shai downed the shot in front of him and turned slowly to face the detectives. "That ain't no threat; it's some cold hard truth." He nodded behind the detectives.

The detectives looked around the restaurant. A bus boy who had been pretending to clean off a table near where they were talking was now focused on the detectives. He had both his hands hidden in a bucket that was used to clear dirty dishes, but it didn't look like there were any plates in it. At that instant, the kitchen door swung open, and a female line cook stepped out. She had a towel over her arm, but it did little to hide the bulge beneath it. The manager Shai had been briefing was now standing by the front door. He flipped the sign from open to close and glared at the detectives. Detective Brown started to reach for his pistol, but Alvarez stopped him short. It would've been stupid for Shai to make such a brazen move against the detectives, but there was no telling what a man backed into a corner would do.

"Have it your way, Shai." Detective Alvarez pulled his partner toward the exit, keeping Shai and his employees in his line of sight. "But when the boogeyman comes knocking at your door, don't dial nine-one-one, because we ain't gonna answer."

Just as the detectives were leaving, Swann was coming in. He accidentally bumped into Detective Brown in passing. "Fuck outta my way." Detective Brown shoved Swann into the door on his way out.

"You did that shit in front of witnesses. I'm suing the department," Swann taunted the detectives. He laughed and continued inside the restaurant, but when he took one look at the expressions of Shai's and Angelo's faces, his smile faded. "What happened? Is everything good?"

"Just these cocksuckers trying to get under my skin as usual." Shai motioned for the bartender to bring him another drink. "You know they're fishing for info about what happened at Sin City."

"Speaking of which, I got the skinny on that from Holiday," Swann told him.

"Let's talk outside." Shai led him from the restaurant and away from prying ears. "What the deal?"

"It's just like I was trying to tell you; King James made his play," Swann said.

Shai shook his head, mad at himself because everyone else saw it coming except him. "That piece of shit. I can't believe he had the balls to try to get at us."

"Well, believe it, because he did," Swann told him. "Holiday says it was little Ashanti who King sent after him. You know he been hanging around King James and them like flies on shit. I guess sending him at Holiday was his initiation into their fold."

"I'm gonna show them a fold when I fold their whole fucking crew. King, Ashanti, . . . All of them niggaz is dead and make it quick."

"That ain't all, Shai," Swann said hesitantly.

There was something about the look on Swann's face that unnerved him. "What is it?"

"Holiday says that Ashanti wasn't alone. He says that Animal was with him."

Shai gave Swann a disbelieving look. "Is Holiday smoking that shit y'all are giving him to sell? Animal is dead."

"Not according to Holiday. He saw his face and from the description he gave me, it was Animal. Ol' boy even introduced himself to make sure Holiday knew just who he was."

The revelation hit Shai like a physical blow. He had tried to tell Honey that she was being paranoid when she brought him up, but obviously, her woman's intuition was more reliable than his sources on the police force. It would be the last time he ever doubted her. "First, this nobody muthafucka King James gets outta pocket, then he resurrects the dead to do his dirty work. Can this shit get any crazier?"

"It sure can. See, Holiday says that Animal spoke with him before he tried to take his head off, and his part in it has nothing to do with King James," Swann informed him.

Shai was confused. "Then what the fuck would make him pop up after all these years and start laying people down?"

"A broad. Apparently the girl that idiot Holiday shot in the club awhile back was none other than Animal's lady, Gucci. He wants the cat who shot her and the man who gave the order." Swann gave Shai a look.

Suddenly, Shai felt weak. He leaned his back against the restaurant wall and rested his hands on his knees. "But I never told

Holiday to shoot that girl. I felt so bad about it that I sent her flowers in the hospital."

"Try telling that to that crazy li'l muthafucka Animal. This shit has officially gotten out of hand, Shai."

"The boogeyman has come a-knockin'," Shai mumbled, thinking back on the detective's words.

"What?"

Shai dismissed it. "Nothing. We gotta get a handle on this shit ASAP."

"I'm all over it," Swann assured him. "I've got every available snitch and gun-boy on the streets looking for signs of Animal. I also sent some extra muscle out to the house to make sure the family is safe."

"Animal is a killer, but an honorable killer. He wouldn't involve my family in this. He'll keep it between us."

"Try telling that to the trail of bodies he's left all over the city. Better safe than sorry, and when dealing with someone as skilled as Animal, we can't leave anything to chance. You want me to cancel the card game tonight?"

"No, we can't do that. We're playing host to some major players tonight, and there's gonna be a lot of money floating around. Even some of Gee-Gee's people are supposed to be showing up. My dad hosted these card games for years, and we're gonna honor the tradition. If we don't go through with it, it'll look suspect. It's bad enough that everybody and they mamas seem to wanna test us, so we don't need to raise anymore doubt over our control of the streets."

"Shai, fuck what people think. This is about your safety. You ain't the prince no more; you're the king, and protecting you is priority number one."

"I respect what you're saying, Swann, but we have to keep up appearances. A Clark has played host to these card games for the past twenty years, and we're going to hold on to that tradition."

"Then let me host it for you. As your underboss, I can speak for the Clark family, and no one will question it," Swann suggested.

Shai wanted to argue the point, but he knew Swann was right. For as long as Animal was running around loose, he couldn't truly breathe easy. "You're a good soldier, Swann, and a better friend."

"You know how we do; from the cradle to the grave, baby boy." Swann gave him dap. "I'll take care of the game, and Angelo can hold you down in my absence."

"A'ight, get everything in order. I'll have Angelo get some guys on the job with this situation with these street monkeys. We're gonna dead Animal, then King James."

Swann nodded. "King James should be easy enough to track down. Niggaz like him don't know nothing outside the projects. Finding Animal is gonna be a little harder."

"Which is why we're gonna make him come to us."

"And how do you plan to do that?"

"The most obvious way, of course. I'm gonna send some of our people to pay a visit to his girlfriend in the hospital. Let's sprinkle a little blood in the water and see if we can catch a shark," Shai smiled wickedly.

THIRTY-EIGHT

THERE WAS BLOOD EVERYWHERE. THE ONCE-WHITE TILED walls of the motel bathroom were now crimson and smeared. In the small bedroom area beyond, two men decorated the floor, marinating in pools of their own blood and intestines. The promise of riches convinced them that they were killers, but the hot touch of lead piercing soft flesh told them the truth. They were collateral damage, but the man held captive in the bathroom was the prize.

Money Mike was slumped in the corner with his arms suspended over his head, chained over the shower curtain rod and as naked as the day he was born. His face was badly bruised, and his eye had swollen shut on the first hit. Two of his teeth were broken, and the inside of his lip was cut so deeply that he knew he would need stitches. He was in a bad way, and the cause for it was standing mere feet away from him.

Animal paced back and forth in the small bathroom like a caged dog. His chest heaved up and down from the cigarettes he'd taken to smoking, cutting off his wind. The white tank top he'd stripped down to before he started in on Money Mike was now an off-shade of pink and soaked. From wrists to knuckles, both of his hands were wrapped in bicycle chains, which dripped blood onto the floor. Before using the chains on Money Mike, he'd pretreated them in bleach so that every time one of the chained blows opened a wound on his victim, it would burn like he'd been doused with acid. It was a brutal, yet affective, method of interrogation, and the subjects never lasted more than eight minutes. Money Mike was on minute seven.

Money Mike was a low-life hustler who had survived years in the game by always making himself appear to be too insignificant to be considered a threat, but a select few knew different. He dealt in something more dangerous than guns or drugs. He dealt in information. He hadn't been on Animal's shit list, or even on his radar, until he became a means to an end.

Against his better judgment and Ashanti's protests, Animal had reached out to Money Mike. They'd done business in the past, and though Mike might not have been the most savory cat, Animal always remembered him to be honorable, but things were different now. Money Mike had grown in status, and Animal had a price on his head. Animal had dealt with Money Mike in the past, and the two had done good business, but when Animal arrived at the motel in Elizabeth, N.J., where Mike had set up the meeting, he realized how much time and greed had changed things. Instead of providing Animal with the information he was paying for, Money Mike decided he wanted to try to collect the bounty on Animal.

The goons were amateurs. They didn't even wait for Animal to get into the motel room fully before they jumped the gun and tried to take him down. By the time the lead goon could finish the movie line he was reciting from *Carlito's Way,* Animal had drawn his Pretty Bitches and gave him two to the chest. By the time the second goon had even gotten the idea in his head to pop off, Animal already had one of the rose-chrome Glocks placed snuggly under his chin. The second goon made eye contact with Animal. The last thing he saw was Animal turn his face away so blood wouldn't splash in it when he blew the top of the goon's skull off.

Money Mike tried to break for the door, but he was stopped by one of Animal's Glocks being jammed roughly into the side of his jaw.

"I paid for some information, and I intend to have it," Animal whispered in his ear. Ten minutes later, he had Money Mike bound and in a world of pain.

"So what's up, Mike? You ready to tell me something good? Where will my chickens come home to roost?" Animal asked.

Money Mike fought against the pain as best he could to reply, "C'mon, man, they'll kill me if I say anything."

Animal struck Monkey Mike in the eye with one of his chain-wrapped fists, spraying the shower curtain with more blood. He grabbed Money Mike by the jowls and watched his eyes began to tear from the bleach fumes. "And what do you think *I'll* do if you don't say anything?"

"Animal, stall me out," Money Mike pleaded. "I got some money stashed not too far from here, about ten stacks. If you let me go, I swear on everything you can have it."

Animal punched Money Mike in the face again. "Don't play with me, Blood. You know I don't play for money; I play for souls. Quit stalling and tell me what I need to know. Where is it going down?"

"I can't do it, man! I just can't," Money Mike rasped. He knew by not talking there was a chance that Animal would kill him, but it would be a clean death. If he talked and Shai Clark found out, he would kill him too, but he would make it slow and painful.

"You must think I'm playing with you, Mikey." Animal slowly undid the chains from his fists. He picked up a paring knife from the bathroom sink. Leaning in, he whispered softly to Money Mike. "Let me see if I can convince you of how serious I am." Animal started at Money Mike's collarbone and traced a blood trail across his chest and stopped at his stomach, where he pushed the knife into the soft skin of Money Mike's gut.

"Please just kill me and get it over with," Money Mike begged.

"I got no intentions on killing you. We're just gonna have a bit of fun." Animal cut him across the chest again. Once he had made a bloody mess of his chest and abdomen he went to work on his arms and legs, jabbing small holes in them with the paring knife. When he moved the knife to Money Mike's eye, preparing to pluck it out, his victim decided he'd had enough.

"Wait," he begged just above a whisper. His throat was raw from screaming, and he felt like he would black out.

"What's that?" Animal cupped his hand to his ear. "You got something you want to tell me?" Money Mike mumbled an address into Animal's ear that brought a broad smile to his face. "See? Was that so hard? You did good, Mikey, and you should be rewarded," Animal drew the knife back.

"You said you wouldn't kill me!" Money Mike said.

"And I am a man of my word," Animal told him before jamming the knife deep into Money Mike's nuts. The pain was so intense that Money Mike couldn't even scream. "I ain't gonna kill you, but you'll probably off yourself rather than live the rest of your days with no dick. Thanks for the information." Animal patted Money Mike on the cheek playfully and left him chained to the shower curtain with the knife still dangling from between his legs.

The plan was for Alonzo to meet Ashanti in front of the building at sundown, but at the last minute, Ashanti had called him and changed the plan. He told Zo to meet him at Grant's Tomb in the park. The moment he hung up with Ashanti Alonzo got a queasy feeling in his gut. What could he possibly want to talk about in the middle of the park that they couldn't talk about in front of the building where they always held counsel? Alonzo smelled a rat, so he made sure he packed his rat killer . . . a long barrel .45.

Alonzo got to the park fifteen minutes early and Ashanti was already there, which was unlike him. That boy would be late to his own funeral, but he showed up early for the super-secret meeting that he had called. The situation was getting fishier by the minute. He checked to make sure his .45 was loaded and easy to get to if he needed it before he approached Ashanti.

"What's goodie?" Ashanti stood and extended his hand.

"Ain't shit." Alonzo pulled him in for an embrace, pressing his body against Ashanti in the process to see exactly where Ashanti had his gun concealed.

"You wanna hit this?" Ashanti held out the blunt that he was smoking.

"I'm good. So what's up, man? Why we out here in the park? What's so secret that we couldn't talk in front of the building or in one of the apartments?"

Ashanti looked around suspiciously before answering. "Got some real heavy shit on my mind and it ain't for everybody's ears, feel me?"

"Yeah, I feel you," Alonzo said in an even tone. "Shit is getting crazy out here, dawg." Ashanti exhaled smoked through his nose. "First, this thing with Shai, and now these two detectives all on a nigga back."

"I peeped that. What was that all about, fam?" Alonzo quizzed him.

Ashanti shrugged. "You know Brown and Alvarez. They always hint at shit, but never come out and actually say what the fuck they're trying to get at. All they do is talk."

"And what they wanna talk to you about, Ashanti?"

"Murders," Ashanti said as if it was nothing. "They're trying to connect King James to the dead bodies that been popping up."

"That don't make sense. King keeps a low profile, so how would the police even know to look in his direction?" Alonzo reasoned. He was trying to give Ashanti an out.

Ashanti looked at him as if it was the dumbest question he'd ever heard. "I think we both know the answer to that one."

"Somebody is talking," Alonzo said.

Ashanti nodded. "And we know the penalty for betrayal, don't we?"

"Death."

"Ain't nothing in the world lower than a snitch, and whoever it is running their mouth gotta get pushed off the man, regardless of who it is," Ashanti said matter-of-factly. "That's part of what I wanted to talk to you about, Zo. I got something I need to get off my chest, and I'm not sure how you'll react to it."

"Only one way to find out," Alonzo said. His voice was calm, but inside, he was going to pieces with each word of Ashanti's confession.

"I know you've been wondering about the way I been acting lately." Ashanti looked up at the stars with his back to Alonzo. "Everything just got so crazy so fast that I'm still trying to figure out how it got to this point. Just when you think you've seen it all, the game throws you a twist. I'm in deep, Zo, real deep, and I ain't sure what to do."

"What did you do, Ashanti?" Alonzo was inching up on his friend with the .45 dangling in his hand. His eyes stung, but he wouldn't let them water.

"It ain't what I've done that concerns me, it's what I'm gonna do. I think I've gone too far to turn back, and I'm sorry to have to bring you into it, but I'm in a real bind. I need your help . . . *we* need your help."

Alonzo paused. "Who the hell is we?"

Ashanti turned around. "I can show you better than I can tell you." He nodded behind Alonzo.

When Alonzo turned around he found himself staring down the barrels of two rose-colored Glocks. The man holding the weapons cracked a half smile, catching the streetlight on his jeweled teeth.

"Ashanti," Animal addressed his protégé but kept his eyes and guns on Alonzo, "if all your friends greet you with guns, I'd hate to meet your enemies."

Alonzo's head whipped back and forth in confusion. "Ashanti, what the fuck going on?"

"Zo, this is the secret I've been keeping. I don't think you've ever met, but I'm sure you've heard of the big homie Animal," Ashanti said proudly.

Alonzo was taken aback. Within a few minutes he had seen two unlikely things: himself about to shoot one of his closest friends thinking he was a snitch and a legend resurrected from the grave. He had heard stories about Animal, his unfortunate rise and fall, but to see him live and in the flesh was almost surreal. His mind was immediately flooded with a million questions. "My nigga, what's this all about?"

"Payback," Ashanti told him. He went on to give Alonzo the short version of what brought them to that point, with Animal occasionally filling in blanks. By the time Alonzo finished hearing the tragic story, his head felt like it was spinning.

"Seems we ain't the only ones with an axe to grind against the Clarks," Alonzo said.

"I'm gonna grind more than an axe," Animal assured him.

"Look, Zo, we kinda short on time, so I'm gonna keep it as tall with you as I possibly can. We about to jump out the window with no parachutes and get at ya man, Shai. The deck is stacked against, but at this point, we ain't got much choice other than finishing the game. I understand if you wanna step off, and I won't hold it against you, but I wouldn't be mad to

have the two cats I love the most on both my flanks in this battle." He looked from Animal to Alonzo. "Whether you're in or
not, this is something I gotta do."

Alonzo looked into Ashanti's eyes and saw no fear, only
determination. He was about to go against insurmountable
odds and would do it with pride, all because it meant something to his friend. Little Ashanti was a real soldier. Alonzo was
sorry he had ever doubted him and would never make that mistake again.

"Fuck it, who wants to live forever anyway, right? What's
the game plan?"

THIRTY-NINE

FRANKIE FELT LIKE SHE HAD JUST LAY down for her nap when she heard her cell phone ringing. She rolled over and plucked it from the nightstand, looking at the caller ID with one eye. She saw Cutty's name flashing across the screen and hit IGNORE. It had been a long day, and she was tired as hell, so the last thing she wanted to do was chitchat with anyone, especially him. As soon as her cell stopped ringing her house phone started. She placed the pillow over her head trying to drown it out, knowing that it was Cutty calling again. When the ringing stopped and the answering machine picked up, she heard his gruff voice come through the speaker.

"Frankie Angels, I know your ass is up there. I'm in front of your building. We got business to discuss, so bring your ass downstairs so we can talk. You hear me, Frankie? Girlie, if you keep ignoring me, then I'm gonna start leaning on this car horn until you come see what I want or somebody calls the police. Stop playing with me, Frankie," he threatened.

Frankie let out a long sigh from beneath her pillow. She knew if she continued to ignore Cutty he would make good on his threat. With a low growl, she rolled out of bed and prepared to go see what the hell he wanted. When she came out of the building she was dressed in sweatpants, a bathrobe, head scarf, and wore mismatched furry slippers. Boots and Vashaun were sitting in their usual spots on the stoop. Vashaun gave her a half-hearted wave, but Bess remained silent. She had been acting like she had an attitude with Frankie ever since she stopped Veronica from taking advantage of Porsha. It made things a bit tense with them living in the same building, but Frankie didn't care. The chicks on her block were cool, but she and Porsha had broken bread. They had been up together and down together, and that held a lot more weight. Frankie returned Vashaun's half-hearted wave and ignored Bess, continuing to Cutty's truck, which was idling near the curb.

"Get in." Cutty nodded in the way of a greeting. "Damn, you look like a hood rat," he joked once she was inside the truck.

"Don't start with me, Cutty. I ain't in the mood for it today." Frankie glanced over at Bess and Vashaun, who were both clocking her hard.

Cutty peeped it too. "These bitches giving you trouble? You know I got a few homegirls that'll come through here and tighten them up on the strength," he offered.

"Nah, it ain't that serious. So what's so important that you couldn't call instead of coming all the way out here?" Frankie asked. She wanted to be rid of Cutty so she could get back to her much-needed nap.

"You know, I don't do them phones like that. Besides, I had some business out this way at Blood Orchid," he told her.

"Blood Orchid? What the hell you doing in there?"

"That's none of your concern, li'l girl. Anyhow, I came out

330

here to holla at you about putting in some work. You down for that?"

"I'm always down to make some paper. What's the lick? Some old-ass trick need fleecing?" she asked.

"Nah, something a li'l heavier. I got the plug on a high-stakes card game that's supposed to be going down tonight."

"Tonight? That's kinda short notice," she said. Normally they cased a spot before they hit it, and it was unlike Cutty to move spontaneously.

"I know, but when opportunity knocks, you gotta be ready to open the door. There's gonna be a lot of money at that game, and we need it, feel me?"

"Yeah, I feel you," Frankie said uncertainly.

Cutty looked at her. "You ain't getting cold feet on me are you, Frankie Angels?"

"Nah, Cutty. I'm just thinking about how we gonna pull this off. If the card game is as heavy as you say, I know there's gonna be security. What are we supposed to do, shoot our way in and out?"

"Frankie, I'm crazy, not stupid. Getting in is the easiest part, especially since we're invited. This bitch-ass nigga uptown who owes me some paper is a guest of this card game, so we're rolling in with him. I'm posing as his muscle, and you'll play the role of his pampered whore," Cutty laughed.

"Why I gotta be his whore? Why can't I just be his girl or his chick?"

"Frankie, you can be whatever your mind tells you to be for this caper. As long as you're on time, I could care less."

"Nigga, you know Frankie Angels is *always* on time. You just do your part and make sure we ain't walking into no bullshit. I ain't with no cowboy shit, Cutty," she warned.

"Frankie, this is easy money, ma. Ain't gonna be nothing but a bunch of old washed-up hustlers who think they still got it and a few young boys hanging around to carry their change purses. Once they see that iron flashing, ain't nobody gonna want no sauce. I can't do this without you, Frankie Angels. You with me?"

Frankie weighed it. She and Cutty had been mostly doing cons or high-end rip-offs, and it had been awhile since she'd had to point a gun at anybody. A part of her was nervous, but on the other hand, she knew if Cutty was jumping out the window with less than a day's preparation there was some heavy paper on the line, and she needed the money.

"I'm with you," she said.

"That's my bitch," Cutty patted her on the leg.

"Don't play with me, Cutty."

"Sorry, I meant my dawg. You know I love you, Frankie Angels."

She twisted her lips. "Love you too, career criminal. Now, if there's nothing else, I'm going back upstairs to get in my bed," she reached for the door handle.

He stopped her. "Actually, there is. You know, after we talked the other day it really got me to thinking . . . you know about how I've been moving."

"So does that mean you're finally gonna start treating Jada right?"

Cutty frowned. "Hell, nah. Fuck that thieving bitch. Jada is gonna continue to be my doormat until her debt is paid. I was talking about Fatima. I got enough paper put away to where I can slow down for a minute and try to take some time out for her. I been in prison so long that I really don't know my kid, and I wanna change that."

Frankie looked at him strangely. "You now, until this moment, I'd have never thought that you had a heart in that nappy chest of yours." She plucked at one of his chest hairs peeking up through his shirt.

"Ouch!" He swatted her. "See, here I am trying to have a moment with you and you wanna go and fuck it up, just like a woman." Cutty shook his head.

"I'm sorry, Cutty. On the real, I think it's a good idea. Little girls need their daddies, no matter how grown they are."

"Yeah, Fatima is a wild one." He laughed. "I guess the apple doesn't fall too far from the tree. I'd really like for you to meet her too."

Frankie smiled. "I'd like that. But first, you two spend some time together trying to mend those fences. We can do the introductions after that."

"Bet. Who knows, maybe me, you, and Fatima can—"

"Let me stop you before you ruin this li'l moment, Cutty," Frankie interrupted. "You know I don't shit where I work. I ain't fucking with you like that."

"Frankie, you act like I'm an ugly nigga or something," he said defensively.

"No, Cutty. You're actually very handsome, but that's only on the outside. I know how you think, so I could never fuck with you like that. If you ever tried to treat me like you treat Jada, I'd kill you in your sleep, so let's not even put ourselves through the motions," she got out of the truck.

"One day, Frankie Angels!" he called after her.

"I doubt it, but you can hold on to hope for as long you like," she said over her shoulder and sashayed toward her building.

As she approached the stoop, she noticed Bess and Vashaun staring at her. From the way they suddenly got quiet she knew that they had been talking about her. When Frankie made eye contact with the girls, Vashaun turned her eyes away, but Bess kept staring. Frankie didn't do *eye battles*; she was more into hand-to-hand combat, so she decided it was time to confront Bess and see just where she wanted to go with it.

"What up?" Frankie stood in front of the stoop and addressed the girls.

"What's going on, Frankie?" Vashaun gave her phony smile. Bess just rolled her eyes.

"That's what I'm trying to figure out. What's good with you, Bess?" Frankie called her out.

"Ain't shit good with me." Bess snaked her neck.

"Obviously, because you walking around with an attitude with me like I kicked your dog," Frankie stated. "You got a problem with me or something, Bess?"

Bess turned and looked up at Frankie. "As a matter of fact, I do. That was some bullshit you pulled the other day, Frankie."

"What, you mean during the fight? Bess, you know homie tripped Porsha, and it wouldn't have been right to let Veronica get at her. That shit was foul," Frankie explained.

"Yeah, well, just staying out of it would've been the smart thing to do. A lot of people from the neighborhood are feeling some type of way about you jumping in."

Frankie looked at Bess as if she had taken leave of her senses. "Shorty, you sound silly. Porsha is like my sister. Ain't no way I was gonna see her go out like no sucker. I don't know how y'all bitches do it down here, but in Harlem, we look out for our own."

"Well, this ain't Harlem; it's Brooklyn," Bess reminded her.

"I wouldn't give a fuck if it was the moon. That rule is universal with me," Frankie shot back. "And as far as muthafuckas on this block feeling some type of way for me defending my girl, anybody who wants it knows where to find me." Frankie stepped over the girls and went up the stairs into her building.

Frankie was stomping her way up the stairs when Dena opened her apartment door and stepped out. "I heard you yelling. Is everything okay?"

"Everything is good. I just had to G-check these bitches real quick," Frankie said in a huff.

"Them hoes still tripping over what happened the other day?" Dena asked.

"You know they are. Bess out there talking about people on this block are feeling some type of way about me getting in the middle—like I give a fuck. She's lucky I didn't decide to bust her ass that day, and Harlem could've had a two for one out here."

"That Bess is something else." Dena shook her head. "Not for nothing, you might wanna keep an eye on her ass, Frankie. Bess ain't the toughest bitch in this hood, but she's the sneakiest."

"That bum bitch don't want no parts of me. If Bess ever try to get outta pocket, I'm gonna molly-wop that broad all up and down Jefferson," Frankie said confidently.

"Well, just be on point. It would make me feel better. You know I would have to wild out if somebody tried to do something to my Frankie Angels." She reached out to touch Frankie's face, but Frankie pulled away.

"Chill out," Frankie said, looking around to make sure no one had seen.

"Stop being so jumpy, Frankie. Ain't nobody out here but us." Dena took a step forward, and Frankie backed up. "What's good with you?"

"Ain't nothing, Dena. I'm just tired and aggravated," Frankie lied. The truth was that Dena was starting to make her feel uncomfortable. She'd initially enjoyed her carefree romps with Dena, but lately, she had been very clingy, and it turned Frankie off. Women with her were more of a vice than a choice, and Dena was starting to crowd her.

"I can dig that. Well, look, why don't I run to the store and get us some heroes. We can chill at your crib, relax, and watch a movie," Dena suggested.

"I'm not really feeling up to it. I'm just gonna go in the crib and crash," Frankie said, continuing to her apartment.

"Okay, so let's hook up later tonight then," Dena called after her.

"I wish I could, but I've already made plans. But I'm gonna call you," Frankie promised and closed the door.

"I'll bet you did," Dena murmured under her breath, thinking of the truck she'd seen Frankie getting out of a few minutes prior. Dena was feeling in a way about how Frankie had brushed her off. The more she thought on it, she realized that Frankie's attitude toward her always changed when she'd seen or spoken to Cutty, which had been a lot lately. Dena knew that she and Frankie had agreed that they wouldn't make their fling complicated with feelings, but Dena had no control over her heart. In Frankie, she found the best of both worlds—a BFF and a lover, and the thought of losing that closeness to someone else panicked her, and she feared something bad was about to befall their relationship.

PART IV

LOVE & GUNPLAY

FORTY

ANIMAL SAT BEHIND THE WHEEL OF HIS trusty rental car, steaming a blunt and listening to the night sounds. Ashanti rode shotgun. He was flicking the safety of the black Mac11 on and off, deep in his own thoughts. The sound of the safety being clicked over and over again irritated Animal, but he let him be. They were about to ride into a tense situation, and everybody seemed to be on edge, except Alonzo.

Animal watched him curiously through the rearview mirror as he moved with almost mechanical precision, loading the big .45, then placed it to the side and began loading his .357. He'd offered Alonzo one of the machine guns stashed in the trunk, but he had declined, opting for his revolvers. His reasoning was that he never had to worry about them jamming on him in a tight situation. Animal had expected Alonzo to show signs of nervousness considering they were about to bet a losing hand, but he was the picture of calm. He was almost like a soldier who had seen several tours of duty but was always ready to sign up for one more. The more time Animal spent around Alonzo, the more comfortable he became with the idea of him riding along.

The car was parked in the lot of a small restaurant which sat right next to a nondescript motel off the 1&9 in Elizabeth, NJ. For all intents and purposes, it looked like nothing more than a seedy motel where you could get your jollies on for a few dollars an hour. The only thing that betrayed its secret was the luxury cars lined up in the parking lot that night. The address to the motel had been the one Money Mike had whispered in Animal's ear before Animal made him a eunuch. It was the location of the high-roller card game and the place where he and Shai Clark would have their day of reckoning.

"Damn, you see that bitch?" Ashanti got closer to the windshield. He was looking at a caramel-colored woman wearing a skintight black dress and thigh-high boots. She strode through the motel parking lot like she owned it.

"Yeah, she is nice," Alonzo watched the girl too.

"That square-ass nigga she with look like he don't even know what to do with all that ass." Ashanti was speaking of the man walking arm in arm with the girl. He was an older cat wearing a fur that looked like the sleeves were too short.

"Probably not," Alonzo laughed. As he continued to watch the girl, something about her walk was familiar. He couldn't see her face because it was covered by long black hair and dark sunglasses, but her body language spoke to him. "I think I know that broad, but I can't really tell."

"Knowing you, you probably smashed," Ashanti teased him.

Alonzo shrugged. "Hey, don't hate the player."

"You think they're going to the card game too?" Ashanti asked Animal.

"If I had to guess, I'd say yes. Don't look like homeboy is carrying no laundry in that bag." Animal pointed to a second man who was trailing behind the couple. Ashanti and Alonzo were so preoccupied with the girl that they hadn't noticed the man, but Animal did. He waited until the trio had disappeared inside the motel before giving the nod that he was ready. "Let's do this." He grabbed the duffel bag he had packed for the occasion and got out of the car.

"*That's* what I'm talking about! No more talking. Time to make these niggaz bleed!" Ashanti said excitedly, jumping out of the car like a kid who had just arrived at an amusement park.

Alonzo simply followed in silence.

The three desperados crept across the parking lot like shadows, with Animal leading the way. He peered in the window of the office and saw that there was only one clerk, so he held one finger up to relay it to his crew. Pulling a red bandana over the lower half of his face, Animal stepped into the office. When the desk clerk heard the bell above the door jingle he looked up from the skin-magazine he had been looking at and found himself confronted with three armed men.

Ashanti stepped forward and chambered a round into the Mac11. "Night-night, nigga," he pointed the machine gun at the frightened desk clerk.

"What the fuck are you doing?" Animal pushed the machine gun away.

Ashanti looked at him quizzically. "You said we coming in here to slump niggaz, so I was gonna slump him."

"Go ahead and blast him and not only will you announce our arrival to every cop within a mile, but you'll also end up on the six o'clock news, genius." Animal pointed at the overhead camera. He leaned over the desk and knocked the clerk out with a blow to the head from his gun. When he was sure the clerk wouldn't get back up he turned to Ashanti. "Now, tuck that hammer until I tell you otherwise and go get the videotapes outta the back."

"Fucking killjoy," Ashanti mumbled on his way to the back office to search for the surveillance system. A few minutes later he came back out holding three VCR tapes, which he shoved into Animal's chest before leaving the office.

"Damn kids." Animal shook his head. "I hope I ain't gotta babysit you too," he looked at Alonzo.

Alonzo laughed at Animal's statement and headed outside.

The three men crept up the exterior stairs to the second floor of the motel. They could hear laughter and music the closer they got to the end of the tier. From what Money Mike had told him, they rented two rooms for the event; one for the actual game and the other for the entertainment, which meant pussy and drugs. Animal stopped in front of the room that Mike had told him the players would be in and set his bag on the ground. He pulled out a railroad spike and a sledgehammer with half the shaft sawed off. He handed the railroad spike to Ashanti and took the sledgehammer.

"Everybody remember what they're supposed to do?" Animal asked his cohorts.

"Hell, yeah," Ashanti leveled the railroad spike with the peephole.

"Once we cross this threshold, there ain't no turning back. Everything changes," Animal reminded them.

Ashanti sucked his teeth. "Blood, you know wherever you go, I go."

"And wherever he goes, I go. Somebody has got to keep his li'l ass out of trouble," Alonzo joked.

"That's my brother's keeper." Ashanti gave Alonzo a nod. "Now you gonna keep giving speeches, or are we gonna go up in there and lay it down for Gucci?"

"Zo, you wanna do the honors?" Animal secured his grip on the sledgehammer.

"It would be my pleasure." Alonzo stepped forward and knocked on the door.

A few seconds passed, then they heard someone come to the door. "Who is it?" a voice called from behind the door.

"Payback, muthafucka!" Animal roared and swung the sledgehammer with everything he had. The hammer made contact with the spike and someone howled in pain on the receiving end.

It was officially on.

Frankie's legs felt like noodles while she walked through the motel parking lot, and it wasn't because of the thigh-high boots she was wearing either. From the moment they'd set out, the whole situation felt wrong.

Cutty's inside man and her date for the night was a slightly older man named Davis. In his heyday, he had been a big-time hustler from out of the Bronx, but now, he was just another aging street legend who tried to get in where he fit in. Before Cutty went to prison, he had fronted Davis some work, and when he got locked up, Davis figured that his debt had been wiped clean. Imagine his surprise when Cutty showed up years later and demanded his money. Davis tried to play Cutty to the left about the old debt, but Cutty was a man who was serious about his money, and to show Davis how serious he was, Cutty had paid a visit to his wife. He made it clear to Davis and his family that if he didn't get his money he would take the debt in blood. Davis had no way of getting Cutty's money, so Cutty offered to turn him onto the high-stakes poker game where Cutty could get what he was owed, and then some. Davis knew what he was doing was risky, but he had no choice.

When they got to the motel room where the card game was being held they were greeted by a young man who was guarding the door. Within the first five seconds of opening his mouth, the young man managed to run afoul of Frankie.

"Entertainment in the next room; only players here," he told her.

"*Excuse* you?" Frankie cocked her head.

"Ain't you one of the 'dancers'?" he held his fingers up in air quotations.

"Nigga, you got me fucked up. I ain't no whore!" Frankie snapped. She looked at Davis and Cutty. "I thought you said these were some classy gentlemen but apparently not when they can't tell the difference between a whore and a boss bitch."

"I didn't mean no disrespect. I just thought you were one of the working girls." The young man looked from Frankie's tight dress to her thigh-high boots.

Davis stepped up and snaked his hand around Frankie's waist, pulling her closer. "It's a simple mistake, baby. No harm no foul," he kissed her on the cheek. "Step aside, youngster," Davis brushed the kid away. "I smell money, and I need some of it." He led Frankie and Cutty into the motel room.

Their coats were taken, and they were shown to the table, where Davis was greeted by some of his old street chums. He got plenty of compliments for the fine young girl on his arm, which he soaked up, while palming Frankie's ass to show just how much of the man he was.

Frankie rested her head on Davis's shoulder and spoke in a hushed tone. "Don't feel yourself too much; this is only an act. If you grab my ass one more time, I'm gonna say fuck this lick and kill you. Are we clear on that?"

"Crystal clear, baby." Davis wisely backed off.

"Watch that temper, Frankie Angels," Cutty whispered. "You're supposed to be in character, remember?"

"Yeah, I remember." Frankie whipped the hair of her wig and walked off.

Davis was shown to a seat at the table with the other card players, while Cutty helped himself to the bar and Frankie sat on a loveseat in the corner where several other ladies sat passing around a blunt and gossiping. They tried to make small talk with Frankie, but she only half-listened. She was too busy watching the room. Cutty had told her that the card party would be full of old heads who had no real power, but it didn't look that way to her. She knew the look of a killer when she saw one, and she was surrounded by them. Cutty had walked her into a nest of vipers, and it was too late for her to turn back.

When someone knocked on the door Frankie almost leaped out of her skin. She watched from the loveseat as the young man who had insulted her went to answer it. He placed his eye to the peephole and ordered the person on the other side to identify himself. The person outside the door shouted something, followed by a loud boom. The young man screamed in pain and staggered backward, drawing the attention of everyone in the room as blood spurted from his face. He dropped to the ground writhing in agony, holding his bloody face. Frankie looked up at the door and almost vomited when she saw his eyeball hanging from the end of a spike where the peephole used to be. Before anyone could process what was going on, the whole door crashed in and two men wearing red bandanas over their faces stormed the room.

FORTY-ONE

ANIMAL WAS THE FIRST ONE THROUGH THE door, Glock in one hand and sledgehammer in the other. Alonzo followed closely behind, his .357 and .45 sweeping back and forth, daring someone to move. They'd decided to leave Ashanti out on the tier to cover their backs. Of course, he complained about it, but Animal wouldn't budge on his decision. He didn't want Ashanti's trigger-happy ass to ruin his moment of truth.

Animal addressed the room. "I think we all know what this is, so let's make it as painless as possible."

An older gentleman who had been sitting near the door leaped to his feet. "You know who the fuck you're trying to rip off?" he snarled at Animal menacingly.

Animal swung the sledgehammer one-handed, caving in the side of the man's face, and killing him instantly. "Anymore dumb-ass questions?" Animal asked the frightened onlookers. "Get that," Animal nodded to Alonzo.

Alonzo moved over to the table and began scooping the

money off it and stuffing it into the duffel bag Animal had used to carry his tools. He could feel the cold stares on the men they were robbing, but he ignored them and focused on collecting every last dollar. He looked over at the ladies on the couch, who were all trembling except one. The girl who they had seen in the parking lot. The way she was staring at Alonzo made him uneasy. At first he thought she was looking at his face trying to figure out who was behind the mask, but her eyes were fixed on his guns. The light of recognition went off in both their heads at the same time. He knew Frankie well enough to know that if she was at the party, it wasn't a social call. It seemed that they had the same agendas, but Alonzo had beat her to the punch. He gave her a knowing wink and continued collecting money.

"Gentlemen," Animal continued, "I don't know you, and this ain't nothing personal. You just happened to be in the wrong place at the wrong time. Once I get what I came for I'll be on my way."

"You got our money, what more you want?" a man wearing a crinkled green suit asked.

"Shai Clark," Animal informed him.

The man in the green suit laughed. "Son, seems like you wasted a trip. We don't know no Shai Clark, do we, fellas?" He looked around the table.

Animal sighed and shot the man in the green suit in the head. Blood splattered all over the table and the man sitting next to him. "Look, if y'all wanna keep playing with my intelligence, I got enough bullets to put this whole room to sleep. I know this is the Clark card party, so somebody bring me a Clark before I really get upset." He pulled the other Glock from his pants and tapped the Pretty Bitches together threateningly.

No one spoke.

"That's the way y'all wanna do it, huh?" Animal began slowly pacing around the table. "I tried to be nice." He stopped short of an older Italian man who had been sitting at the card table. "Now it's time to be nasty." He pressed both guns against the back of the man's head.

A younger Italian man with thick black hair, wearing a tracksuit, jumped up from the table. "Hey, now you're crossing the line. If you blacks wanna kill each other in the streets, that's one thing, but leave us out of it. We're with Gee-Gee."

"You're gonna be with God if you don't give me who I came for," Animal assured him.

The young Italian man swallowed hard. He had been against coming to the card game, but their boss Gee-Gee had insisted they attend as a sign of respect to Shai. The young man didn't care that Gee-Gee looked at Shai as an associate. To him and the rest of their organization, he was a nigger street punk, and he wasn't willing to sacrifice one of their own to protect him.

"Look," the young Italian man began, "this is Shai's card game, but he ain't here."

"Well, then, who the fuck is running this circus?" Animal asked.

Suddenly, the sound of shattering glass came from the bathroom. Without having to be told, Alonzo darted to the back to investigate. He returned a few seconds later with a worried expression on his face. "Somebody bolted out the bathroom window. I'm gonna dip outside and see if I can catch whoever it was."

"Don't bother." Ashanti walked into the room with the Mac11 jammed into the back of the man who tried to escape. "Look who I caught trying to make a break for it."

Animal smiled from ear to ear behind his bandana at the sight of who Ashanti had captured. "Nice of you to join us, Swann."

Tionna was just coming back from the vending machines with an arm full of snacks for Gucci and her. She was glad to see her friend getting her appetite back because it meant that she was one step closer to getting back to where she needed to be. What Gucci had gone through would've broken most people, but the fact that she was pulling through it was a testament to her strength. The physical wounds would take a while to heal, and the mental ones even longer, but no matter how long it took, Tionna would be by her side.

She and Gucci had been crime partners since grade school, always having each other's backs against any and all odds. When they got older, their problems got bigger, but that only made their bond stronger. When Tionna was assed out with nothing but the clothes on her back, Gucci and her mom had been right there for her, even going as far as letting Tionna and her two sons move in with Ms. Ronnie when Don B. had her apartment burned down. Tionna and Gucci were more than friends; they were sisters.

Tionna entered Gucci's hospital room, smiling from ear to ear because the vending machine had her favorite toasted almond ice cream snacks, but the smile faded when she saw two men standing over Gucci's bed. At first she thought that they were the detectives that had come back to ask more questions about the shooting, but that thought faded when she saw one of them injecting something into Gucci's IV.

"What are y'all doing? You're not supposed to be here!" Tionna yelled, trying to draw the attention of the hospital staff.

"Grab that bitch!" one of the men ordered.

Tionna turned and tried to run but was grabbed roughly by her hair and dragged into the room. The man tried to close the door, but Tionna stuck her foot in the doorjamb to stop him. He slammed the door repeatedly on Tionna's foot to try to get her to remove it, but she wouldn't. She knew if that door closed they were finished, so he was going to have to break her foot to get her to move it. But instead of bothering to break her foot, he slugged her in the gut and knocked the wind out of her. Then he dragged her across the room and tossed her at the feet of the guy Tionna had seen injecting the foreign substance into Gucci's IV. He was a slightly older, brown-skinned man wearing a gray suit and black tie with a white shirt.

"Now, why do you wanna go and stir up trouble unnecessarily?" Angelo asked with a shake of his head.

"What are you doing to her?" Gucci mumbled groggily from her bed. Whatever Angelo had put in the IV was starting to kick in, but she wasn't too far gone yet to know that something wasn't right.

"Don't you worry your pretty little head about it, doll. Once that cocktail kicks in, this will be the least of your concerns." Angelo patted Gucci's leg.

"Whatever you're thinking about doing to her, you better un-think it or else," Tionna threatened.

"Or else what? Big bad Animal gonna come for me?" Angelo

asked. "I sure hope so, because if he don't, that means I wasted a trip, and you bitches are dead."

"What do you want?" Gucci asked. She was starting to see double.

"We want your boyfriend, and you're gonna give him to us." Angelo handed Gucci a cell phone.

Gucci laughed weakly. "Fuck you."

Angelo grabbed her by the neck and shook her. "Bitch, I ain't playing games with you. Now either you get on the phone and call that nigga, or I'm gonna put a crease in your brain." He placed his gun to the top of her head.

Gucci was frightened, but she wouldn't give the men the satisfaction of showing it. If they'd come for Animal, then nine times out of ten she and Tionna would be killed anyway. The two things she regretted most was that she was going to lose Animal again and the fact that her love had condemned her best friend to death with her.

Gucci pursed her dry lips together like she was trying to say something, and when Angelo leaned in to hear what it was, she spat in his face. "When you kill me, it's gonna start the shot-clock on the rest of your worthless-ass life because Animal is gonna kill you!"

Angelo wiped the saliva from the side of his face with Gucci's bedsheet. "If you like it, I love it." He cocked the hammer back on the gun.

"Wait!" Tionna cried out. "She can't bring you Animal, but I can."

"You?" Angelo asked curiously.

"Tionna, don't," Gucci pleaded with tears in her eyes.

"Gucci, they're gonna kill us if we don't," Tionna said, her eyes also filled with tears. "He gave me a number to reach him at, but he'll only pick up if I call from this phone." She handed Angelo the phone.

"How could you?" Gucci cried, looking at Tionna in disbelief.

"I'm sorry, Gucci, but I'm doing this for us. I don't wanna die," Tionna tried to explain. She looked at her pleading friend, and her heart broke. Gucci may have seen what she was doing as betrayal, but Tionna saw it as their best chance at survival.

"Then let's get Mr. Lover Man on the line." Angelo hit send on the phone.

Animal eyeballed Swann like he was a Porterhouse steak that had just been set before a starving man. The beef between Swann and Animal went back even further and deeper than the one between him and Shai. At one time, Swann had been a comrade in arms and, to an extent, even considered a brother, but somewhere along the path, he had lost his way. When he murdered Tech on the word of an outsider, Shai Clark, it put him out of favor, but most were hesitant to touch him because of his affiliation with the Clarks. Animal had no such reservations. He had come for Shai Clark, but Swann was a welcomed consolation prize.

With his eyes still locked on Swann, Animal spoke to the room. "Ladies and gentlemen, if you have no affiliation with the Clark family and don't wish to die, please take this time to leave with my sincere apologies. But if you're loyal to these traitorous rats and have a problem with what I'm about to do to ol' Swann, then feel free to stick around and we can settle up."

"Yes, indeed," Alonzo cosigned, holding his two revolvers.

All at once, men and women spilled out of the motel room in a near stampede. Alonzo watched Frankie and a dark-skinned dude exchange heated words in the corner. It looked like she was trying to urge him to leave, and he wanted to stay. Alonzo gave Frankie a *get-the-fuck-out-of-here* look, hoping that she could convince her friend to do the same. There was no doubt in his mind that Animal meant to kill anyone who remained, and he didn't want Frankie to be among that number. Finally, she got her two male guests to move for the exit. On the way out, the one who had been holding the bag looked over at Alonzo and smirked. Alonzo didn't think that Frankie would be foolish enough to let her friend in on their secret, but he planned to look into it later and deal with all parties accordingly.

Slowly, Animal walked over to Swann, pulling his bandana from his face so Swann could see just who he was up against. "Long time no see, *Blood*," Animal said the last word as if it left a foul taste in his mouth.

"Not long enough, if you ask me," Swann retorted. The deck was stacked against him, but regardless, he was a gangsta and wouldn't fold. "I hear you've been busy."

"If you call pushing your pussy-ass team off the earth busy, then I guess so," Animal replied. "Blood, do you know how long I've dreamt of this moment?"

"Not hardly as long as I have. You know, when Shai had me put Tech in his place, I told him that we needed to whack you out too, but he didn't listen."

"He should've," Animal told him. "You know, for years I've looked at the li'l rift in our family from every angle, and I still haven't been able to figure out what made you betray your homies."

Swann shook his head. "All these years, and you still don't get it, which is why you niggaz will always be the low men on the totem pole. Me killing Tech wasn't about betrayal; it was about maintaining order. No matter how many times y'all were warned, you continued to run around like rabid dogs, killing and taking what you wanted, and that wasn't good for business."

"So, you call killing a nigga a *business* decision?" Animal scowled.

"No, I call it a tender mercy. Better I killed him clean than Shai sending somebody to make a mess outta him like he's gonna do with you. You should've stayed in hiding, Animal."

"Ironically, I probably would've, but you crossed the line when yo' people let Gucci fall under his bullet," Animal told him.

Swann laughed. "I'd heard this was all over a bitch, but I gave you more credit than that, Animal. I could've respected you if you'd come back to avenge your homie, but you're throwing your life away over a bitch! And you wonder why you'll always be looked at as a li'l nigga."

Animal punched Swann in the face, sending him crashing into the card table. "This li'l nigga hits hard, don't he?" He yanked Swann to his feet. Animal fired another fist into Swann's face, bloodying his nose. "Who do you think you're talking to?" Animal slapped Swann viciously across the face with one of his guns. "You got Shai thinking you're the supreme street general, but that's because he don't know you as good as he thinks he does." Animal slapped him with the gun again. He pressed Swann against the wall and crammed his Glock into his mouth. "Beneath that gangsta persona, I

355

know your true face, and so did Tech, which is why you were so willing when the order came down to kill him. You went through a lot to protect your secret, but maybe I'll tell it after I body you." The feeling of his cell phone vibrating in his pocket gave Animal pause.

Swann's eyes went from Animal's face to his vibrating pocket and back again. "If I were you, I'd answer that," he mumbled around the Glock that was shoved firmly in his mouth.

Animal was going to ignore the call, but it could've only been one person, and if she was calling, then something might've been wrong. Keeping his gun in Swann's mouth, he slipped his phone from his pocket and placed it to his ear. "What you need, T? I kinda got my hands full right now."

"I got my hands full too. Wanna guess what I'm holding?" a masculine voice said on the other end of the line.

"Who the fuck is this, and where's my girl?" Animal roared into Angelo's ear.

"Tsk, tsk! Such language," Angelo taunted him. "Your shorty is good . . . for now. How long she stays that way is on you, li'l homie."

"On everything I love, if you touch her I'm gonna hunt you down and make you wish your mama had swallowed you," Animal promised.

"I don't doubt that you'd give it the old college try, but for as long as I got your bitch, you ain't gonna do shit but shut your fucking mouth and listen," Angelo barked. "You thought that shit you were doing running around town was real cute, didn't you? Instead of keeping your head in the sand like a good little ostrich, you're strutting around Harlem like a peacock.

You wanted our attention; well, li'l nigga, you got it. Our friend wants to have a chat with you."

"That bitch ass-nigga Shai ain't no friend of mine, and the only thing we got to say to each other will be said over gun smoke," Animal capped. "You got something of mine, and I got something of yours. You touch one hair on Gucci's head, and I'm gonna blow Swann's muthafucking brains out, ya dig?"

Angelo sighed. "You still think you're calling the shots, huh?" Angelo put the phone on speaker. "You listening, li'l fella?"

"What're you playing at?" Animal asked nervously.

"I ain't playing at shit. I'm actually quite serious, and I'm about to show you how serious I am. Ayo," Angelo called to his henchman, "since these bitches think they're so fly, let's see if they got wings."

The henchman smiled and dragged Tionna to her feet. She tried to put all of her weight down so he couldn't move her, but she was too light in the ass. He dragged her like a rag doll over to the hospital window and held her in front of it so she could see the street far below.

"Please don't!" Gucci called out frantically.

Hearing her voice made Animal panic. "Don't you do it!" Animal said in an almost pleading tone.

"You wanna roll with the big dogs, then you need to know how it feels to get bit," Angelo spat venomously at the phone. "Do that bitch!" he ordered his henchman.

"You ain't gotta do this!" Tionna clung to the henchman for dear life.

"Sorry, shorty. I got my orders." He took a step back and

kicked Tionna as hard as he could, sending her through the window like a battering ram and into the cool night air.

"Gucci!" Animal howled when he heard the scream through the phone. It was a sound so eerie that it would stick with him for the rest of his days. He stood there with the phone glued to his ear in shock. He was so numb that he couldn't do much other than stand there. Animal turned his tear-filled eyes to Swann, and Swann knew that it was over for him. "Your boy just forfeited your life, homie."

"Animal . . ." He heard Gucci's voice coming through the phone softly.

Animal's face lit up. "Gucci?" he pressed the phone harder to his ear so he could hear her. "Baby, I thought . . . are you okay?"

"Animal, I don't know what's going on . . . these guys . . . Tionna is dead," Gucci mumbled, the cocktail Angelo had given her was kicking in and she could barely stay awake. "Help me, baby."

"Gucci, I'm coming for you!" Animal declared.

"Ain't that sweet?" Angelo was back on the phone. "You can rush on out here to the hospital, but we'll probably be gone by then. It's like I told you. My peoples wants to have a conversation with you, and this sweet little piece of candy will make sure you play nice when you show up."

They had Animal by the balls. He knew that whatever scenario laid out for him was a death trap, but what choice did he have? If he had to give his life for Gucci's, he'd do it readily. "Name your terms."

"I'm gonna holla at you later on with an address. You show

up—alone—and your bitch walks. You play games, and I'm gonna clap her pretty ass. Sound fair to you?" Angelo asked.

"A'ight," Animal reluctantly agreed. "I'll be waiting for your call. But, my nigga, you better turn her over the same way you found her or I'm gonna make you wear that."

"Don't worry, I ain't gonna let my niggaz deflower this whore. You do your part, and we'll do ours," Angelo assured him. "Oh, and before I forget, cut my partner loose. If Swann doesn't call me in three minutes to let me know he's good, all bets are off. Not only am I gonna kill this bitch, but I'm gonna make sure I fuck her until she bleeds on my dick first. The pussy gotta be the bomb if your dumb ass was willing to commit suicide over it." Angelo laughed and ended the call.

Animal looked at the silent phone as if it was the most vile thing he had ever seen. He had so many emotions running ramped inside him that his chest swelled to the point where he felt like it would pop. Alonzo and Ashanti were looking at him waiting for word of what the next move was, but he couldn't even form his lips to tell them what he'd just learned. He happened to look up and catch Swann giving him a smug look.

"Fuck you smirking at?" Animal snarled.

Swann held his hands up. "Don't pay me no mind, *Blood*. As a matter of fact, it's about time I take my leave of you, ain't it? You know, my nigga, Angelo is a stickler for time," he chuckled.

Animal felt his body begin to tremble from the mounting rage. The more he stared at the half smirk on Swann's face, the angrier he got. "You got that, Swann," Animal placed his guns on the table, "but before you dip, let me give you something to look forward to for the next time we meet." Instantly,

Animal hit Swann flush in the mouth. Swann tried to throw his hands up to defend himself, but Animal was relentless in his onslaught of punches. Swann was so disoriented that he tripped over his own feet and fell into the waiting arms of Alonzo and Ashanti.

"What's hood, big homie? You ready to earth this nigga?" Ashanti asked, jamming the Mac11 into Swann's ribs. He was so thirsty to murk him that a trail of slobber escaped over his bottom lip.

"No, let him go," Animal said, not believing his own words.

Ashanti looked at him as if he had lost it. "You can't be fucking serious! Swann is the root of Shai's power in the streets. We kill this nigga, and we cripple the Clarks!"

"They got Gucci, homie," Animal confessed. "Let him go."

Hurt crossed Ashanti's face. "That's how y'all playing?" Ashanti looked at Swann in disgust.

Swann was leaning against the wall, wiping the blood from his mouth with the sleeve of his shirt. "Time is ticking, fellas," he snickered.

"I'm gonna see you again, *Blood*," Animal told Swann.

"Not if I see you first," Swann said before slipping from the motel room.

"Why do I feel like a rape victim right now?" Alonzo spoke up. He knew what was at stake, and he knew what it meant to let Swann walk. If he wasn't before, he was definitely a marked man now.

"You ain't the only one feeling in a way about this, Zo. They already killed Tionna and got Gucci hostage," Animal filled them in.

"Damn, these niggaz playing dirty," Ashanti said sadly.

"Shai wants me to meet with him; in exchange, they'll let Gucci go."

"You know it's a setup, don't you?" Alonzo asked.

"Yeah, but I ain't got a whole lot of choices right now. I left Gucci hanging once, and I can't do it again. For right now, the ball is in Shai's court," Animal told him.

"Fam, I can't sit by and watch you throw yourself to the dogs like that," Ashanti said emotionally. He couldn't lose his big brother again so soon.

Animal smirked. "Baby boy, you should know me better than that. Me and Shai gonna have our meeting, but I plan on walking outta that muthfucka with my lady and on my own two legs."

"Well, if you got a plan, I'm listening," Alonzo told him.

Animal nodded. "I got a plan, but I doubt if y'all like it."

FORTY-TWO

FRANKIE WAS QUIET FOR THE WHOLE RIDE back to New York. Cutty was going on and on about the masked bandits beating them to the lick and what he was gonna do to Davis if he didn't find a way to get him the money he owed. Frankie was only half-listening. She was too busy thinking about how close they'd come to dying.

Frankie had seen people killed before; she had even taken a life to protect her own, but the motel slayings were different. The lead bandit was ruthless and killed without conscience. There was no doubt in her mind that he had been belched out from the very pits of hell to do the devil's work, which raised a nagging question in the back of her mind; what was Alonzo doing with him? Had it not been for his choice in weapons Frankie probably would've never suspected it was him, but there were very few people who handled the duel cannons so well. They had always been Alonzo's calling card. She knew Alonzo was dabbling in the streets, but if he was robbing Shai Clark and murdering recklessly then he had slipped further back into his

362

old ways than anyone thought. She wondered if she should tell Porsha or just mind her own business. Either way, she planned to confront Alonzo about it. The last thing she wanted was her friend getting caught in the middle of some shit that Alonzo had stirred up.

"Frankie, do you hear me?" Cutty drew her out of her thoughts.

"What?" Frankie asked with an attitude.

"We're here." He nodded to her building, which they had just pulled up in front of. "What the hell is your problem? You've been in a pissy mood the whole ride back."

"Let's see." Frankie tapped her chin. "You say we're going to pull an easy caper, but you walk me into a room full of killers that would've probably murdered us if we'd gone through with it. Then to top it off, you neglect to mention that somebody else was planning to rob the joint too. So what the fuck do you think my problem is, Cutty? Jesus, we almost tried to rob Shai Clark. Do you know what he would've done to us if we had?" Frankie lowered her head in her hands.

"You act like this is my fault. I didn't know whose party it was," he told her.

"Did you bother to check? Of course, you didn't because you were too worried about getting paid. I told you this felt wrong from the beginning, but you wouldn't listen."

"Hold on now. Don't try to act like I put a gun to your head and made you run up in there with me. All I did was present the opportunity. You're right, Frankie, I should've done more research instead of going off on Davis's word, but even if I had found out it was Shai's party, that don't mean I wouldn't have tried to rip it off anyway."

"Then you're a damn fool. Fucking with people like Shai is suicide," she said.

"Try telling that to them three niggaz who right now are sitting somewhere, very much alive, counting *our* paper. I gotta admit those was some cold young niggaz. You see the way the leader blew ol' boy's head off? Reminds me of myself when I was in my twenties," Cutty said proudly.

"I can't believe you're idolizing them for almost killing us!" Frankie said in disbelief.

"They wasn't gonna kill us. You heard what he said. They were there looking for Shai. Besides, I have a feeling regardless of what might of happened, we were gonna walk out of there untouched, at least you would've," he told her.

"What the hell is that supposed to mean?"

Cutty turned to her. "I saw something pass between you and the cat holding the revolvers. I'm not sure what it was, but I know there was something."

"Cutty, you're bugging," Frankie lied. She didn't think anyone saw, but apparently Cutty did.

"We really gonna play this game?" Cutty eased his gun onto his lap. He didn't point it at Frankie, but he made sure she saw it. "Most people would've chalked somebody robbing our robbery was a coincidence, but I don't believe in those. Then when I saw the funny business between you two, a thought entered my head. Maybe they showed up to rob that card game because somebody tipped them off."

"What are you trying to say to me, Cutty?" Frankie asked defensively.

"I'm not trying to say anything to you, Frankie. I'm asking you a question. Did you tip them boys off about the card game?"

Hurt flashed across Frankie's face. "I can't believe you just asked me that." Granted, she was lying about knowing one of the robbers, but she would never betray Cutty.

"Better I come out and ask you than the alternative, right?" He glanced down at the gun on his lap.

"Are you threatening me?" Frankie looked from the gun to Cutty.

"No, I'm waiting for you to answer my question."

"You know what? I don't need this shit. Go fuck yourself, Cutty," Frankie spat.

She opened the door to get out of the truck, but Cutty grabbed her arm roughly and snatched her back inside.

He yanked Frankie's head back, pinning her to the seat, and pressed his gun under her chin. With a fist full of Frankie's hair he snarled in her face. "Look here, li'l girl, don't think because I got love for you that I won't paint the inside of this whip with your brains if you're trying to put shit on me. Now, I'm gonna ask you one more time; did you cross me for them niggaz?"

"Cutty, we're partners! I would never cross you," she pleaded.

"I've seen brother turn against brother in the name of a dollar, so I don't put nothing past nobody. Did you tip them niggaz?" he repeated.

Frankie was frantic. She tried to think of something . . . anything that would guarantee she didn't meet her end in that truck. "How could I tip them off if I didn't know where the game was until we got there, remember?"

Cutty studied her face for a few minutes more before releasing her. "Okay."

Frankie wiped the tears from her eyes with her hands. "You accuse me of betraying you and shoving a gun to my throat and all you've got to say is *okay*?"

"Look, I'm sorry, Frankie. I didn't mean to hurt you, but I had to make sure you were on the up and up. You can't take chances with anyone, even the ones you love. This is a cold game we're playing, baby girl."

"Too cold for me."

"What the hell does that mean?" Cutty asked.

"I'm out," Frankie told him.

"Frankie, I think you're overreacting."

"No, overreacting would be me waiting to catch you slipping and killing you for what you did. This is just me knowing when to throw in the towel." Frankie got out of the truck.

"Wait a second, we had an arrangement," Cutty reminded her.

"Don't worry, I'll get the rest of your money," she assured him.

"I don't know how. You jump ship on me and ain't no other crew in the city gonna work with you," Cutty threatened.

"Then I'll get a job. I'll get *two* jobs if I have to. I just want you out of my hair and my life." She slammed his door.

"You can't just walk away, Frankie!" Cutty called out the window.

"Watch me." She turned and sashayed toward her building.

Dena had been dozing off when she heard Frankie's raised voice out her window. She had been waiting for her all night to tell her what she had heard through the grapevine. She looked outside and saw Cutty's truck idling at the curb. She couldn't see very well through the heavily tinted windows, but from the way the truck was rocking they were either fighting or fucking, and neither sat well with Dena. Jumping into her sweatpants, she grabbed her trusty baseball bat by the door and headed downstairs.

She was just coming out of the building when Frankie was getting out of the truck. She was surprised by the vulgar outfit Frankie was wearing, but more surprised to see Frankie crying. In all the time she had known her, she couldn't ever remember seeing Frankie cry. "You okay?" Dena asked, meeting Frankie halfway.

"I'm good." Frankie brushed past her.

"Frankie, I need to talk to you," Dena told her.

"Not now." Frankie never broke her stride.

"But it's important," Dena grabbed her by the arm.

Frankie spun and in a fit of anger and hurt, took out her frustrations toward Cutty on Dena. "What the fuck is your problem? I said not now, so why don't you just let it go and leave me the fuck alone!" She snatched away from Dena and continued into the building. She hadn't meant to be so sharp with Dena, but she was going through a lot and wasn't thinking straight at the moment.

Dena stood there, feeling the tears welling up in her eyes. Frankie speaking to her like that hurt worse than when she had found out Lazy was cheating on her back in the days. She really liked Lazy, but she was in love with Frankie. Dena looked up and saw Cutty eyeing her like she was a piece of meat. His gaze made her feel dirty.

"Why you looking at me like that? You wanna get in and

maybe hang out for a while?" Cutty asked her as if he hadn't just threatened to kill her lover less than five minutes prior.

"Not if my ass was on fire and you had the last extinguisher on earth." She stuck her middle finger up at Cutty and walked into the building.

Cutty shook his head. "All these bitches are crazy," he mumbled and pulled off.

FORTY-THREE

BY THE NEXT DAY, NEWS OF THE Shai's card game getting robbed was all over the streets. Everybody was whispering about the masked bandits who had the audacity to stick the boss of bosses and the handsome bounty placed on their heads. Shai had offered fifty thousand dollars a piece for the bandits and one hundred thousand for the man who had led them. It was safe to say that Alonzo had finally made it to the big times, but how long he lived to celebrate his newfound notoriety remained the question.

Animal had assured them that Shai would be so focused on him that Alonzo and Ashanti were safe, but it didn't make Alonzo sleep any easier. It was as if at every turn he expected one of Shai's soldiers to jump out and try to finish him, but as of yet, it hadn't happened. For the moment they were safe, but deep down, each of them knew it was only a matter of time for the other shoe to drop. It was too late to worry about it at that point, however; all he could do was wait and see how it would play out.

A knock on his front door brought Alonzo to his feet. He pulled on a tank top and grabbed his .357 from the table and tiptoed to the door. With his gun at the ready he peered through the peephole to see who it was. When he saw the smiling face on the other side, he hid the gun on the bookshelf and opened the door.

Porsha stepped into his apartment looking good enough to eat. She was wearing a green tennis skirt with a white Polo shirt and some white and green Stan Smiths. "Think it took you long enough to answer the door? I was starting to think you might've been in here with another chick," Porsha said playfully and invited herself in.

"Knock it off." Alonzo shoved her in the back playfully. "And you got a lot of nerve complaining about how long it took me to open the door, when I called you to come over almost two hours ago. What took *you* so long?"

"I had to stop off and get pretty for you." She held up her freshly manicured nails that were painted green and white to match her outfit. "Besides, I had to get the latest gossip from those nosey heifers."

"What's the good word?" Alonzo didn't care much for gossip, but he was curious to see what people were saying.

"Well," Porsha sat on the couch and crossed her oiled legs, "everybody is talking about what happened at Harlem Hospital last night."

"Harlem Hospital? What the hell happened there?" He had been expecting her to bring up the robbery.

"Boy, you got that big-ass television and don't watch the news?" She nodded to the flat-screen mounted on the wall, then picked up the remote and turned the television to NY1.

They were just in time to catch the recap of the murder that had everyone talking. Alonzo watched in shock as the news anchor recounted the events of the night before. The way they were spinning it, a girl from Harlem had been visiting her mentally unstable friend in the hospital when apparently they'd gotten into an argument over a man. The argument turned physical and ended with one of the girls falling from the window to her death. Whether it was an accident or foul play was unclear, but the missing patient was now a person of interest in the case.

Alonzo was too stunned to speak. The murder of the young girl was a sad thing, but the obvious con job that was being run on the American public was even sadder. Gucci was fresh out of a coma with a bullet to the stomach. There was no way she was pushing anybody out of the window. Even at full strength, the two girls had been like sisters and there was no way anybody who knew them was buying into it, but the general public believed what the news reported to them. Shai had obviously gotten to the media and flexed his muscle. The fact that he had that kind of reach taught Alonzo a newfound respect for his opponent.

"Ain't that some sad shit?" Porsha shook her head.

"Yeah, fucking tragic," Alonzo said trying to shake off the shock. "Other than that, what've you been up to, besides holding down your reputation as being the finest li'l muthafucka in Harlem?" he sat on the couch next to her.

"Just Harlem?" Porsha crossed her arms defensively.

"It would've amounted to the same thing had I said the world, because Harlem is the world to me. It's the only one I know."

Porsha smiled. "How come you always know the right things to say?"

"Because when I speak to you, I speak from the heart." He took her hand and placed it over his chest. "It keeps it one hundred even when the brain doesn't want to."

Porsha let her hand linger on his chest, appreciating the firmness of it. His heart beat rapidly under her palm like a scared teenager about to go on his first date. The rapid thumping in his chest beat in time with the thumping of her own because she felt it too. There was a natural rhythm between them.

"You play too much." Porsha moved her hand and scooted further down on the couch.

"How is it that I'm the one playing when you're the one doing all the running?" Alonzo closed the distance. "Damn, Porsha, everybody else sees the chemistry between us, so why do you keep acting like it ain't there?"

"It's not that, Zo. I know how you feel about me and I like you too, but . . ."

"But what? You worried about me hurting you like the rest? If you don't see by now that I'm better than that, then you need to get your eyes checked. Damn, what do I have to do, crawl over broken glass to prove how far I'm willing to go for you?" his voice was heavy with emotion.

"Zo, I dig what you're saying, but you know a bitch got baggage," she reminded him.

"Your luggage ain't no heavier than mine," he shot back. Alonzo slipped his hand to the nape of Porsha's neck and looked her dead in the eyes. "Let's break these two suitcases down to one and sort the clothes out when we get to our destination."

"Zo—"

He silenced her with a gentle finger over the lips. "Stop talking so much and live in the moment." He kissed her deeply.

Porsha was shocked, but she didn't resist. Alonzo's lips were softer in reality than they had been in her dreams. When his hands explored her frame they were firm and assertive, but not groping as she had become accustomed to. Alonzo handled her like a flower instead of a weed. She straddled his lap and traced her fingers along his cheeks. He was clean shaven as always but she could feel the light stubble tickling her fingertips. She wasn't sure when it had happened, but at some point, Alonzo had slipped her Polo shirt over her head, and clamped his mouth on her nipples through her bra. Porsha pulled him away from her breasts and shoved her tongue down his throat. She was so wet that she could almost hear the sloshing of her saturated panties while she grinded on his lap.

Alonzo ran his tongue over every piece of exposed flesh on Porsha's body that he could find. She tasted like the food of the gods, and he intended to gorge on her. He peeled their bodies apart and forced Porsha on her back. The ravenous look in his eyes told her what he meant to do, but she still wasn't prepared for it when he flipped her skirt up and nipped at her panties with his teeth. When he was done teasing her, he dipped his tongue into her box like a hot spear.

Porsha's eyes crossed when Alonzo invaded her. Alonzo munched on her box like a starved man, not wasting a drop of her essence. She locked her legs around his neck and forced his face and tongue deeper into her womb. Porsha clawed at the back of Alonzo's head and rolled her hips, smearing her womanly foam across his chin.

Alonzo's arms trembled as he braced on his knuckles and hovered above Porsha's body. His dick was so hard that he had trouble getting it out of his pants, but Porsha helped him spring it. She tugged on it, smiling silently, letting him know that she was pleased with his package. Alonzo balanced on one arm while he used his free hand to try to guide himself inside of her. She was soaking wet, but her womb was tight and hard to enter. Tighter than he would've expected, in fact. Alonzo could feel the heat of her gripping his wood as he slid deeper and deeper into her. He had just reached the Promised Land when there was another knock on the door and he froze.

Porsha's eyes snapped open, and she looked up at Alonzo. "Fuck that door, get this." She gripped his ass cheeks and tried to force him deeper.

Her walls felt like the finest silk, and for as much as he wanted to explore her further he couldn't ignore the knocking. "Give me a second." He pulled out of her and got off the couch.

Porsha propped on one elbow. "Are you *kidding* me?" She watched Alonzo duck-walk to the door, holding his pants up with one hand. She was about to bark at him for leaving her hanging until she saw him grab the gun off the bookshelf on his way to the door.

Alonzo's heart pounded in his chest a little harder the closer he got to the door. He hardly ever had visitors, and they were never unannounced. When he looked though the peephole and saw nothing but the tanned flesh of someone's palm, his mind automatically went into war mode. He looked over the shoulder and gave Porsha the signal to get clear. Then he swung the door open, ready to lay his murder game down—and was confronted by a face that looked much like his own.

"If that's how you greet your family, I'd hate to see how you greet your enemies." Lakim pushed the gun aside and stepped in the apartment. On the couch, Porsha was putting herself together. He sized her up. "Nice."

"Slow ya roll, pimp. That ain't community property." Alonzo took Lakim by the arm and steered him back toward the front door. "Fuck are you doing here?"

"Apparently fucking up your afternoon," Lakim chuckled, trying to peer around Alonzo at Porsha. "But on some G-shit," Lakim lowered his voice, "we gotta talk."

"And you couldn't call me on the phone?" Alonzo was tight.

"Not for this kinda talk. King need to holla about some shit, and he needs you there."

Alonzo sucked his teeth. "A'ight, I'll come through later." He tried to shove Lakim out the door so he could get back to Porsha.

"Nah, he needs to see you *now*. This can't wait. Baby bro, you know I wouldn't even be over here fucking with you if it wasn't *important*," Lakim told him.

Alonzo glanced over at Porsha, who looked like she was wound up tighter than a clock, then back to Lakim, who was doing a poor job of hiding the worried expression on his face. As usual, duty trumped personal interest. "Give me a minute," he told Lakim, holding the door open for him to wait in the hall. He turned to Porsha and found her giving him a look that said she wasn't pleased. "Ma—" he began, but she didn't want to hear it.

"Zo, don't even say nothing because whatever you say is probably gonna make me feel cheaper than I already do," she said in a disappointed tone. "I know how it is. The streets call, and you answer, right?"

"It ain't like that, Porsha. I just gotta handle this thing—"

"What about handling *this* thing?" she motioned to herself. "You know what? Nevermind, Zo." she gathered her purse and headed for the door.

"Porsha, I'm sorry," he said. He couldn't believe that he had worked so hard for the prize and couldn't enjoy it.

"Alonzo, I don't want you to be sorry, I want you to be considerate. And that's what I've been trying to say from the beginning. Thanks for the nut, Zo. I'll see you around." She left the apartment.

"Nice seeing you again, love," Lakim said sarcastically to Porsha as she passed him in the hall. Porsha just rolled her eyes and kept it moving. "Yo, wasn't that shorty from Brick City?" Lakim asked Alonzo after Porsha had gone.

"Please don't piss on my parade any further," Alonzo sighed. "What the fuck does King wanna talk about that's so urgent anyway?"

"Murder. What else?"

FORTY-FOUR

FRANKIE WOKE WITH HER MOUTH FEELING LIKE she had gargled with sand and a splitting headache, no doubt from Cutty pulling her hair. She was shocked and hurt that he had carried her like that, but she didn't know why she was. She saw Cutty treat Jada like shit, and she was the mother of his child, so it was foolish of her to think the snake wouldn't turn and bite her one day.

"Fuck him," Frankie said and rolled out of bed. She grabbed her cell phone from the dresser and saw that she had fourteen missed calls and several voice mails. Cutty had called her a few times and Porsha once, but the rest were from Dena. Frankie recalled the way she had spoken to Dena and felt bad.

Frankie had been meaning to have a talk with Dena for a while, but hadn't gotten around to it. She was cool as hell but becoming way too possessive, and Frankie didn't need anymore complications in her life. She intended on breaking it to her gently, but Dena caught her at the wrong time and all of the resentment came out in a wave instead of a trickle. She had gone way too hard on Dena and would make it her business to apologize to her.

Before calling Dena back, Frankie decided to check in with Porsha. Of course, Porsha had given her an earful of the latest gossip, but what really shocked her was when Porsha revealed the details of her encounter with Alonzo.

"I knew your hot ass would give in sooner or later," Frankie smiled.

"Shut up," Porsha giggled on the other end of the phone. "I didn't go over there to sleep with him, but one thing led to another and you know . . ."

"Well, I need to know *all* the nasty details. How was it?" Frankie asked excitedly.

"It was beautiful, right up into the point that he left me with a soaked pussy and feeling like a two-dollar whore," Porsha said with a sigh. She went on to fill in the blanks about how Alonzo had left her hanging when Lakim came for him. "You wanna talk about burnt? I could've killed him and his cock-blocking-ass brother."

"That's messed up. Well, I know the next time y'all get up you're gonna put it on him."

"Ain't gonna be no next time, Frankie. Never in my life have I had a man jump outta this sweet pussy and rush off because he had something better to do. I ain't fucking with Alonzo."

"Maybe it was important and he had to leave. You might be overreacting a bit, Porsha."

"What do you mean overacting? Do you know what kind of blow that was to my self-esteem? This is the reason why I didn't want to get emotionally attached to Zo in the first place. I'm not doing this to myself, Frankie. I can't."

Frankie could tell that her friend was hurting, and she hurt for her. Porsha acted like she wasn't, but she was really into Alonzo and anyone with eyes could see that he was into her too. Frankie knew that if Zo rushed out suddenly with Lakim, then it had to be tied into his extracurricular activities. She'd said she would confront Alonzo before telling Porsha his secret, but the truth might've been the only thing that could save their promising relationship.

"Porsha, before you do something you might regret, I need to holla at you about Alonzo," Frankie told her.

"What, he got another bitch? I *knew* that nigga was foul!" Porsha fumed.

"Nah, it's nothing like that. It's just . . . I don't wanna have this conversation on the phone. What're you doing in a couple of hours?"

"Sitting in my house wondering why I have such poor judgment when it comes to men."

"A'ight. After I get dressed I'm gonna come uptown to check you. Don't do anything until we talk," Frankie told her.

"Okay, but whatever you have to say better be damn good because I'm two seconds from calling him and cursing him out."

"Just hold your head until I get there." Frankie ended the call.

Frankie quickly showered and began to get dressed. She threw on a Fila sweat suit with the matching sneakers. She didn't have time to do her hair, so she just threw on a fitted cap and kept it moving. On her way out the door her cell phone went off. She looked at the screen and when she saw Dena's name, she hit ignore. She would talk to her when she came back from delivering the news to Porsha.

Feeling like she was about to save the world, Frankie set out to start her journey uptown. When she came out of the building she found Bess and Vashaun sitting on the stoop with two guys she had seen before but didn't know. The way they were spread out there was no way for Frankie to come down the stairs. She waited for them to notice her and move, but they acted like they didn't notice her at all.

"Excuse y'all," Frankie said with an attitude.

"My bad, li'l mama," one of the dudes said, looking up at her.

"Thank you," Frankie said, and descended the last few steps. As she passed she felt the dude grab her ass.

"Soft as cotton," he laughed.

Frankie didn't even reply, she just punched the dude in his face. He tried to get up, and she rocked him twice more. His friend grabbed her from behind and locked her arms over her head in a full nelson. She struggled, but the dude was too strong. Frankie watched in horror as Bess stepped in front of her and extended a long box cutter.

"You punk bitch, you couldn't see in a fair one!" Frankie shouted.

"Guess we'll never know, will we?" Bess laid the box cutter against Frankie's throat. "Maybe this will teach you that it ain't where you're from, it's where you're at." She ripped the blade across Frankie's neck.

Dena came out of the corner store just in time to see Bess and the others scatter from in front of the building. She shook her head, wondering what kind of fuckery the two stoop rats had stirred up. When she reached her building she found out.

"Oh my God!" Dena dropped the bag of groceries she had been carrying. Frankie lay on the stoop, clutching at her neck and gasping for air. "No, no, no, no!" She rushed to Frankie's side. "Why'd you have to be so hardheaded, Frankie? I've been trying to tell you they were gonna get at you, but you never had time to listen to me," she sobbed.

"Why they do this to me?" Frankie croaked. She was now bleeding from her mouth too.

"Don't talk! It's gonna be okay. We're gonna get you some help." Dena placed her hands over Frankie's throat to try to stop the bleeding. "Somebody help! Help us!" Dena roared, but no one stirred. She knelt on the stoop next to her lover, wailing as she was forced to helplessly watch Frankie bleed out onto the stairs.

FORTY-FIVE

ALONZO HAD EXPECTED LAKIM TO DRIVE BACK to the projects where King held council, but instead, he jumped on the FDR and headed downtown. He'd tried quizzing his brother about the big meeting, but all he could get out of him was "King will explain when we get there." Generally, Lakim couldn't wait to boast on whatever plans they had brewing, but he was tight-lipped about this one, which immediately raised Alonzo's antennas. He and Lakim had come from the same womb, so the thought of his brother betraying him never entered his mind, but he didn't like going into situations blindly, no matter who was leading him.

Their journey ended in a housing project on the Lower East Side, where they parked and headed inside the projects. Alonzo wasn't familiar with that particular project, but he could tell that Lakim had been there more than a few times by the way he expertly navigated the maze. The brothers ventured deeper into the heart of the projects to a playground. There were a group of men loitering on the playground, some he recognized and some he didn't. Off to the side he spotted Ashanti. When they made eye contact, Ashanti gave Alonzo a look that he didn't like. King James stood off to the side speaking to a Spanish cat. When he noticed Lakim and Alonzo enter the park, he excused himself and moved to intercept them.

"Peace, peace." King gave Lakim dap, then Alonzo.

"What's good, King?" Alonzo greeted him.

"You tell me. We ain't seen too much of you lately," King said.

Alonzo shrugged. "I been around, just lying low like you told us to."

"So I've noticed. I guess it ain't been too hard for you to get MIA since you've been so preoccupied lately, huh?"

Alonzo was thrown by the question. "What do you mean by that?" he asked King, but his eyes involuntarily cut to Ashanti who had just joined them.

"I'm talking about your shorty. You've been kicking it heavy with the joint from Brick City, haven't you?"

Alonzo was both relieved and surprised. "How'd you know?"

King smirked. "C'mon, God. You know I make it a point to know what my peoples are up to at *all* times."

"So what's up? I know you didn't call me all the way down here to ask me about my love life. What're we doing here, and what's up with all them Germans?" Alonzo was speaking of the Spanish cats who were out there with them.

"We're holding a war council, what does it look like?" King motioned to the hardened faces congregating around them. "It seems as if things have heated up unexpectedly. Somebody hit Shai Clark's card game last night. You heard about that?" King stared at Alonzo as if he could see directly into his soul.

Alonzo hesitated. "Yeah, I heard about it."

"The whole hood is talking about it. These cats had to be some real cowboys or real stupid to disrespect Shai so blatantly. Now, I'd love for our team to take the credit for something so brazen, but I know none of my young boys would jump out the window like that, especially without my approval ... would they?"

Alonzo opened his mouth to say something, but King James stopped him with a raised finger.

"Before you answer," King James continued, "just know that loyalty and honesty are all I've ever asked or expected in exchange for eating off my plate."

Alonzo started to gamble on a lie, but when he saw the hurt look in King's eyes he couldn't bring himself to do it. "I took the spot," he confessed.

King shook his head as Alonzo confirmed what he already knew. "Zo, are you fucking stupid? If I was able to find out you were there, how many other muthafuckas do you think placed you at the scene? Do you know what Shai Clark is gonna do to you if he finds out you were there?"

"Then he's gonna have to do it to both of us, because I was there too." Ashanti stepped forward.

King looked at the two of them as if they had both lost their minds. "It's a fucking mutiny." He threw his hands up in frustration. "I hear there were three of you. Who was the other cat?"

"Just some nigga I was locked up with," Alonzo lied. King didn't look like he believed him, but that was the story he intended to stick to.

"Who's to say this clown y'all rode out with decides to start running his mouth?" King asked.

"Nah, niggaz like him don't break," Ashanti assured him.

"You willing to bet your life on it?"

"Absolutely," Ashanti said without hesitation.

"Good, because you just did. I won't have nobody's careless-ass antics fucking up my grove, Ashanti, feel me?"

"Yeah," Ashanti nodded. He didn't miss the threat in King's tone.

"Fuck it, we can't do much about it now other than damage control. It's only a matter of time before Shai puts this together . . . if he hasn't already, so the first thing we need to do is get dumb and dumber out of his reach." He pointed at Alonzo and Ashanti respectively.

"I got a bitch who stays down in Philly that they can crash with for a week or so until we sort this out," Lakim offered.

"Bet, get on it," King told him.

"Wait a second. I don't remember agreeing to go nowhere. If Shai wanna get it on, then I'm gonna stay right here. I ain't no coward."

"Zo, we ain't trying to *son* you, but this is for your own good. You a working dude now, Zo, and instead of encouraging you to keep at that, I let you get caught up in this bullshit," Lakim said sadly. "This isn't a request, baby bro." Lakim placed his hand on Alonzo's shoulder.

"La, I love you for wanting to look out for me, but I'm not the same kid brother you used to send to stay with relatives whenever you went to war in the streets. I carry my own weight."

"Zo, I know you're a tough nut, but I'm not sure if you're built for where this is about to go."

Alonzo looked his brother dead in the eyes and spoke slowly and clearly so that there was no misunderstanding. "I'm built for more than even you understand, big bro. I wasn't *given* the name Zo-Pound; I earned it. Thanks for the ride down, but I'll take the train back to Harlem." He walked off.

Ashanti stood there looking confused. He wasn't sure if he should follow Alonzo or stay with King and Lakim. He looked at King with questioning eyes.

"You know damn well you wanna follow him, so go ahead," King told him. He watched as Ashanti jogged off to catch up with Alonzo. They were promising soldiers and would make more promising generals but only when they outgrew the ignorance of youth.

"You believe that shit about the third dude being some nigga Zo was locked up with?" Lakim asked King once Alonzo and Ashanti had gone.

"Hell, no," King said.

"Who do you think it was?"

King took a long pause. "I have a theory, but I hope I'm wrong."

FORTY-SIX

IF THERE HAD EVER BEEN A SHADOW of a doubt in Animal's mind as to what Shai's true intentions were, seeing the massive scrap yard looming in the distance removed it. Before he even approached the gates he could smell the stench of death reeking from the place. Shai meant to make the yard Animal's final resting place, and even knowing this didn't stop him from coming.

His cell phone vibrated on the center console. Animal looked at the caller ID and hit ignore. Ashanti and Zo had been taking turns blowing his phone up all day, but he hadn't answered any of their calls. The two young men had pledged their loyalties to Animal and their lives to his cause. For as noble as their selfless acts had been, Animal didn't fool himself. It was a fool's mission that he was on, and the chances of survival were slim to none. They were good soldiers but too young to die, so he left them and made *other* arrangements.

Animal pulled up to the high gate and flashed the headlights on the rental twice, as he had been instructed to. A few seconds passed, then Animal heard the engine that powered the automatic gate roar to life. Gravel crunched under the tires of the rental as Animal drove slowly into the yard. Though it was nearly pitch-black, he could see figures moving around in the shadows. There had to be at least a dozen of them, give or take. He absently rubbed the grip of one of the Pretty Bitches for comfort. Behind him the automatic gate rolled closed, letting him know he had reached the point of no return.

Every few yards Animal would see the flick of a flashlight, letting him know which way to go. By the time he had navigated the twists and turns of the scrap yard, he was so disoriented that he doubted he could find his way back out without some assistance. After a while, the rows of cars opened up into a clearing that was brightly lit by the headlights of the ring of cars that formed a horseshoe around it. Sitting tied to a chair in the middle of the ring of light, like a shining angel of mercy, was the woman he had come to rescue . . . Gucci.

Animal threw the car in park so quick that it jerked forward. Ignoring the fact that he was surrounded by armed men who all wanted him dead, he rushed to Gucci's side. "Baby, are you okay? They didn't hurt you, did they?"

Gucci looked up and strained her eyes to focus. "Tayshawn, is that you? You shouldn't have came. They're gonna kill you."

"Don't worry about none of that shit, ma. I'm gonna make sure you get outta here, I promise."

"Never have a saw a more touching scene." Shai stepped forward from the shadows. Instead of his usual business suit, he was dressed in jeans and Timberlands with a dark colored hoodie. "The tortured lover flies headfirst into danger to rescue his lady." He clapped his hands. "Bravo!"

Animal looked up at Shai with rage in his eyes. "You piece of shit," he whipped one of his Pretty Bitches out and aimed it at Shai. "I should blow your brains out for touching what's mine."

"You're welcome to try if you like," Shai said coolly. Suddenly, a dozen infrared lights winked to life all around them. There were more beams than Animal could count, and they were all trained on Gucci's head like a crown of cherries. "But I wouldn't if I were you."

Animal kept the gun aimed at Shai. He wanted to shoot him so bad that his finger trembled on the trigger. One shot and his nemesis would finally be dead, but so would Gucci. Reluctantly, Animal lowered his weapon.

"Good boy." Shai smiled. "Disarm this fool before he gets any big ideas," he said over his shoulder.

Swann stepped from the darkness. His face was a mass of bruises and cuts from the beating Animal had put on him, but the smirk on his face remained intact. He took both guns from Animal, then checked him for any more concealed weapons. When he was sure that Animal wasn't hiding anything else he leaned in and whispered, "When Shai gives me the order to clip you, I ain't gonna be as merciful as I was with Tech. I'm gonna kill you slow . . . *real* slow." Swann punched Animal in the stomach, doubling him over and dropped him when he brought both of the Pretty Bitches down on the back of his head.

Animal saw the most beautiful stars before the ground slamming into his face dissipated his vision. The metallic taste of blood mixed with dirt filled his mouth. He braced his fist against the ground and pushed himself up, but the moment he tried to stand he was overcome with a wave of dizziness, so the best he could manage was a kneeling position. He heard the crush of gravel under a boot and looked up expecting to see Swann, but it was Shai.

"The mighty Animal down on bended knee." Shai looked at him pitifully. "You have no idea how long I've been waiting to see this."

The knot on Animal's head throbbed, but it was nothing compared to his wounded pride. Fighting against the pain, he got to his feet. "Don't get too used to it, because you'll never see it again."

"Doesn't matter because I got it stored in here." Shai tapped his temple. "I can replay this movie anytime I want. You know," Shai began pacing in a tight circle around Animal, "we've never seen eye to eye, but I've always respected you. You're loyal and fearless. Had things played out differently, we might've been able to keep doing business together, but you got cocky."

Animal laughed. "I didn't get cocky, Shai, I got tired. Tired of people like you who sit in your big houses getting fat while your soldiers die in the street. Tired of muthafuckas who have earned nothing, claiming everything. I'm tired of arrogant li'l pussies like you spoon-feeding real niggaz shit and expecting us to smile and ask for a second helping. They call you the king of Harlem, but what kind of king puts innocent people in harm's way?" He nodded at Gucci.

"One who is willing to do whatever it takes to hold on to his crown," Shai told him. "Watching my father and brother fall taught me one simple truth: he who is willing to go the furthest shall rule the longest. Pardon my arrogance, but I'd kill this bitch and ten more that looked just like her to get a pesky nigga like you outta my hair."

"Spoken like a true Clark," Animal told him. "A'ight, Shai,

you got your prize. I'm at your mercy, so honor your word and let Gucci go."

Shai raised an eyebrow. "Did you ever hear me agree to that?"

"Don't play me, Shai. Your peoples promised that if I came quietly, you'd let Gucci go."

"The word of my people ain't the word of the king. I think I'd sleep better if I washed this problem as a whole from the face of the earth. Don't worry, I'll make sure you two lovebirds are buried together."

Animal laughed mockingly. "I kinda had the feeling you would pull a bitch move, so I came prepared. Before I die, I *will* see you laid low." Animal thrust his fist into the air. He waited for a few seconds and nothing happened, so he did it again. Still nothing. Animal whipped his head back and forth frantically, scanning the darkness.

"Lose something?" Shai asked with a sinister grin. He signaled someone behind him to step forward.

Angelo and another man stepped forward, dragging a woman between them. Blood stained the front of her shirt, and it looked like her legs could barely support her. When she got closer, Animal could see the woman was none other than his insurance policy, Kastro. She had been his last hope of him and Gucci making it out alive.

"No," Animal said weakly.

"Yes," Shai said enthusiastically. "We found this li'l bitch hiding in here and armed with a rifle that could've done some real nasty damage had she ever had the chance to use it."

"I tried, big homie," Kastro mumbled through her bloodied lips.

"And you failed," Shai told her.

"Shai, keep this between me and you. Let these women go," Animal pleaded.

"Everyone must be held accountable for their actions. Ain't that what you was running around screaming when you was killing my people?" Shai reminded him. "If you play pussy, you're bound to get fucked."

"Then allow me to provide the condoms," Kastro said, surprising her captors by playing possum. She jerked away from Angelo and spun, revealing the last ace she had been hiding in her deck, a Gemstar razor. The blade opened Angelo's face from temple to jaw, spraying blood on both of them. Kastro drew her hand back for another strike, but Angelo caught her by the wrist in midswing.

"Bitch, you're gonna pay for what you did to my face!" He placed a gun to her chest.

"No!" Animal screamed, but his voice was drowned out by the roar of the gun when Angelo pulled the trigger.

The impact of the bullet knocked Kastro across the scrap yard and slammed her into a pile of junked cars. Even with the gaping hole in her chest, she was still on her feet and still holding her razor. She staggered forward, swinging the razor blindly, trying to get to Angelo. He fired another shot, then another, dropping Kastro to her knees. Angelo came to stand over her with the gun to her forehead.

"Any last words?" Angelo asked her.

"Yeah . . . fuck you." Kastro spit bloody phlegm into his face. It was her last great act before Angelo put her lights out with a single shot to the head.

"Muthafucka!" Animal tried to rush Shai but was pounced

on by his henchmen. It took four of them to keep the struggling man from their boss. They eventually wrestled Animal down and tied his hands behind his back. "You're dead, Shai. You are *so* fucking dead!"

"Yeah, yeah, yeah . . . you sound like a broken record," Shai dismissed him. "I want you to carve him up real nice before you let him die," Shai ordered someone who was hidden in the shadows.

"Just like a bitch, too scared to do his own dirty work."

"Nah, murder has never been my thing, so why would I even play at it when I have an expert on my team." Shai waved the man forward he had been talking to. Animal's eyes almost popped out of his head when the priest he had been talking to at the church emerged. He had shed his army jacket and jeans and was now dressed in full priest's robes. "Let me introduce you to my executioner, Priest."

"You?" Animal asked in disbelief.

Priest shrugged. "I told you I wasn't always a man of the cloth." He drew a gun from the folds of his robe.

Animal felt dizzy. All he ever wanted to do was the right thing, but fate forced his hand to do wrong at every turn. As a result of his decisions, the kiss of death had touched everyone he loved. He felt defeated, like he had nothing left. In a last act of desperation, he rushed Priest to try to get through him to Shai.

Being that his hands were bound, his charge was awkward. He dropped his shoulder and tried to hit Priest with everything he had. The older and more seasoned killer easily sidestepped the charge and grabbed Animal by his hair as he passed. Priest whipped Animal across the yard like a rag doll, sending him skidding across the ground. Animal tried to get to his feet, but Priest put him back down with a kick to the gut. He tried to get up again and was rewarded with another kick. This one knocked the wind out of him and stilled his rage.

"Don't make it harder on yourself, kid," Priest whispered to him. He dragged Animal by the hair back to where Gucci was sitting and tossed him at her feet. Then he produced a knife and approached Gucci.

"Please don't," Gucci begged as she watched the upraised knife. When it came down, she closed her eyes expecting to meet her end, but instead, the knife only grazed her flesh when it cut through the ropes that had been binding her to the chair. Gucci spilled forward and landed on the ground beside Animal. He then cut Animal's bindings. The two lovers hugged each other tightly, knowing that it would be the last hug they ever shared in this life.

"Priest, we don't have time for your games. Just kill them and be done with it!" Shai ordered. He underestimated Animal's resilience once and it had cost him soldiers and money. He didn't intend to make the same mistake twice.

Priest glared at Shai. "I am the wolf of the Clark family, not the lap dog, and you'd do well to remember that, little one. I take no pleasure in murdering the helpless. You'll have Animal's life, but it will be an honorable death. A real soldier deserves as much."

Shai was angry, but he tried not to show it. He knew arguing with Priest was pointless because he lived by his own rules. "Fine, just be done with it. Come by the house and collect your money when you're finished." Shai gathered his troops, and the entourage left the scrap yard.

394

When Shai and his men had left the yard, Priest turned his attention back to the couple. They were kneeling, wrapped in each other's arms. Even wrapped in Animal's comforting embrace, Gucci couldn't stop trembling.

"It's gonna be okay," Animal cooed in her ear.

"I'm scared," she sobbed.

"No need to be, Gucci. We'll be together again, in this life or the next," Animal promised. Gucci closed her eyes, preparing for the end, but Animal glared menacingly at Priest. He would look death in the face when it came for him. "So I guess this is God showing me how much he loves me again, huh?" Animal asked sarcastically.

"No, this is man showing you the error of your ways." Priest raised his gun. "I wish you'd listened to me. Now it's too late. Make your peace with God, children, for you shall soon sit with him."

Shai and Swann lounged in the back of a Lincoln Town Car, making their way from the parking garage. Swann was smoking a blunt and smiling like the cat who had swallowed the canary. To him, it was time to celebrate a long-awaited victory, but Shai's face wore a troubled expression.

"What's good with you?" Swann asked his friend.

"Nothing, man. I'm just thinking about everything that's happened," Shai told him.

"If that's the case, then why aren't you smiling? Shai, you've just gotten rid of a hell of a thorn in your side, so I'm trying to figure out why you're looking all sad instead of jumping for joy?"

"Swann, you know I've never taken pleasure in having people killed."

"But you do it so well." Swann meant it as a joke, but Shai didn't laugh. "Come on, fam, you did what you had to do. It was either you or him. Animal had to die."

"I know, but the girl . . ." Shai trailed off. "I just wonder if I could've handled this situation differently." In his heart he wanted to let Gucci go, but killing her would send a message to any and all watching that Shai was willing to do whatever it took to hold onto his throne.

Two gunshots rang out from somewhere in the scrap yard.

Swann shrugged. "Sounds like it's too late to worry about that now."

FORTY-SEVEN

FRANKIE LAY IN THE HOSPITAL BED AT King's County, nodding in and out of a drug-induced stupor. She kept telling the nurses that she didn't want to be sedated, but they told her it was for the pain. She'd just had a serious operation, and it would take some time for the wound to heal.

Bess had cut her open and left her for dead, and she would've died if it hadn't been for Dena. While Frankie lay there knocking on heaven's door, she could remember hearing Dena's voice the whole time, assuring her that everything would be okay. It was Dena's voice that Frankie had held on to until the paramedics had gotten there. She'd treated Dena like a nuisance, but she turned out to be a godsend. When she got out of the hospital, the fence between her and Dena would be the first one she mended along the road of her new life.

Frankie heard someone enter her room, and when she tried to turn her head to see who it was, she immediately regretted it, as pain shot through her neck when she almost dislodged the stitches the doctors had used to close her wound. "Who is that?" Frankie called out, deciding against trying to continue turning her head.

"Hello," a soft voice answered. A young, light-skinned girl of about seventeen stepped into Frankie's line of vision. She was holding a bouquet of flowers. "I'm sorry. I hope I didn't wake you."

"Nah, when you're in as much pain as I'm in, sleep don't come easy. Who are you again?" Frankie asked, as she had never seen the girl before.

"Oh, I'm sorry. My name is Fatima—"

"Cutty's daughter," Frankie finished her sentence. As she really took a good look at the girl, she saw the resemblance. Fatima had her mother's complexion but her father's face.

"Yeah, Cutty is my dad," Fatima said, not knowing whether she should be proud or ashamed. "He sent these for you." She held up the flowers for Frankie to see.

Frankie smirked. "That's Cutty for you. Always sending other people to do his dirty work. I guess you can set them wherever you find a space for them."

Fatima set the flowers in the chair at the foot of Frankie's bed. "Listen, I don't really know what kind of relationship you have with my father, but I know what kind of man he is, so I can respect your bitterness, but don't disrespect my father in front of me. For as foul of a nigga as he might be, the fact that he sent you flowers says you mean something to him. I'll get out of your hair now." Fatima turned to leave.

"Wait," Frankie stopped her. "I didn't mean to come across like a bitch. I'm sorry. It's nice to finally meet you, Fatima."

"Likewise," Fatima nodded.

"So, how come ol' Cutty sent you up hear instead of coming himself? You know he loves a grand entrance," Frankie smirked.

"That he does," Fatima laughed. "He's actually downstairs. He sent me up because he didn't think you wanted to see him, but he wanted to let you know that he was concerned."

"Tell your dad that I said thank you for the flowers, but plants won't buy him a ticket out of the doghouse. It's a good start, but I'm gonna need some time," Frankie said honestly.

Fatima placed her hand over Frankie's reassuringly. "Take all the time you need. It was nice meeting you and get better soon." Fatima waved as she exited the hospital room.

Frankie lay there looking at her flowers and contemplating her next move. This was the second time in less than a year that she had almost lost her life, and frankly, she was tired of playing the odds. It was time for her to get out of New York City and go back to the only place that had ever felt like home. She just hoped that Mama Jae would accept her back, considering the circumstances surrounding how they parted.

Just as Cutty had said, he made an attempt to put in extra time with Fatima. When he'd called her expectedly that morning and asked about spending the day together, she was skeptical. In the seventeen years she had known her father, keeping promises had never been high on his list of strong points. Still, she agreed just to have one more tally mark against him when he showed up . . . or not. To her surprise, he was where he said he would be, when he said he would be there.

Fatima was initially apprehensive, but ended up enjoying the outing with her dad. He'd kicked off the morning by taking her to the shooting range, followed by lunch at a nice restaurant and a movie. Fatima had been resistant at the beginning of the date, but as she hung out with him, she realized her father was a cool-ass dude and more in tune with what she was going through than she'd given him credit for. One date couldn't repair their relationship, but it was a start.

When he'd gotten word about what had happened to Frankie, Cutty was distraught. His hidden feelings for her had made him overreact about the card game debacle, which caused a rift between them, but he still had love for Frankie. He was hesitant about asking Fatima to detour their date so he could see about Frankie, but she was surprisingly understanding. She had even offered to take the flowers upstairs in case Frankie didn't want to see him, and if she didn't, he couldn't say that he blamed her. He had been a real asshole to Frankie, but if she allowed him to change, he was going to make it right.

Cutty spotted Fatima coming out of the hospital. She wasn't carrying the flowers so that was a good sign. He opened the door to the truck so he could get out and meet her halfway and found his path blocked by a female. He didn't recognize her at first, but he placed her face as the girl who lived in Frankie's building. He opened his mouth to say hello, but his words froze in his throat when she pointed the gun at him.

"What the fuck are you doing?" Cutty asked her.

"Making everything right. You caused this shit," Dena said emotionally.

Cutty tried to reason with her. "Shorty, whatever you're thinking, I can promise you that you're wrong."

"We were good together . . . we didn't need nobody, but then you came around with your broken promises of fast cash.

Frankie was fooled, but I knew you were a snake from the moment I first laid eyes on you," Dena told him.

"You don't wanna do this," Cutty told her.

"The hell I don't. If Frankie hadn't been so caught up in your bullshit, then I might've had a chance to warm her." Tears ran down Dena's cheeks. "You took her from the world, and now it's time for you to make your exit."

There was a loud boom. Reflexively, Cutty closed his eyes waiting on the familiar burning of a bullet through his flesh. After a few seconds, the bullet still hadn't come so he opened his eyes. Dena stood there, still pointing the gun at him. A small red dot appeared on her forehead, which eventually became a fountain of blood. She dropped face-first to the floor, dead as a doornail. Standing behind her holding a smoking gun was Fatima.

"What did you do?" Cutty looked at his daughter in shock.

"She was going to hurt you, and I just—" Fatima began, but couldn't finish. This was the second time in less than a week that she had found herself staring at a dead body.

Being so close to the hospital, it was only a few seconds before sirens could be heard in the distance. There wasn't enough time to run and there was no story that Cutty could think of to hide the obvious. "Give me the gun." He snatched the murder weapon from Fatima's hand. He immediately began wiping the gun with his shirt, making sure to remove her prints.

"What're you doing?" Fatima asked nervously.

"Making up for seventeen years of lost time." Cutty fired another shot into Dena's dead body to ensure that there was powder residue on his hands when the police tested them.

"No!" Fatima tried to snatch the gun back, but Cutty held it out of her reach.

Half a dozen police cars carrying a dozen police officers converged on their location. Cutty placed the gun on the ground right before the police swooped in on him and cuffed him.

"Why?" Fatima asked with tears in her eyes as they dragged her father away in shackles.

Cutty looked over his shoulder. "When you have kids of your own, you'll understand. I love you, Fatima." Those were his last words to her before he was shoved roughly into the squad car.

EPILOGUE

KING JAMES STOOD IN THE MIDDLE OF the playground dressed in all-black. The few members of his crew were also dressed in black. The similarities of what they had on hadn't been a coincidence; it had been an order. The night before they had officially lost one of the realest cats alive . . . for the second time.

It had come as no shock to him to hear that Animal hadn't perished after the jail break. Animal was a much bigger part in the grand scheme than most understood, so King James knew it would only be a matter of time before he resurfaced, but he never imagined the circumstances or the fact that their destinies would overlap. If only Ashanti had connected them instead of keeping Animal's presence a secret things could've played out different and they'd be celebrating the murder of one of Shai's instead of mourning the loss of one of their own. When he looked over at Ashanti and saw the crushed look on his face, he knew that no amount of lecturing could teach him a harder lesson than the one Animal's death had just taught him. He lost his best friend.

When Ashanti got word of what had happened in the scrap yard, he was destroyed. He'd had a bad feeling when he was trying to reach Animal unsuccessfully, and when he'd gotten the news of his murder that morning from King James, his worst fears were confirmed. Fatima had been calling and texting him all day, but Ashanti never answered. For as bad as he needed to be close to her at that moment, he wouldn't let himself do it. She was supposed to be spending the day hanging out with her dad, and he didn't want his tragedy to taint their reunion.

Ashanti had spent the better half of the day in his apartment, crying and drinking until he was numb. He couldn't wrap his mind around the fact that someone he had always looked at as invincible was no longer with them. Ashanti had always been a wayward soul with no real direction or purpose in his life, but that changed the moment Shai Clark had killed Animal. His new purpose in life was to whack Shai. There was so much going on inside his young mind at that moment that he felt like his head would explode if he didn't get it out, so he turned to his comrade, Alonzo.

Alonzo sat on a crate, dressed in a black T-shirt and black Yankee fitted. He bobbed his head to the sounds of Animal's first mix tape bumping from someone's car speakers. He hadn't gotten a chance to spend much time around Animal, but he understood why the hood loved him. He was a cat who would live and die by what he believed in. Animal's loss was a tragedy, but what was more tragic was the stain it had left on Ashanti's spirit. Ashanti idolized Animal, and losing him for the second time killed off whatever youthful innocence that Ashanti had been holding on to. He had crossed the threshold, and nothing

Alonzo said would convince him to turn back. All he could do was hold Ashanti down and try to make sure he didn't meet with the same unfortunate end as his predecessor.

The first thing Animal could remember thinking was that hell smelled like an old gym locker. He rolled off the army cot he was lying on and got into a sitting position where he could better take stock of his surroundings. Animal blinked, trying to adjust his eyes to the darkness, and instead of fiery pits, he was greeted by the stained glass mural that he had stood before a few nights prior. He knew where he was but wasn't sure how he had gotten there.

"Glad to have you back with us," a voice called behind Animal. He turned and saw Priest sitting on the front pew.

"You!" Animal snarled. He leaped from the cot and tried to attack Priest, but the shackle that went from his ankle to the floor tripped him, causing him to fall flat on his face.

"There's that mindless anger again. That's how you got here in the first place," Priest reminded him.

"What am I doing here, and where's my lady?" Animal asked hostilely.

"I'm here, baby," Gucci called from the aisle. She had traded her hospital gown and slippers for a sweat suit and sneakers. The girl Animal had met during his first visit to the church was helping her down the aisle. She was still weak from the surgery, but moving around far better now that all of the different medications were out of her system.

"Are you okay?" Animal asked when she had finally reached him.

"I'm fine." She hugged Animal. "They didn't hurt me."

"What the fuck is your game, Priest?" Animal turned to him.

"This ain't about no game. This is about redemption," Priest told him. "Shai's reasons for wanting you dead are petty. My reasons for wanting you alive go much deeper. I see something in you that I wish someone had seen in me as a young man, which is why I've given you a second chance at life. As soon as you're able, you and your lady are free to leave and start your lives over. To the world at large, you're dead now . . . I mean *really* dead, not like that fucked-up job your buddies did a few years back. As we speak, there's a medical examiner verifying your identities in some lab downtown. Animal and Gucci no longer exist."

Animal looked at him suspiciously. "Old man, you must think I'm a fool. If it was that simple, then why the hell do you have me chained to the floor? What're your terms?"

"That chain is to ensure that you sit still long enough to listen to what I have to say, and my terms are simple. As far as Shai is concerned, the two of you are dead and gone. You are gonna leave this beef alone and ride off into the sunset with your lady."

"I can't do that," Animal said.

"You've been given a pass. Take it and do with your life what you will," Khallah added.

"Sweety, where I'm from, we don't abandon our comrades. Even if I dip off now, Alonzo and Ashanti are marked for death for helping me. I can't have that on my conscience," Animal told her.

"Animal, I pulled you from the fire once, and there's no guarantee that I can do it again," Priest told him.

"I'm not asking you to. I appreciate what you did, getting me and Gucci out of there, but I can't turn away now. I gotta at least make sure Zo and Ashanti are good before I can put all this behind me."

Priest shook his head and smirked. "You're determined to keep putting your life on the line until you eventually lose it, huh?"

"They helped me, and I can't leave them for dead."

Priest studied his face for a minute. "So be it. If you're determined to tackle a king cobra, then I guess it's only right that I show you how to kill it."

"Priest, I don't want to sound ungrateful or anything, but why are you helping me? You know what Shai is liable to do to you if he finds out, don't you?" Animal asked.

Priest nodded. "Indeed I do, but there's nothing he can do to me that I haven't already done to myself. Think of it as an old man trying to make his peace in the twilight of his years." He handed Animal an old photograph.

Animal studied the photo, which was of a much younger Priest with a woman and a small child. Upon closer inspection of the photo, he realized that the woman was his estranged mother and the child cradled lovingly in Priest's arms was him. "What the fuck is this, some kinda trick?"

"It's no trick; the photo is real."

"Then that means—"

"Yes," Priest cut him off. "You've grown into a fine young man, son, and every bit as dangerous as your dad."

THE BEGINNING

 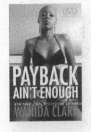 

 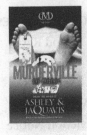 

ALSO BY K'WAN

TITLE LIST:
Gangland
Road Dawgz
Street Dreams
Hoodlum
Eve
Gutter

HOOD RAT SERIES:
Hood Rat
Still Hood
Section 8
Welfare Wifeys
Eviction Notice

SHORTS/NOVELLAS:
The Game
Blow
Flirt
Flexin & Sexin (vol. 1)
From Harlem With Love
Love & Gunplay (Animal story)
Purple Reign (Vol 1: Purple City Tales)